BY **KIRKMAN**
& **AZACETA**

VOLUME **2**: A VAST AND UNENDING RUIN

OUTCAST BY KIRKMAN & AZACETA
VOL. 2: A VAST AND UNENDING RUIN
October 2015
First printing

ISBN: 978-1-63215-448-4

Published by Image Comics, Inc.

Office of publication: 2001 Center Street, 6th Floor,
Berkeley, CA 94704.

Printed in the U.S.A.

For information regarding the CPSIA on this printed
material call: 203-595-3636 and provide reference #
RICH - 647720.

IMAGE COMICS, INC.
Robert Kirkman – Chief Operating Officer
Erik Larsen – Chief Financial Officer
Todd McFarlane – President
Marc Silvestri – Chief Executive Officer
Jim Valentino – Vice-President

Eric Stephenson – Publisher
Corey Murphy – Director of Sales
Jeremy Sullivan – Director of Digital Sales
Kat Salazar – Director of PR & Marketing
Emily Miller – Director of Operations
Branwyn Bigglestone – Senior Accounts Manager
Sarah Mello – Accounts Manager
Drew Gill – Art Director
Jonathan Chan – Production Manager
Meredith Wallace – Print Manager
Randy Okamura – Marketing Production Designer
David Brothers – Branding Manager
Ally Power – Content Manager
Addison Duke – Production Artist
Vincent Kukua – Production Artist
Sasha Head – Production Artist
Tricia Ramos – Production Artist
Emilio Bautista – Digital Sales Associate
Chloe Ramos-Peterson – Administrative Assistant
IMAGECOMICS.COM

For SKYBOUND ENTERTAINMENT

Robert Kirkman - CEO
David Alpert - President
Sean Mackiewicz - Editorial Director
Shawn Kirkham - Director of Business Development
Brian Huntington - Online Editorial Director
June Alian - Publicity Director
Rachel Skidmore - Director of Media Development
Arielle Basich - Assistant Editor
Dan Petersen - Operations Manager
Sarah Effinger - Office Manager
Nick Palmer - Operations Coordinator
Genevieve Jones - Production Coordinator
Andres Juarez - Graphic Designer
Stephan Murillo - Administrative Assistant

International inquiries: foreign@skybound.com
Licensing inquiries: contact@skybound.com

WWW.SKYBOUND.COM

Robert Kirkman
Creator, Writer

Paul Azaceta
Artist

Elizabeth Breitweiser
Colorist

Rus Wooton
Letterer

Paul Azaceta
Elizabeth Breitweiser
Cover

Arielle Basich
Assistant Editor

Sean Mackiewicz
Editor

Rian Hughes
Logo Design

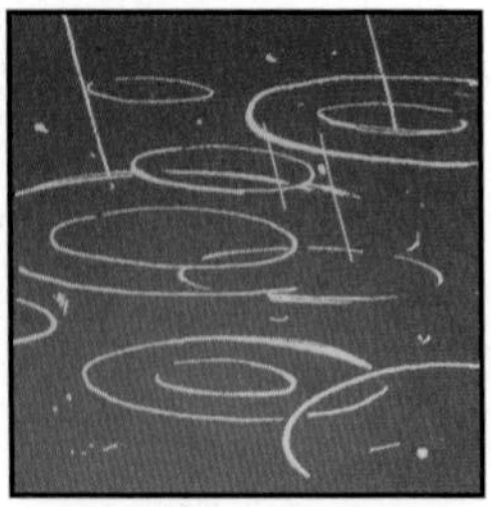

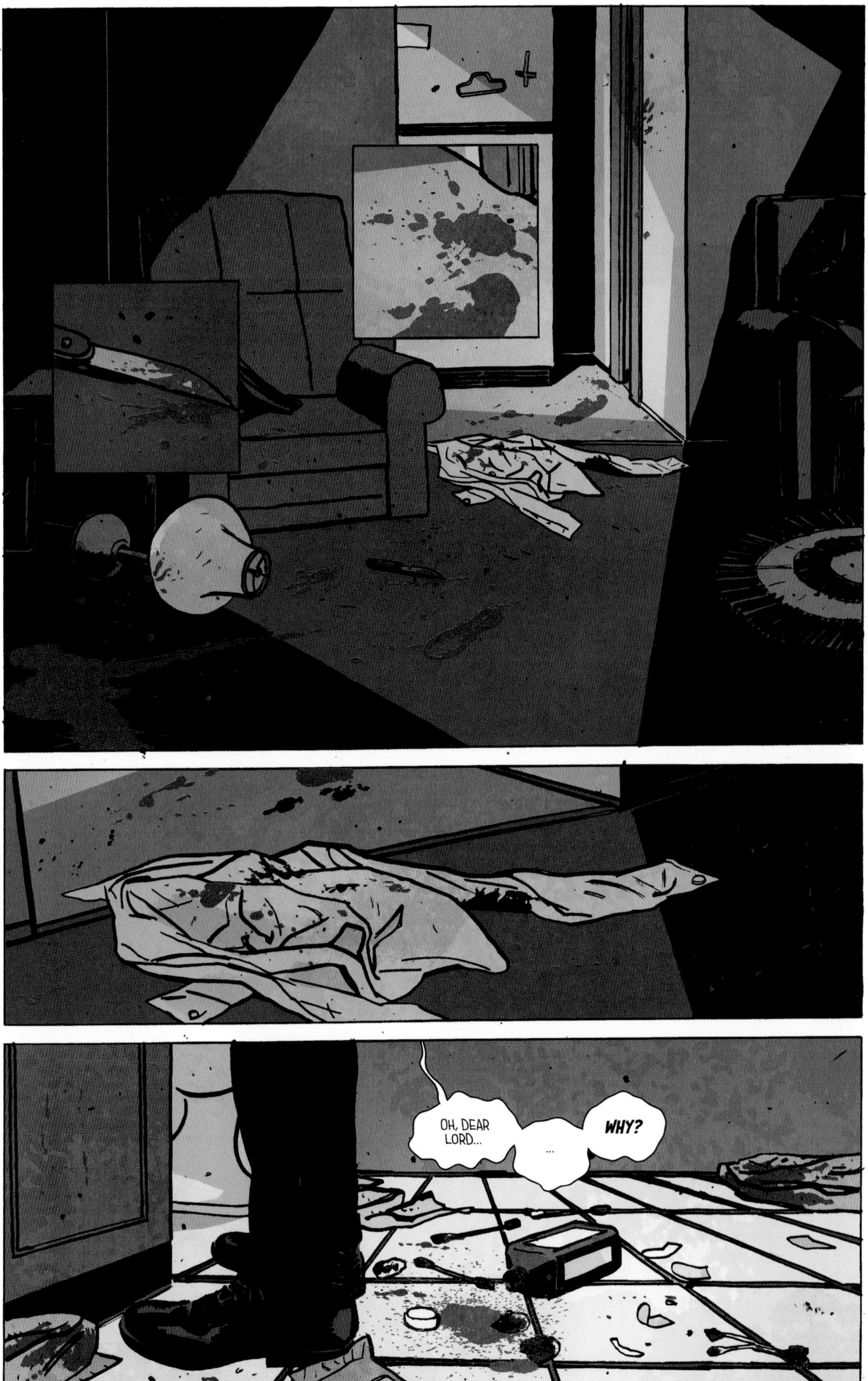
OH, DEAR LORD...
...
WHY?

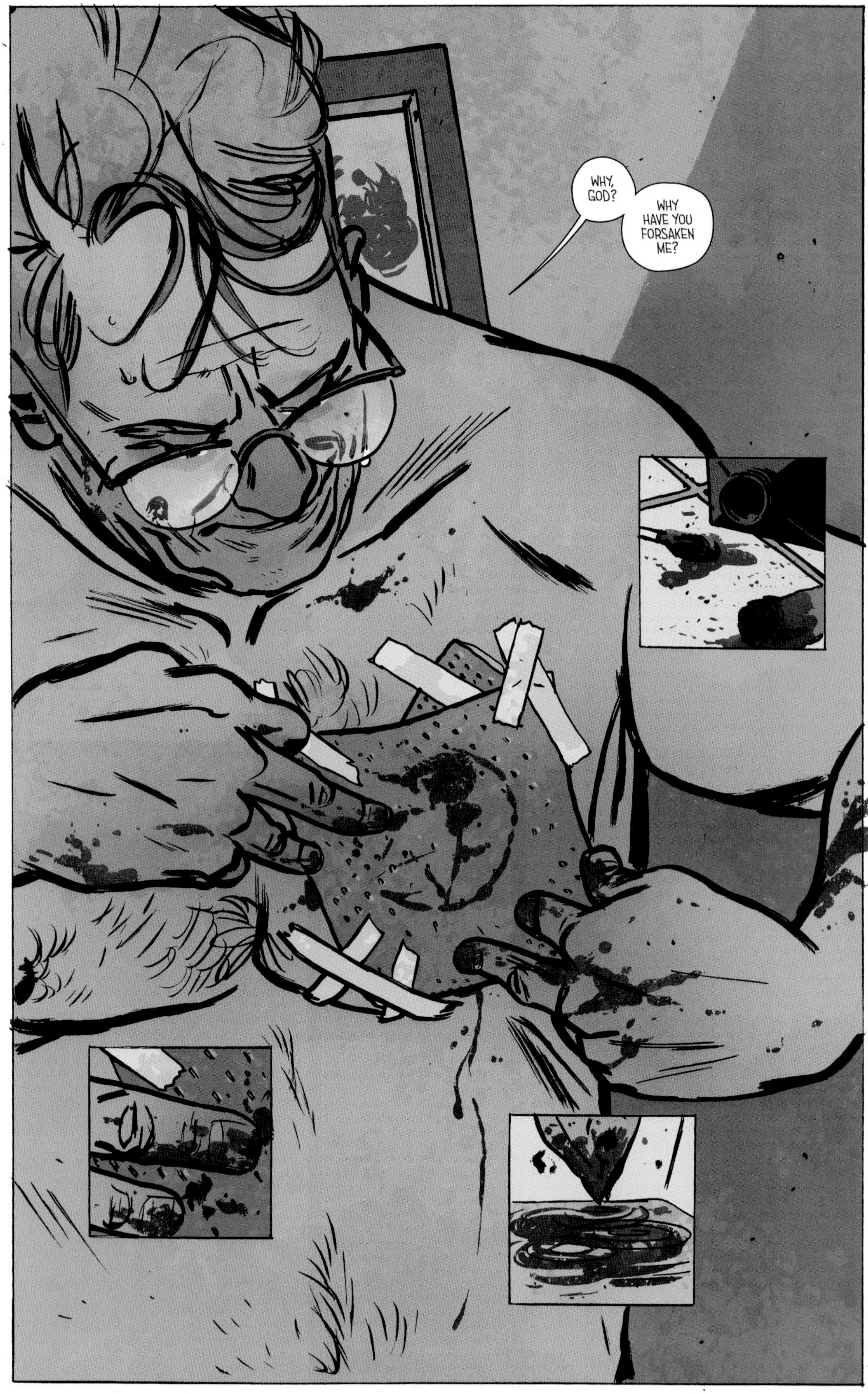
WHY, GOD?
WHY HAVE YOU FORSAKEN ME?

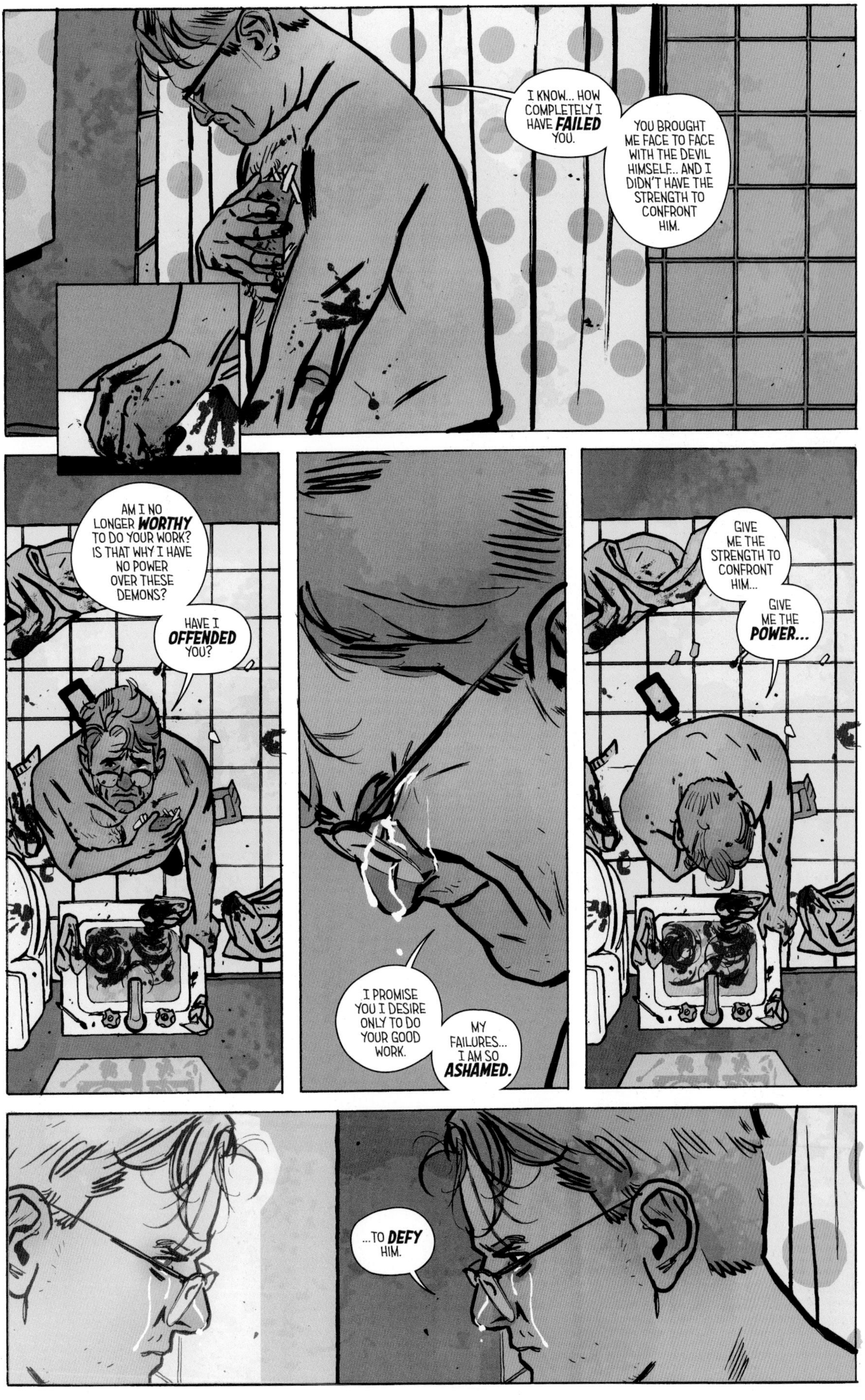
I KNOW... HOW COMPLETELY I HAVE FAILED YOU.
YOU BROUGHT ME FACE TO FACE WITH THE DEVIL HIMSELF... AND I DIDN'T HAVE THE STRENGTH TO CONFRONT HIM.
AM I NO LONGER WORTHY TO DO YOUR WORK? IS THAT WHY I HAVE NO POWER OVER THESE DEMONS?
HAVE I OFFENDED YOU?
I PROMISE YOU I DESIRE ONLY TO DO YOUR GOOD WORK.
MY FAILURES... I AM SO ASHAMED.
GIVE ME THE STRENGTH TO CONFRONT HIM...
GIVE ME THE POWER...
...TO DEFY HIM.

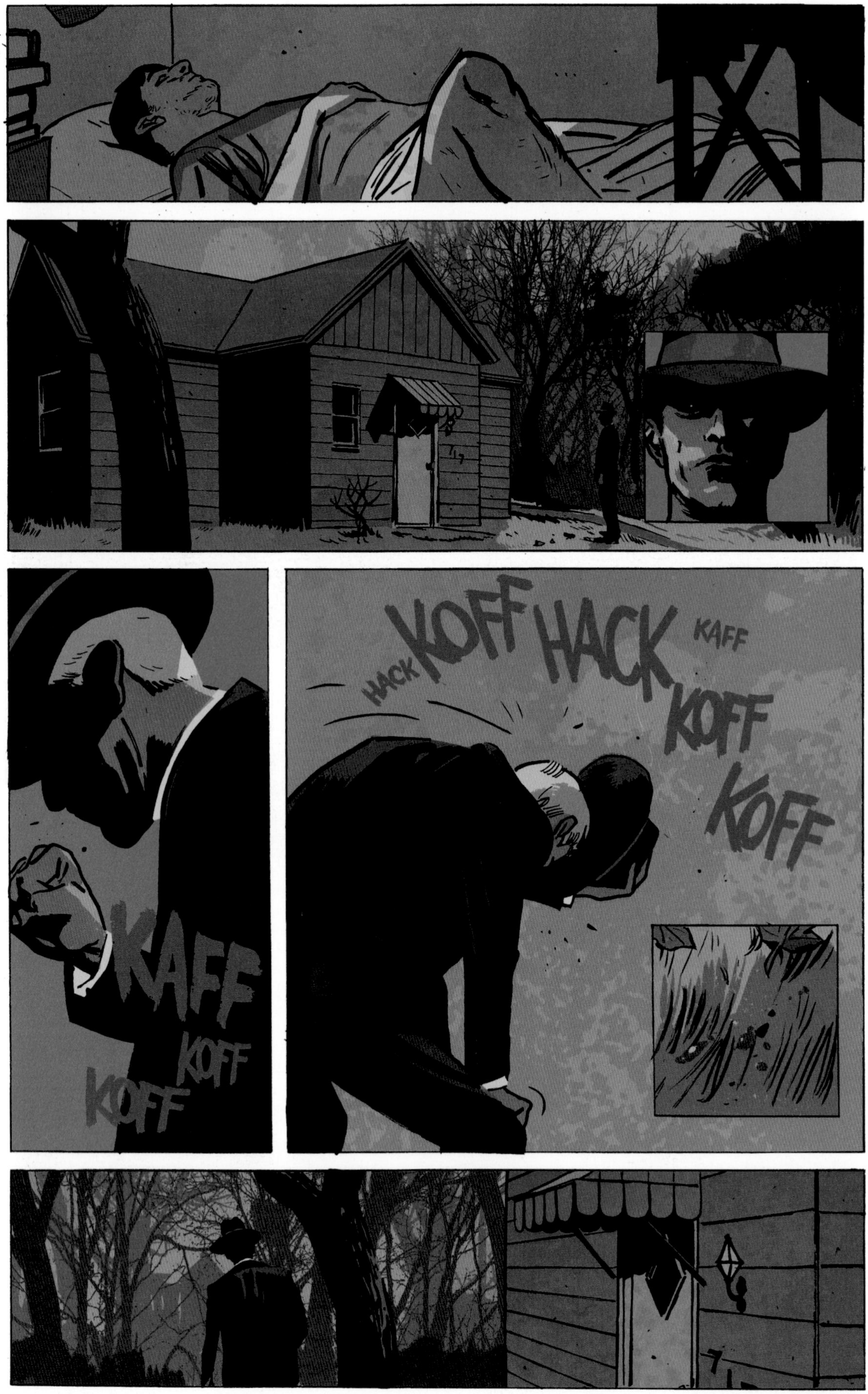
KAFF
KOFF
KOFF
HACK KOFF HACK KAFF
KOFF
KOFF

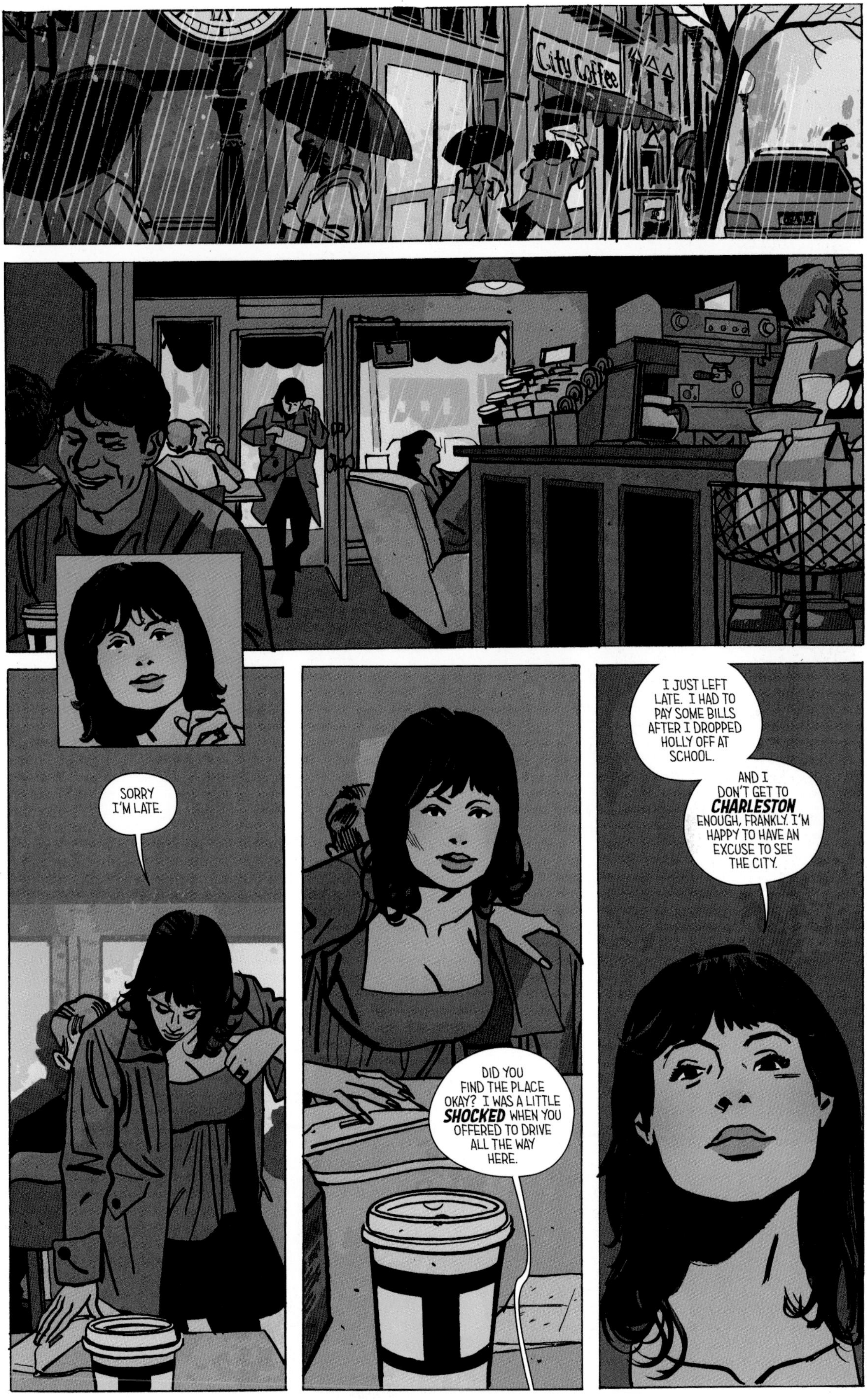
City Coffee
SORRY I'M LATE.
DID YOU FIND THE PLACE OKAY? I WAS A LITTLE SHOCKED WHEN YOU OFFERED TO DRIVE ALL THE WAY HERE.
I JUST LEFT LATE. I HAD TO PAY SOME BILLS AFTER I DROPPED HOLLY OFF AT SCHOOL.
AND I DON'T GET TO CHARLESTON ENOUGH, FRANKLY. I'M HAPPY TO HAVE AN EXCUSE TO SEE THE CITY.

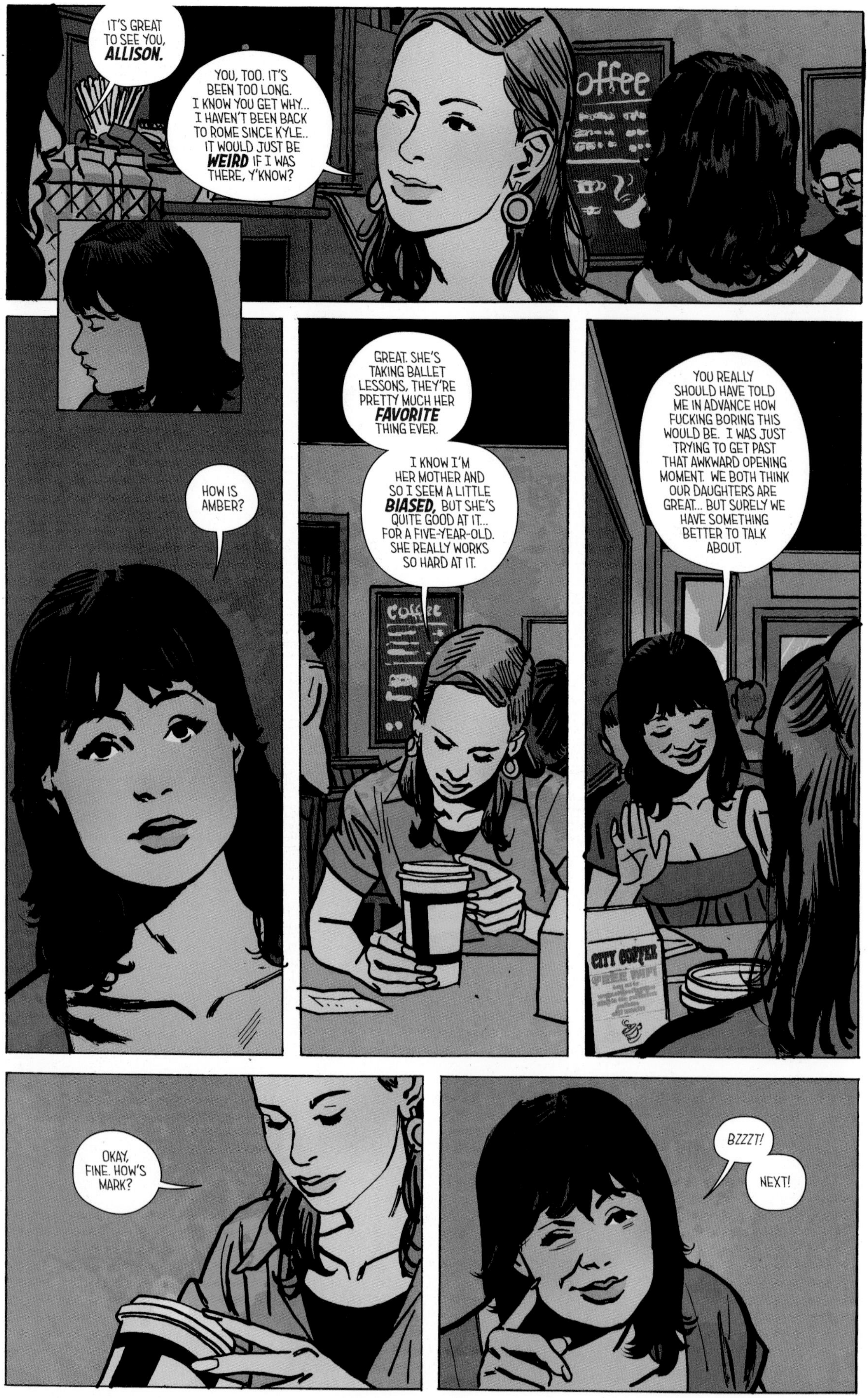
IT'S GREAT TO SEE YOU, ALLISON.
YOU, TOO. IT'S BEEN TOO LONG. I KNOW YOU GET WHY... I HAVEN'T BEEN BACK TO ROME SINCE KYLE.. IT WOULD JUST BE WEIRD IF I WAS THERE, Y'KNOW?
HOW IS AMBER?
GREAT. SHE'S TAKING BALLET LESSONS, THEY'RE PRETTY MUCH HER FAVORITE THING EVER.
I KNOW I'M HER MOTHER AND SO I SEEM A LITTLE BIASED, BUT SHE'S QUITE GOOD AT IT... FOR A FIVE-YEAR-OLD. SHE REALLY WORKS SO HARD AT IT.
YOU REALLY SHOULD HAVE TOLD ME IN ADVANCE HOW FUCKING BORING THIS WOULD BE. I WAS JUST TRYING TO GET PAST THAT AWKWARD OPENING MOMENT. WE BOTH THINK OUR DAUGHTERS ARE GREAT... BUT SURELY WE HAVE SOMETHING BETTER TO TALK ABOUT.
CITY COFFEE
FREE WIFI
OKAY, FINE. HOW'S MARK?
BZZZT!
NEXT!

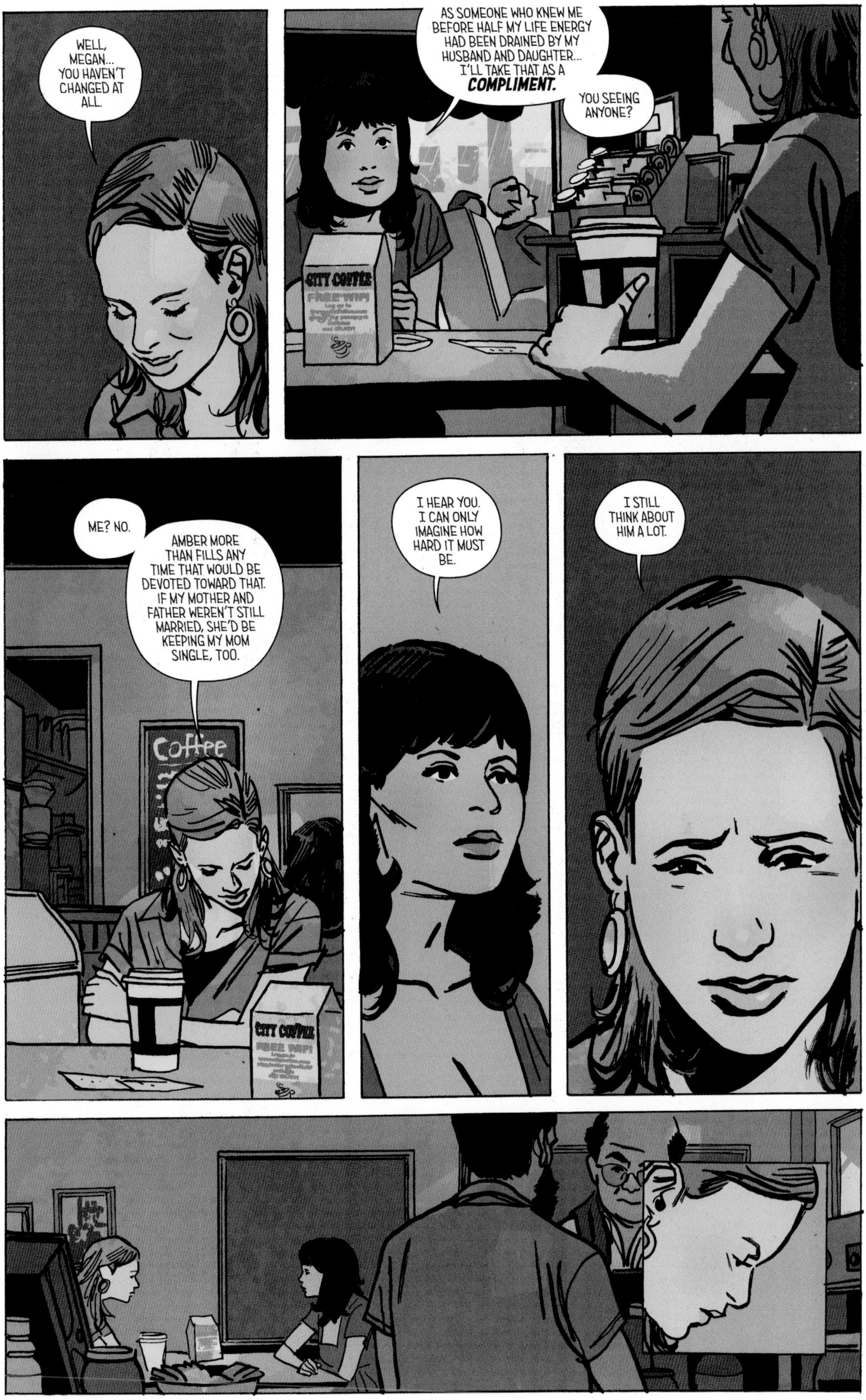
WELL, MEGAN... YOU HAVEN'T CHANGED AT ALL.
AS SOMEONE WHO KNEW ME BEFORE HALF MY LIFE ENERGY HAD BEEN DRAINED BY MY HUSBAND AND DAUGHTER... I'LL TAKE THAT AS A COMPLIMENT.
YOU SEEING ANYONE?
CITY COFFEE
ME? NO.
AMBER MORE THAN FILLS ANY TIME THAT WOULD BE DEVOTED TOWARD THAT. IF MY MOTHER AND FATHER WEREN'T STILL MARRIED, SHE'D BE KEEPING MY MOM SINGLE, TOO.
Coffee
CITY COFFEE
I HEAR YOU. I CAN ONLY IMAGINE HOW HARD IT MUST BE.
I STILL THINK ABOUT HIM A LOT.

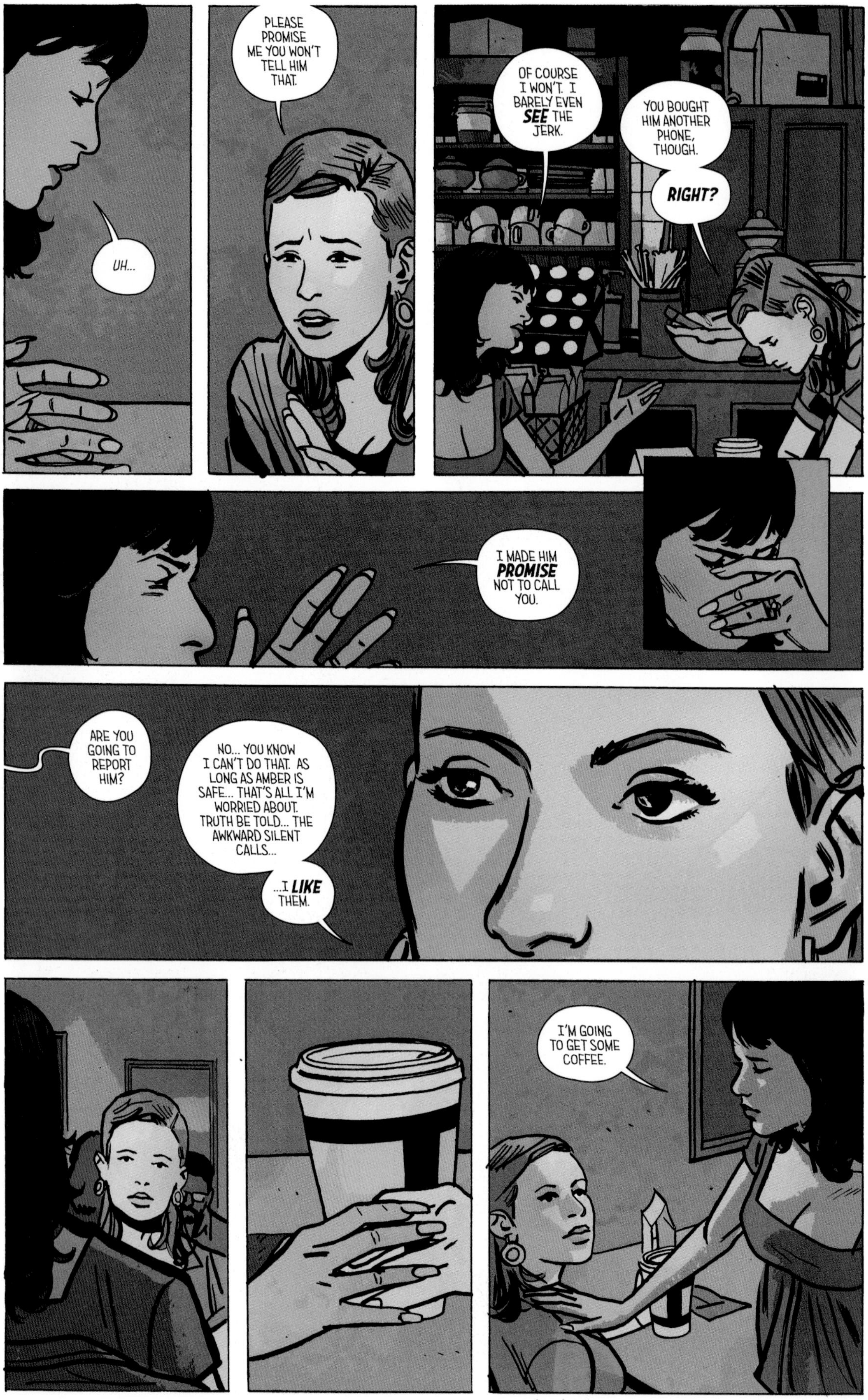
UH...
PLEASE PROMISE ME YOU WON'T TELL HIM THAT.
OF COURSE I WON'T. I BARELY EVEN SEE THE JERK.
YOU BOUGHT HIM ANOTHER PHONE, THOUGH.
RIGHT?
I MADE HIM PROMISE NOT TO CALL YOU.
ARE YOU GOING TO REPORT HIM?
NO... YOU KNOW I CAN'T DO THAT. AS LONG AS AMBER IS SAFE... THAT'S ALL I'M WORRIED ABOUT. TRUTH BE TOLD... THE AWKWARD SILENT CALLS...
...I LIKE THEM.
I'M GOING TO GET SOME COFFEE.

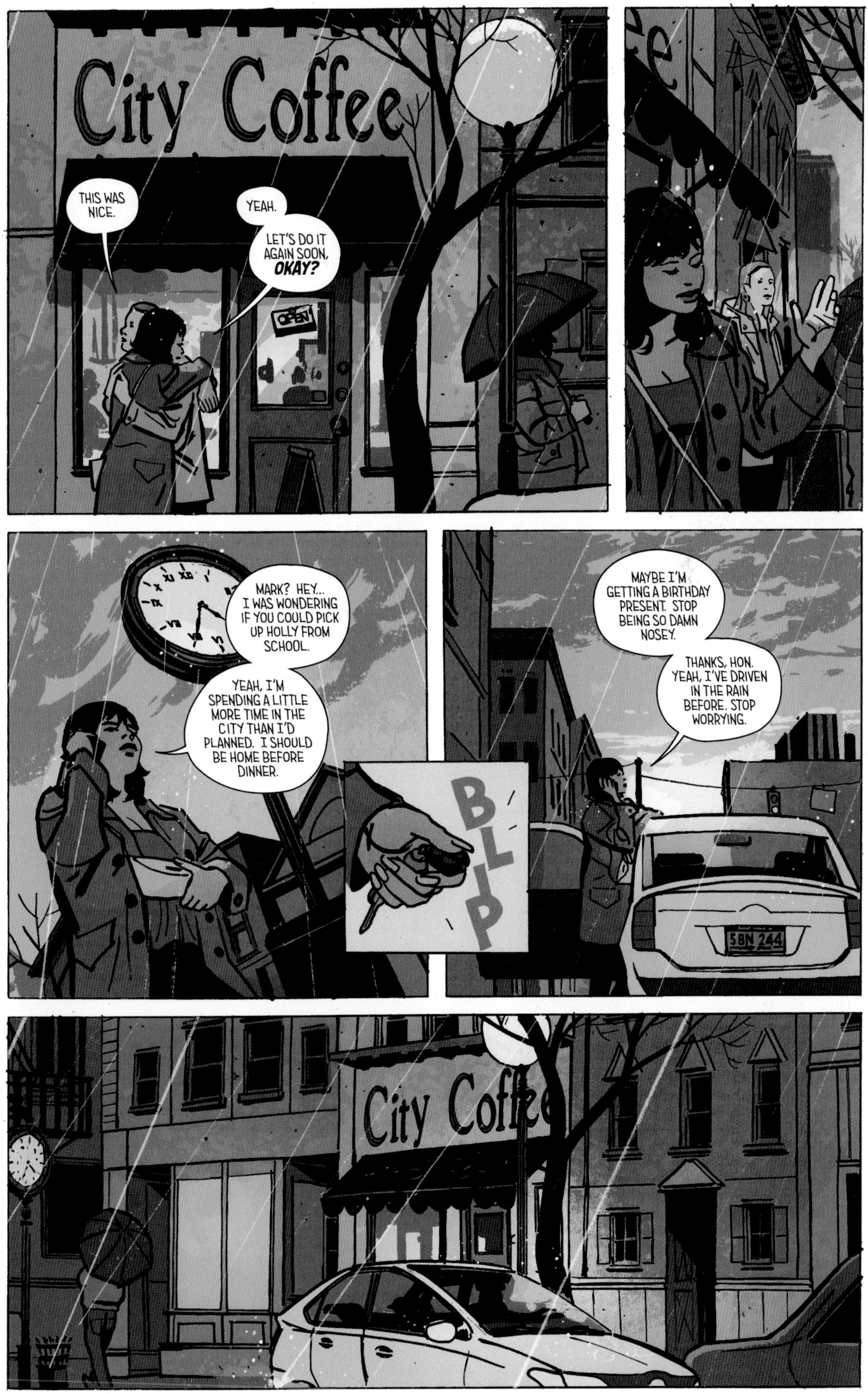
City Coffee
THIS WAS NICE.
YEAH.
LET'S DO IT AGAIN SOON, **OKAY?**
OPEN
MARK? HEY... I WAS WONDERING IF YOU COULD PICK UP HOLLY FROM SCHOOL.
YEAH, I'M SPENDING A LITTLE MORE TIME IN THE CITY THAN I'D PLANNED. I SHOULD BE HOME BEFORE DINNER.
BLIP
MAYBE I'M GETTING A BIRTHDAY PRESENT. STOP BEING SO DAMN NOSEY.
THANKS, HON. YEAH, I'VE DRIVEN IN THE RAIN BEFORE. STOP WORRYING.
5BN 244
City Coffee

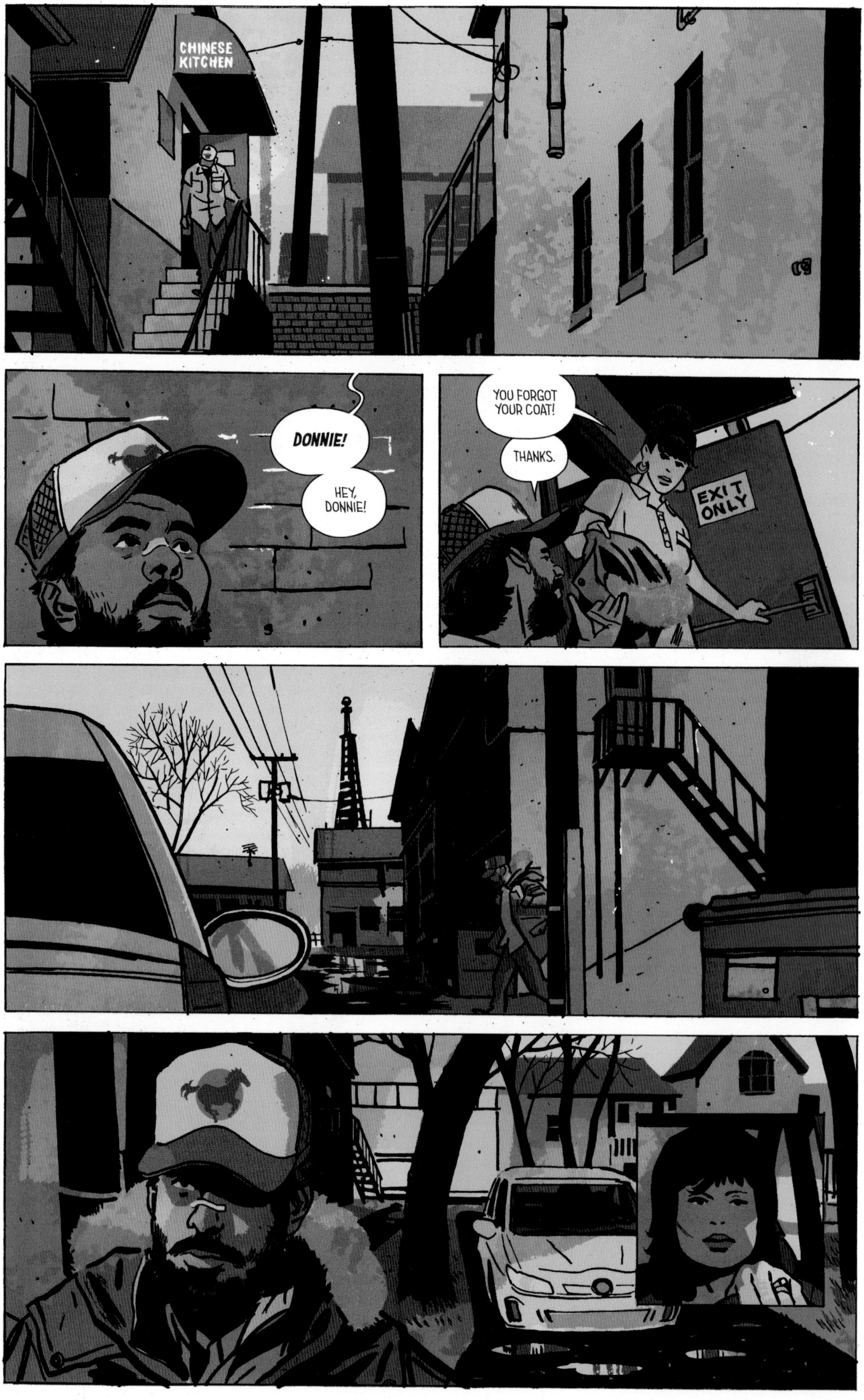
CHINESE KITCHEN
DONNIE!
HEY, DONNIE!
YOU FORGOT YOUR COAT!
THANKS.
EXIT ONLY

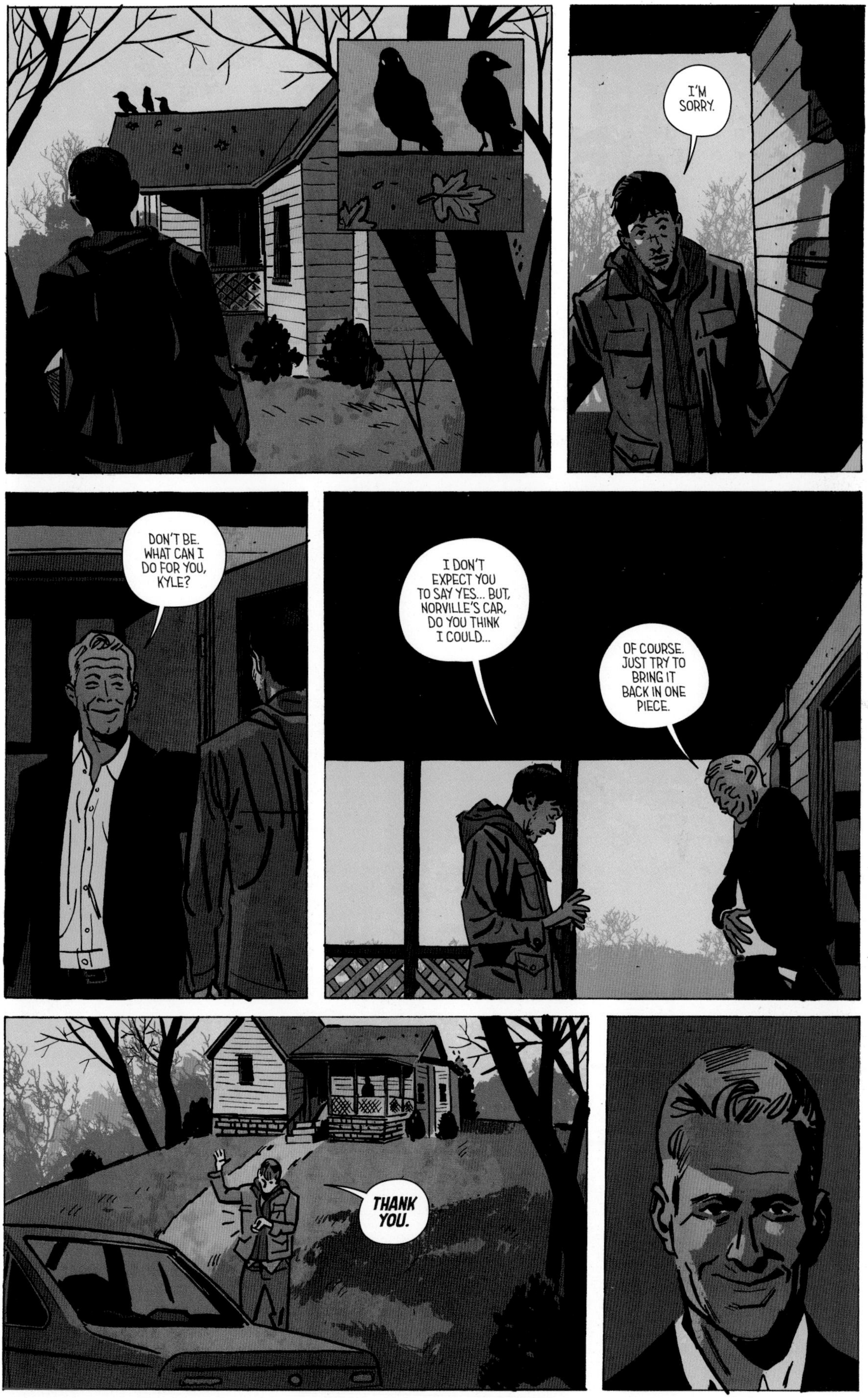
I'M SORRY.
DON'T BE. WHAT CAN I DO FOR YOU, KYLE?
I DON'T EXPECT YOU TO SAY YES... BUT, NORVILLE'S CAR, DO YOU THINK I COULD...
OF COURSE. JUST TRY TO BRING IT BACK IN ONE PIECE.
THANK YOU.

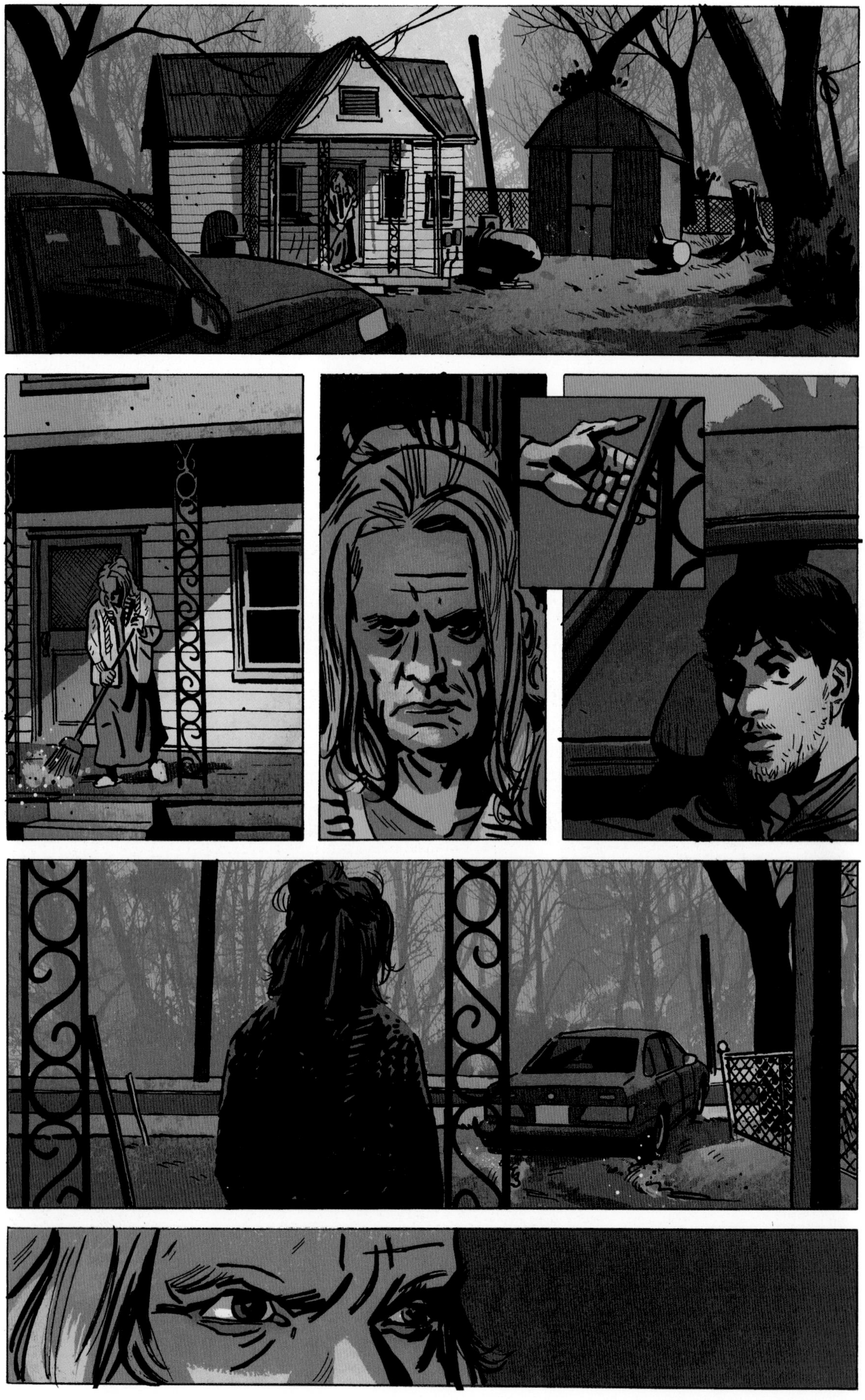

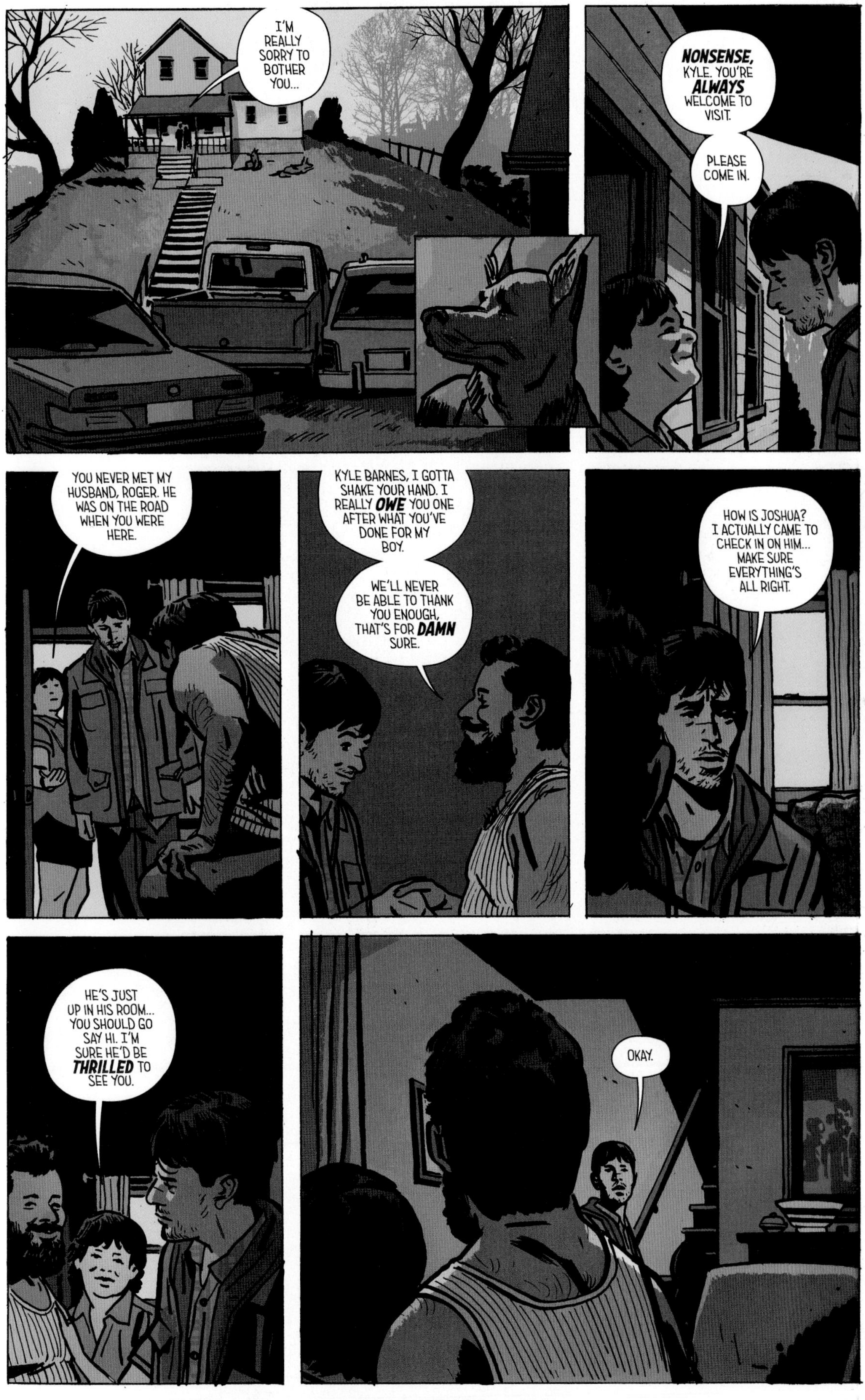

I'M REALLY SORRY TO BOTHER YOU...
NONSENSE, KYLE. YOU'RE ALWAYS WELCOME TO VISIT.
PLEASE COME IN.
YOU NEVER MET MY HUSBAND, ROGER. HE WAS ON THE ROAD WHEN YOU WERE HERE.
KYLE BARNES, I GOTTA SHAKE YOUR HAND. I REALLY OWE YOU ONE AFTER WHAT YOU'VE DONE FOR MY BOY.
WE'LL NEVER BE ABLE TO THANK YOU ENOUGH, THAT'S FOR DAMN SURE.
HOW IS JOSHUA? I ACTUALLY CAME TO CHECK IN ON HIM... MAKE SURE EVERYTHING'S ALL RIGHT.
HE'S JUST UP IN HIS ROOM... YOU SHOULD GO SAY HI. I'M SURE HE'D BE THRILLED TO SEE YOU.
OKAY.

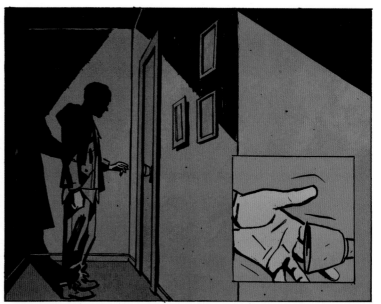

UM...

HELLO?

JOSHUA?

YEAH?

DO YOU REMEMBER ME?

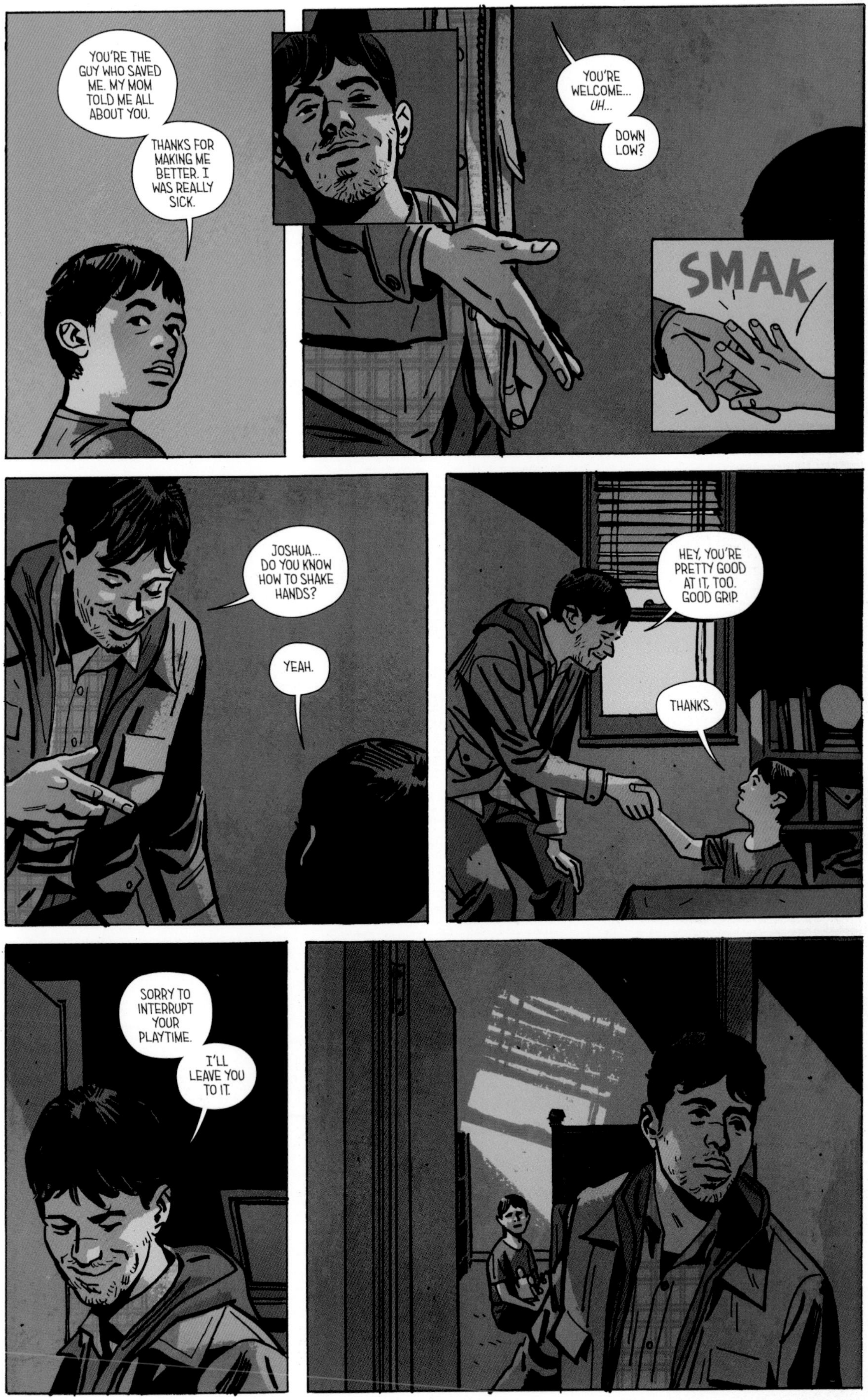
YOU'RE THE GUY WHO SAVED ME. MY MOM TOLD ME ALL ABOUT YOU.
THANKS FOR MAKING ME BETTER. I WAS REALLY SICK.
YOU'RE WELCOME... UH...
DOWN LOW?
SMAK
JOSHUA... DO YOU KNOW HOW TO SHAKE HANDS?
YEAH.
HEY, YOU'RE PRETTY GOOD AT IT, TOO. GOOD GRIP.
THANKS.
SORRY TO INTERRUPT YOUR PLAYTIME.
I'LL LEAVE YOU TO IT.

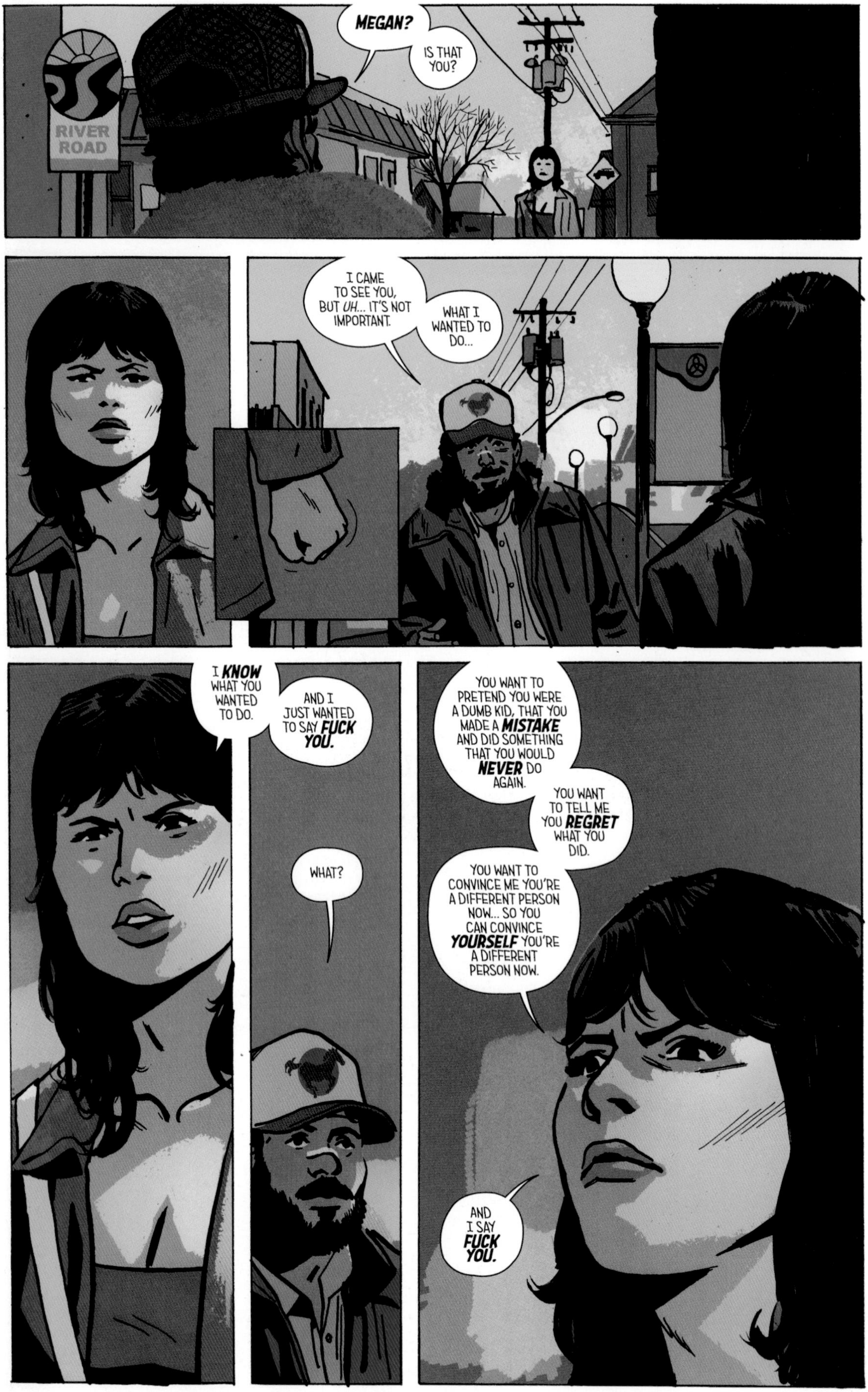

RIVER ROAD
MEGAN?
IS THAT YOU?
I CAME TO SEE YOU, BUT UH... IT'S NOT IMPORTANT.
WHAT I WANTED TO DO...
I KNOW WHAT YOU WANTED TO DO.
AND I JUST WANTED TO SAY FUCK YOU.
WHAT?
YOU WANT TO PRETEND YOU WERE A DUMB KID, THAT YOU MADE A MISTAKE AND DID SOMETHING THAT YOU WOULD NEVER DO AGAIN.
YOU WANT TO TELL ME YOU REGRET WHAT YOU DID.
YOU WANT TO CONVINCE ME YOU'RE A DIFFERENT PERSON NOW... SO YOU CAN CONVINCE YOURSELF YOU'RE A DIFFERENT PERSON NOW.
AND I SAY FUCK YOU.

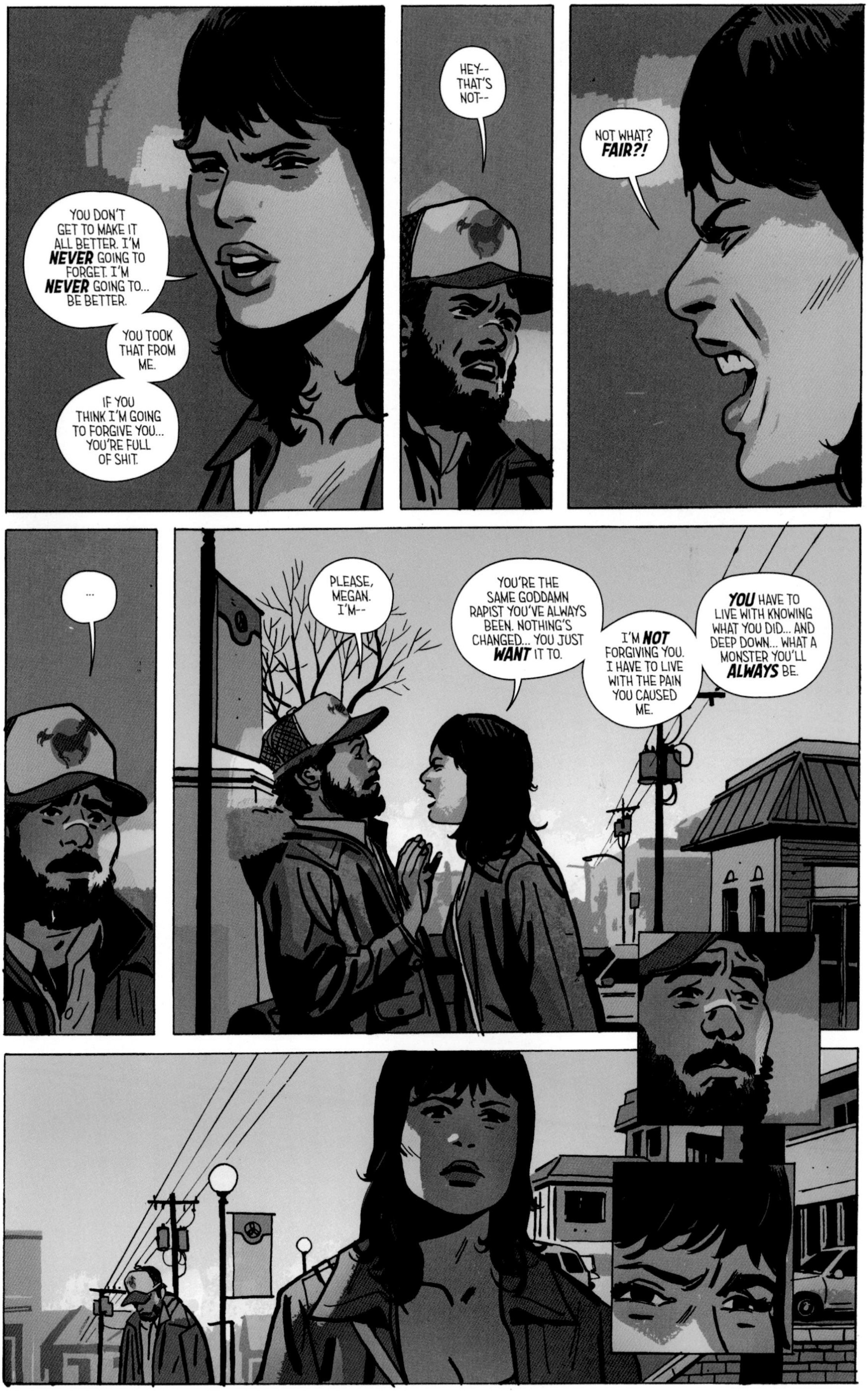

YOU DON'T GET TO MAKE IT ALL BETTER. I'M **NEVER** GOING TO FORGET. I'M **NEVER** GOING TO... BE BETTER.
YOU TOOK THAT FROM ME.
IF YOU THINK I'M GOING TO FORGIVE YOU... YOU'RE FULL OF SHIT.
HEY-- THAT'S NOT--
NOT WHAT? **FAIR?!**
...
PLEASE, MEGAN. I'M--
YOU'RE THE SAME GODDAMN RAPIST YOU'VE ALWAYS BEEN. NOTHING'S CHANGED... YOU JUST **WANT** IT TO.
I'M **NOT** FORGIVING YOU. I HAVE TO LIVE WITH THE PAIN YOU CAUSED ME.
YOU HAVE TO LIVE WITH KNOWING WHAT YOU DID... AND DEEP DOWN... WHAT A MONSTER YOU'LL **ALWAYS** BE.

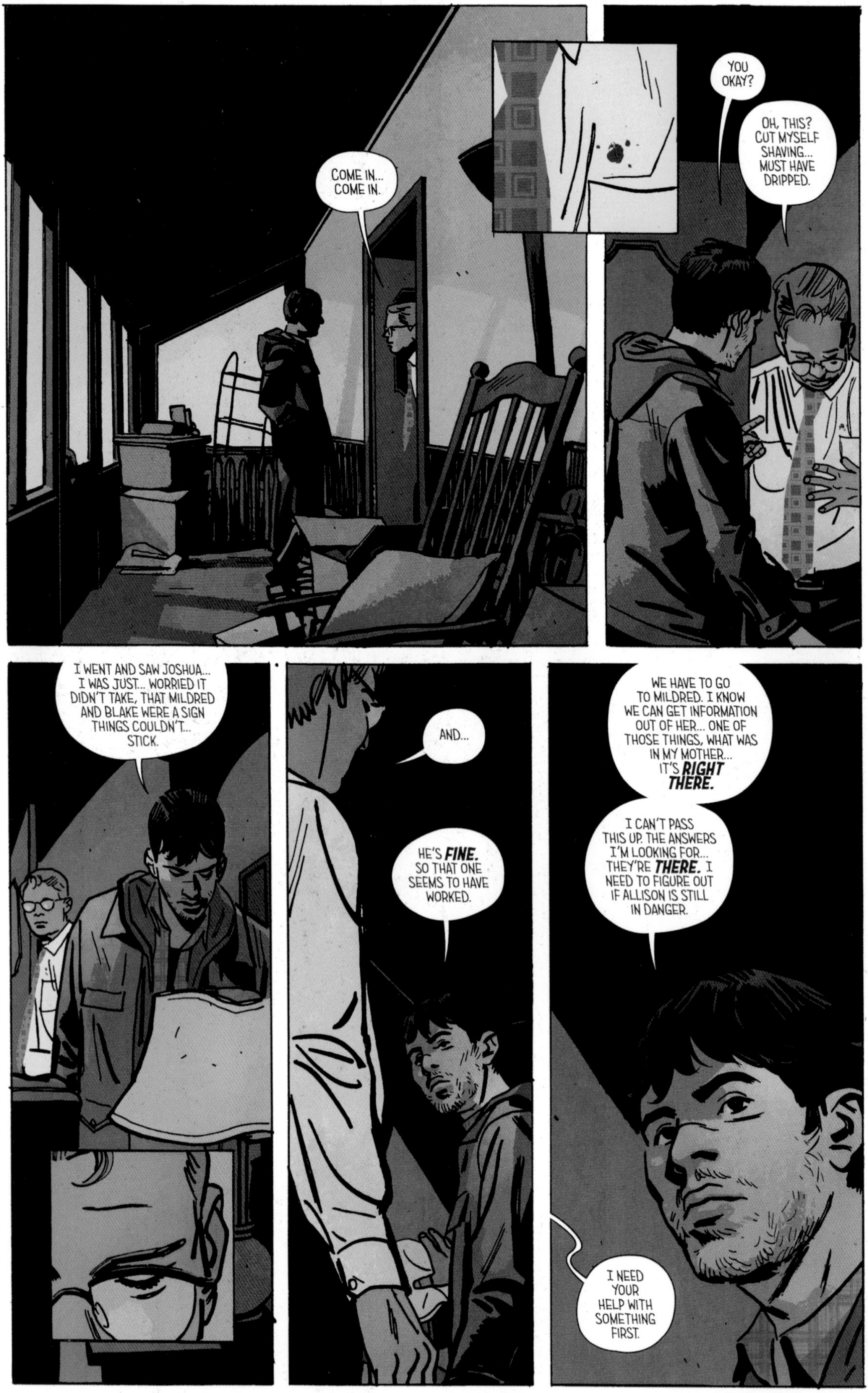
COME IN... COME IN.
YOU OKAY?
OH, THIS? CUT MYSELF SHAVING... MUST HAVE DRIPPED.
I WENT AND SAW JOSHUA... I WAS JUST... WORRIED IT DIDN'T TAKE, THAT MILDRED AND BLAKE WERE A SIGN THINGS COULDN'T... STICK.
AND...
HE'S **FINE.** SO THAT ONE SEEMS TO HAVE WORKED.
WE HAVE TO GO TO MILDRED. I KNOW WE CAN GET INFORMATION OUT OF HER... ONE OF THOSE THINGS, WHAT WAS IN MY MOTHER... IT'S **RIGHT THERE.**
I CAN'T PASS THIS UP. THE ANSWERS I'M LOOKING FOR... THEY'RE **THERE.** I NEED TO FIGURE OUT IF ALLISON IS STILL IN DANGER.
I NEED YOUR HELP WITH SOMETHING FIRST.

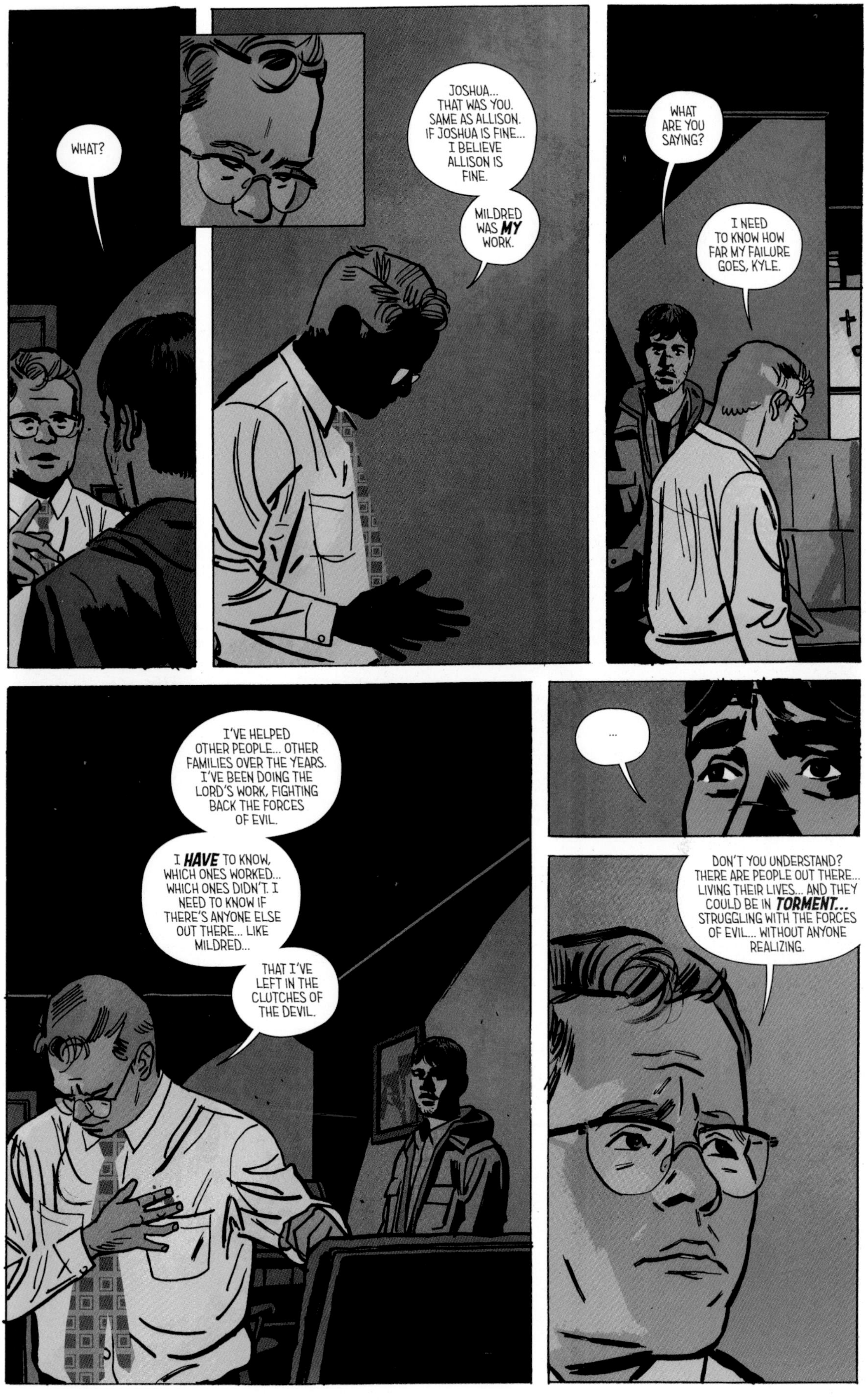
WHAT?
JOSHUA... THAT WAS YOU. SAME AS ALLISON. IF JOSHUA IS FINE... I BELIEVE ALLISON IS FINE.
MILDRED WAS MY WORK.
WHAT ARE YOU SAYING?
I NEED TO KNOW HOW FAR MY FAILURE GOES, KYLE.
I'VE HELPED OTHER PEOPLE... OTHER FAMILIES OVER THE YEARS. I'VE BEEN DOING THE LORD'S WORK, FIGHTING BACK THE FORCES OF EVIL.
I HAVE TO KNOW, WHICH ONES WORKED... WHICH ONES DIDN'T. I NEED TO KNOW IF THERE'S ANYONE ELSE OUT THERE... LIKE MILDRED...
THAT I'VE LEFT IN THE CLUTCHES OF THE DEVIL.
...
DON'T YOU UNDERSTAND? THERE ARE PEOPLE OUT THERE... LIVING THEIR LIVES... AND THEY COULD BE IN TORMENT... STRUGGLING WITH THE FORCES OF EVIL... WITHOUT ANYONE REALIZING.

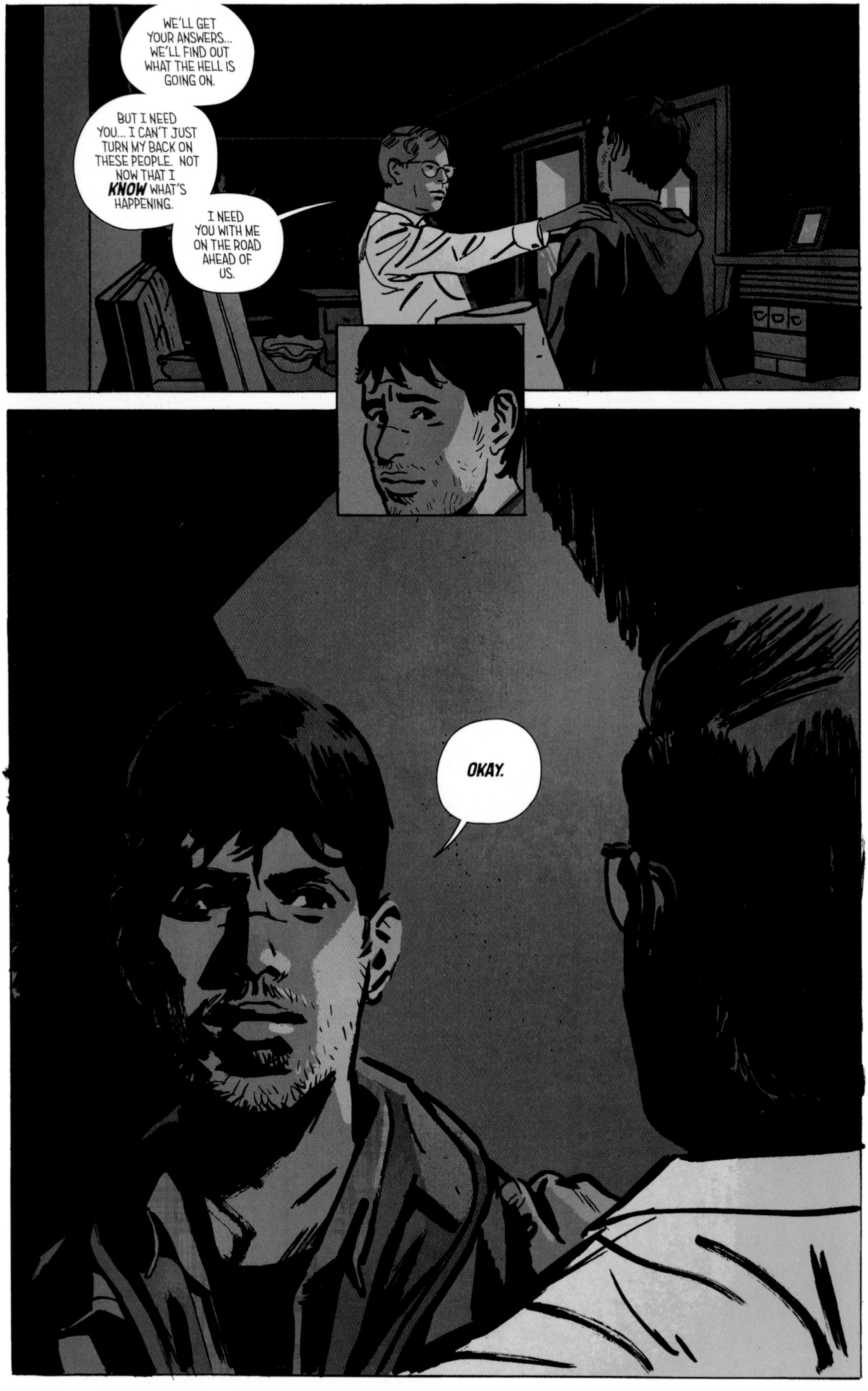
WE'LL GET YOUR ANSWERS... WE'LL FIND OUT WHAT THE HELL IS GOING ON.
BUT I NEED YOU... I CAN'T JUST TURN MY BACK ON THESE PEOPLE. NOT NOW THAT I **KNOW** WHAT'S HAPPENING.
I NEED YOU WITH ME ON THE ROAD AHEAD OF US.
OKAY.

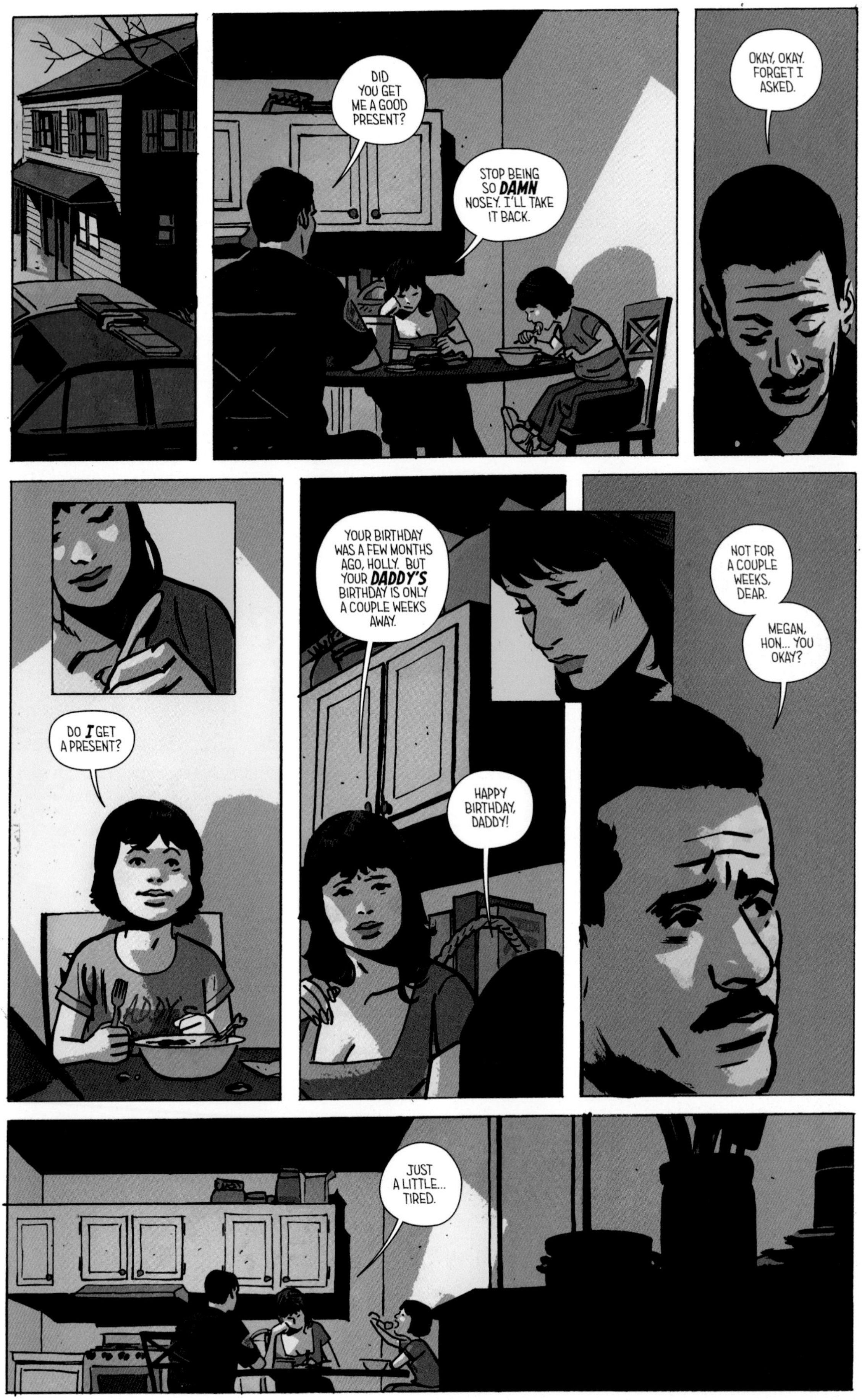
DID YOU GET ME A GOOD PRESENT?
STOP BEING SO **DAMN** NOSEY. I'LL TAKE IT BACK.
OKAY, OKAY. FORGET I ASKED.
DO **I** GET A PRESENT?
YOUR BIRTHDAY WAS A FEW MONTHS AGO, HOLLY. BUT YOUR **DADDY'S** BIRTHDAY IS ONLY A COUPLE WEEKS AWAY.
HAPPY BIRTHDAY, DADDY!
NOT FOR A COUPLE WEEKS, DEAR.
MEGAN, HON... YOU OKAY?
JUST A LITTLE... TIRED.

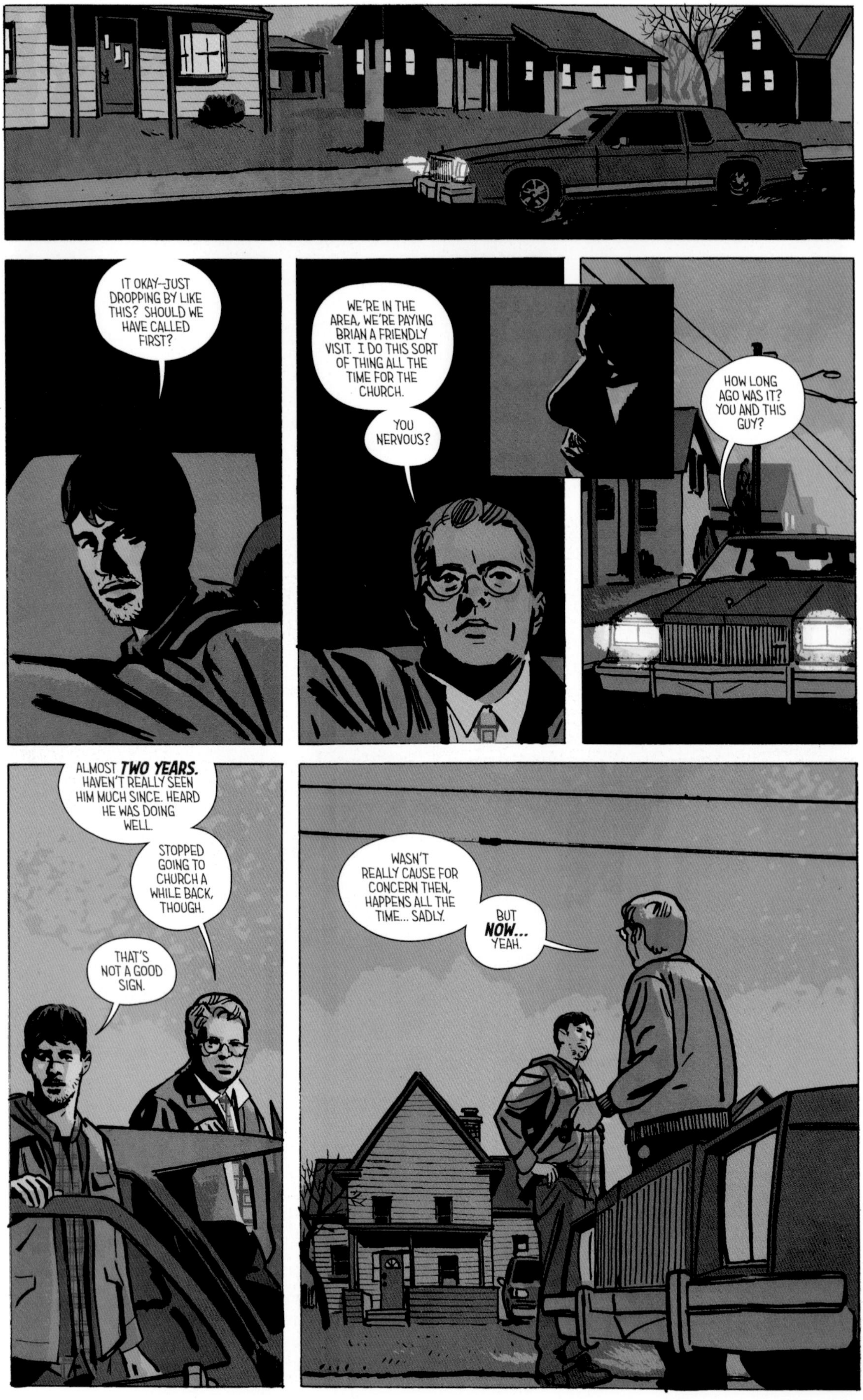

IT OKAY--JUST DROPPING BY LIKE THIS? SHOULD WE HAVE CALLED FIRST?
WE'RE IN THE AREA, WE'RE PAYING BRIAN A FRIENDLY VISIT. I DO THIS SORT OF THING ALL THE TIME FOR THE CHURCH.
YOU NERVOUS?
HOW LONG AGO WAS IT? YOU AND THIS GUY?
ALMOST **TWO YEARS.** HAVEN'T REALLY SEEN HIM MUCH SINCE. HEARD HE WAS DOING WELL.
STOPPED GOING TO CHURCH A WHILE BACK, THOUGH.
THAT'S NOT A GOOD SIGN.
WASN'T REALLY CAUSE FOR CONCERN THEN, HAPPENS ALL THE TIME... SADLY.
BUT **NOW...** YEAH.

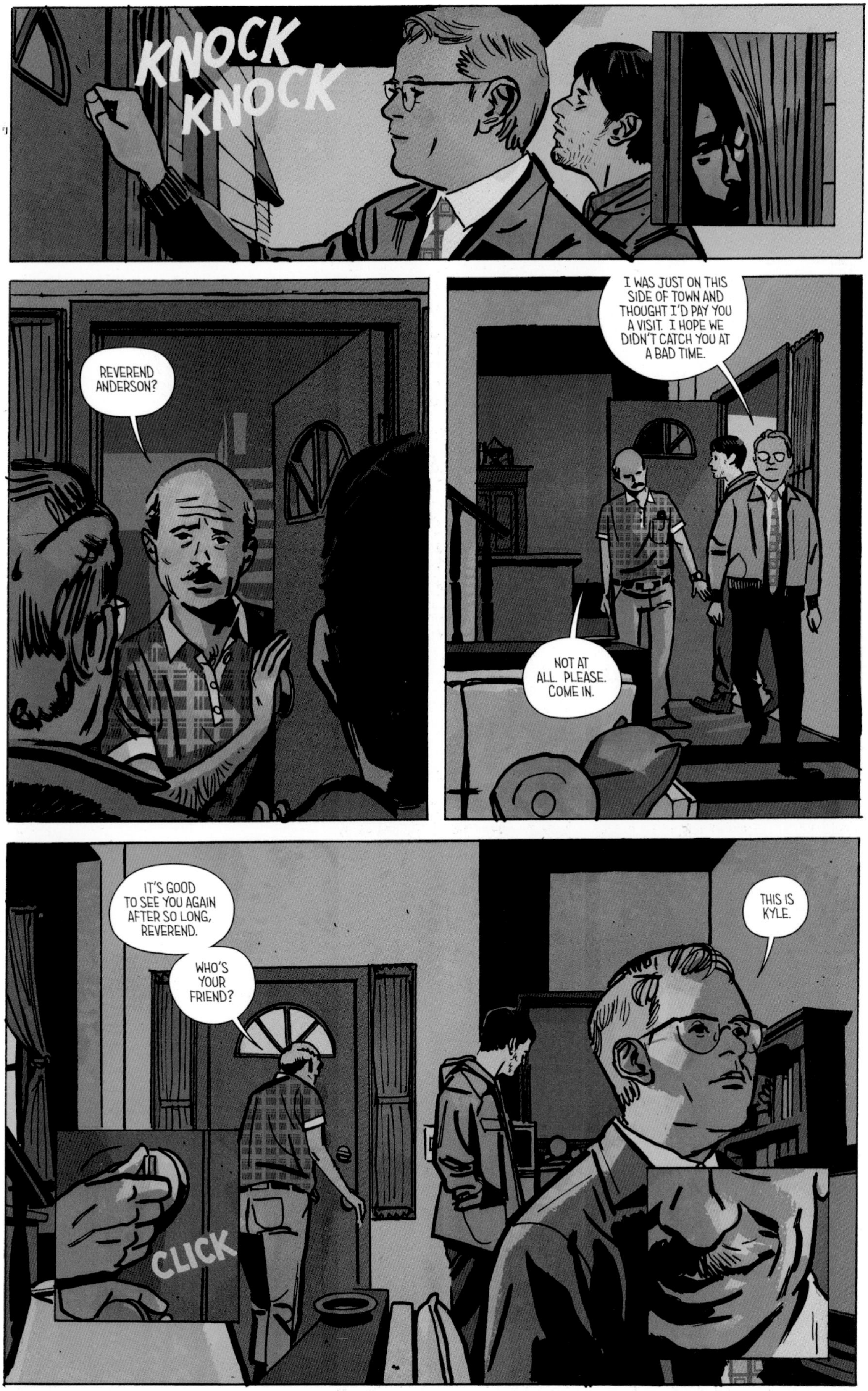
KNOCK KNOCK
REVEREND ANDERSON?
I WAS JUST ON THIS SIDE OF TOWN AND THOUGHT I'D PAY YOU A VISIT. I HOPE WE DIDN'T CATCH YOU AT A BAD TIME.
NOT AT ALL. PLEASE. COME IN.
IT'S GOOD TO SEE YOU AGAIN AFTER SO LONG, REVEREND.
WHO'S YOUR FRIEND?
THIS IS KYLE.
CLICK

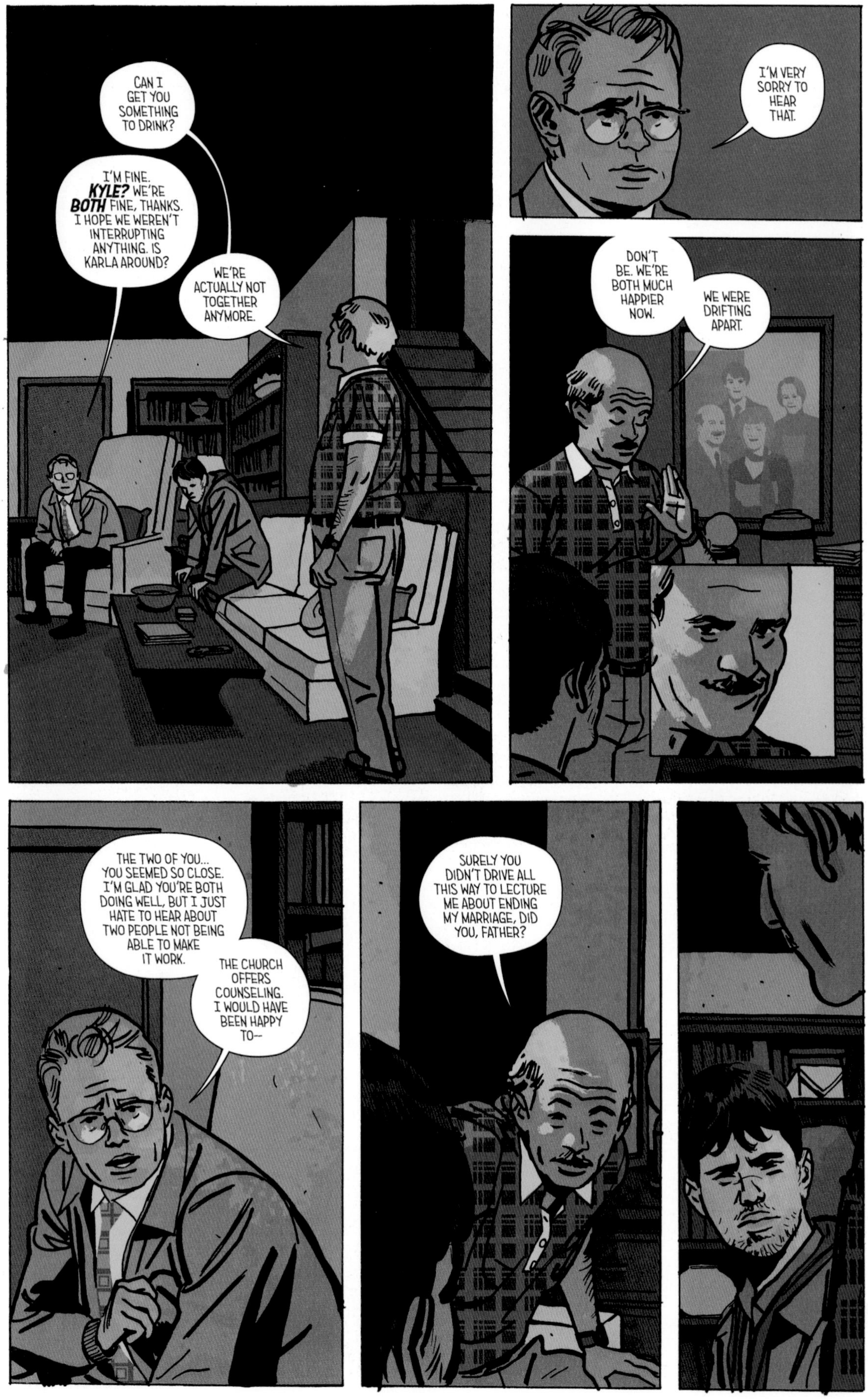
CAN I GET YOU SOMETHING TO DRINK?
I'M FINE. **KYLE?** WE'RE **BOTH** FINE, THANKS. I HOPE WE WEREN'T INTERRUPTING ANYTHING. IS KARLA AROUND?
WE'RE ACTUALLY NOT TOGETHER ANYMORE.
I'M VERY SORRY TO HEAR THAT.
DON'T BE. WE'RE BOTH MUCH HAPPIER NOW.
WE WERE DRIFTING APART.
THE TWO OF YOU... YOU SEEMED SO CLOSE. I'M GLAD YOU'RE BOTH DOING WELL, BUT I JUST HATE TO HEAR ABOUT TWO PEOPLE NOT BEING ABLE TO MAKE IT WORK.
THE CHURCH OFFERS COUNSELING. I WOULD HAVE BEEN HAPPY TO--
SURELY YOU DIDN'T DRIVE ALL THIS WAY TO LECTURE ME ABOUT ENDING MY MARRIAGE, DID YOU, FATHER?

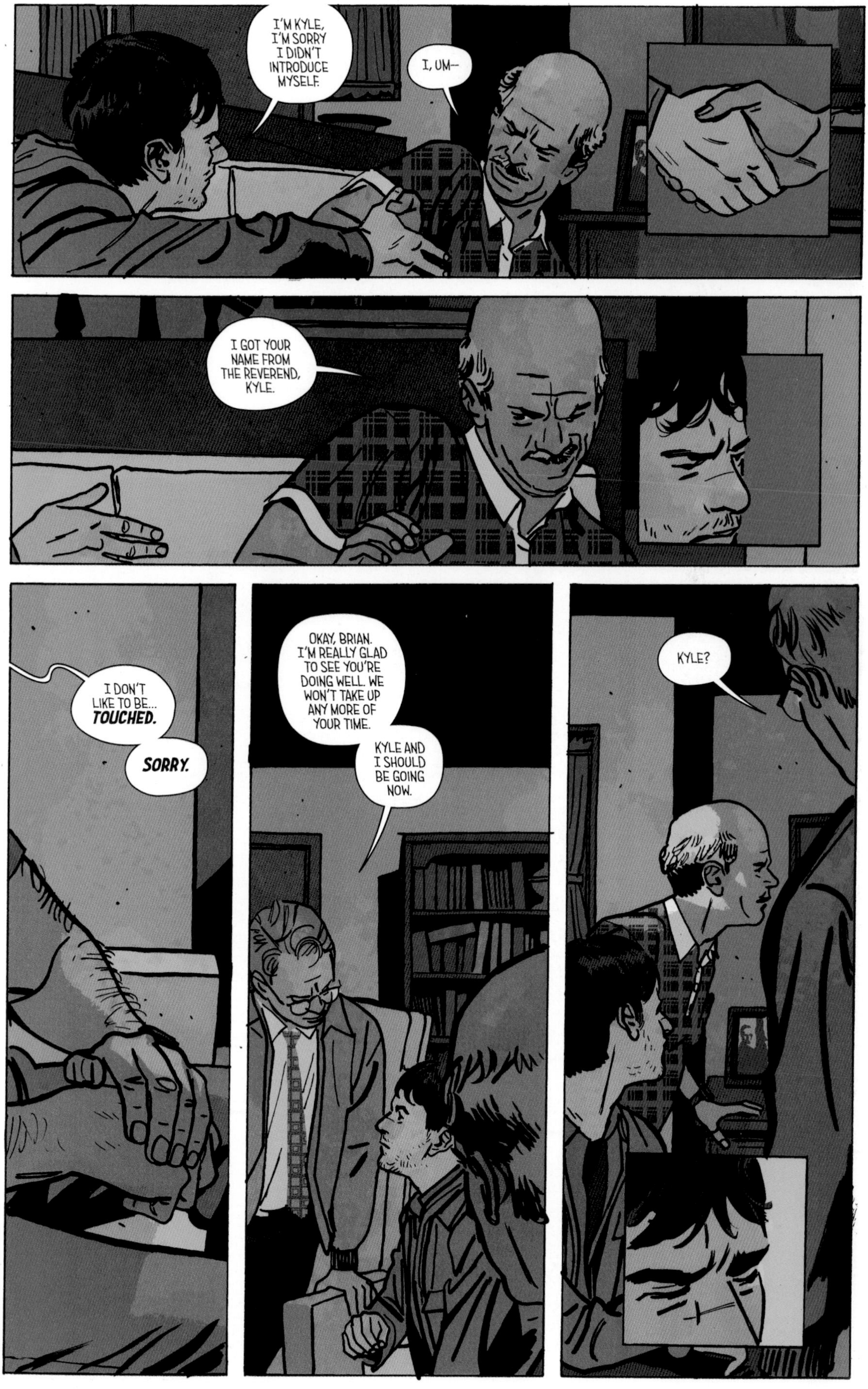
I'M KYLE, I'M SORRY I DIDN'T INTRODUCE MYSELF.
I, UM--
I GOT YOUR NAME FROM THE REVEREND, KYLE.
I DON'T LIKE TO BE... TOUCHED.
SORRY.
OKAY, BRIAN. I'M REALLY GLAD TO SEE YOU'RE DOING WELL. WE WON'T TAKE UP ANY MORE OF YOUR TIME.
KYLE AND I SHOULD BE GOING NOW.
KYLE?

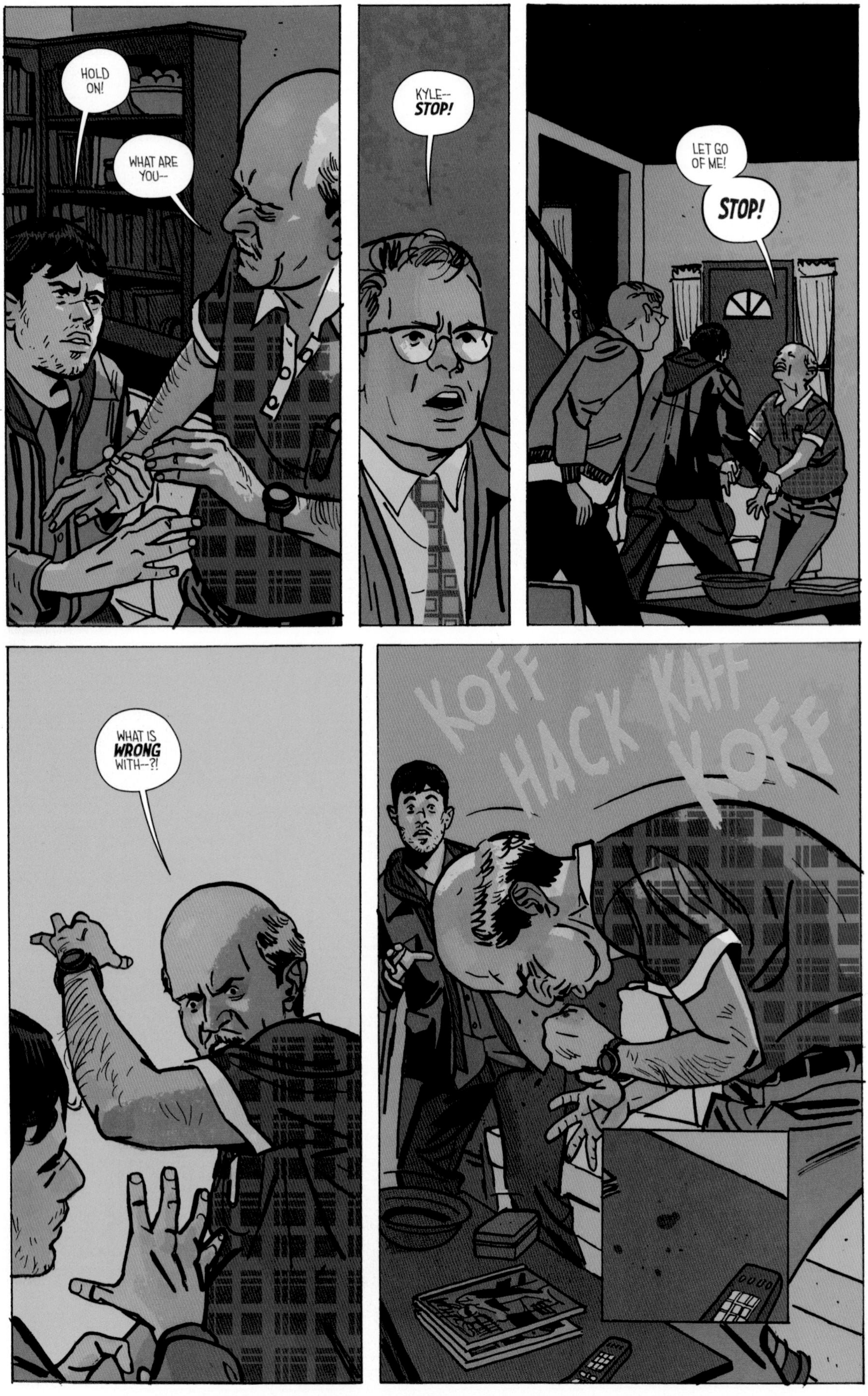
HOLD ON!
WHAT ARE YOU--
KYLE-- **STOP!**
LET GO OF ME!
STOP!
WHAT IS **WRONG** WITH--?!
KOFF
HACK
KAFF
KOFF

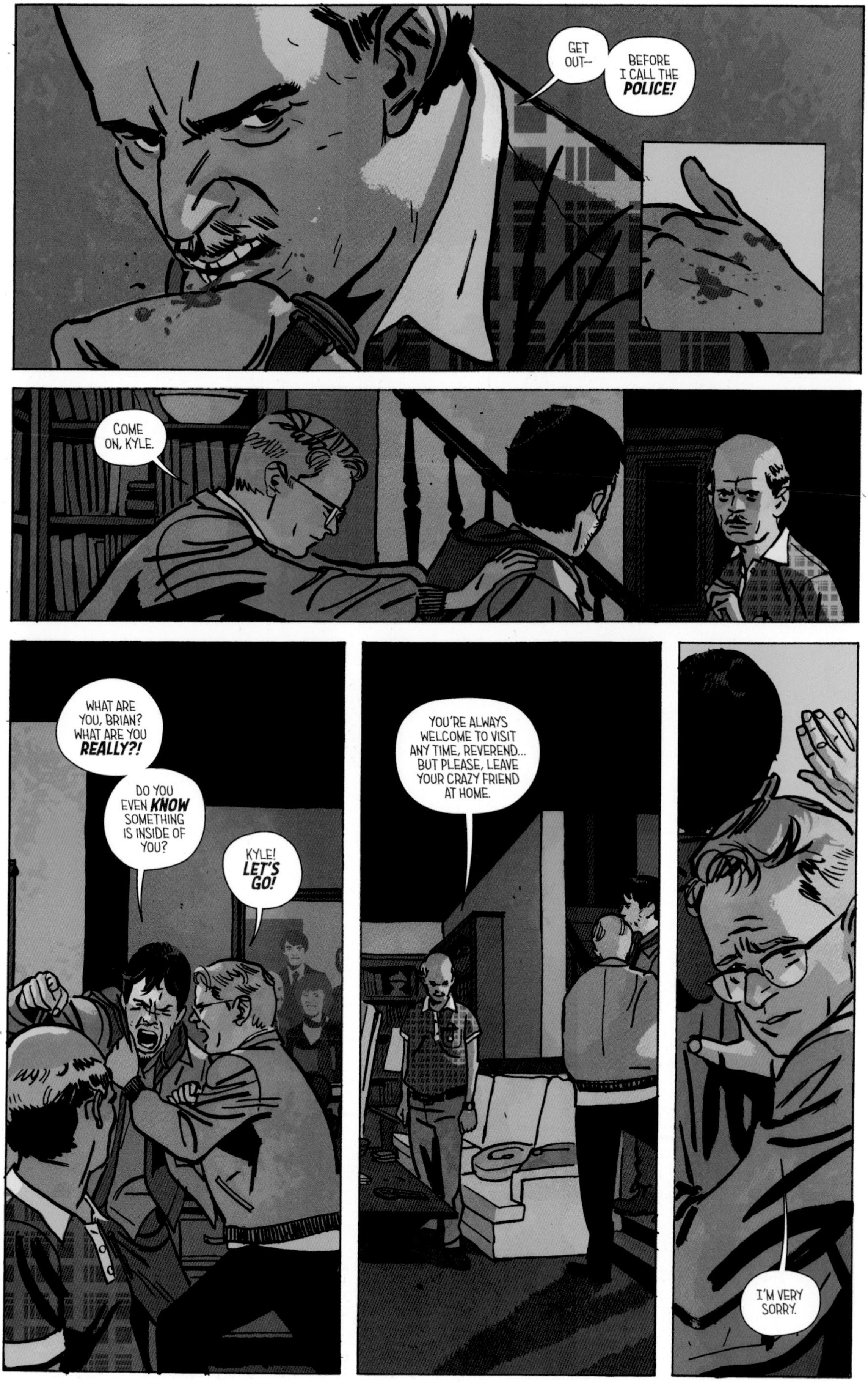
GET OUT--
BEFORE I CALL THE **POLICE!**
COME ON, KYLE.
WHAT ARE YOU, BRIAN? WHAT ARE YOU **REALLY?!**
DO YOU EVEN **KNOW** SOMETHING IS INSIDE OF YOU?
KYLE! **LET'S GO!**
YOU'RE ALWAYS WELCOME TO VISIT ANY TIME, REVEREND... BUT PLEASE, LEAVE YOUR CRAZY FRIEND AT HOME.
I'M VERY SORRY.

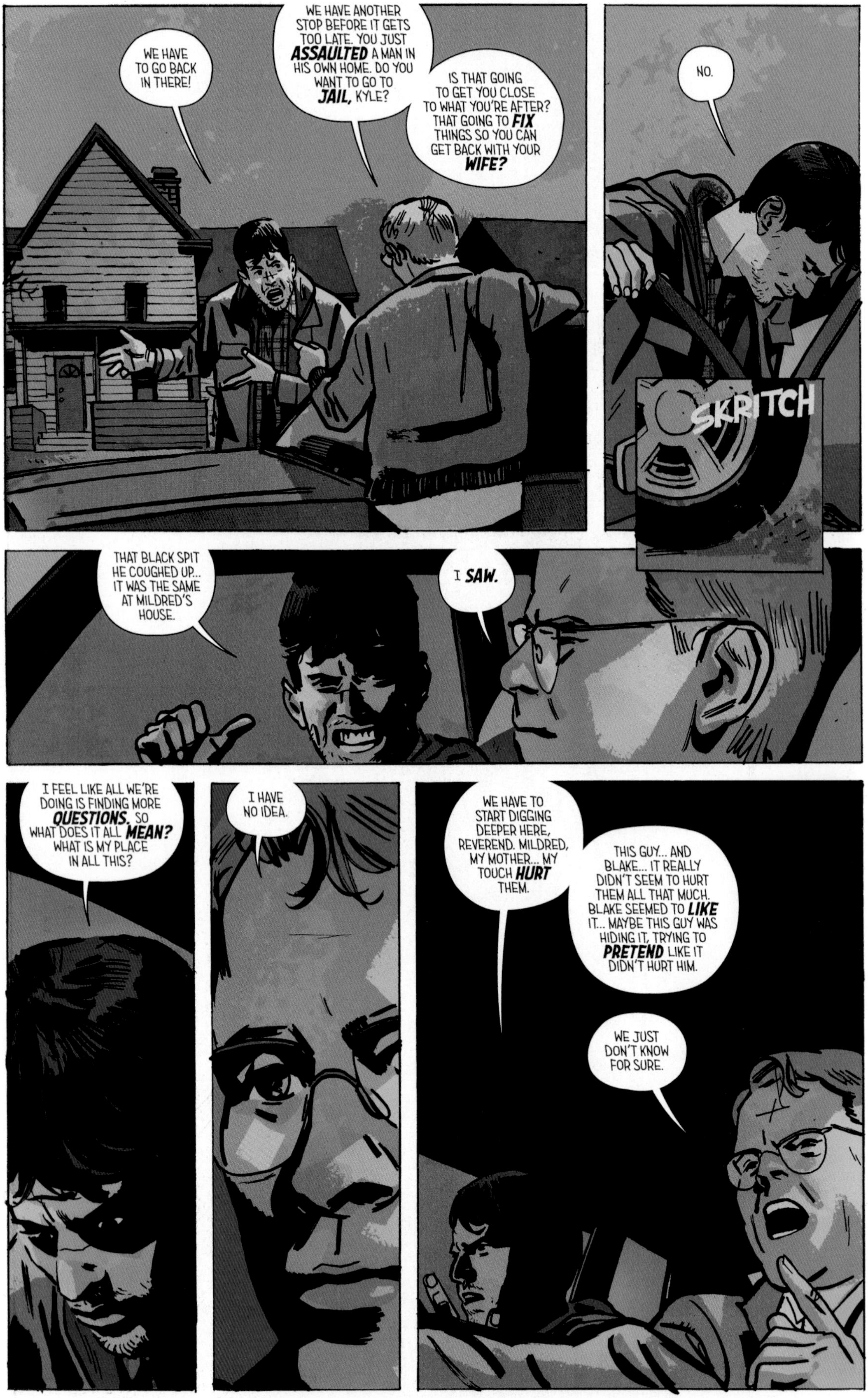

WE HAVE TO GO BACK IN THERE!
WE HAVE ANOTHER STOP BEFORE IT GETS TOO LATE. YOU JUST ASSAULTED A MAN IN HIS OWN HOME. DO YOU WANT TO GO TO JAIL, KYLE?
IS THAT GOING TO GET YOU CLOSE TO WHAT YOU'RE AFTER? THAT GOING TO FIX THINGS SO YOU CAN GET BACK WITH YOUR WIFE?
NO.
SKRITCH
THAT BLACK SPIT HE COUGHED UP... IT WAS THE SAME AT MILDRED'S HOUSE.
I SAW.
I FEEL LIKE ALL WE'RE DOING IS FINDING MORE QUESTIONS. SO WHAT DOES IT ALL MEAN? WHAT IS MY PLACE IN ALL THIS?
I HAVE NO IDEA.
WE HAVE TO START DIGGING DEEPER HERE, REVEREND. MILDRED, MY MOTHER... MY TOUCH HURT THEM.
THIS GUY... AND BLAKE... IT REALLY DIDN'T SEEM TO HURT THEM ALL THAT MUCH. BLAKE SEEMED TO LIKE IT... MAYBE THIS GUY WAS HIDING IT, TRYING TO PRETEND LIKE IT DIDN'T HURT HIM.
WE JUST DON'T KNOW FOR SURE.

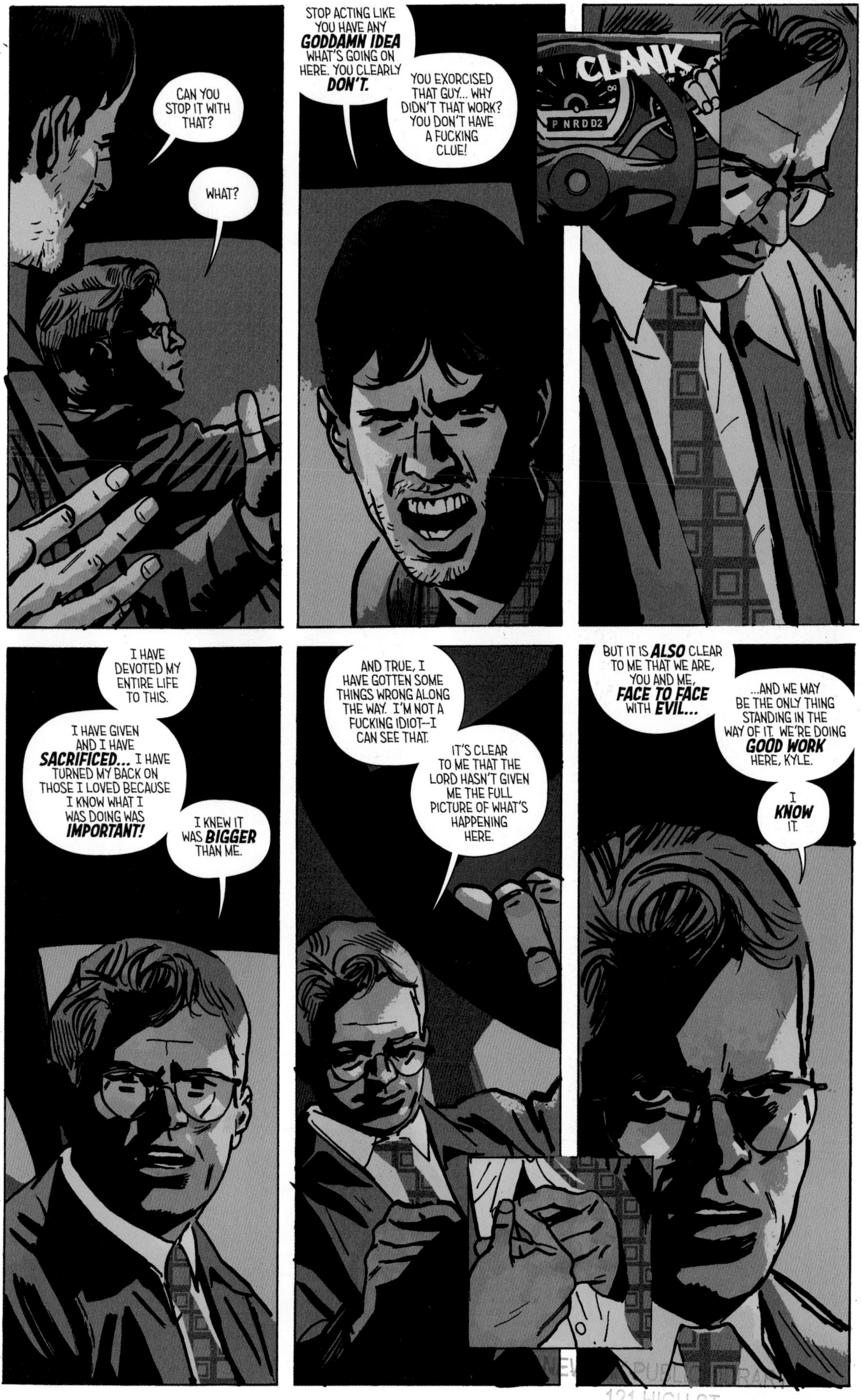
CAN YOU STOP IT WITH THAT?
WHAT?
STOP ACTING LIKE YOU HAVE ANY GODDAMN IDEA WHAT'S GOING ON HERE. YOU CLEARLY DON'T.
YOU EXORCISED THAT GUY... WHY DIDN'T THAT WORK? YOU DON'T HAVE A FUCKING CLUE!
CLANK
P N R D D2
I HAVE DEVOTED MY ENTIRE LIFE TO THIS.
I HAVE GIVEN AND I HAVE SACRIFICED... I HAVE TURNED MY BACK ON THOSE I LOVED BECAUSE I KNOW WHAT I WAS DOING WAS IMPORTANT!
I KNEW IT WAS BIGGER THAN ME.
AND TRUE, I HAVE GOTTEN SOME THINGS WRONG ALONG THE WAY. I'M NOT A FUCKING IDIOT--I CAN SEE THAT.
IT'S CLEAR TO ME THAT THE LORD HASN'T GIVEN ME THE FULL PICTURE OF WHAT'S HAPPENING HERE.
BUT IT IS ALSO CLEAR TO ME THAT WE ARE, YOU AND ME, FACE TO FACE WITH EVIL...
...AND WE MAY BE THE ONLY THING STANDING IN THE WAY OF IT. WE'RE DOING GOOD WORK HERE, KYLE.
I KNOW IT.

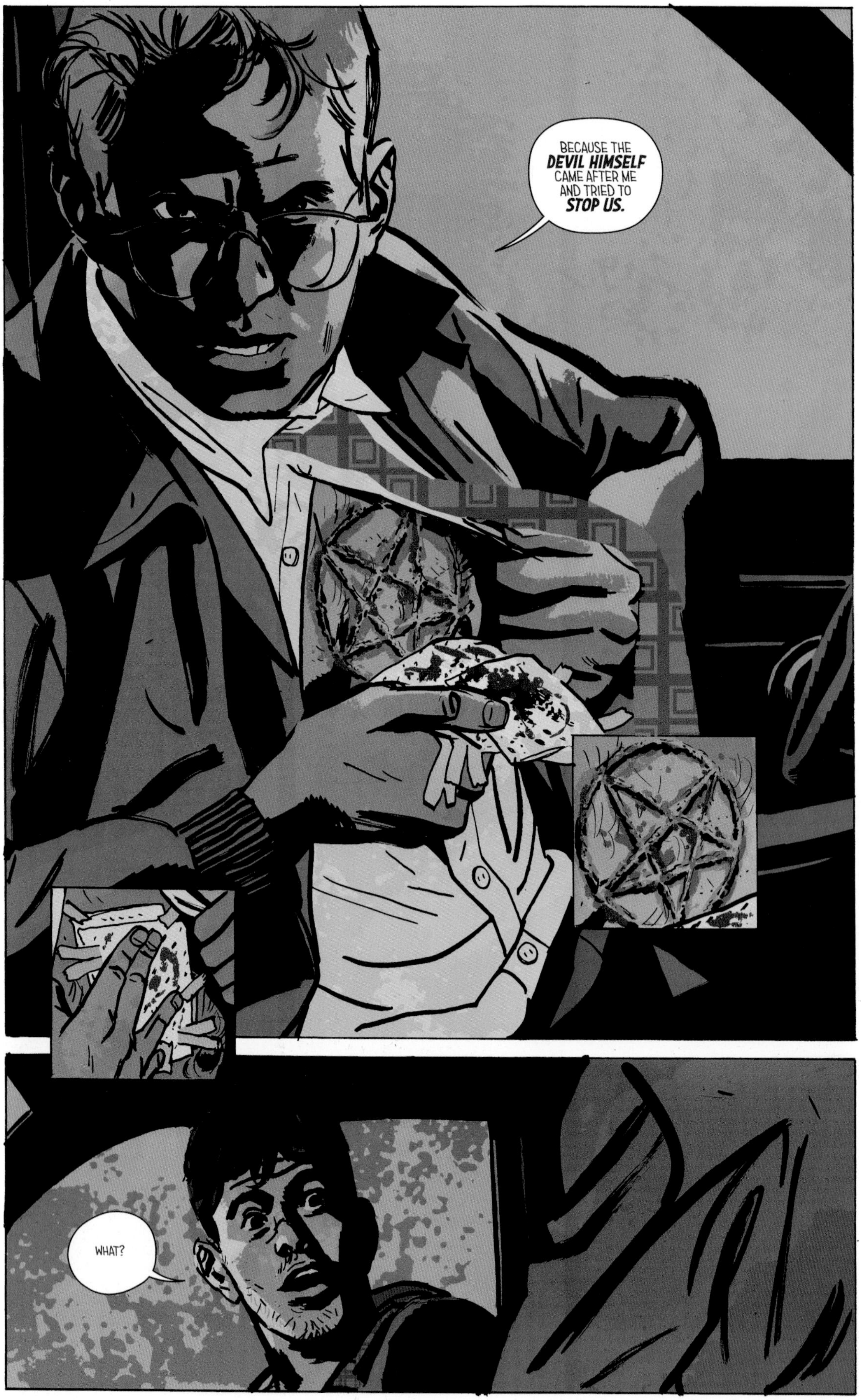
BECAUSE THE **DEVIL HIMSELF** CAME AFTER ME AND TRIED TO **STOP US.**
WHAT?

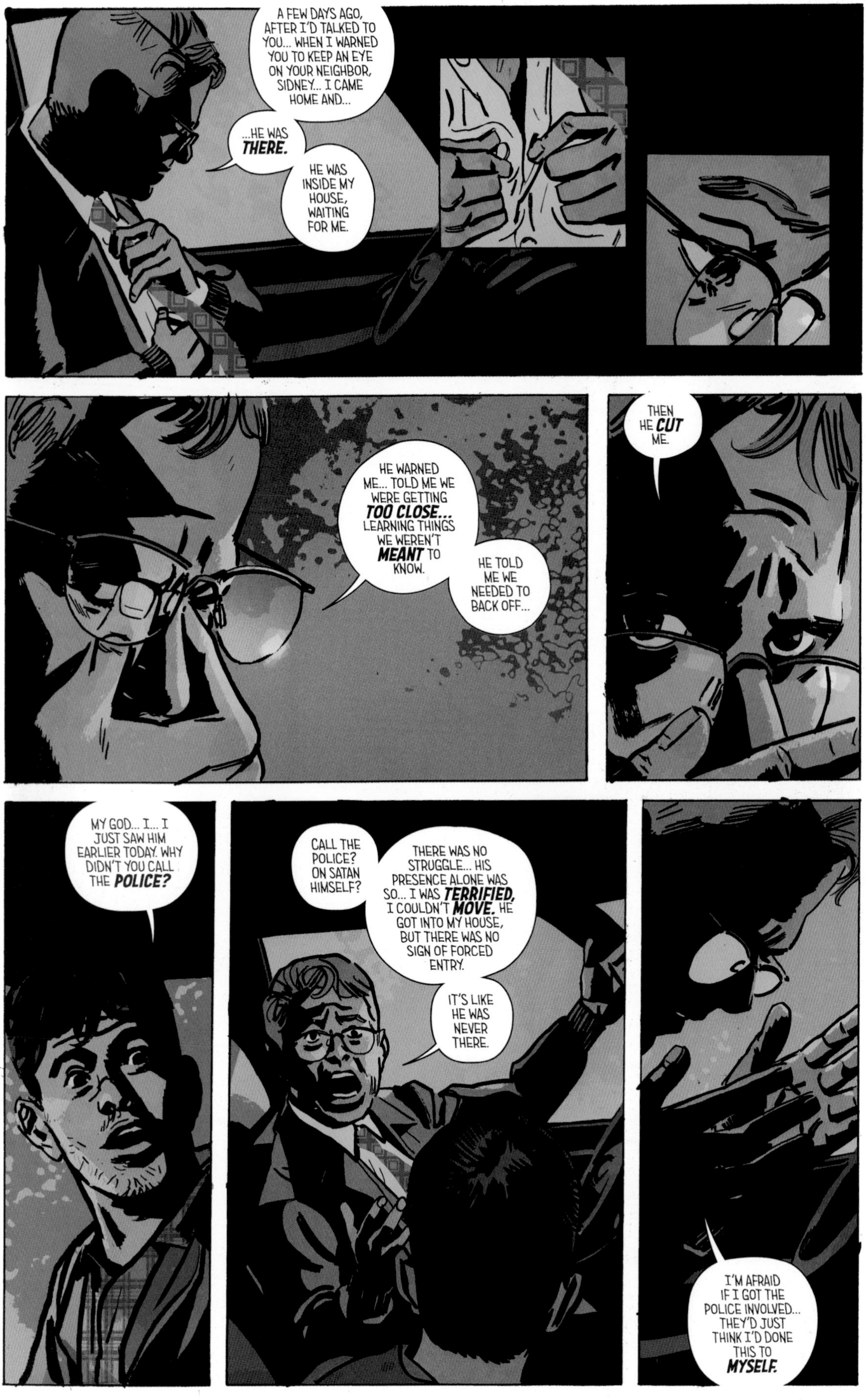
A FEW DAYS AGO, AFTER I'D TALKED TO YOU... WHEN I WARNED YOU TO KEEP AN EYE ON YOUR NEIGHBOR, SIDNEY... I CAME HOME AND...
...HE WAS THERE.
HE WAS INSIDE MY HOUSE, WAITING FOR ME.
HE WARNED ME... TOLD ME WE WERE GETTING TOO CLOSE... LEARNING THINGS WE WEREN'T MEANT TO KNOW.
HE TOLD ME WE NEEDED TO BACK OFF...
THEN HE CUT ME.
MY GOD... I... I JUST SAW HIM EARLIER TODAY. WHY DIDN'T YOU CALL THE POLICE?
CALL THE POLICE? ON SATAN HIMSELF?
THERE WAS NO STRUGGLE... HIS PRESENCE ALONE WAS SO... I WAS TERRIFIED, I COULDN'T MOVE. HE GOT INTO MY HOUSE, BUT THERE WAS NO SIGN OF FORCED ENTRY.
IT'S LIKE HE WAS NEVER THERE.
I'M AFRAID IF I GOT THE POLICE INVOLVED... THEY'D JUST THINK I'D DONE THIS TO MYSELF.

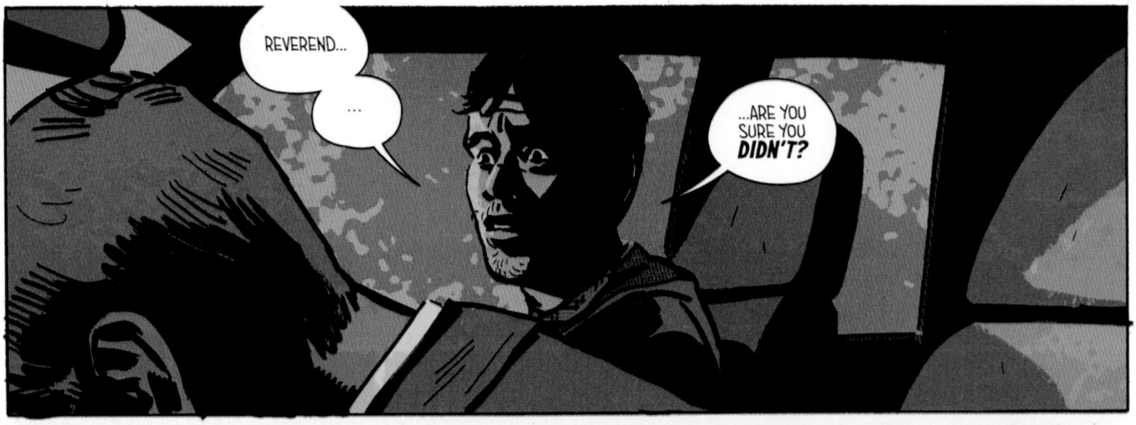
REVEREND...
...
...ARE YOU SURE YOU **DIDN'T?**

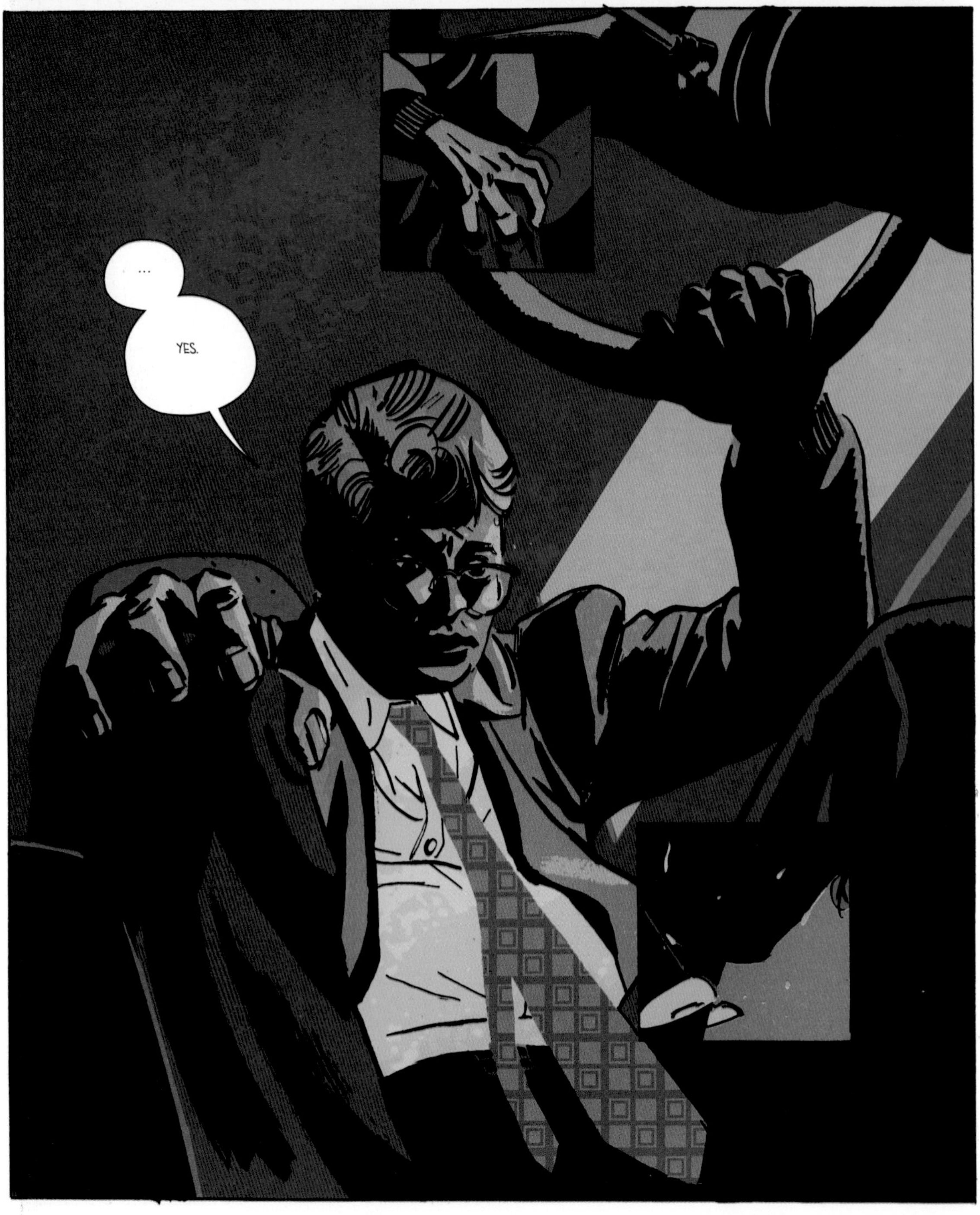
...
YES.

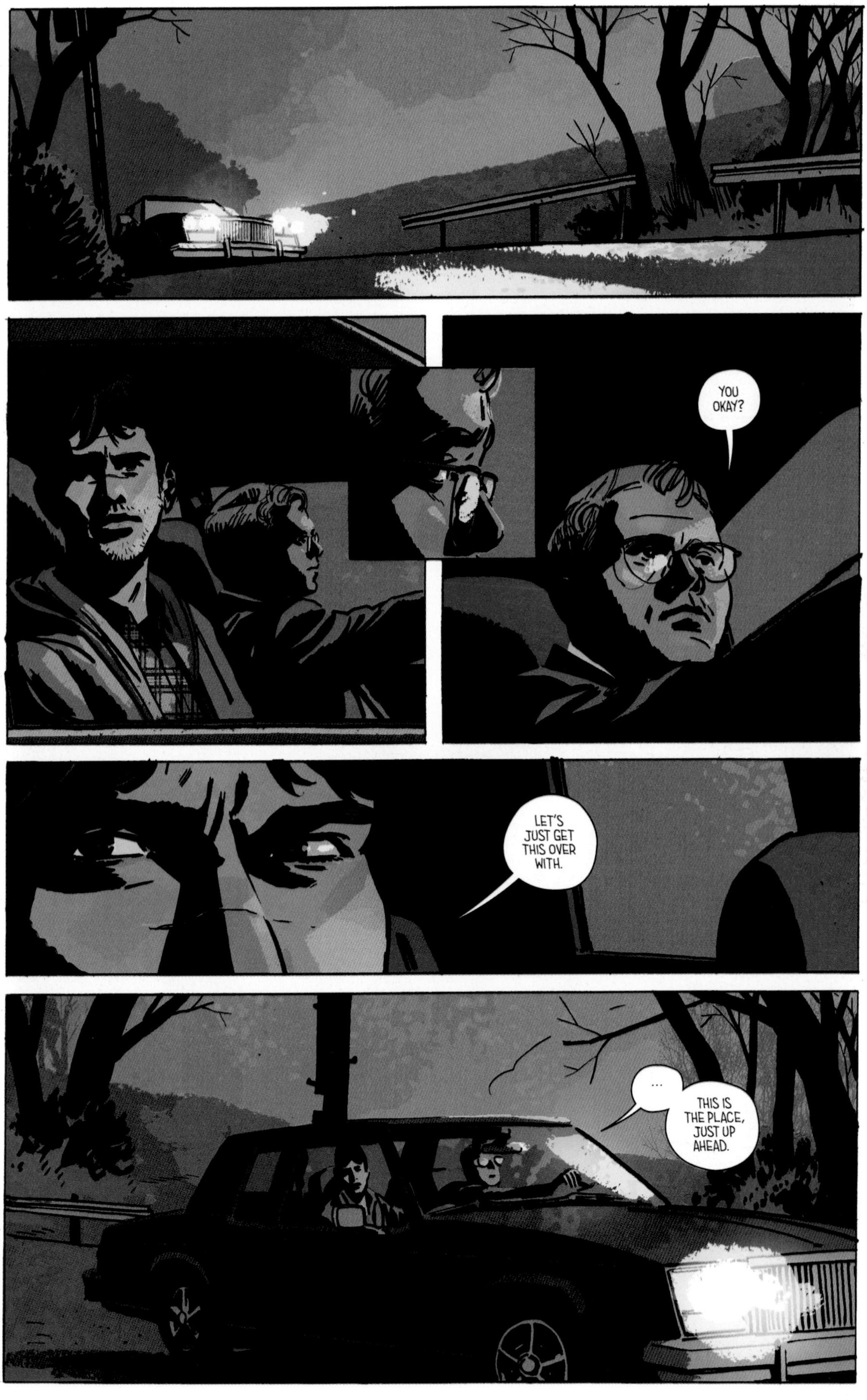
YOU OKAY?
LET'S JUST GET THIS OVER WITH.
...
THIS IS THE PLACE, JUST UP AHEAD.

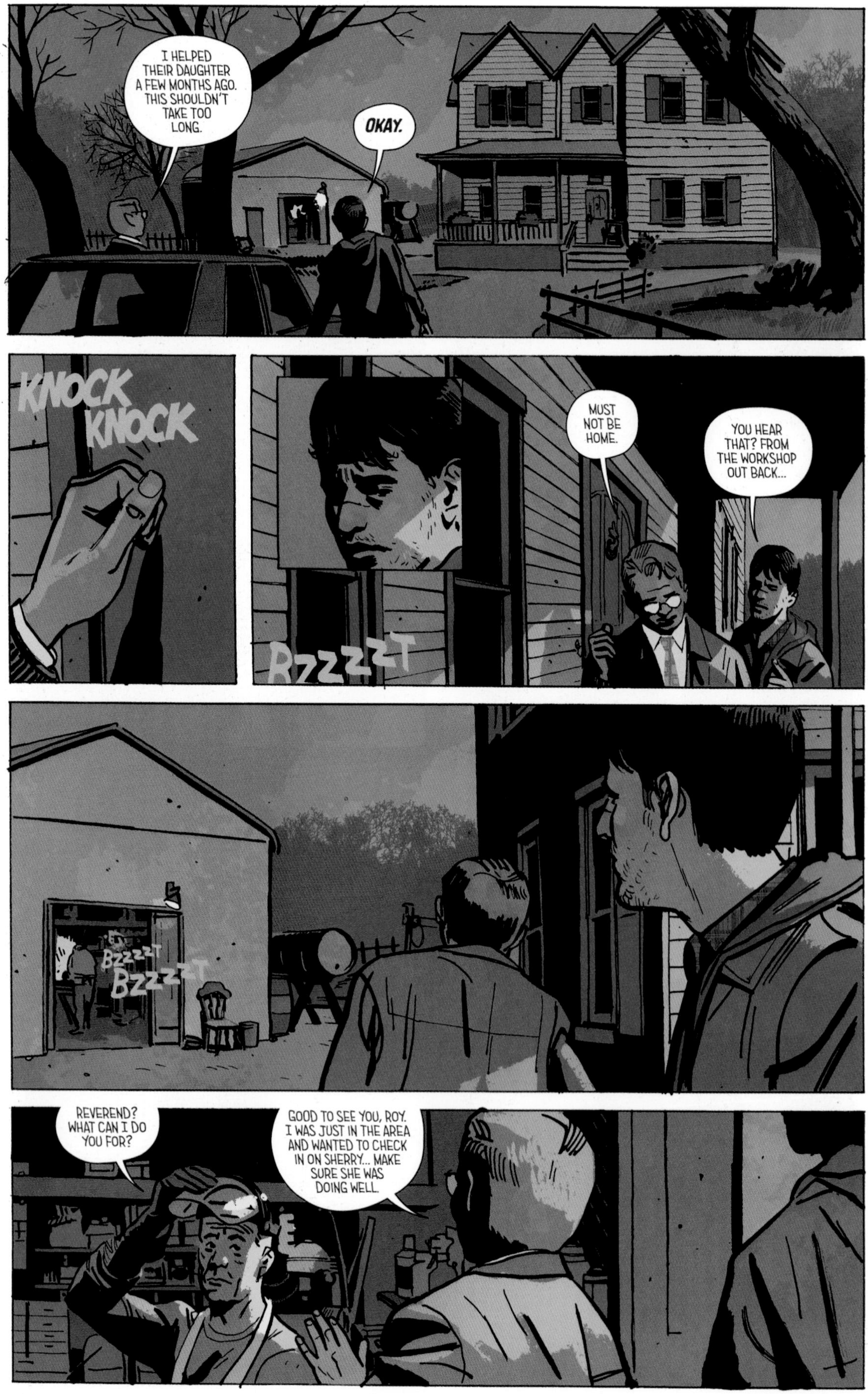
I HELPED THEIR DAUGHTER A FEW MONTHS AGO. THIS SHOULDN'T TAKE TOO LONG.
OKAY.
KNOCK KNOCK
MUST NOT BE HOME.
YOU HEAR THAT? FROM THE WORKSHOP OUT BACK...
BZZZZZT
BZZZZZT BZZZZZT
REVEREND? WHAT CAN I DO YOU FOR?
GOOD TO SEE YOU, ROY. I WAS JUST IN THE AREA AND WANTED TO CHECK IN ON SHERRY... MAKE SURE SHE WAS DOING WELL.

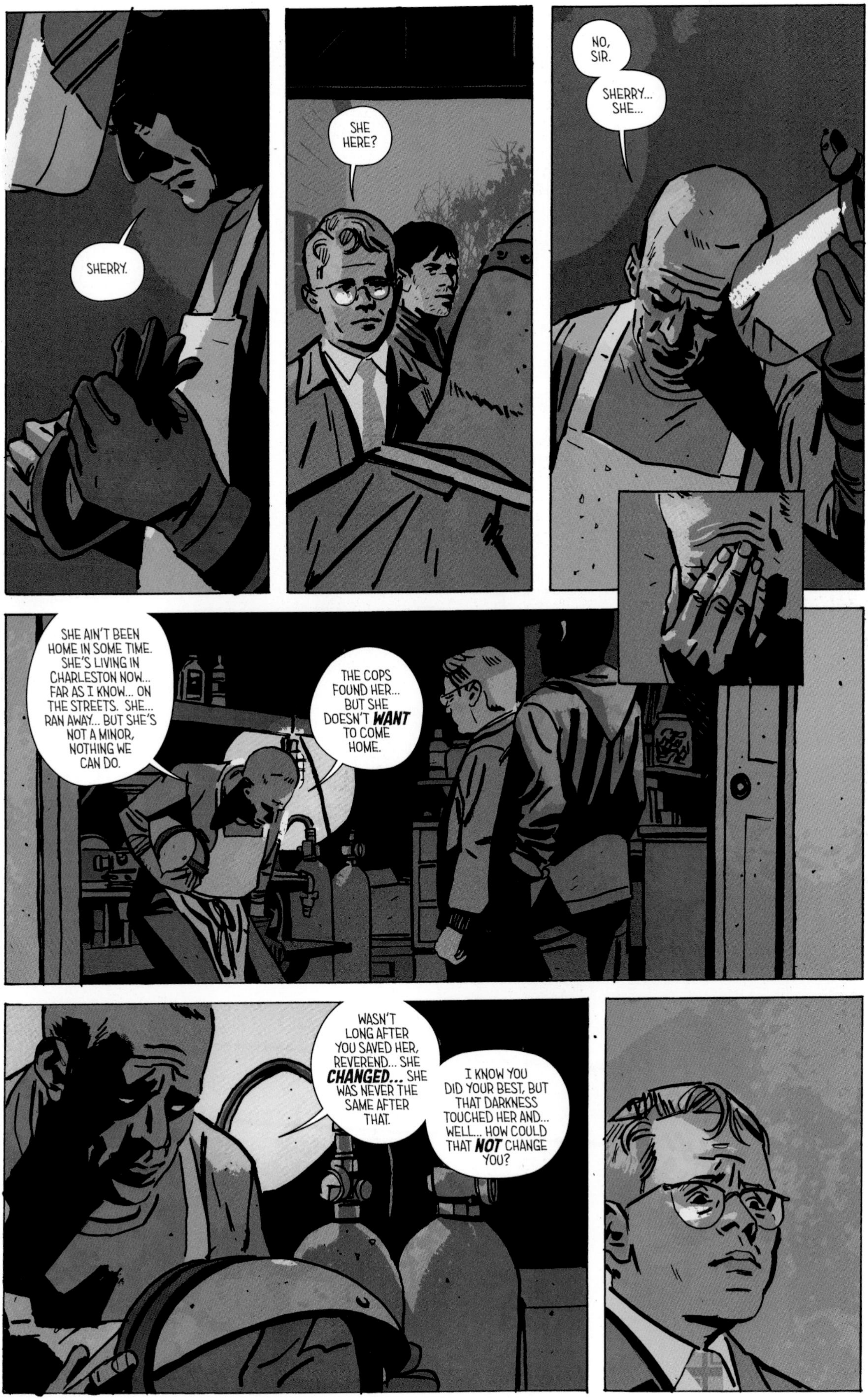

SHERRY.
SHE HERE?
NO, SIR.
SHERRY... SHE...
SHE AIN'T BEEN HOME IN SOME TIME. SHE'S LIVING IN CHARLESTON NOW... FAR AS I KNOW... ON THE STREETS. SHE... RAN AWAY... BUT SHE'S NOT A MINOR, NOTHING WE CAN DO.
THE COPS FOUND HER... BUT SHE DOESN'T **WANT** TO COME HOME.
WASN'T LONG AFTER YOU SAVED HER, REVEREND... SHE **CHANGED...** SHE WAS NEVER THE SAME AFTER THAT.
I KNOW YOU DID YOUR BEST, BUT THAT DARKNESS TOUCHED HER AND... WELL... HOW COULD THAT **NOT** CHANGE YOU?

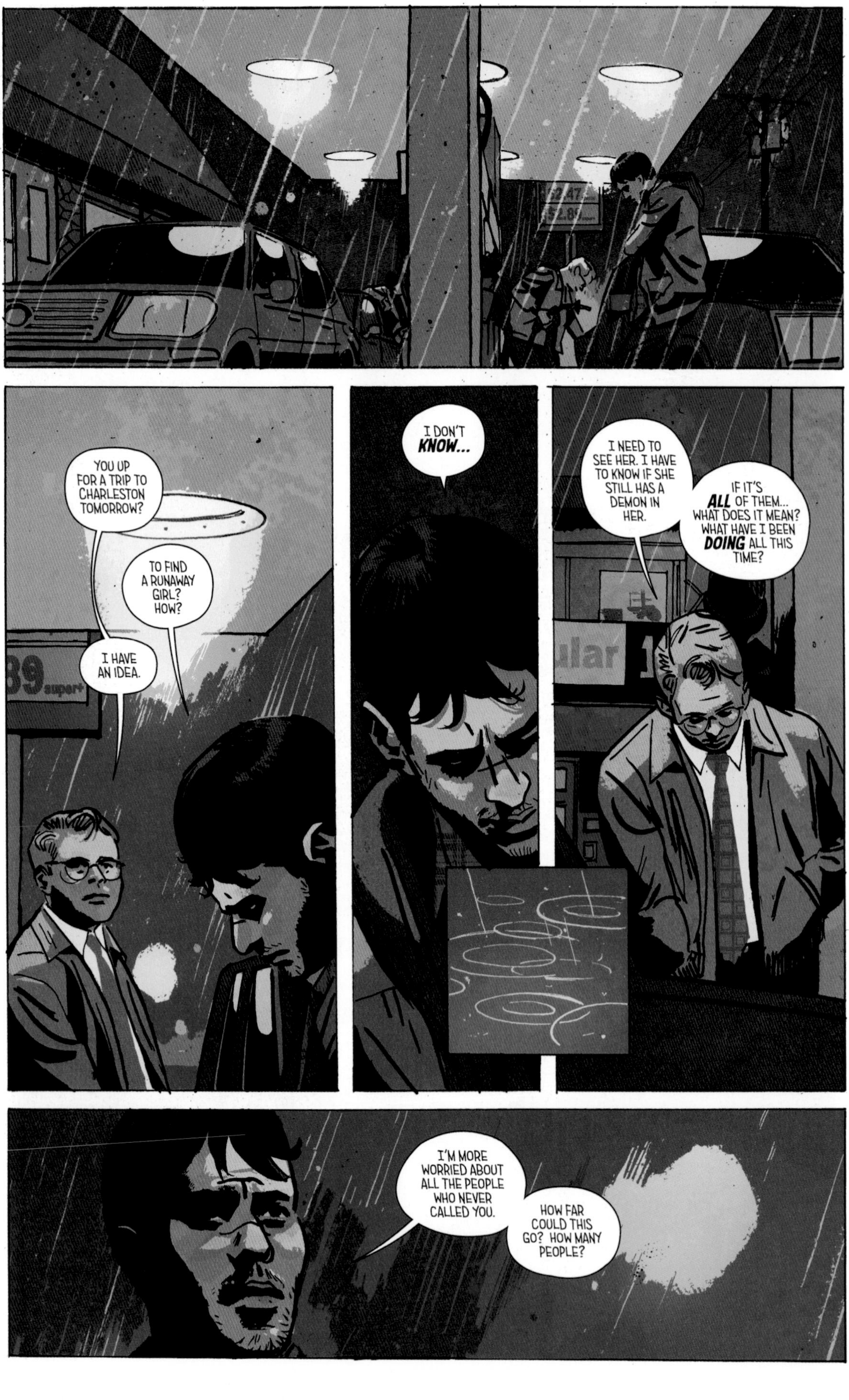
YOU UP FOR A TRIP TO CHARLESTON TOMORROW?
TO FIND A RUNAWAY GIRL? HOW?
I HAVE AN IDEA.
I DON'T *KNOW...*
I NEED TO SEE HER. I HAVE TO KNOW IF SHE STILL HAS A DEMON IN HER.
IF IT'S *ALL* OF THEM... WHAT DOES IT MEAN? WHAT HAVE I BEEN *DOING* ALL THIS TIME?
I'M MORE WORRIED ABOUT ALL THE PEOPLE WHO NEVER CALLED YOU.
HOW FAR COULD THIS GO? HOW MANY PEOPLE?

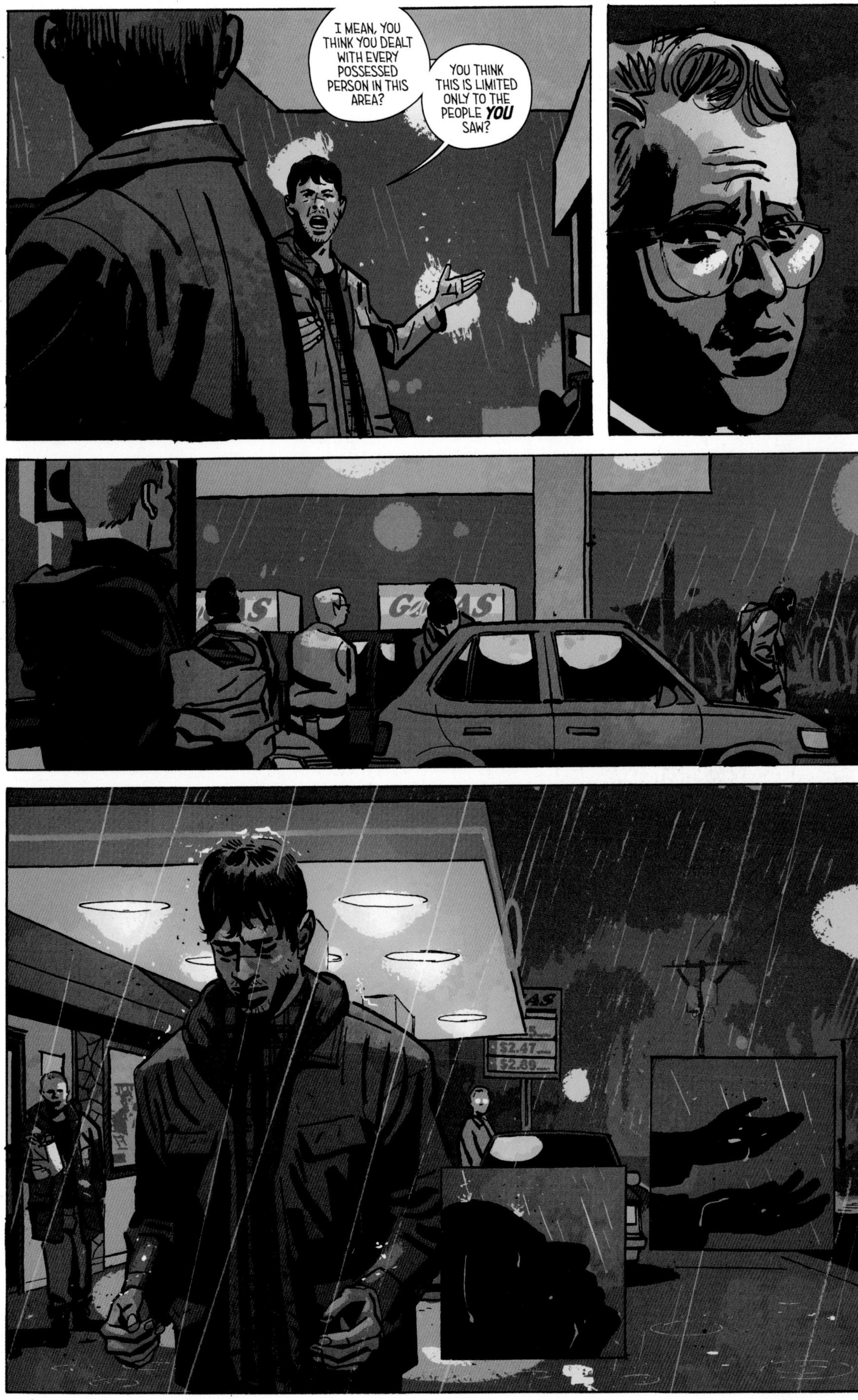
I MEAN, YOU THINK YOU DEALT WITH EVERY POSSESSED PERSON IN THIS AREA?
YOU THINK THIS IS LIMITED ONLY TO THE PEOPLE *YOU* SAW?

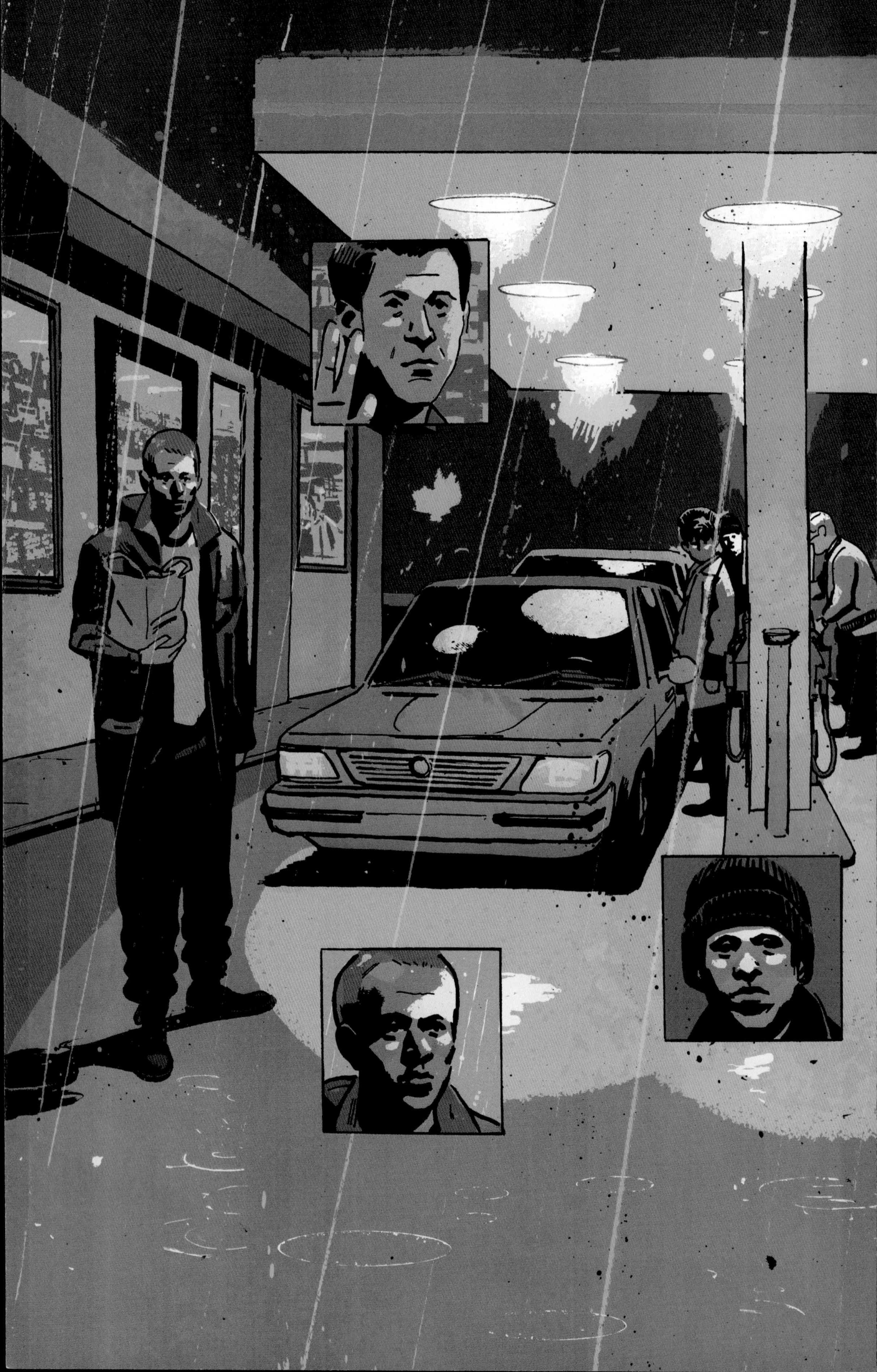

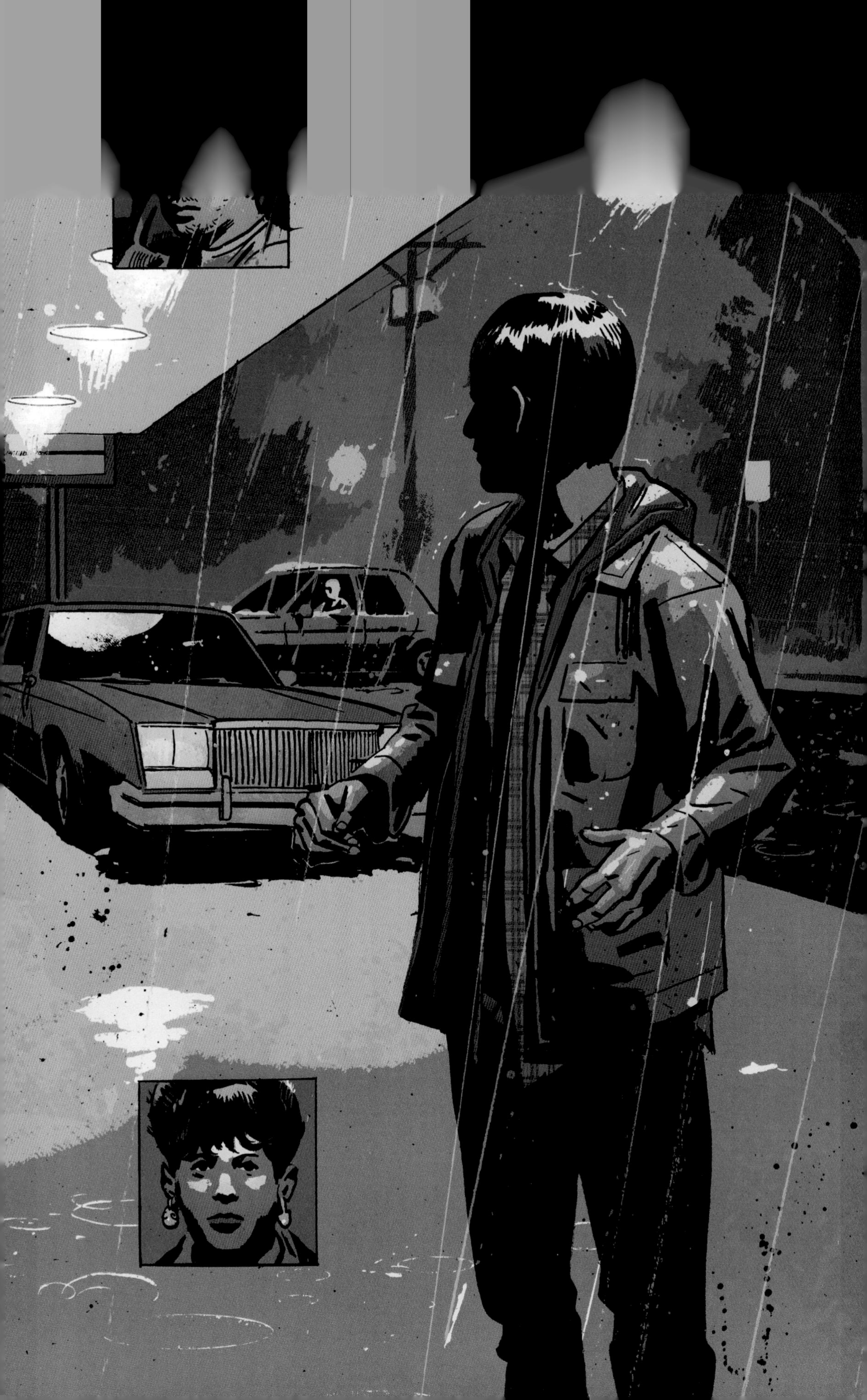

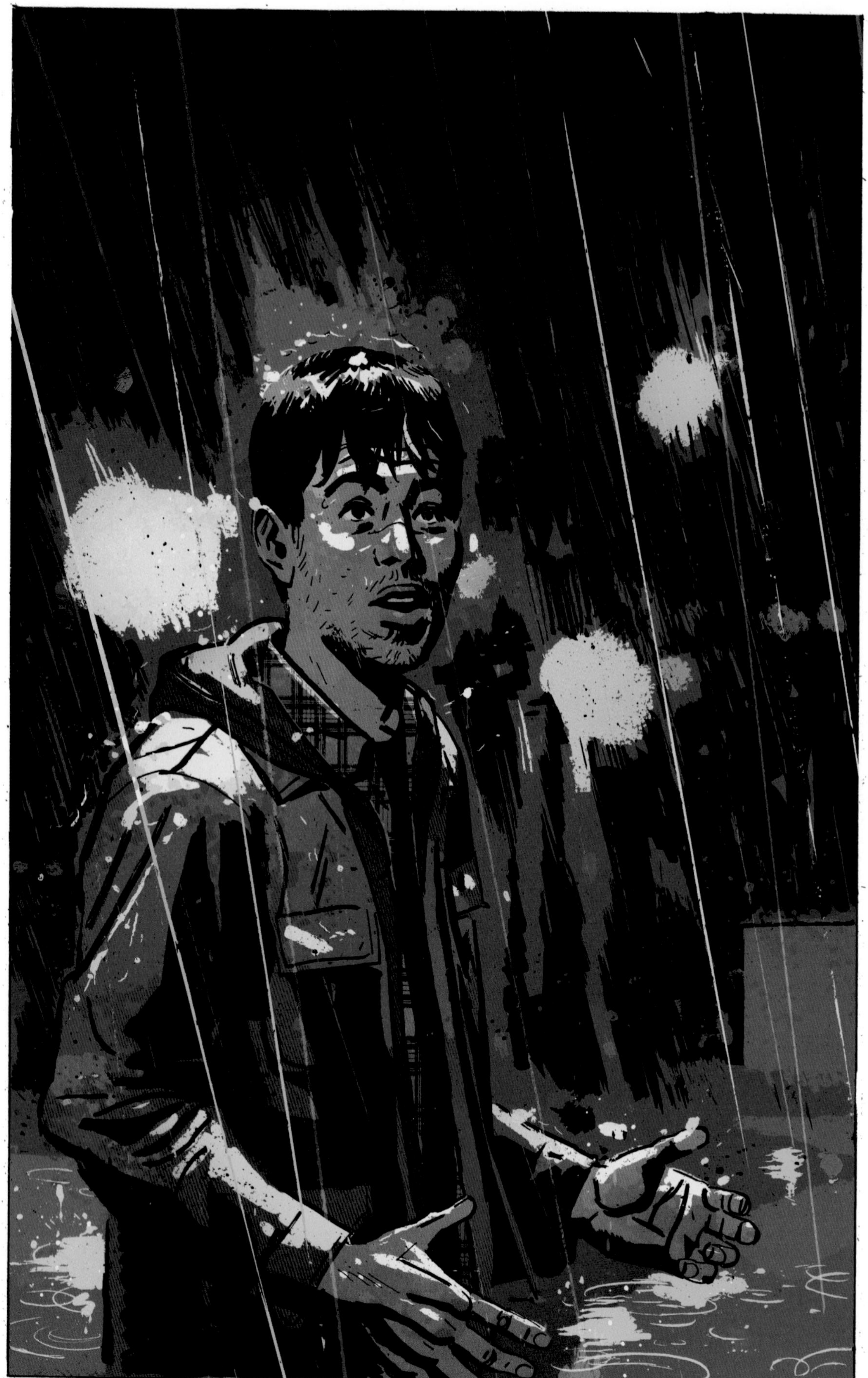

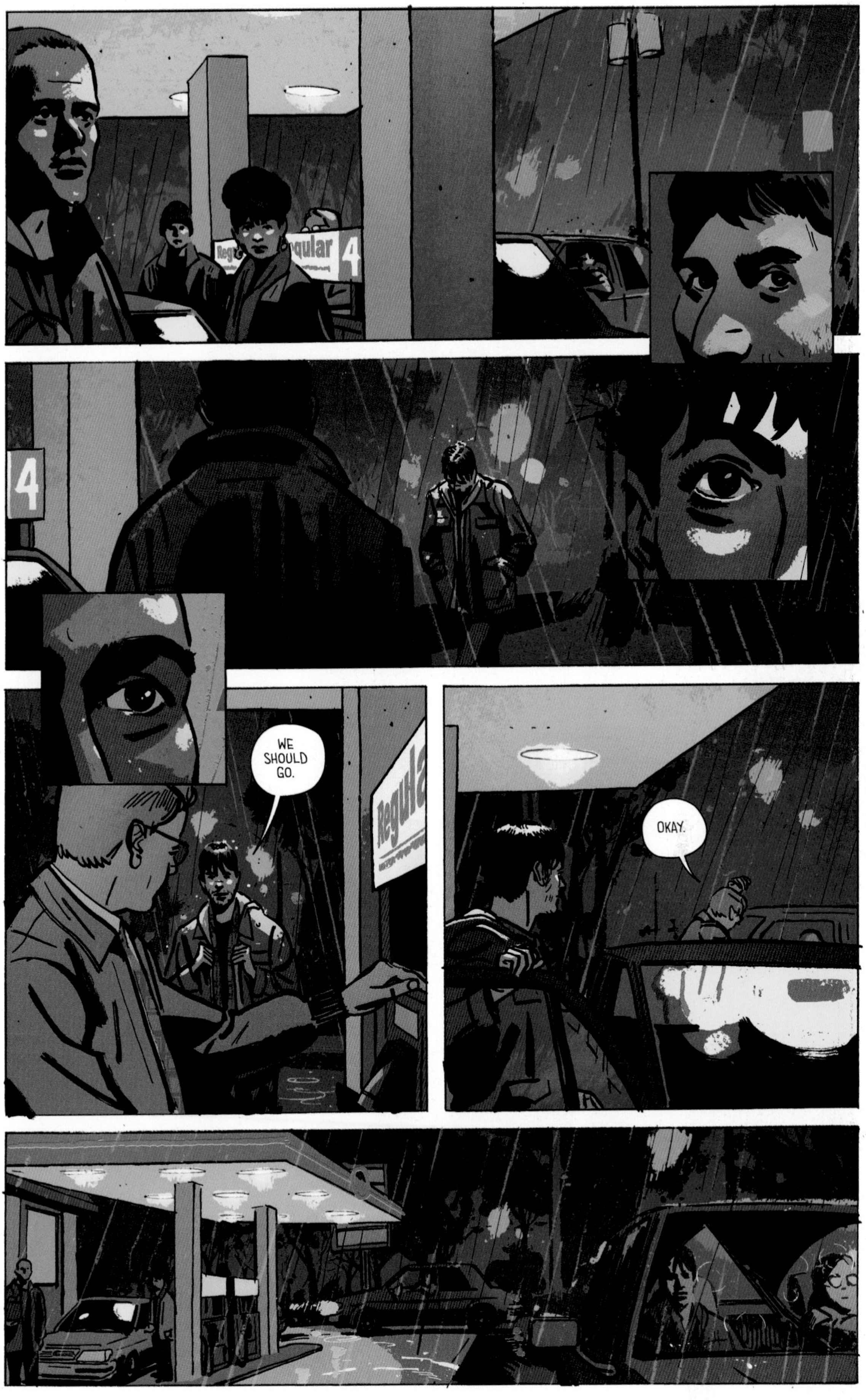
Regular 4
WE SHOULD GO.
OKAY.

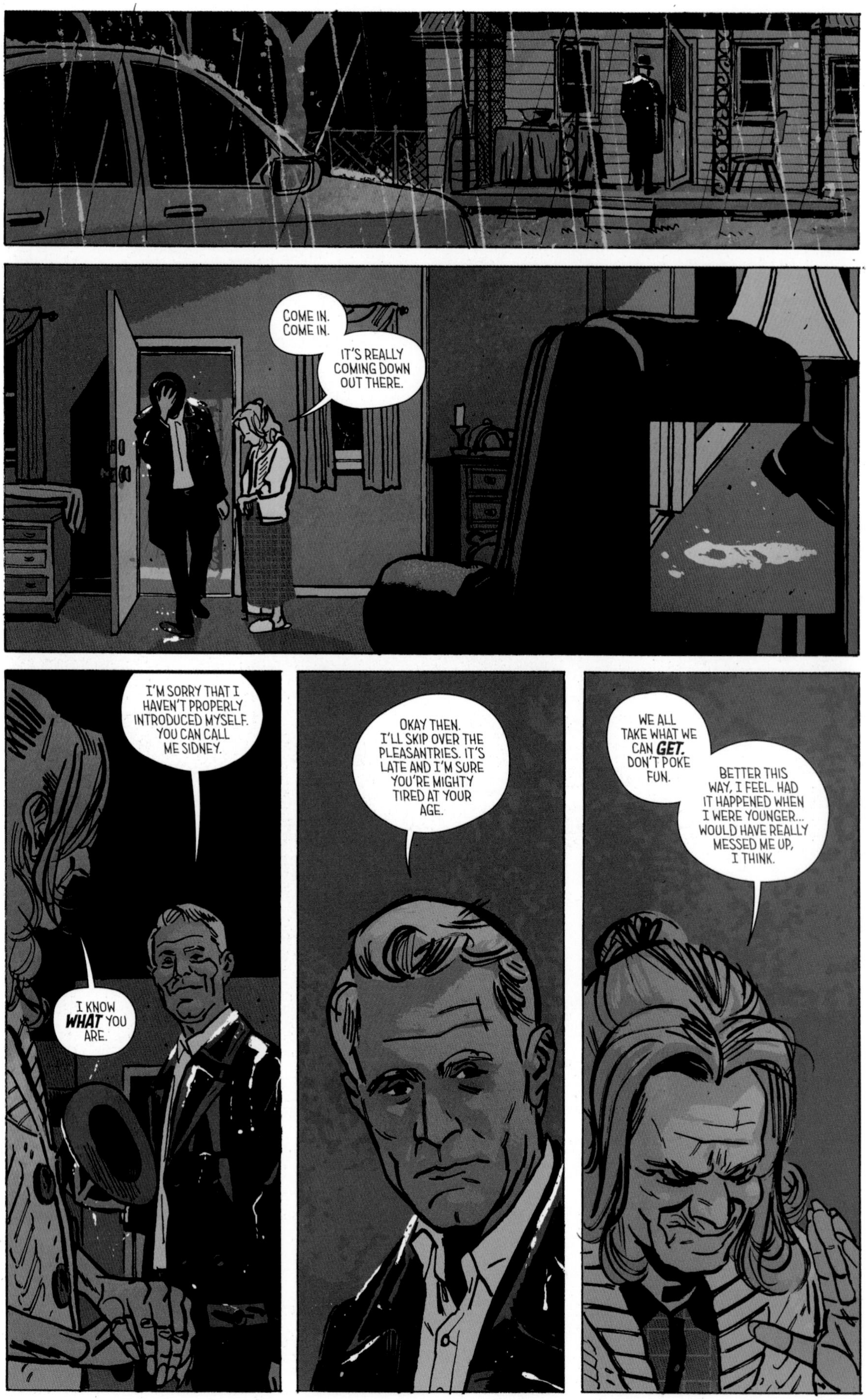
COME IN. COME IN.
IT'S REALLY COMING DOWN OUT THERE.
I'M SORRY THAT I HAVEN'T PROPERLY INTRODUCED MYSELF. YOU CAN CALL ME SIDNEY.
I KNOW **WHAT** YOU ARE.
OKAY THEN. I'LL SKIP OVER THE PLEASANTRIES. IT'S LATE AND I'M SURE YOU'RE MIGHTY TIRED AT YOUR AGE.
WE ALL TAKE WHAT WE CAN ***GET.*** DON'T POKE FUN.
BETTER THIS WAY, I FEEL. HAD IT HAPPENED WHEN I WERE YOUNGER... WOULD HAVE REALLY MESSED ME UP, I THINK.

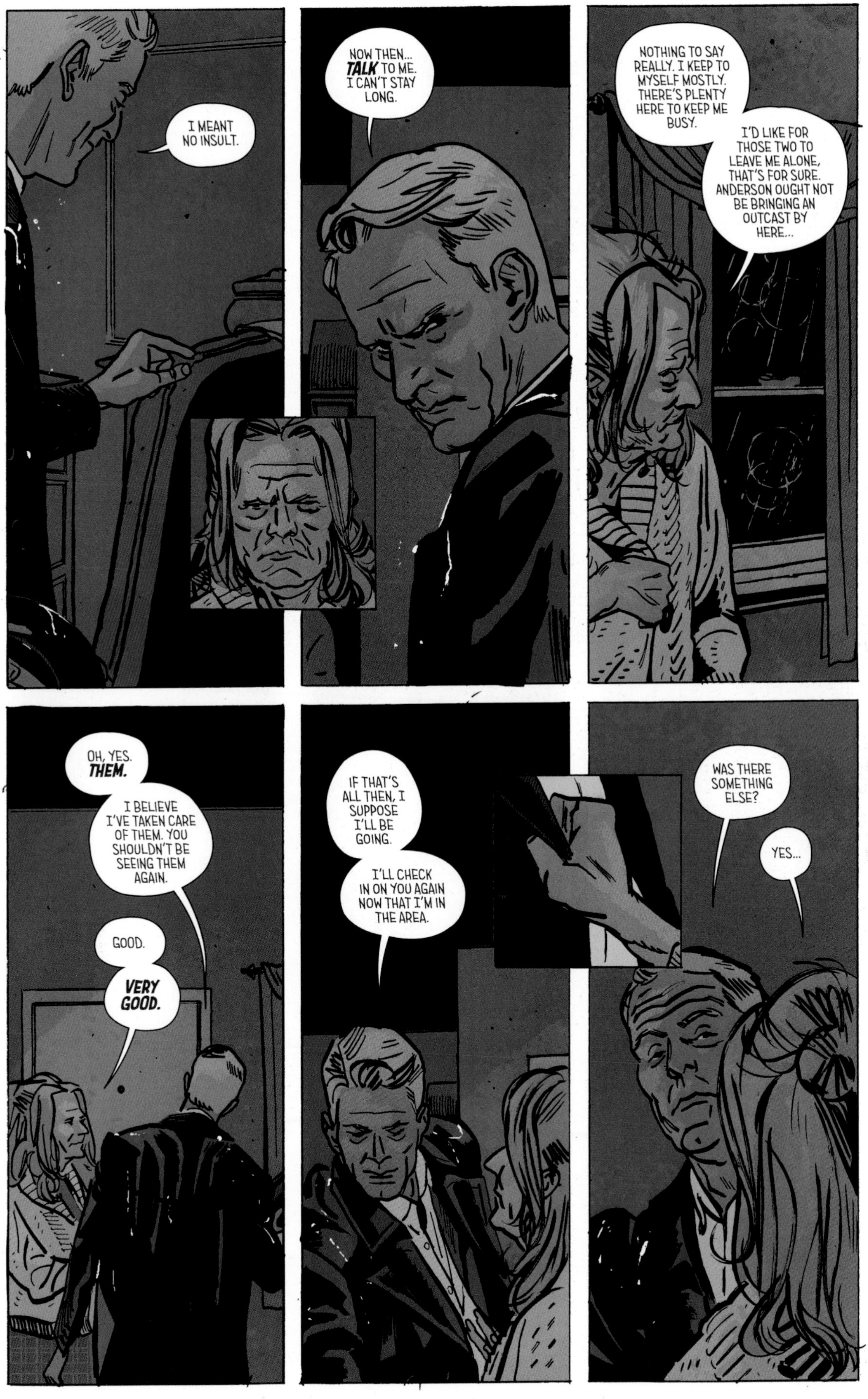
I MEANT NO INSULT.
NOW THEN... TALK TO ME. I CAN'T STAY LONG.
NOTHING TO SAY REALLY. I KEEP TO MYSELF MOSTLY. THERE'S PLENTY HERE TO KEEP ME BUSY.
I'D LIKE FOR THOSE TWO TO LEAVE ME ALONE, THAT'S FOR SURE. ANDERSON OUGHT NOT BE BRINGING AN OUTCAST BY HERE...
OH, YES. THEM.
I BELIEVE I'VE TAKEN CARE OF THEM. YOU SHOULDN'T BE SEEING THEM AGAIN.
GOOD.
VERY GOOD.
IF THAT'S ALL THEN, I SUPPOSE I'LL BE GOING.
I'LL CHECK IN ON YOU AGAIN NOW THAT I'M IN THE AREA.
WAS THERE SOMETHING ELSE?
YES...

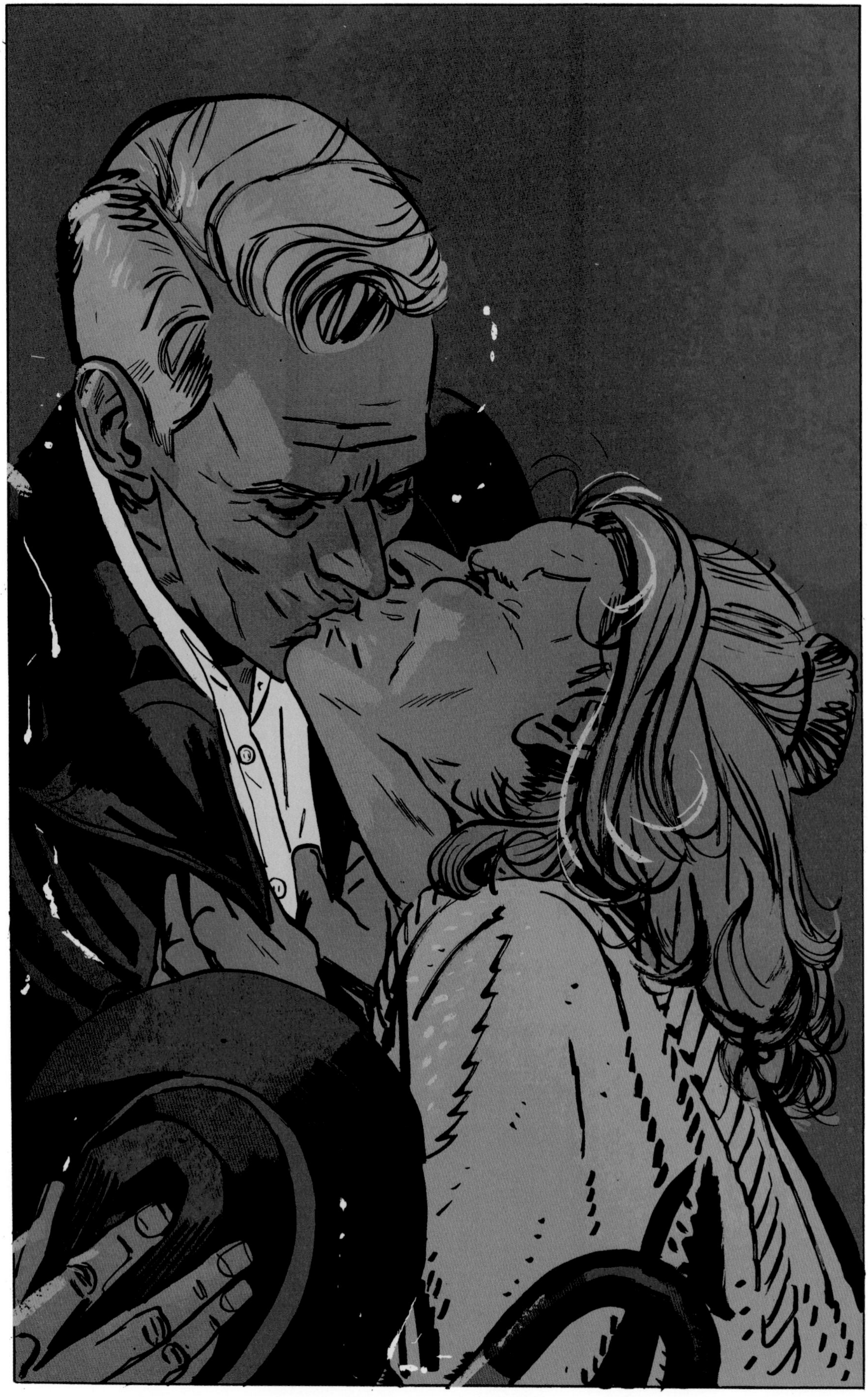

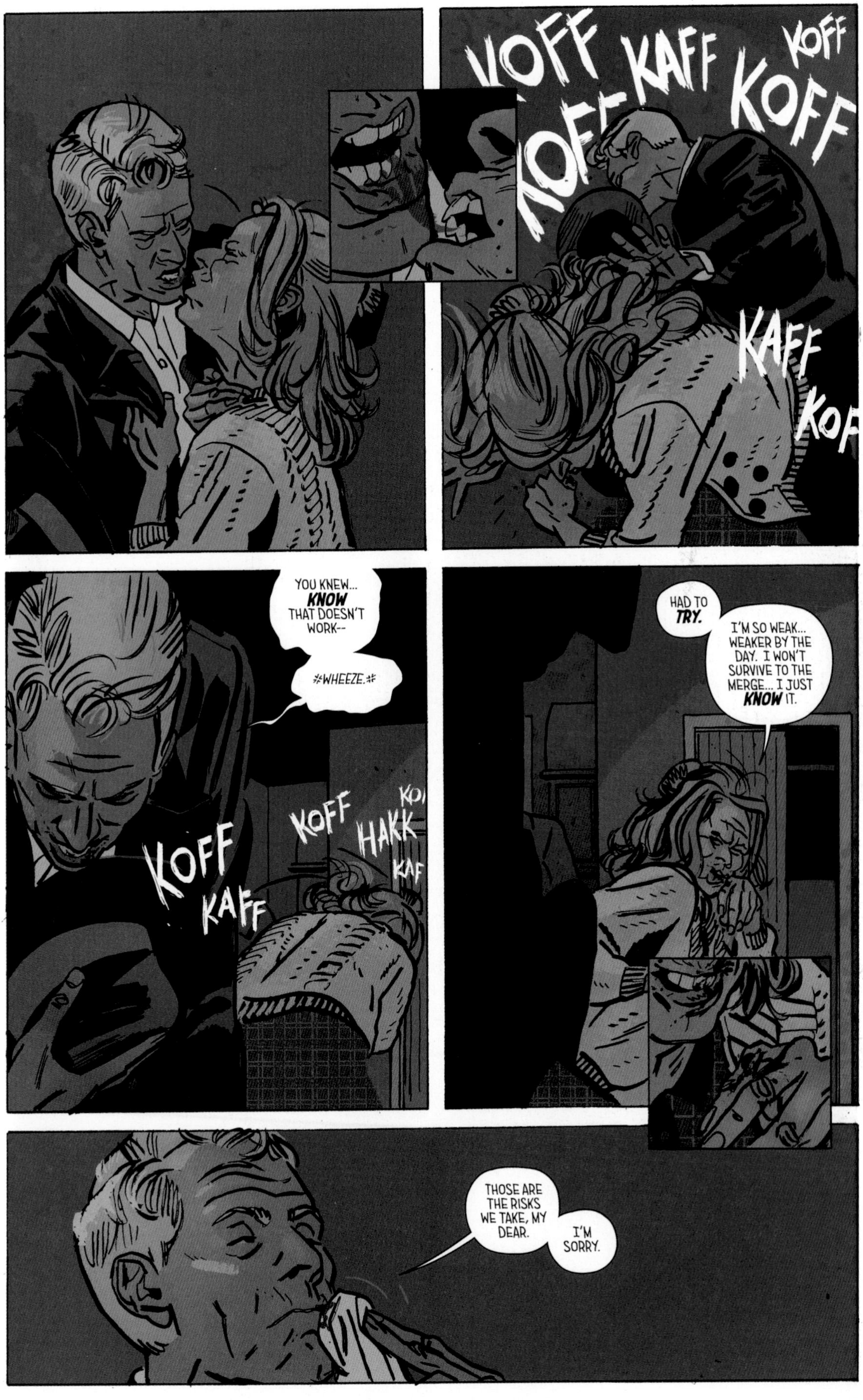
KOFF
KAFF
KOFF
KOFF
KAFF
YOU KNEW... **KNOW** THAT DOESN'T WORK--
#WHEEZE.#
KOFF
KAFF
KOFF
HAKK
KAF
HAD TO **TRY.**
I'M SO WEAK... WEAKER BY THE DAY. I WON'T SURVIVE TO THE MERGE... I JUST **KNOW** IT.
THOSE ARE THE RISKS WE TAKE, MY DEAR.
I'M SORRY.

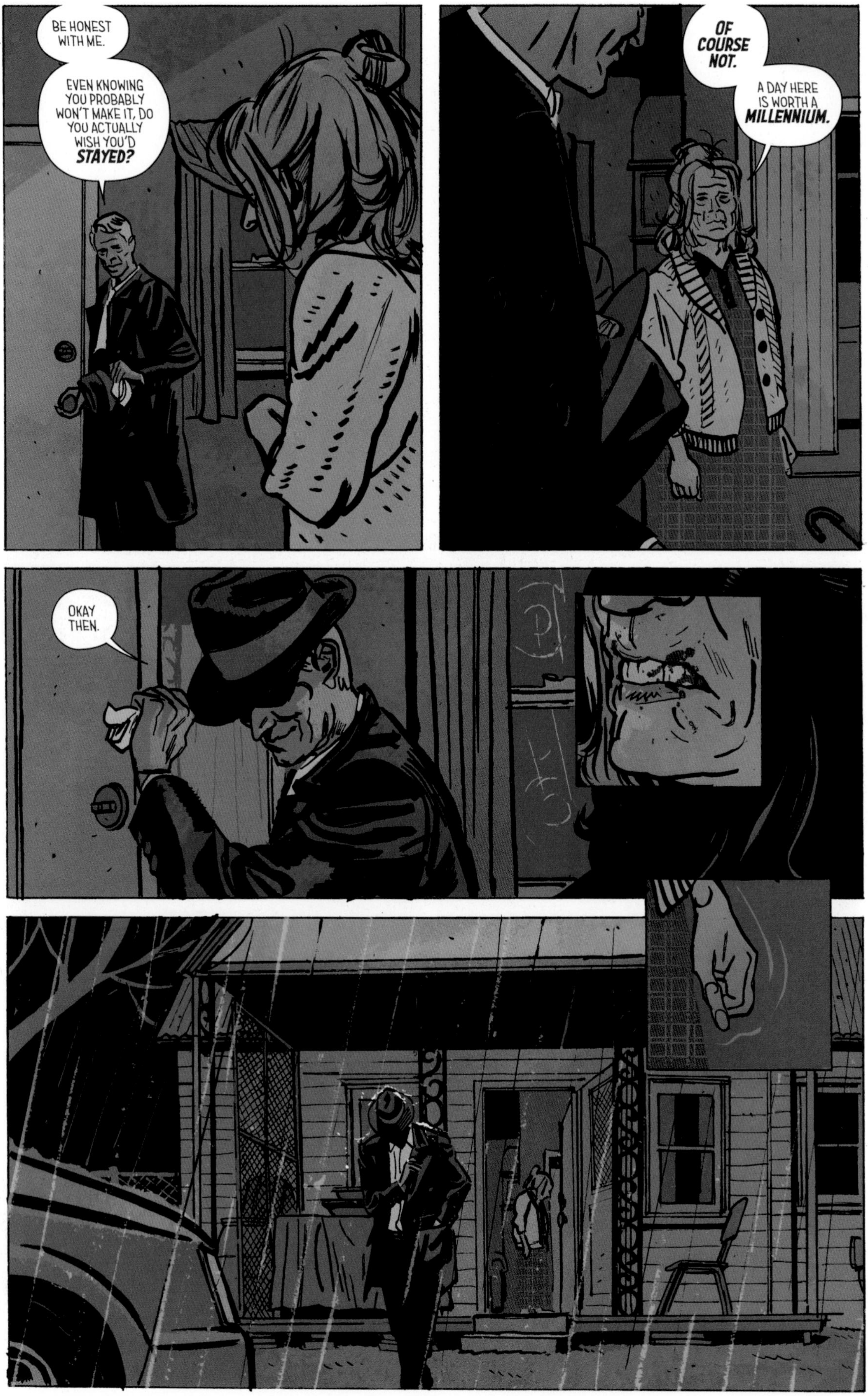
BE HONEST WITH ME.
EVEN KNOWING YOU PROBABLY WON'T MAKE IT, DO YOU ACTUALLY WISH YOU'D STAYED?
OF COURSE NOT.
A DAY HERE IS WORTH A MILLENNIUM.
OKAY THEN.

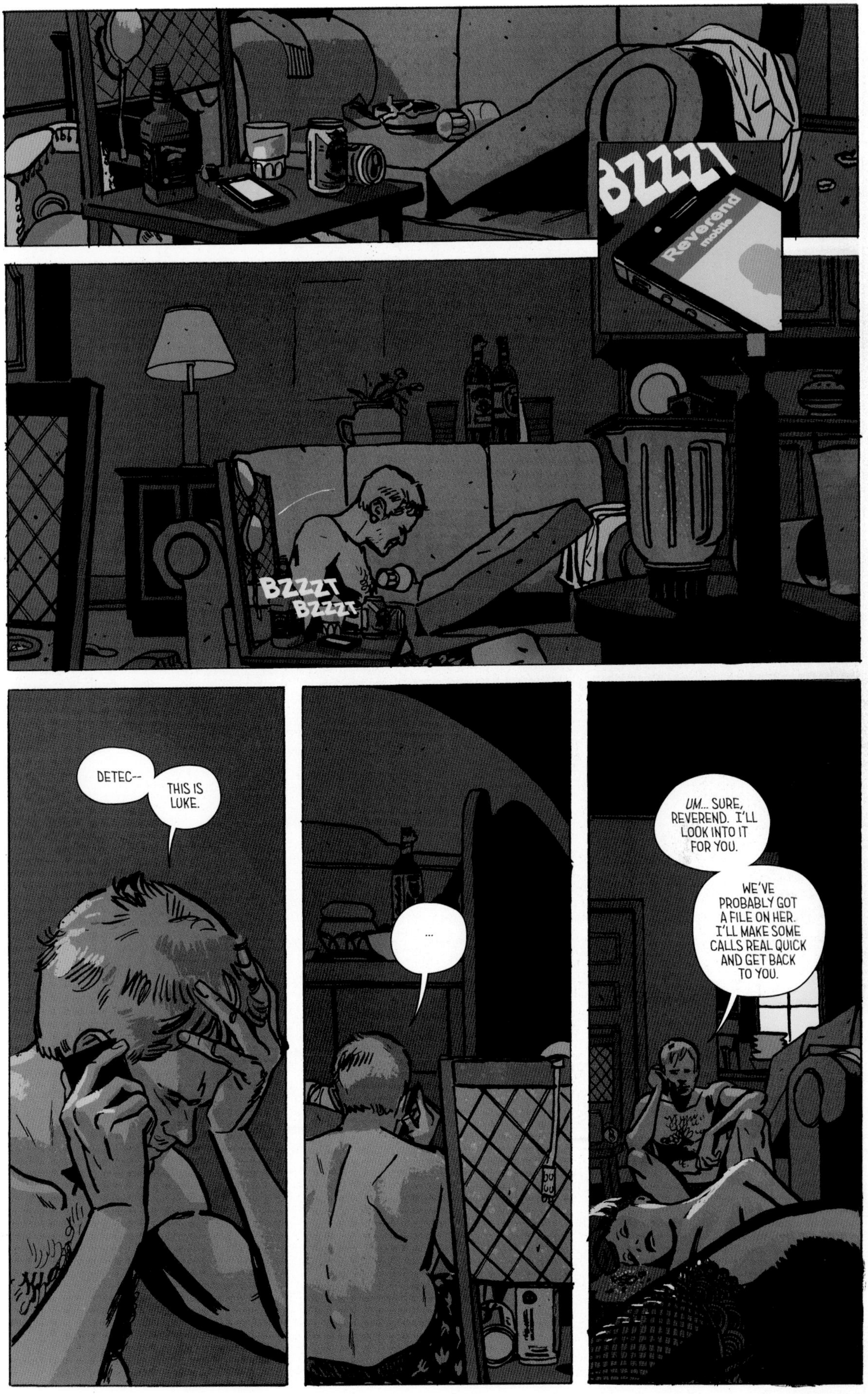
BZZZT
Reverend
mobile
BZZZT
BZZZT
DETEC--
THIS IS LUKE.
...
UM... SURE, REVEREND. I'LL LOOK INTO IT FOR YOU.
WE'VE PROBABLY GOT A FILE ON HER. I'LL MAKE SOME CALLS REAL QUICK AND GET BACK TO YOU.

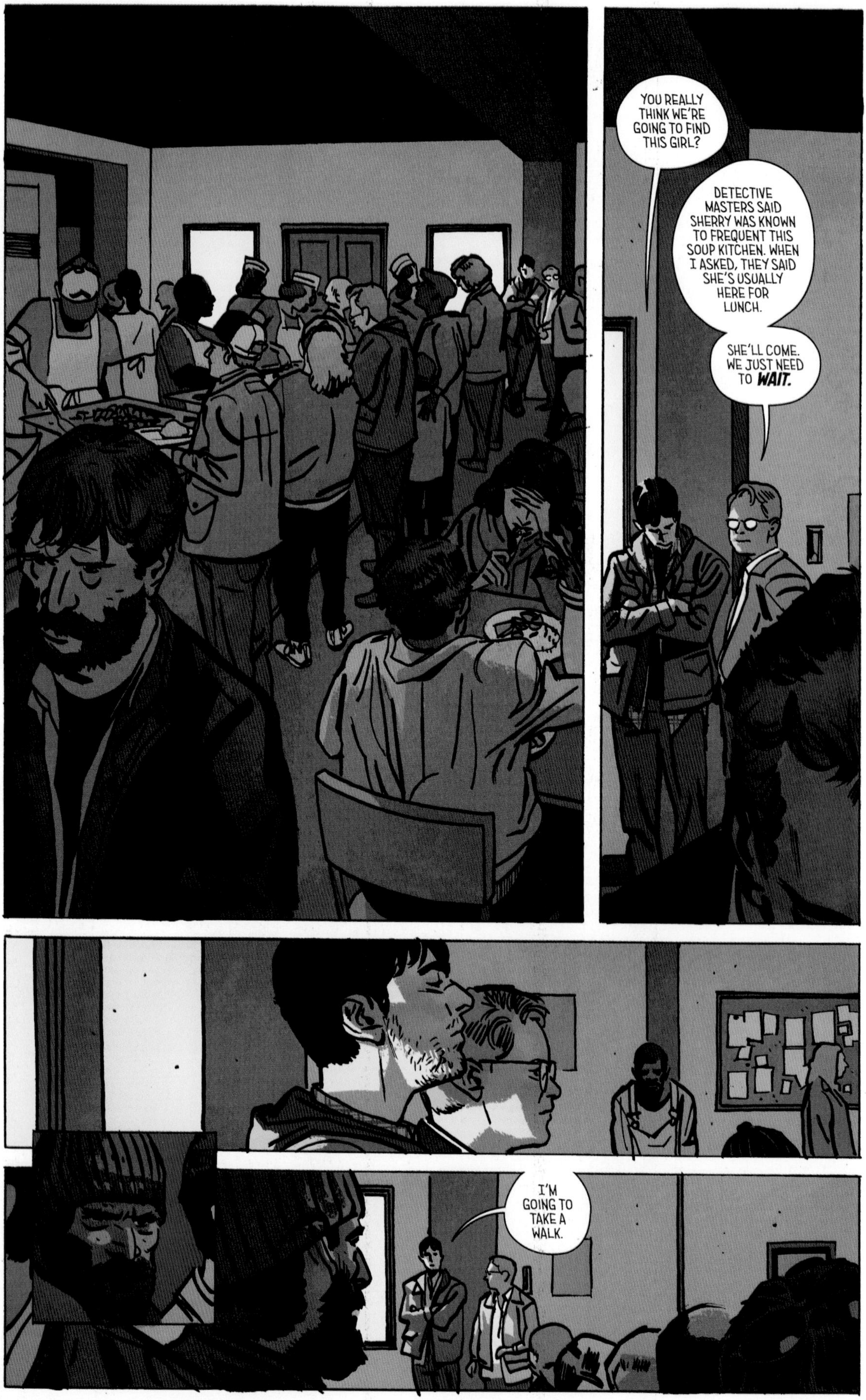
YOU REALLY THINK WE'RE GOING TO FIND THIS GIRL?
DETECTIVE MASTERS SAID SHERRY WAS KNOWN TO FREQUENT THIS SOUP KITCHEN. WHEN I ASKED, THEY SAID SHE'S USUALLY HERE FOR LUNCH.
SHE'LL COME. WE JUST NEED TO **WAIT.**
I'M GOING TO TAKE A WALK.

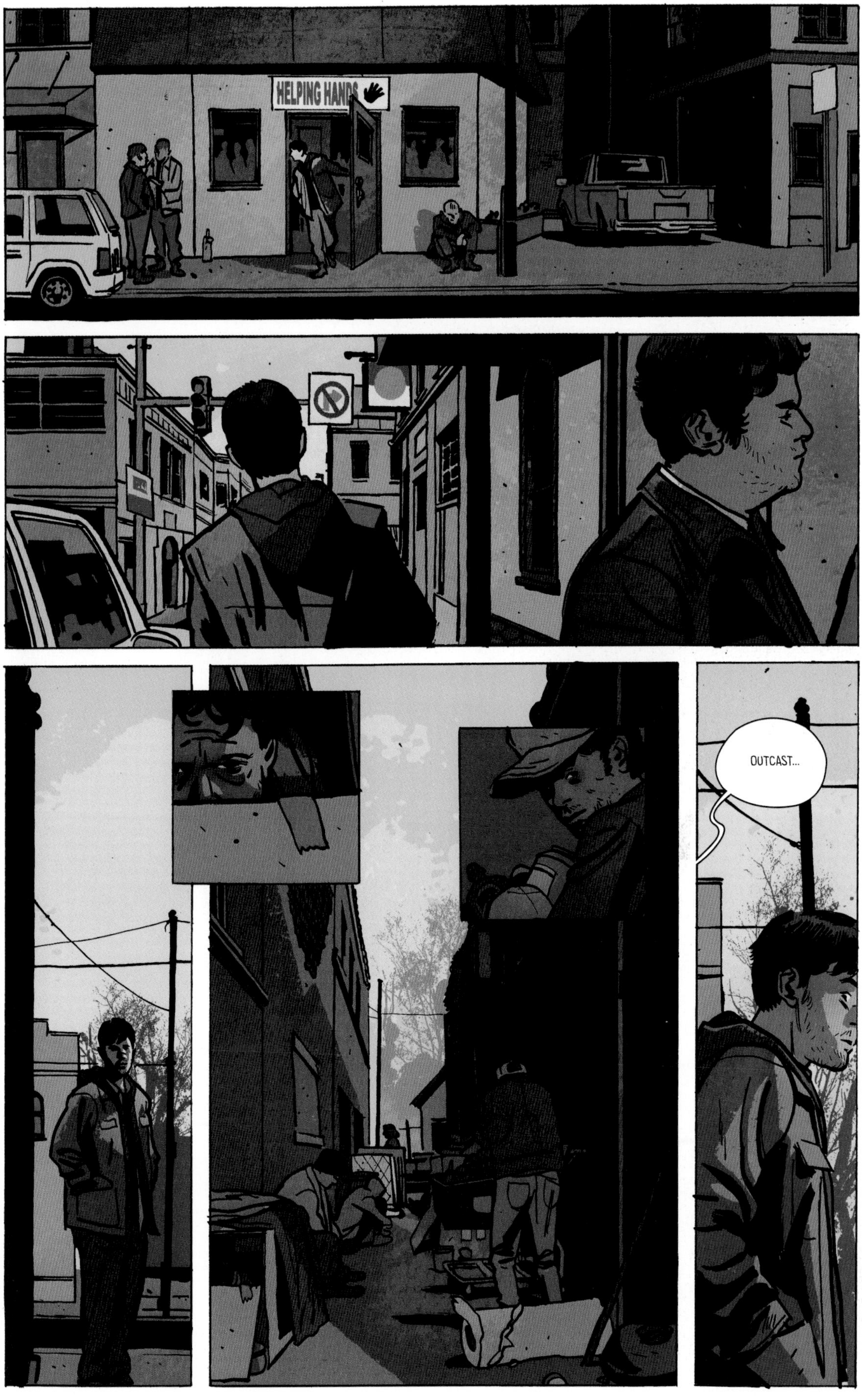
HELPING HANDS
OUTCAST...

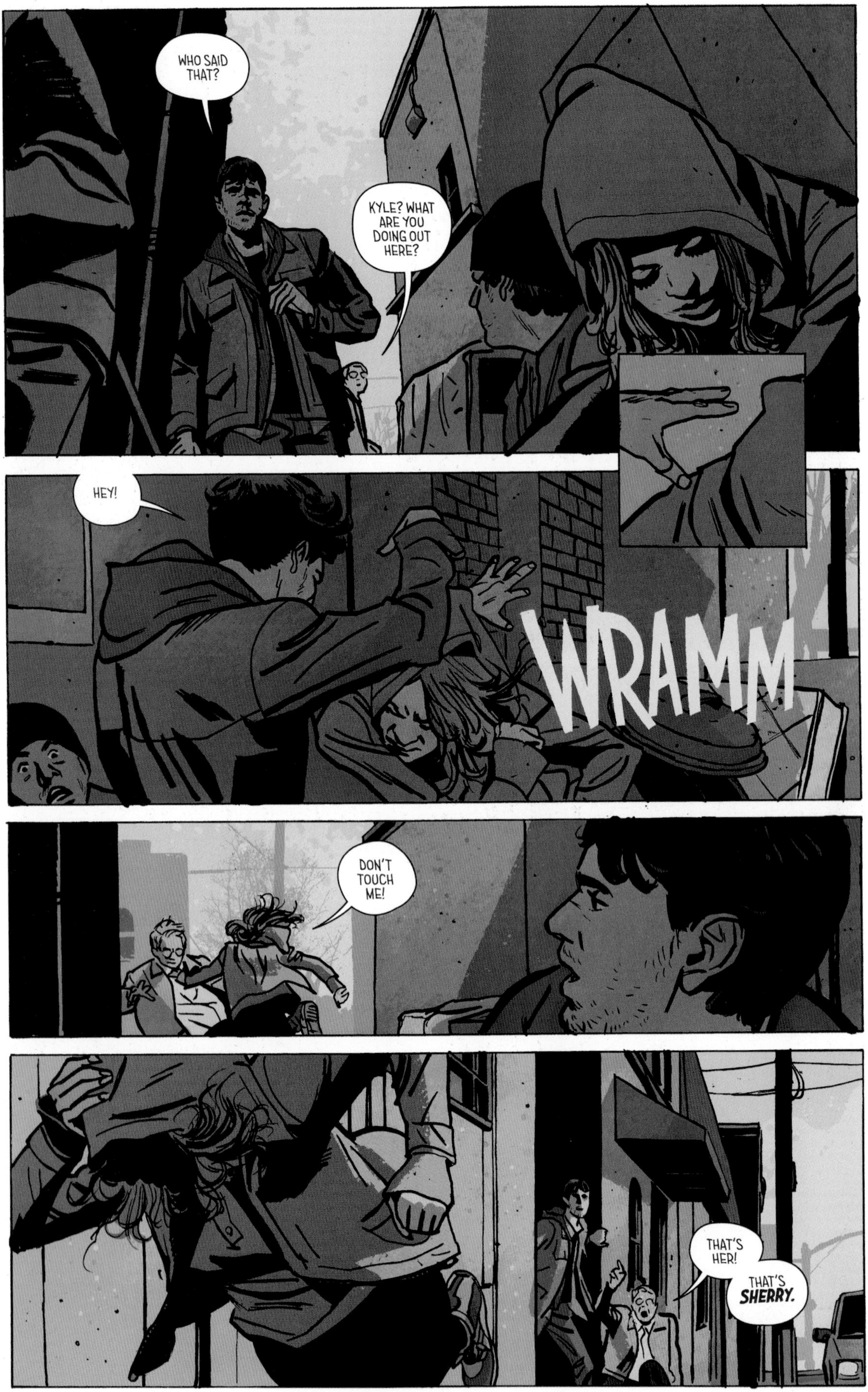
WHO SAID THAT?
KYLE? WHAT ARE YOU DOING OUT HERE?
HEY!
WRAMM
DON'T TOUCH ME!
THAT'S HER!
THAT'S **SHERRY.**

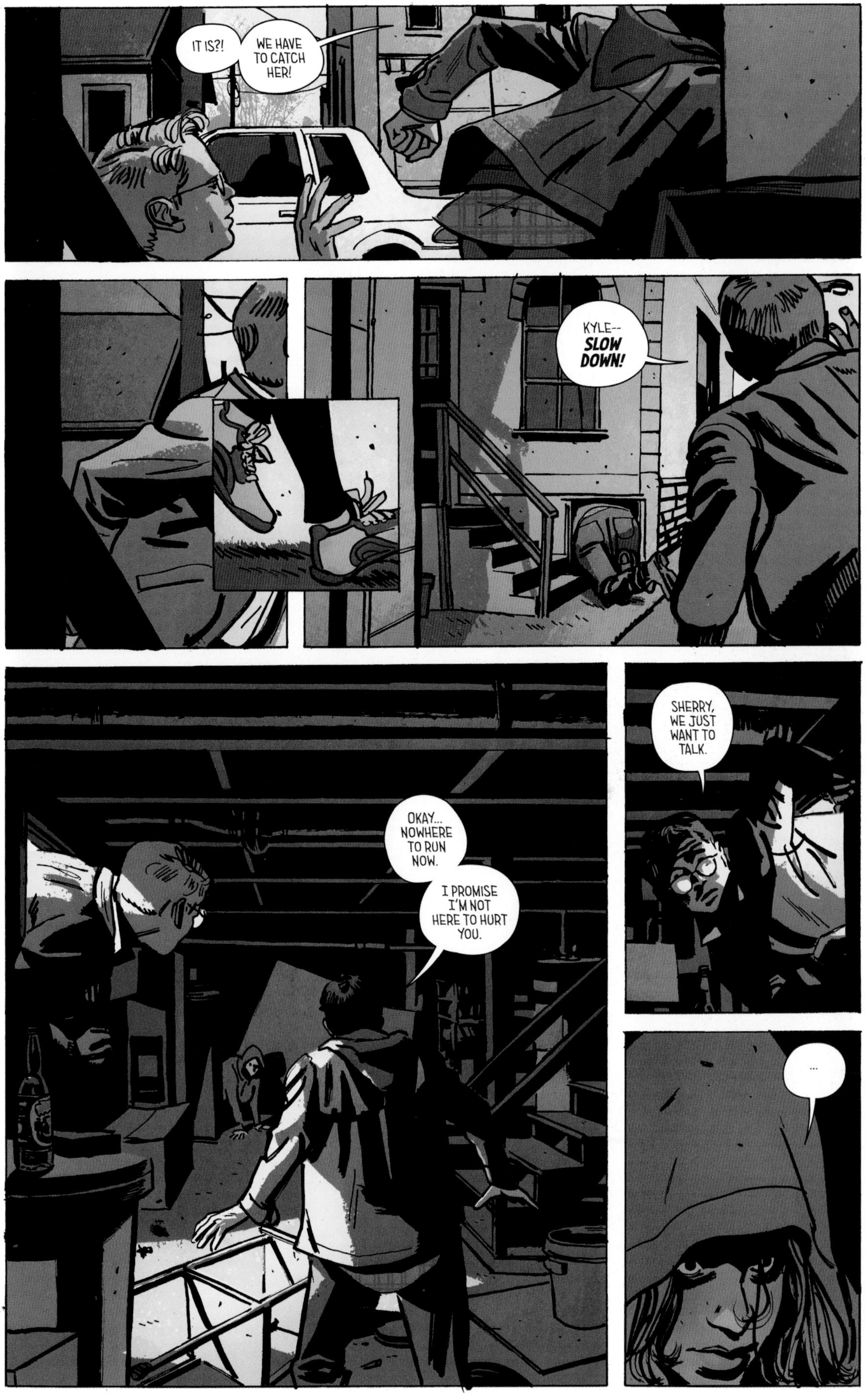
IT IS?!
WE HAVE TO CATCH HER!
KYLE-- SLOW DOWN!
OKAY... NOWHERE TO RUN NOW.
I PROMISE I'M NOT HERE TO HURT YOU.
SHERRY, WE JUST WANT TO TALK.
...

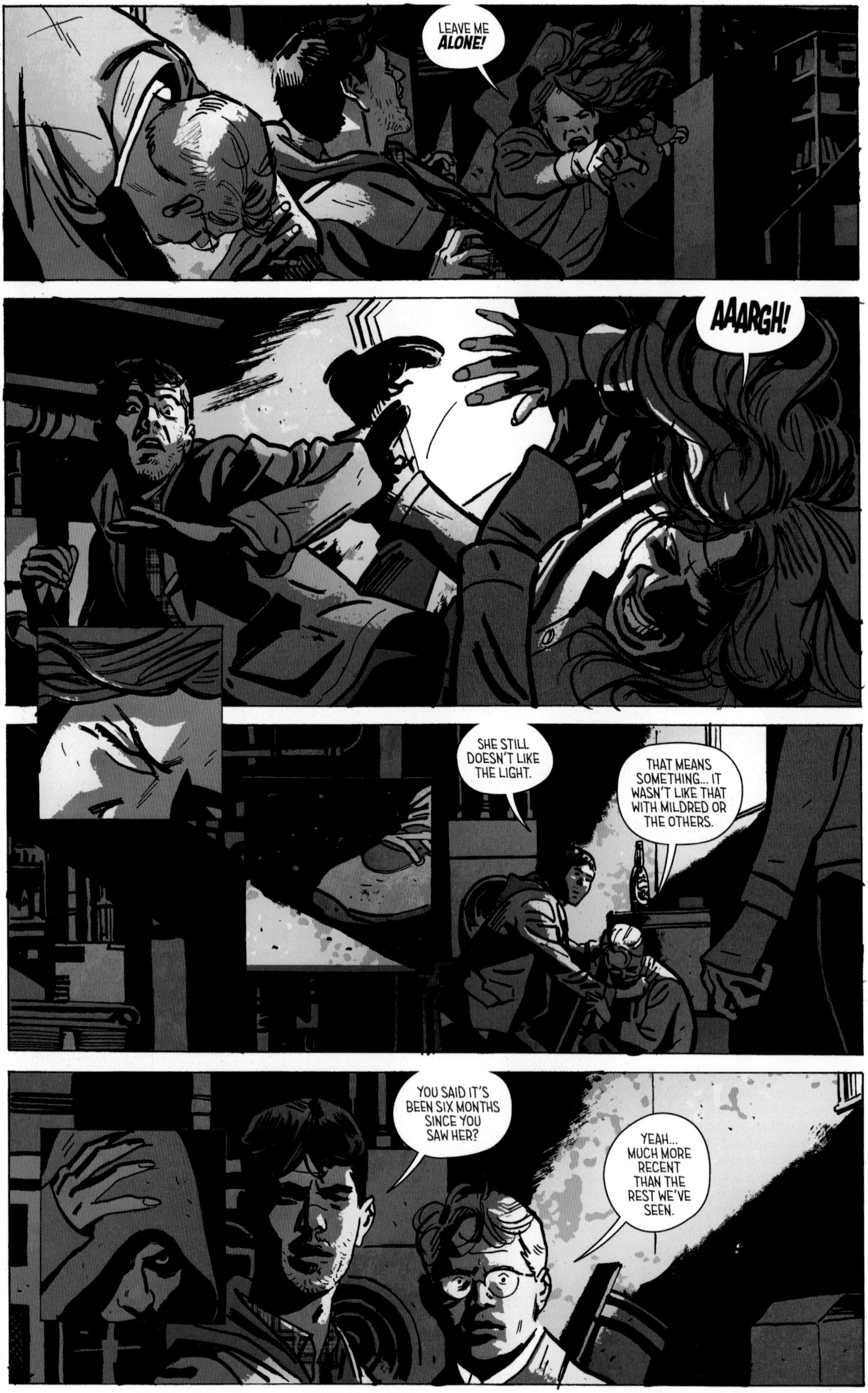
LEAVE ME ALONE!
AAARGH!
SHE STILL DOESN'T LIKE THE LIGHT.
THAT MEANS SOMETHING... IT WASN'T LIKE THAT WITH MILDRED OR THE OTHERS.
YOU SAID IT'S BEEN SIX MONTHS SINCE YOU SAW HER?
YEAH... MUCH MORE RECENT THAN THE REST WE'VE SEEN.

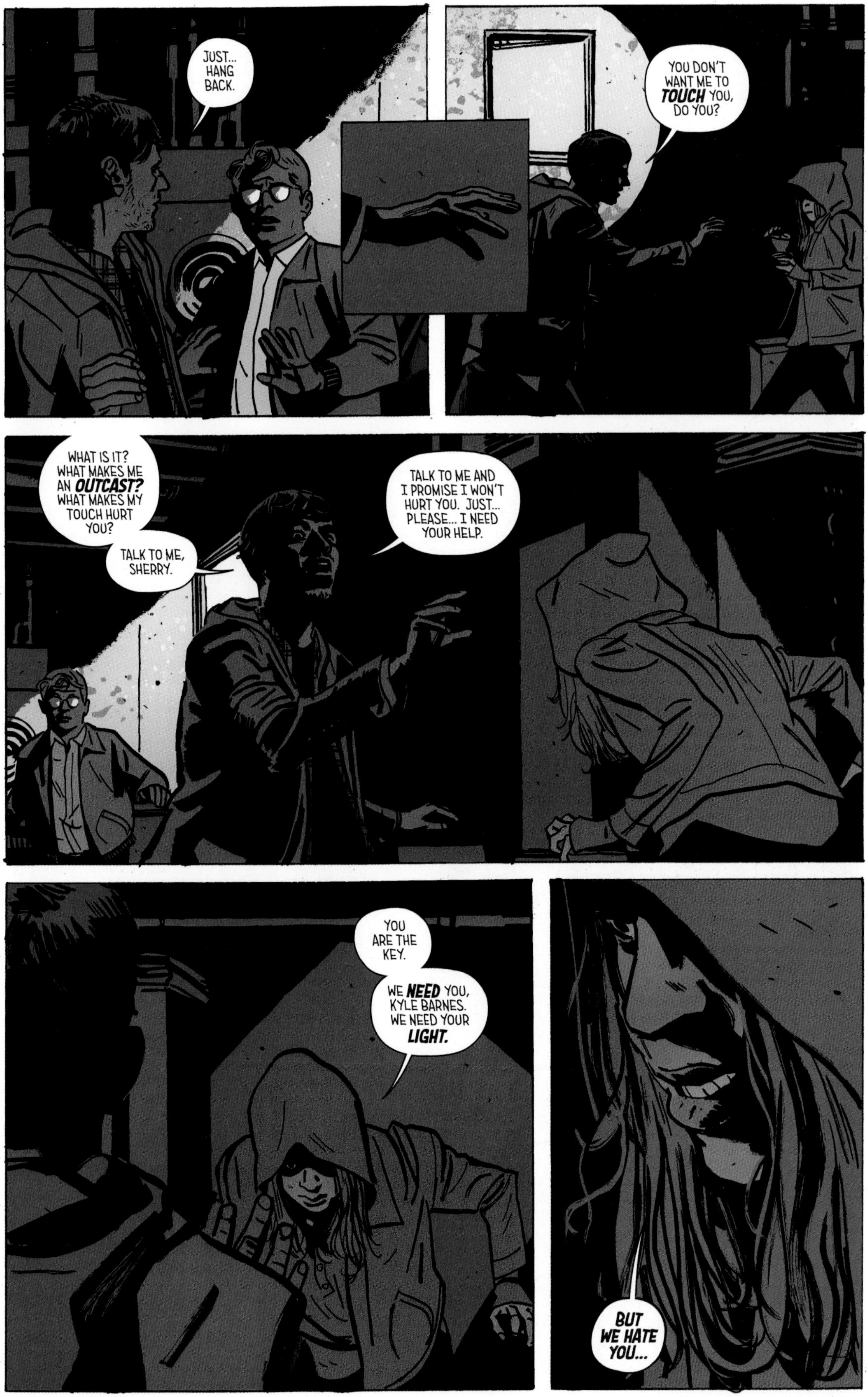
JUST... HANG BACK.
YOU DON'T WANT ME TO **TOUCH** YOU, DO YOU?
WHAT IS IT? WHAT MAKES ME AN **OUTCAST?** WHAT MAKES MY TOUCH HURT YOU?
TALK TO ME, SHERRY.
TALK TO ME AND I PROMISE I WON'T HURT YOU. JUST... PLEASE... I NEED YOUR HELP.
YOU ARE THE KEY.
WE **NEED** YOU, KYLE BARNES. WE NEED YOUR **LIGHT.**
BUT WE HATE YOU...

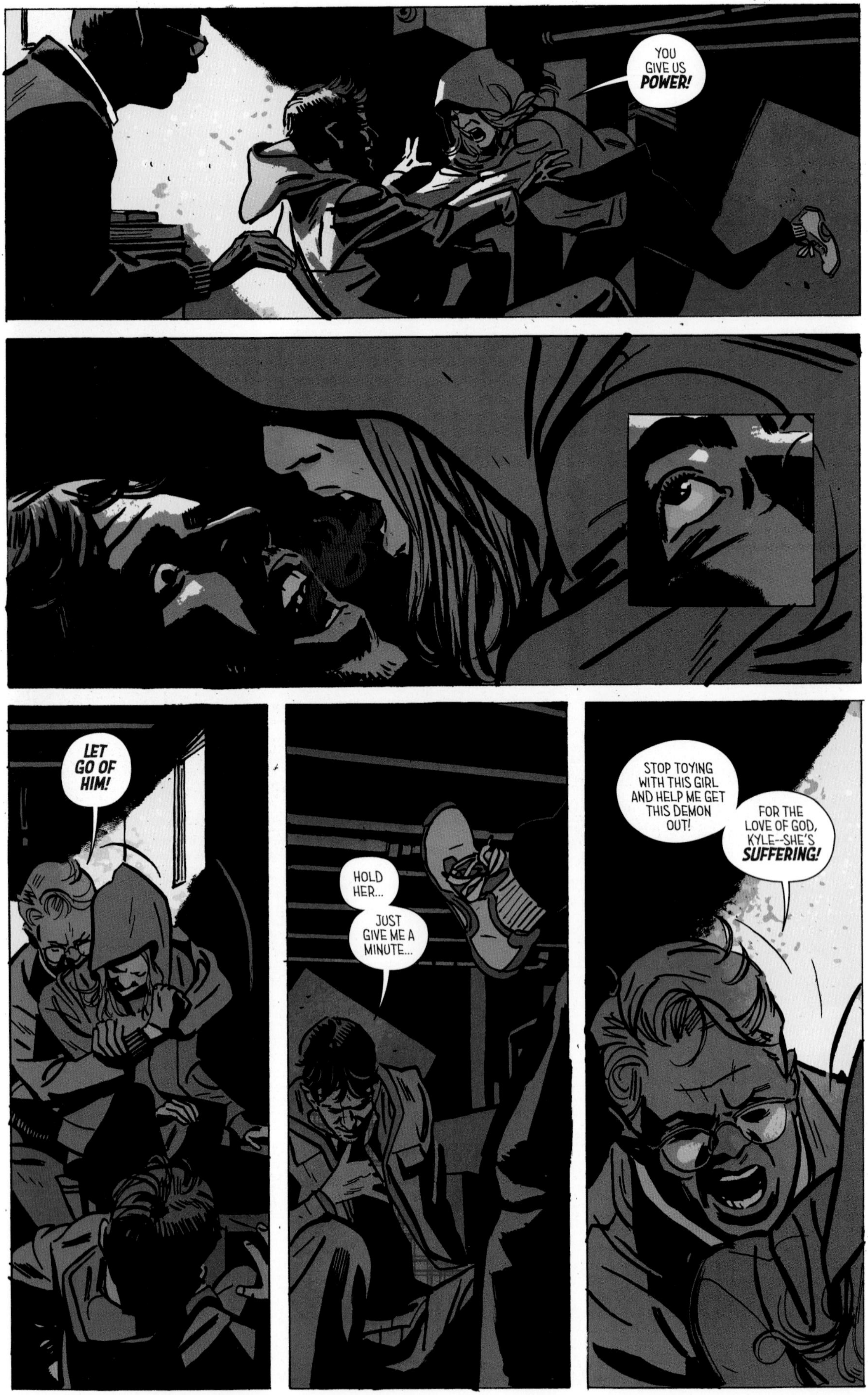
YOU GIVE US **POWER!**
LET GO OF HIM!
HOLD HER...
JUST GIVE ME A MINUTE...
STOP TOYING WITH THIS GIRL AND HELP ME GET THIS DEMON OUT!
FOR THE LOVE OF GOD, KYLE--SHE'S **SUFFERING!**

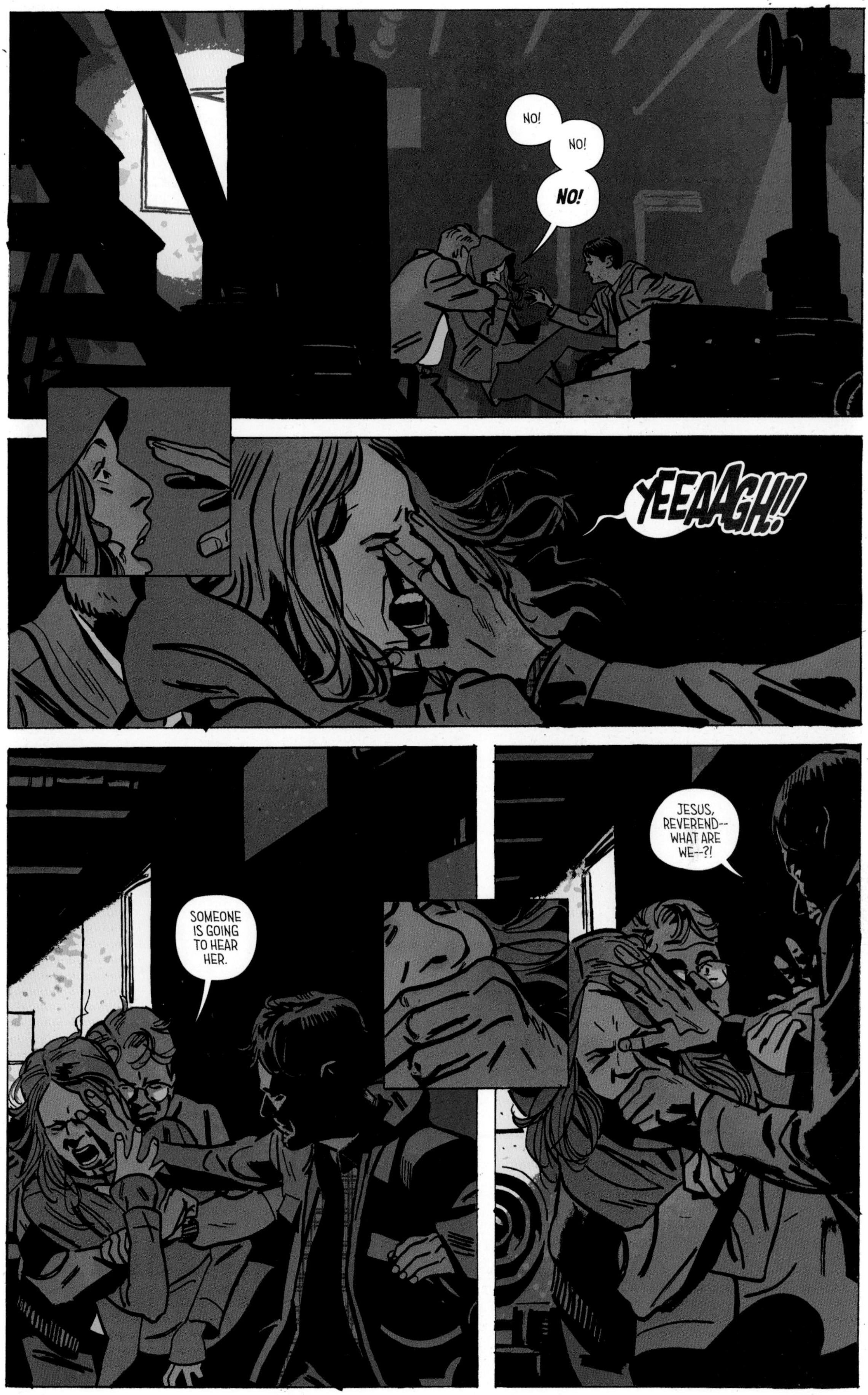
NO!
NO!
NO!
YEEAAGH!!
SOMEONE IS GOING TO HEAR HER.
JESUS, REVEREND-- WHAT ARE WE--?!

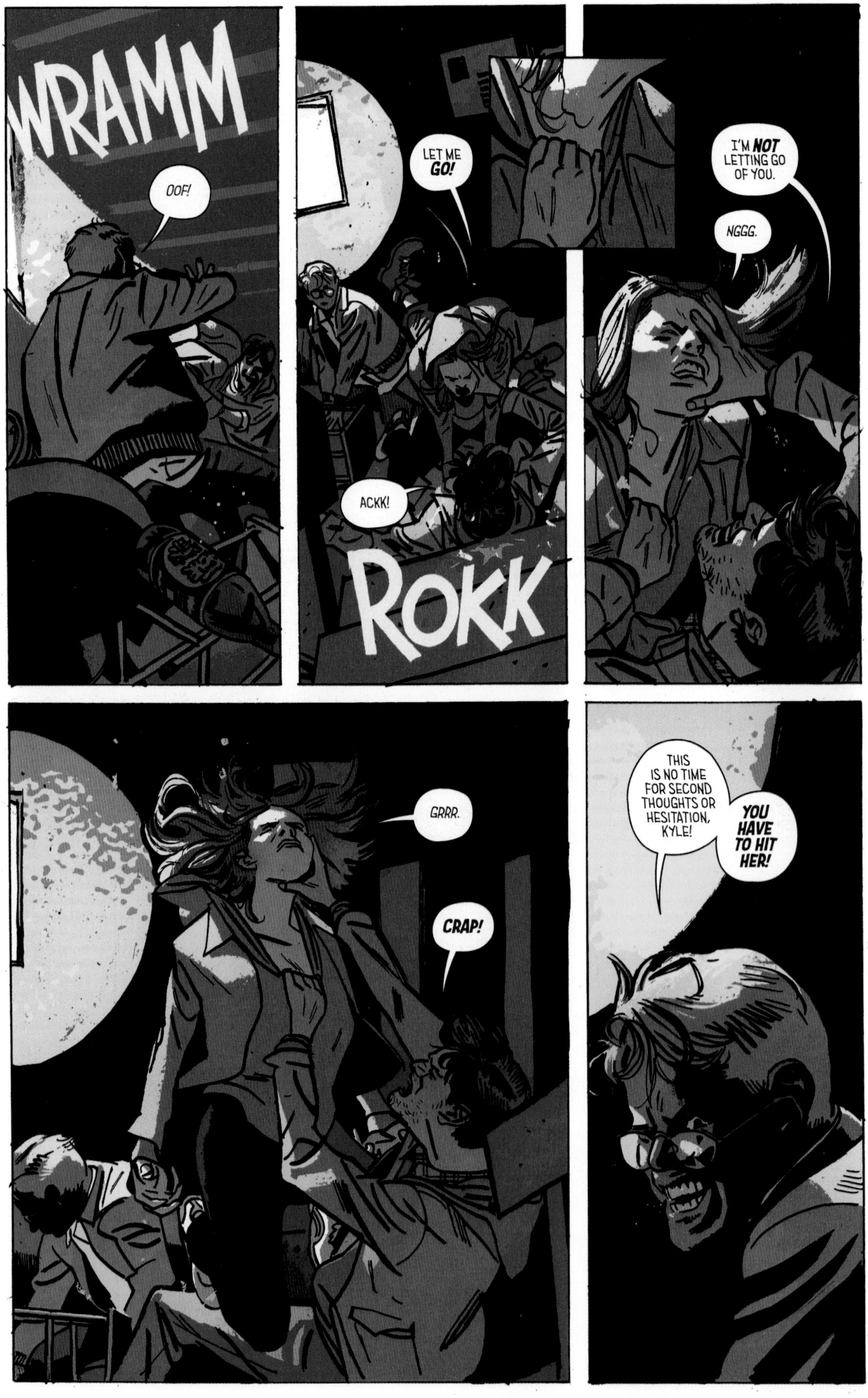
WRAMM
OOF!
LET ME GO!
ACKK!
ROKK
I'M NOT LETTING GO OF YOU.
NGGG.
GRRR.
CRAP!
THIS IS NO TIME FOR SECOND THOUGHTS OR HESITATION, KYLE!
YOU HAVE TO HIT HER!

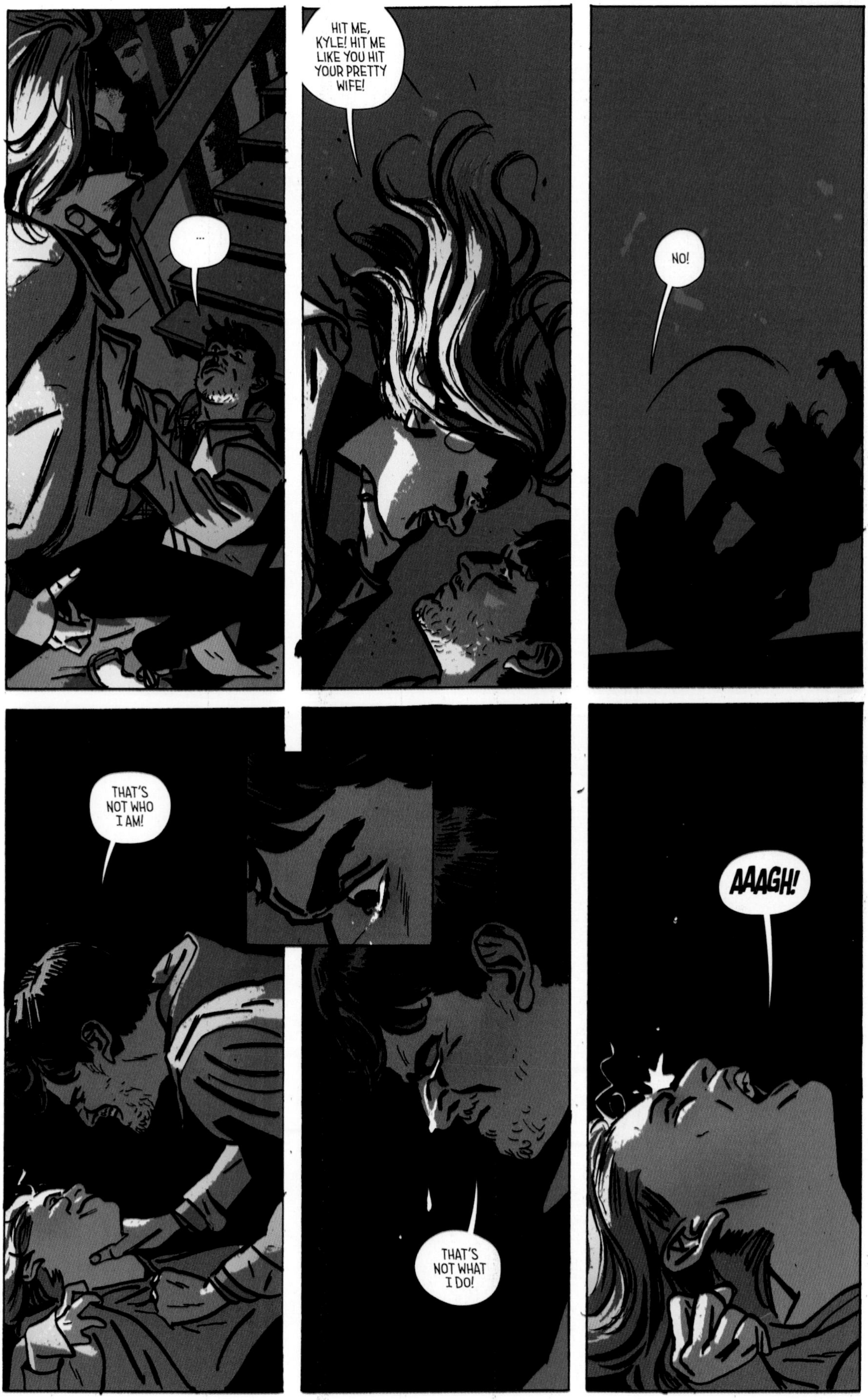
...
HIT ME, KYLE! HIT ME LIKE YOU HIT YOUR PRETTY WIFE!
NO!
THAT'S NOT WHO I AM!
THAT'S NOT WHAT I DO!
AAAGH!

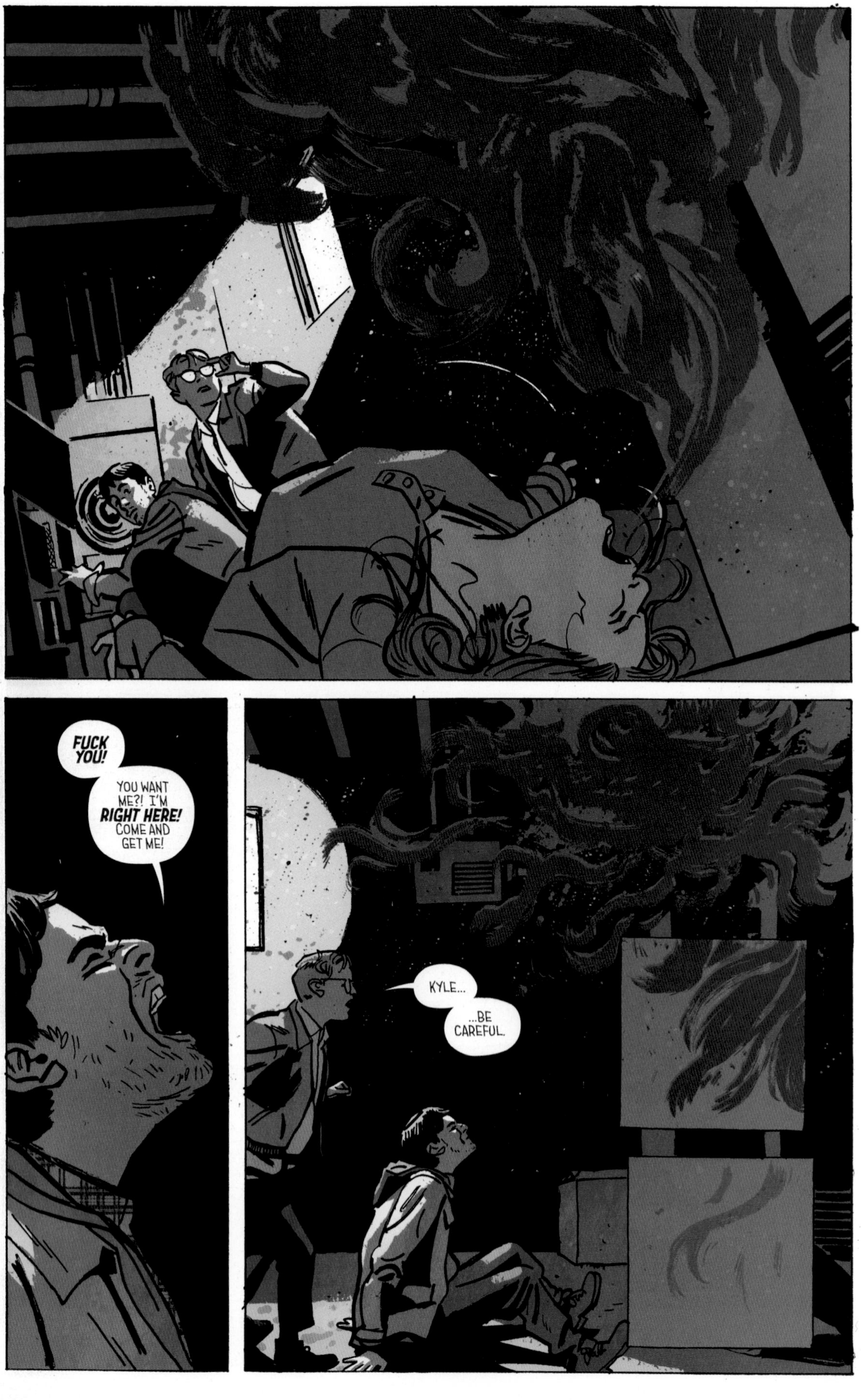
FUCK YOU!
YOU WANT ME?! I'M RIGHT HERE! COME AND GET ME!
KYLE...
...BE CAREFUL.

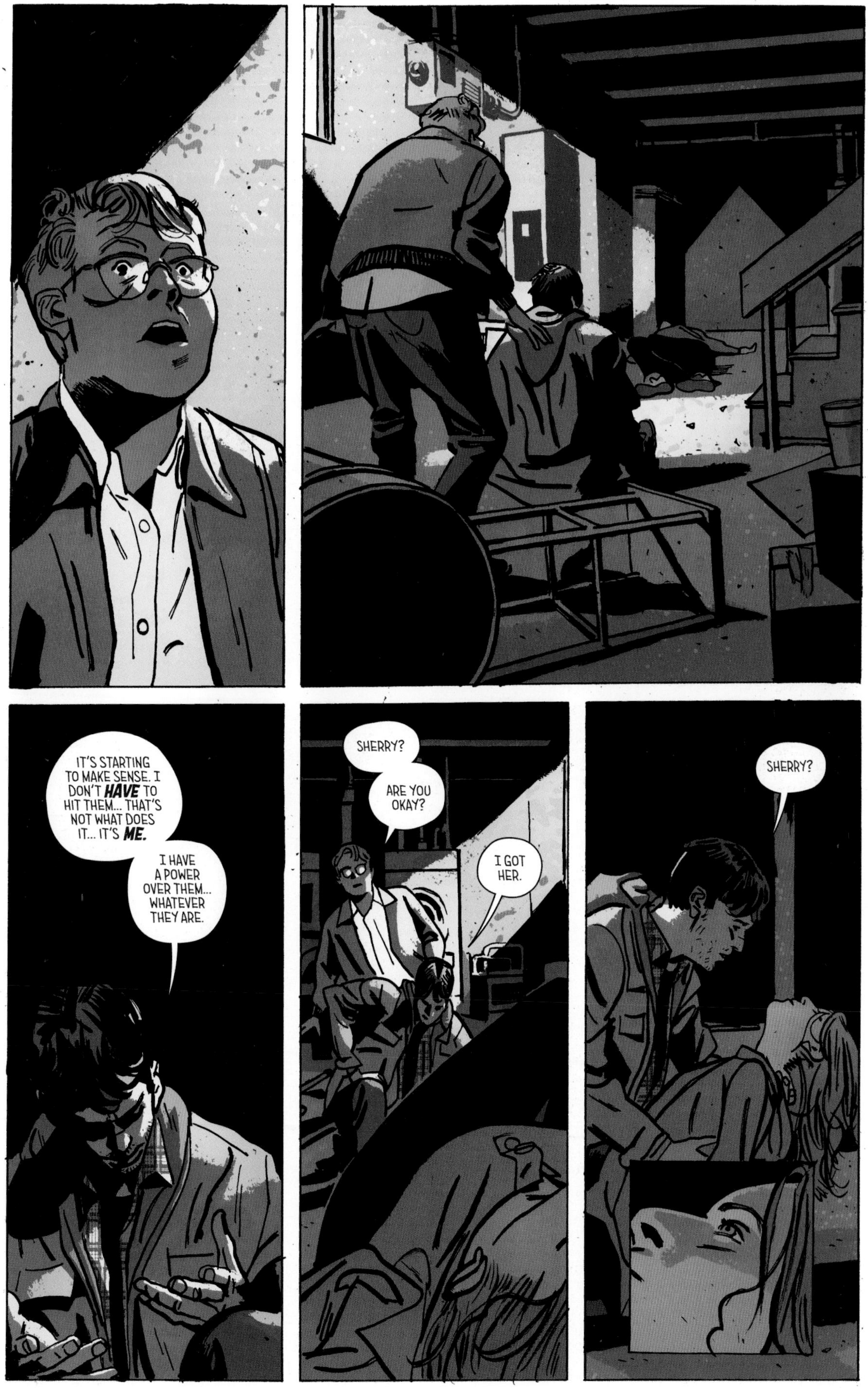
IT'S STARTING TO MAKE SENSE. I DON'T **HAVE** TO HIT THEM... THAT'S NOT WHAT DOES IT... IT'S **ME.**
I HAVE A POWER OVER THEM... WHATEVER THEY ARE.
SHERRY?
ARE YOU OKAY?
I GOT HER.
SHERRY?

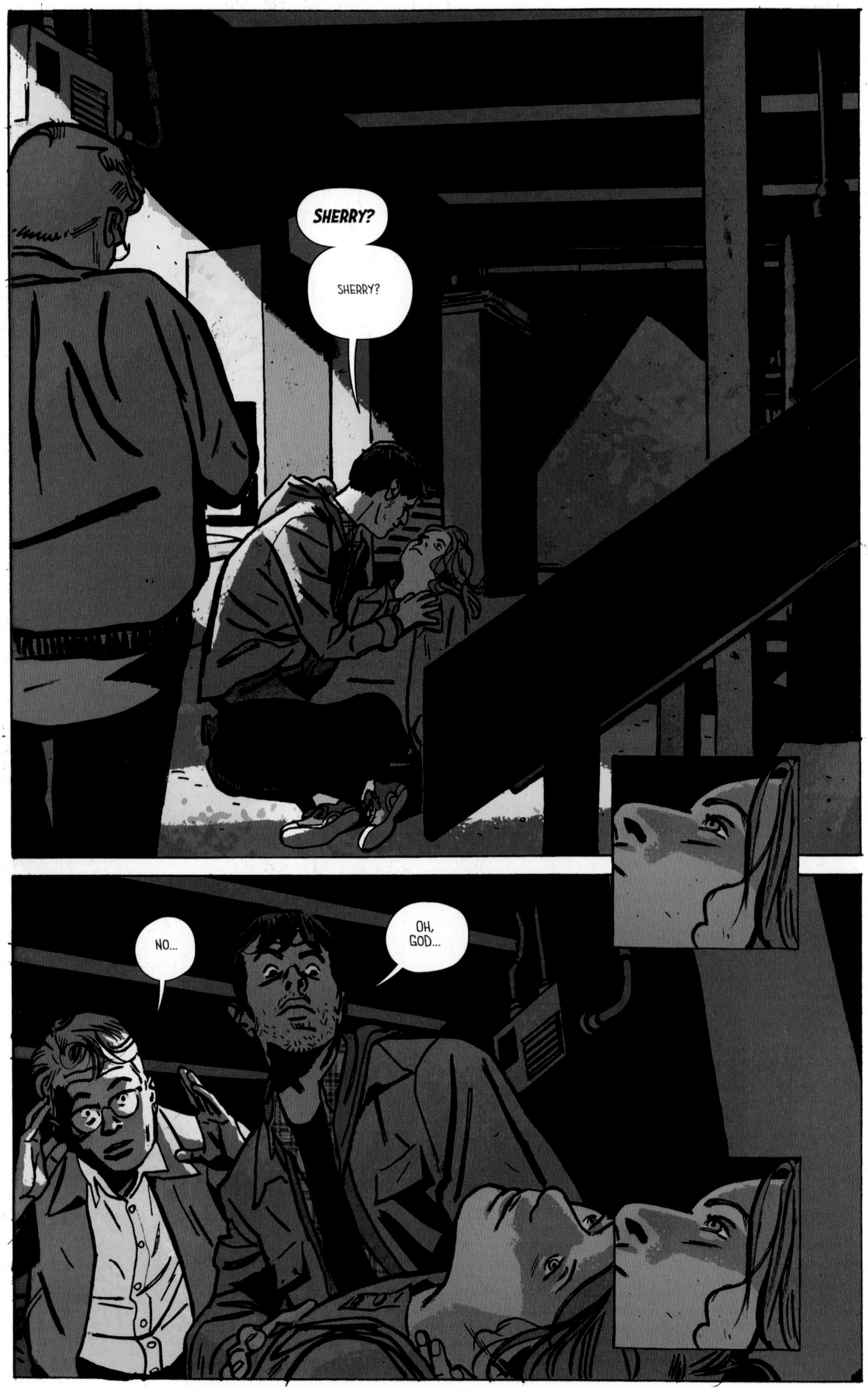
SHERRY?
SHERRY?
NO...
OH, GOD...

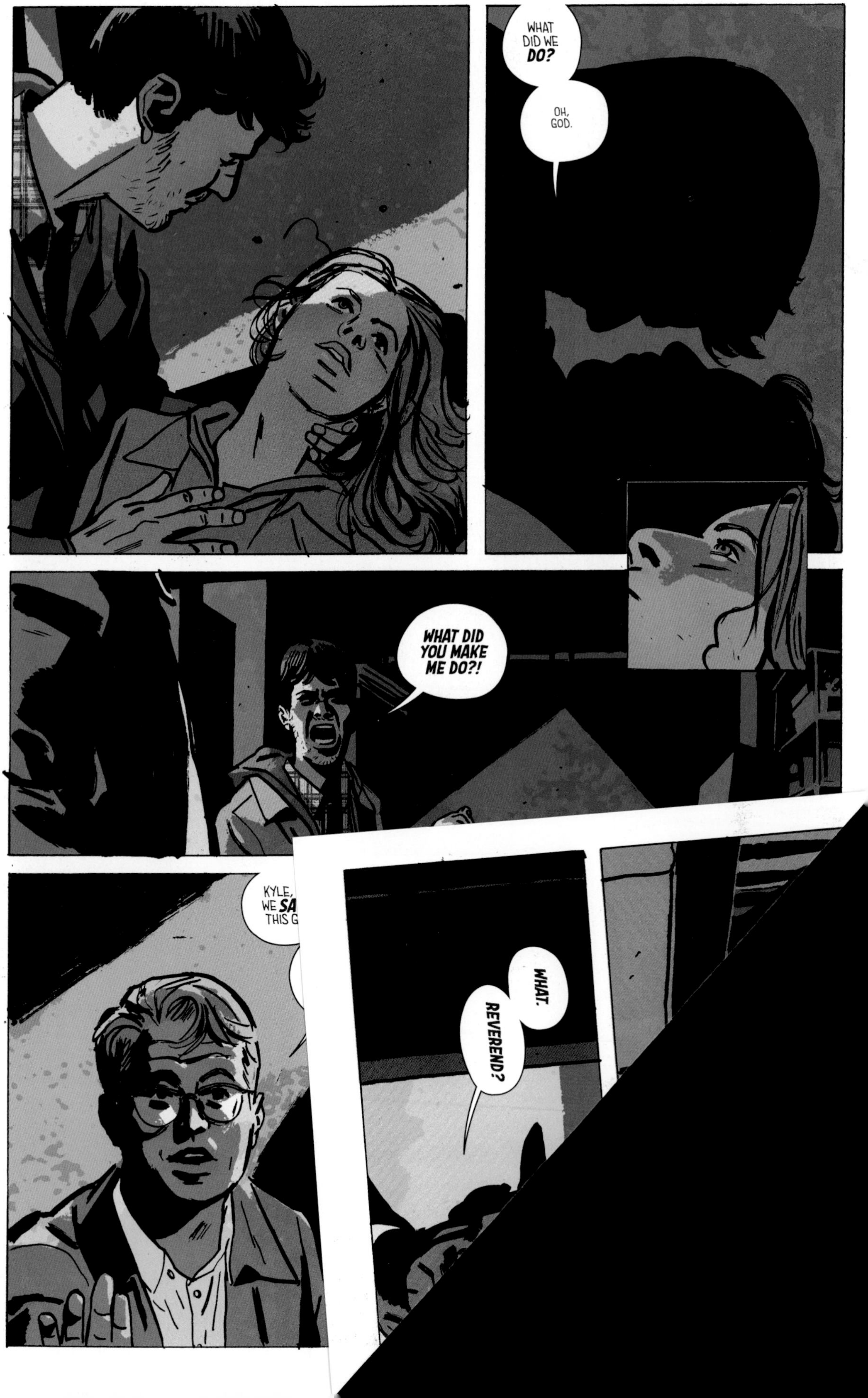
WHAT DID WE DO?
OH, GOD.
WHAT DID YOU MAKE ME DO?!
KYLE,
WHAT.
REVEREND?

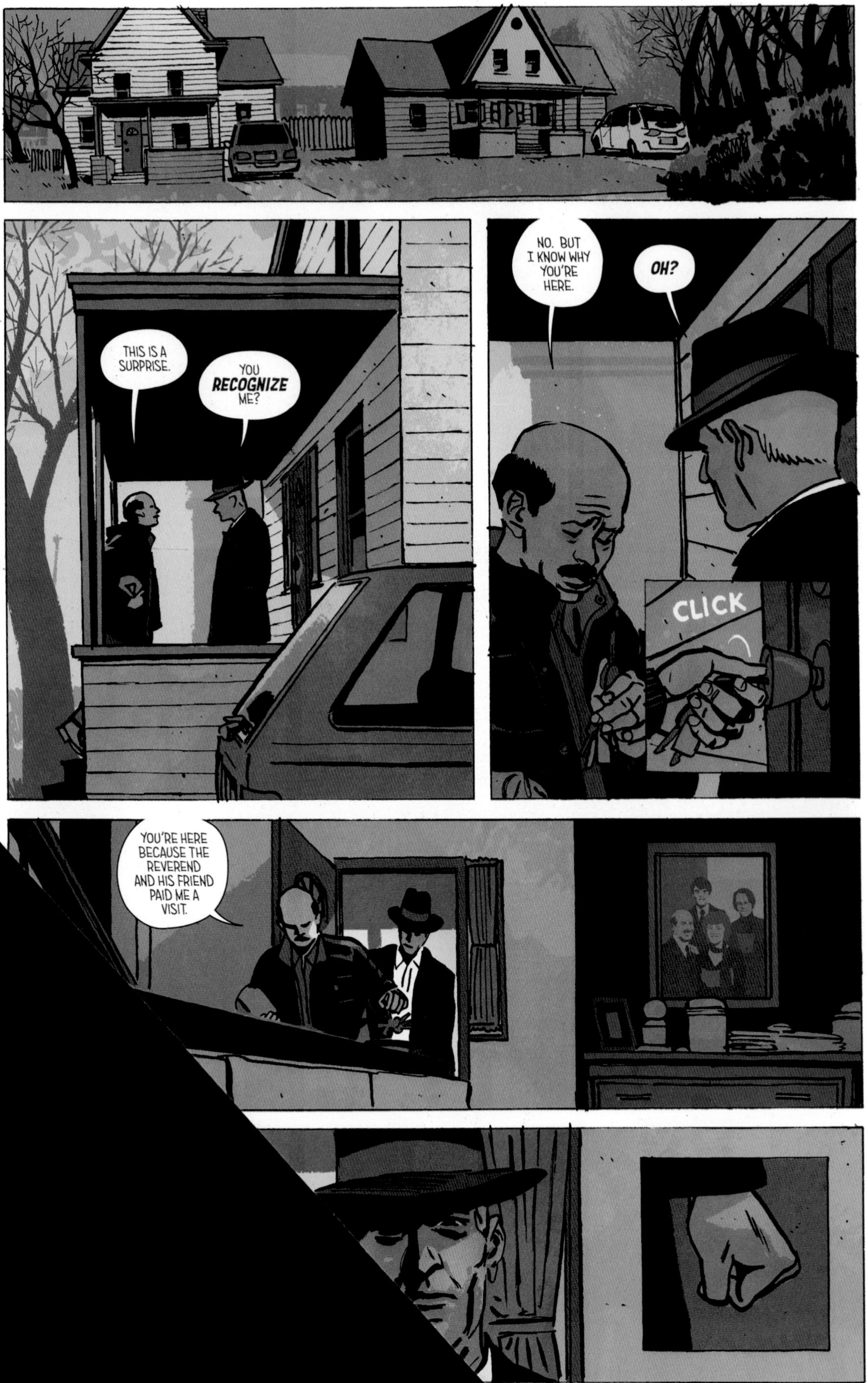
THIS IS A SURPRISE.
YOU RECOGNIZE ME?
NO. BUT I KNOW WHY YOU'RE HERE.
OH?
CLICK
YOU'RE HERE BECAUSE THE REVEREND AND HIS FRIEND PAID ME A VISIT.

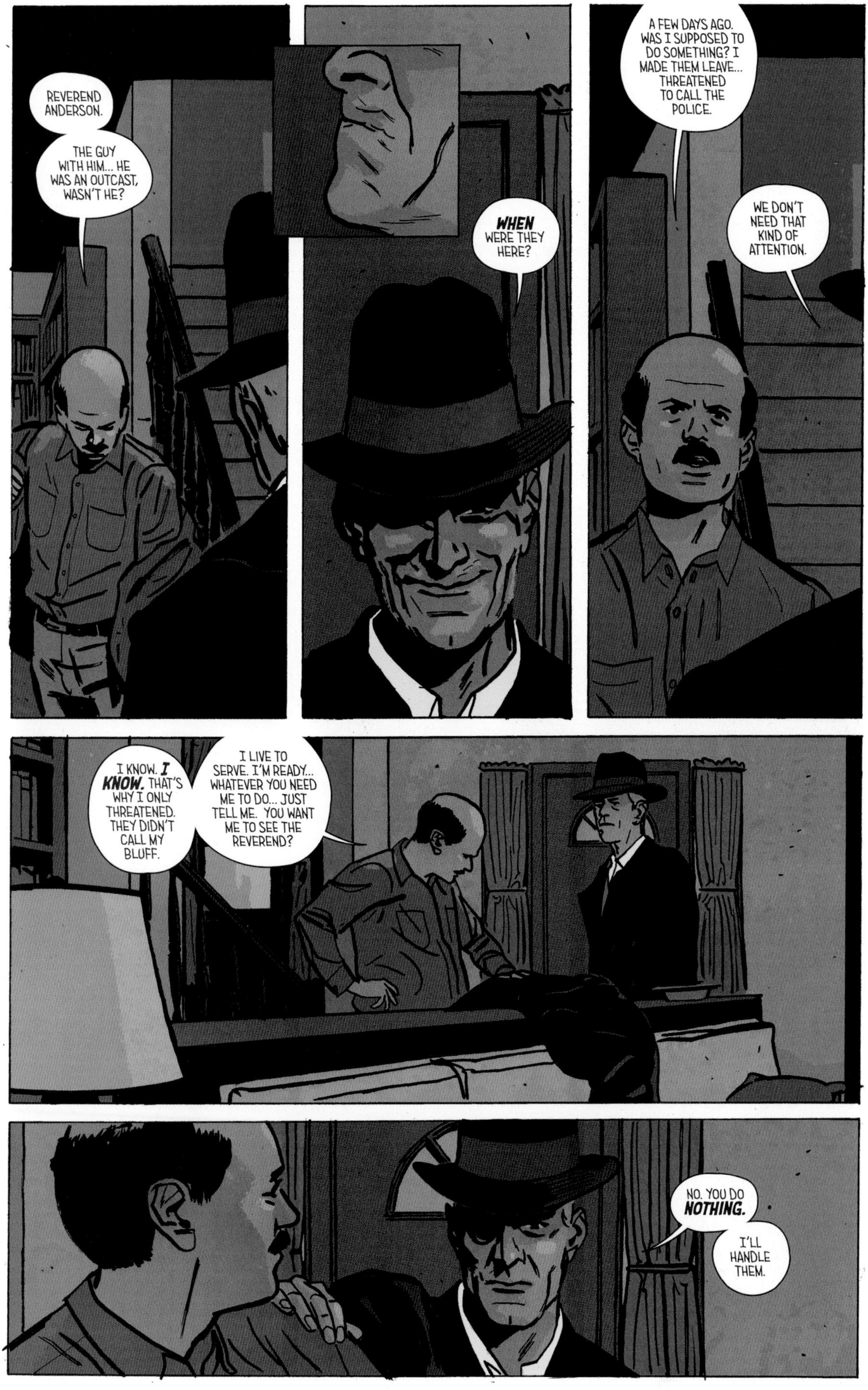
REVEREND ANDERSON.
THE GUY WITH HIM... HE WAS AN OUTCAST, WASN'T HE?
WHEN WERE THEY HERE?
A FEW DAYS AGO. WAS I SUPPOSED TO DO SOMETHING? I MADE THEM LEAVE... THREATENED TO CALL THE POLICE.
WE DON'T NEED THAT KIND OF ATTENTION.
I KNOW. I KNOW. THAT'S WHY I ONLY THREATENED. THEY DIDN'T CALL MY BLUFF.
I LIVE TO SERVE. I'M READY... WHATEVER YOU NEED ME TO DO... JUST TELL ME. YOU WANT ME TO SEE THE REVEREND?
NO. YOU DO NOTHING.
I'LL HANDLE THEM.

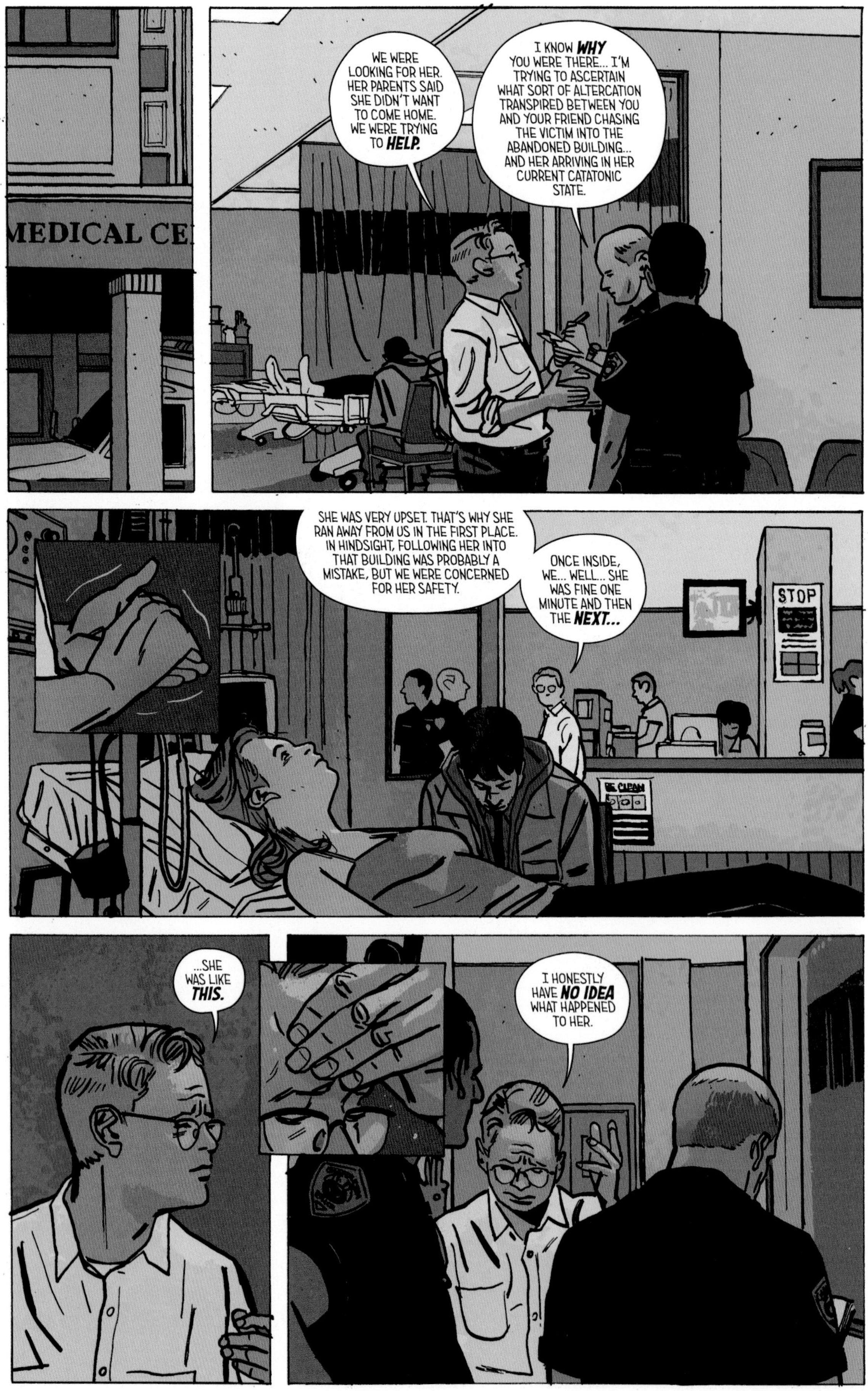
MEDICAL CE
WE WERE LOOKING FOR HER. HER PARENTS SAID SHE DIDN'T WANT TO COME HOME. WE WERE TRYING TO **HELP.**
I KNOW **WHY** YOU WERE THERE... I'M TRYING TO ASCERTAIN WHAT SORT OF ALTERCATION TRANSPIRED BETWEEN YOU AND YOUR FRIEND CHASING THE VICTIM INTO THE ABANDONED BUILDING... AND HER ARRIVING IN HER CURRENT CATATONIC STATE.
SHE WAS VERY UPSET. THAT'S WHY SHE RAN AWAY FROM US IN THE FIRST PLACE. IN HINDSIGHT, FOLLOWING HER INTO THAT BUILDING WAS PROBABLY A MISTAKE, BUT WE WERE CONCERNED FOR HER SAFETY.
ONCE INSIDE, WE... WELL... SHE WAS FINE ONE MINUTE AND THEN THE **NEXT...**
STOP
...SHE WAS LIKE **THIS.**
I HONESTLY HAVE **NO IDEA** WHAT HAPPENED TO HER.

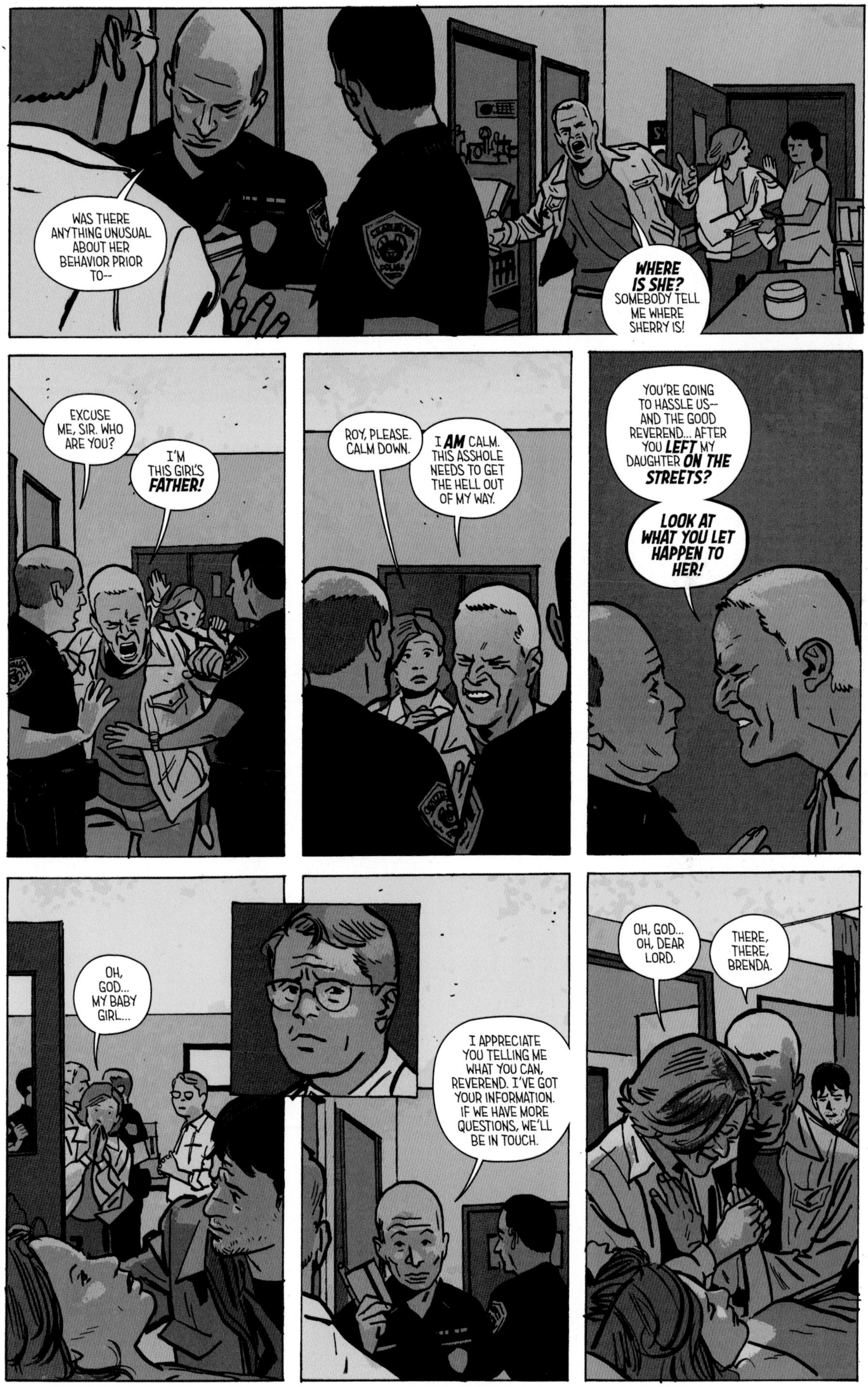
WAS THERE ANYTHING UNUSUAL ABOUT HER BEHAVIOR PRIOR TO--
WHERE IS SHE? SOMEBODY TELL ME WHERE SHERRY IS!
EXCUSE ME, SIR. WHO ARE YOU?
I'M THIS GIRL'S FATHER!
ROY, PLEASE. CALM DOWN.
I AM CALM. THIS ASSHOLE NEEDS TO GET THE HELL OUT OF MY WAY.
YOU'RE GOING TO HASSLE US-- AND THE GOOD REVEREND... AFTER YOU LEFT MY DAUGHTER ON THE STREETS?
LOOK AT WHAT YOU LET HAPPEN TO HER!
OH, GOD... MY BABY GIRL...
I APPRECIATE YOU TELLING ME WHAT YOU CAN, REVEREND. I'VE GOT YOUR INFORMATION. IF WE HAVE MORE QUESTIONS, WE'LL BE IN TOUCH.
OH, GOD... OH, DEAR LORD.
THERE, THERE, BRENDA.

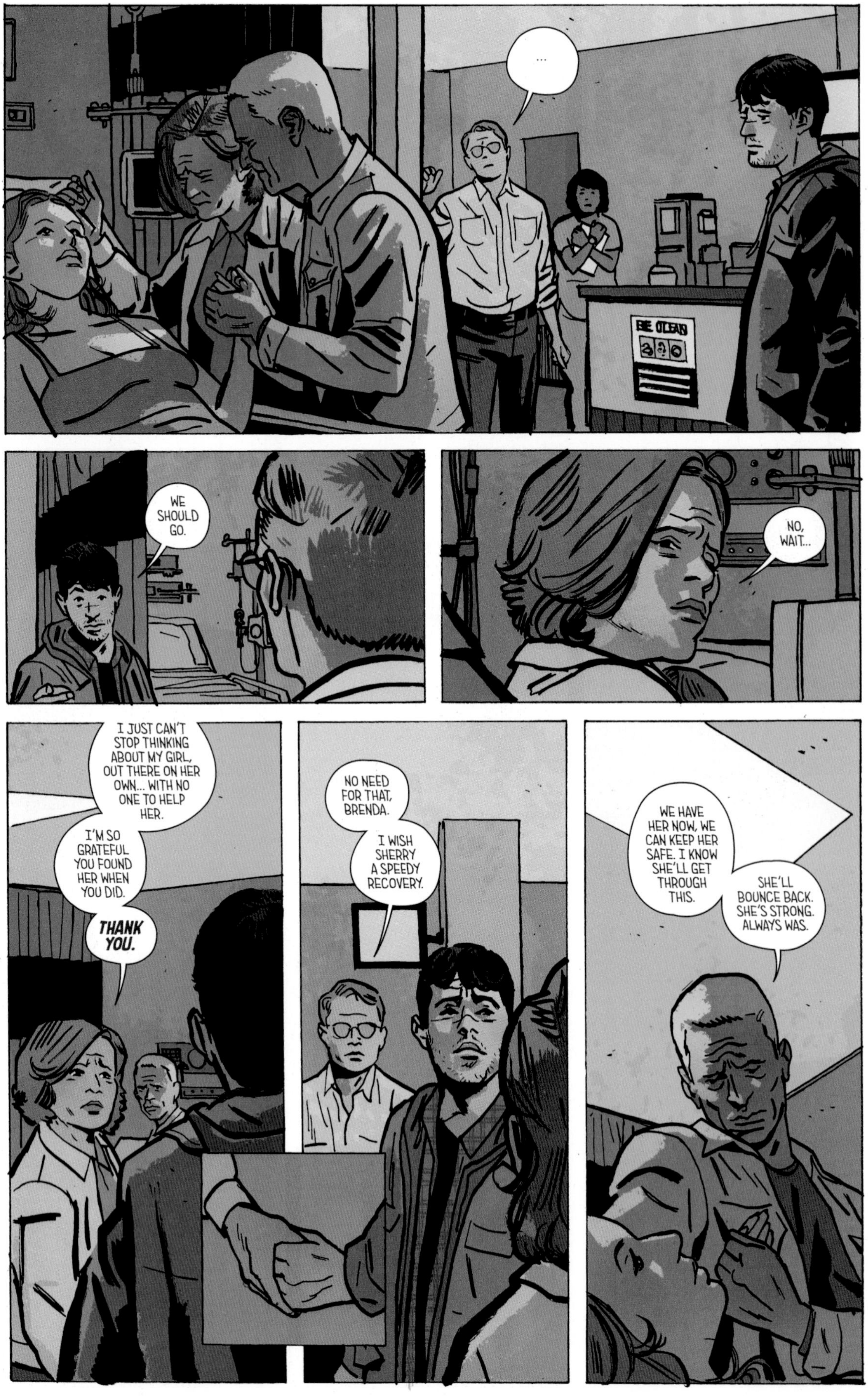
...
WE SHOULD GO.
NO, WAIT...
I JUST CAN'T STOP THINKING ABOUT MY GIRL, OUT THERE ON HER OWN... WITH NO ONE TO HELP HER.
I'M SO GRATEFUL YOU FOUND HER WHEN YOU DID.
THANK YOU.
NO NEED FOR THAT, BRENDA.
I WISH SHERRY A SPEEDY RECOVERY.
WE HAVE HER NOW, WE CAN KEEP HER SAFE. I KNOW SHE'LL GET THROUGH THIS.
SHE'LL BOUNCE BACK. SHE'S STRONG. ALWAYS WAS.

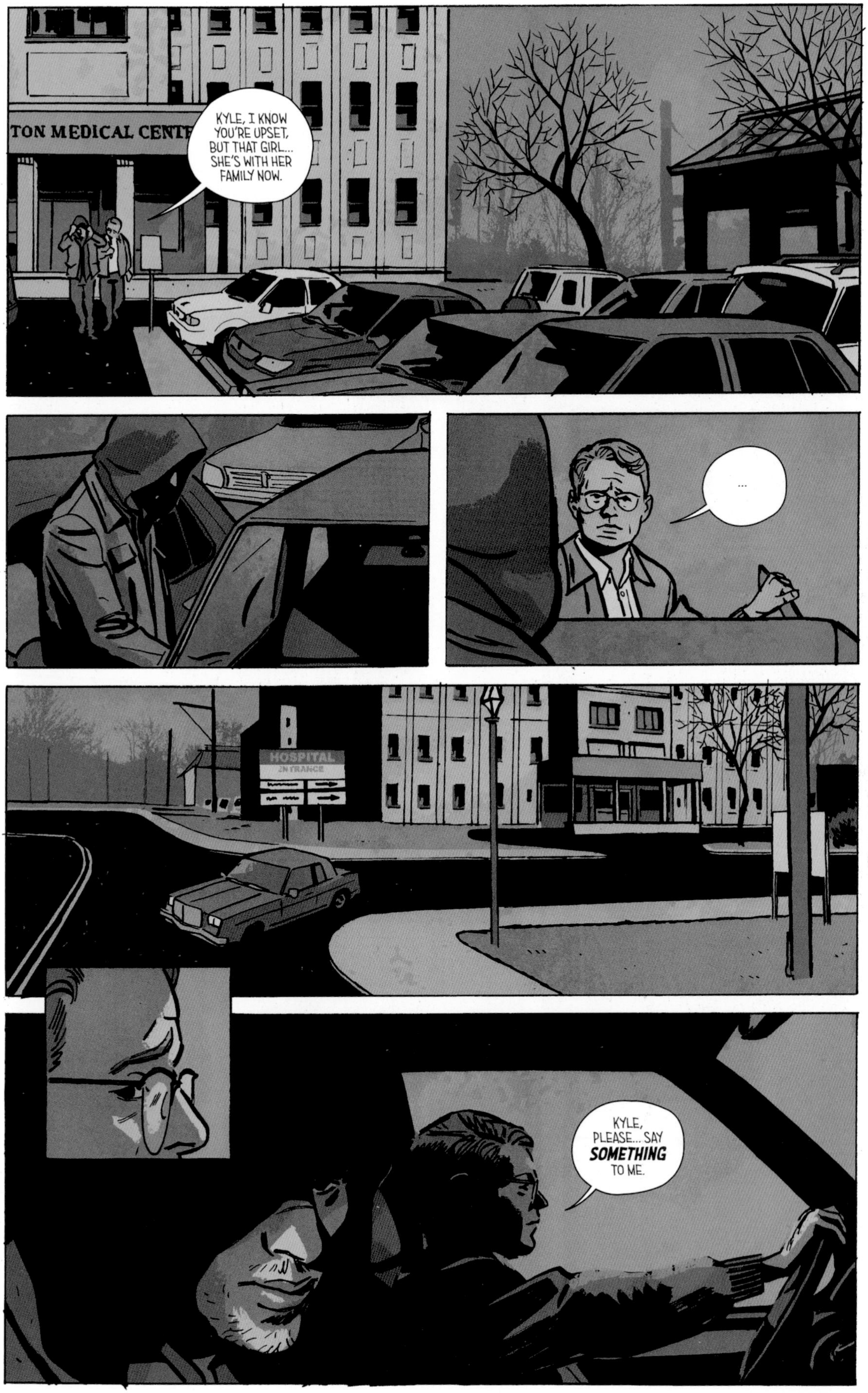
TON MEDICAL CENTE
KYLE, I KNOW YOU'RE UPSET, BUT THAT GIRL... SHE'S WITH HER FAMILY NOW.
...
HOSPITAL
ENTRANCE
KYLE, PLEASE... SAY SOMETHING TO ME.

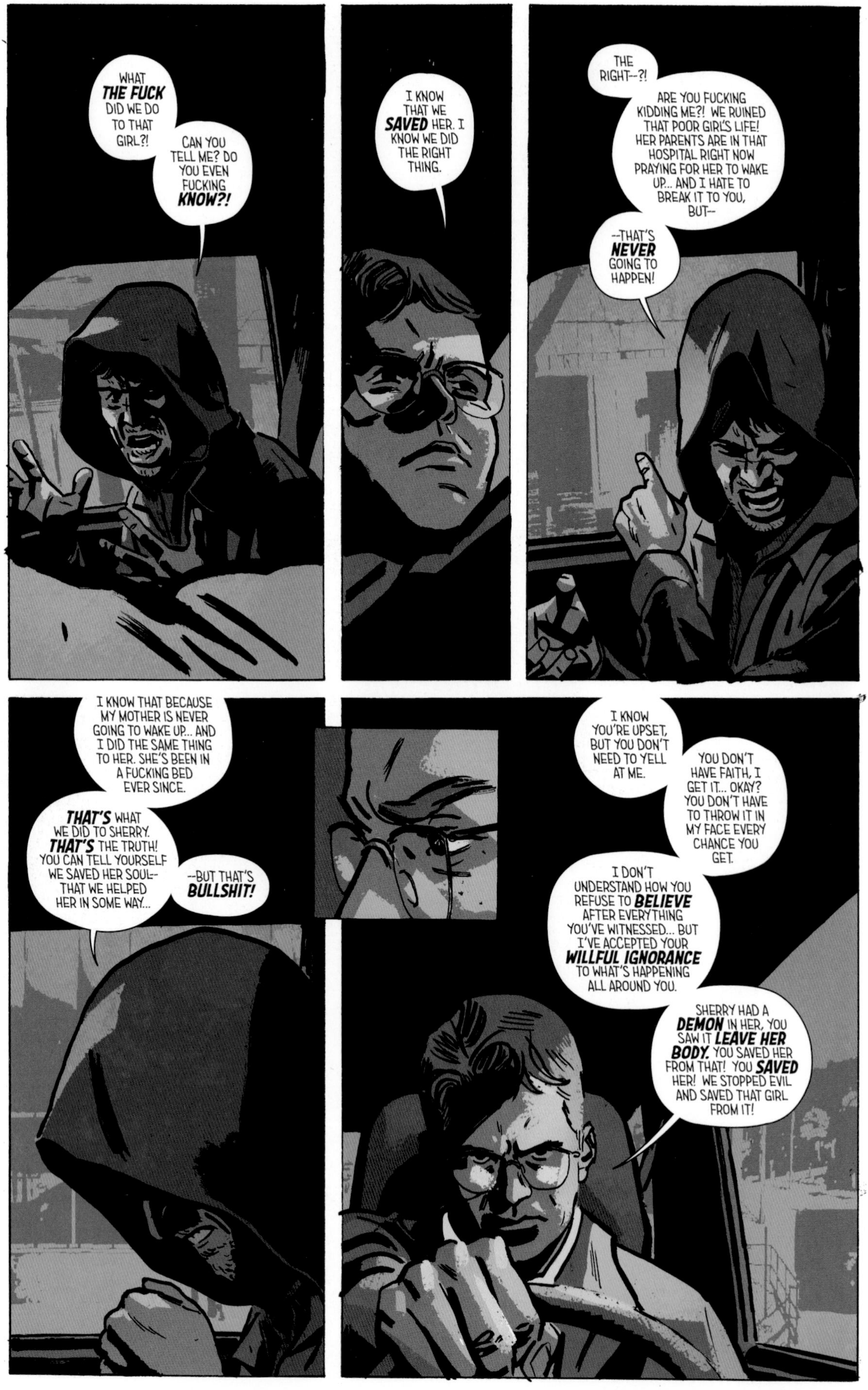
WHAT THE FUCK DID WE DO TO THAT GIRL?!
CAN YOU TELL ME? DO YOU EVEN FUCKING KNOW?!
I KNOW THAT WE SAVED HER. I KNOW WE DID THE RIGHT THING.
THE RIGHT--?!
ARE YOU FUCKING KIDDING ME?! WE RUINED THAT POOR GIRL'S LIFE! HER PARENTS ARE IN THAT HOSPITAL RIGHT NOW PRAYING FOR HER TO WAKE UP... AND I HATE TO BREAK IT TO YOU, BUT--
--THAT'S NEVER GOING TO HAPPEN!
I KNOW THAT BECAUSE MY MOTHER IS NEVER GOING TO WAKE UP... AND I DID THE SAME THING TO HER. SHE'S BEEN IN A FUCKING BED EVER SINCE.
THAT'S WHAT WE DID TO SHERRY. THAT'S THE TRUTH! YOU CAN TELL YOURSELF WE SAVED HER SOUL-- THAT WE HELPED HER IN SOME WAY...
--BUT THAT'S BULLSHIT!
I KNOW YOU'RE UPSET, BUT YOU DON'T NEED TO YELL AT ME.
YOU DON'T HAVE FAITH, I GET IT... OKAY? YOU DON'T HAVE TO THROW IT IN MY FACE EVERY CHANCE YOU GET.
I DON'T UNDERSTAND HOW YOU REFUSE TO BELIEVE AFTER EVERYTHING YOU'VE WITNESSED... BUT I'VE ACCEPTED YOUR WILLFUL IGNORANCE TO WHAT'S HAPPENING ALL AROUND YOU.
SHERRY HAD A DEMON IN HER, YOU SAW IT LEAVE HER BODY. YOU SAVED HER FROM THAT! YOU SAVED HER! WE STOPPED EVIL AND SAVED THAT GIRL FROM IT!

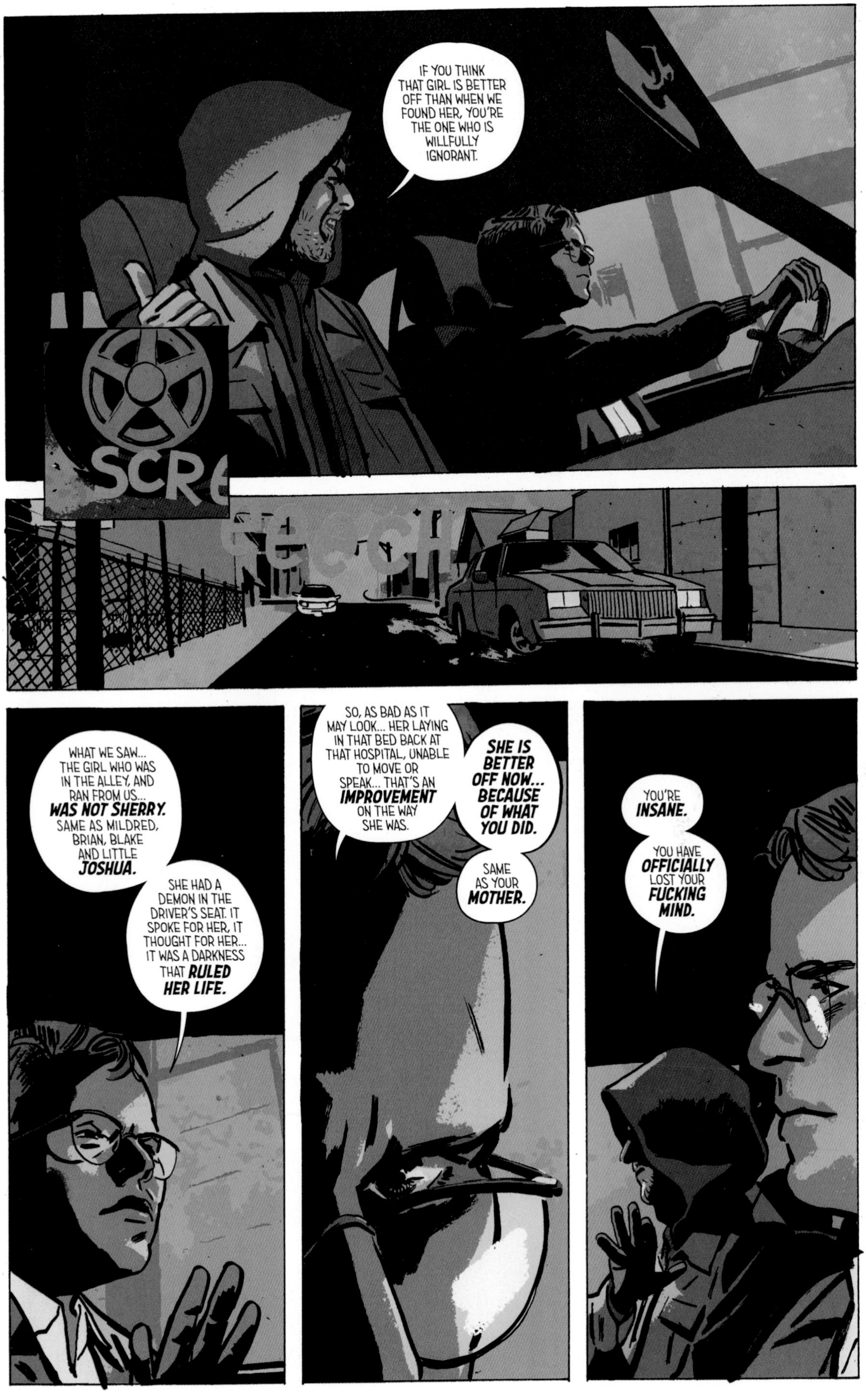
IF YOU THINK THAT GIRL IS BETTER OFF THAN WHEN WE FOUND HER, YOU'RE THE ONE WHO IS WILLFULLY IGNORANT.
SCREEECH
WHAT WE SAW... THE GIRL WHO WAS IN THE ALLEY, AND RAN FROM US... WAS NOT SHERRY. SAME AS MILDRED, BRIAN, BLAKE AND LITTLE JOSHUA.
SHE HAD A DEMON IN THE DRIVER'S SEAT. IT SPOKE FOR HER, IT THOUGHT FOR HER... IT WAS A DARKNESS THAT RULED HER LIFE.
SO, AS BAD AS IT MAY LOOK... HER LAYING IN THAT BED BACK AT THAT HOSPITAL, UNABLE TO MOVE OR SPEAK... THAT'S AN IMPROVEMENT ON THE WAY SHE WAS.
SHE IS BETTER OFF NOW... BECAUSE OF WHAT YOU DID.
SAME AS YOUR MOTHER.
YOU'RE INSANE.
YOU HAVE OFFICIALLY LOST YOUR FUCKING MIND.

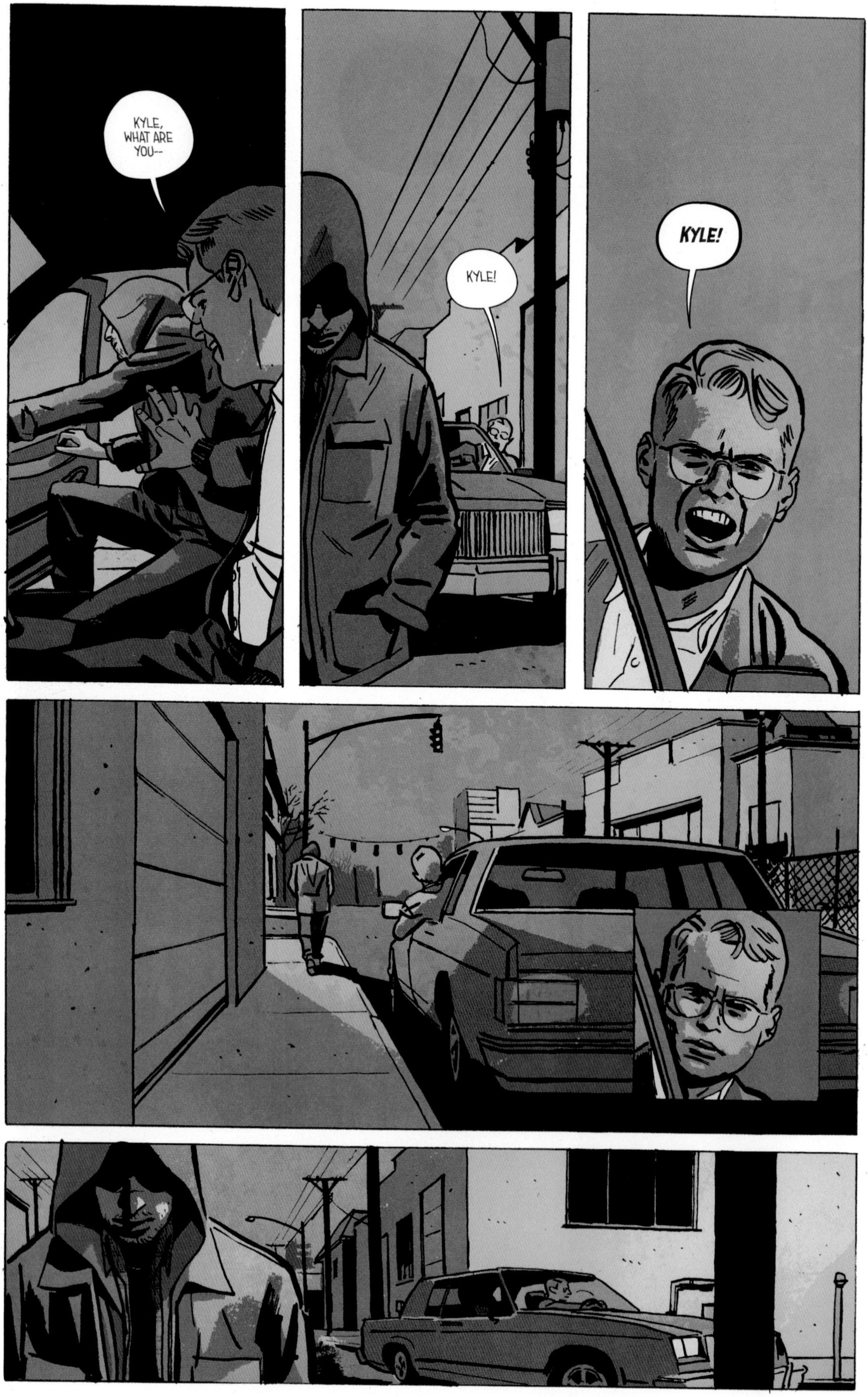
KYLE, WHAT ARE YOU--
KYLE!
KYLE!

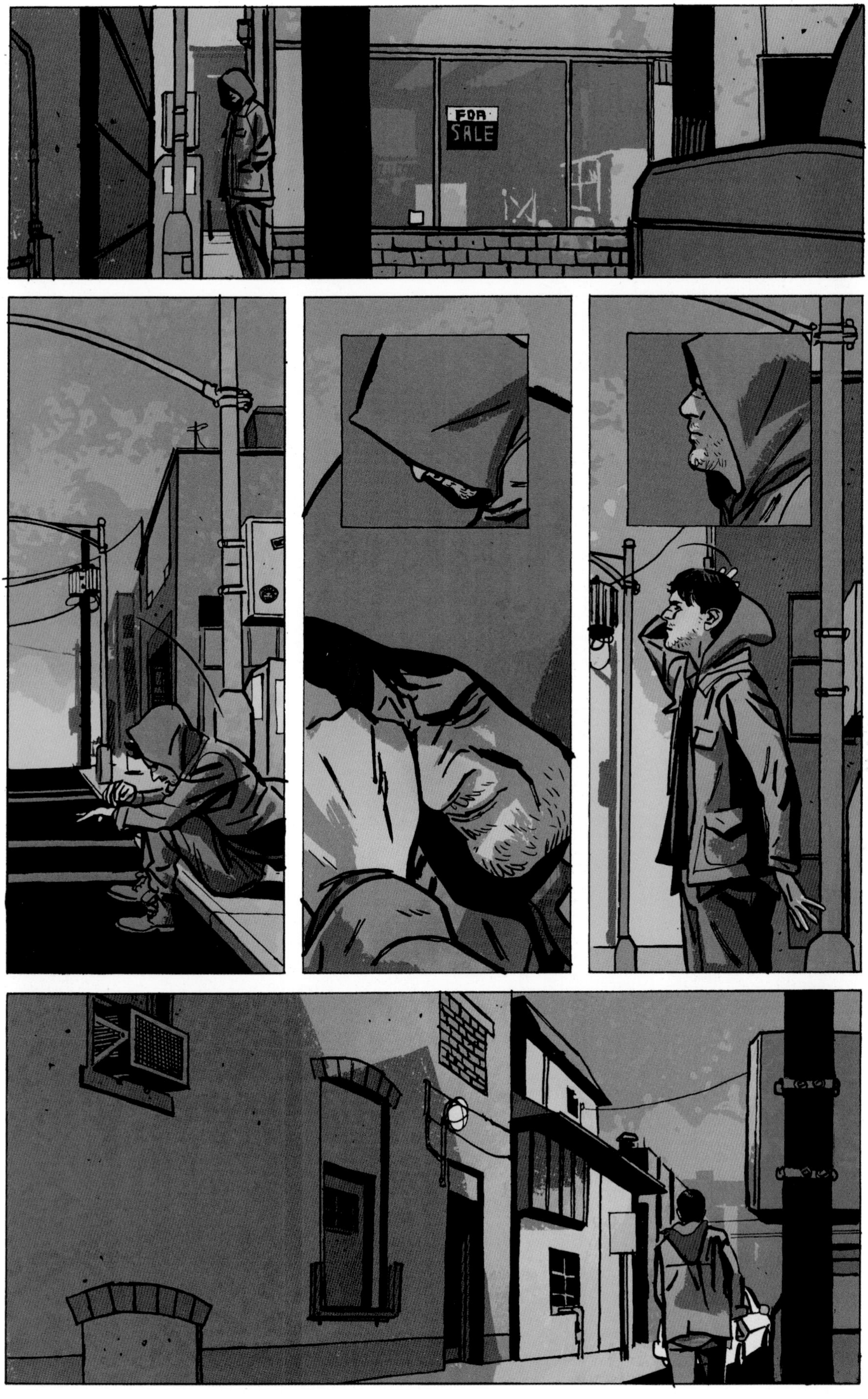
FOR SALE

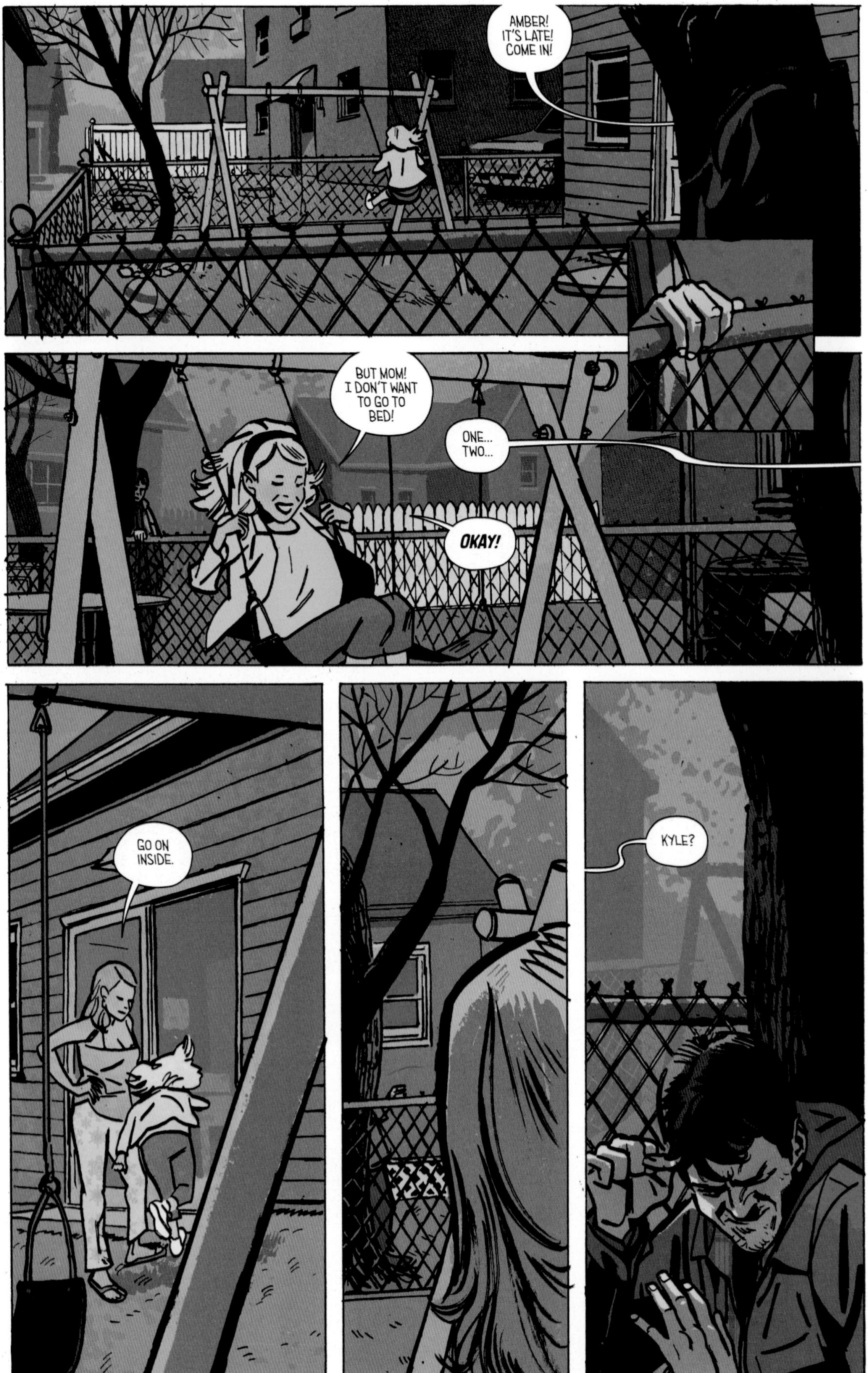
AMBER! IT'S LATE! COME IN!
BUT MOM! I DON'T WANT TO GO TO BED!
ONE... TWO...
OKAY!
GO ON INSIDE.
KYLE?

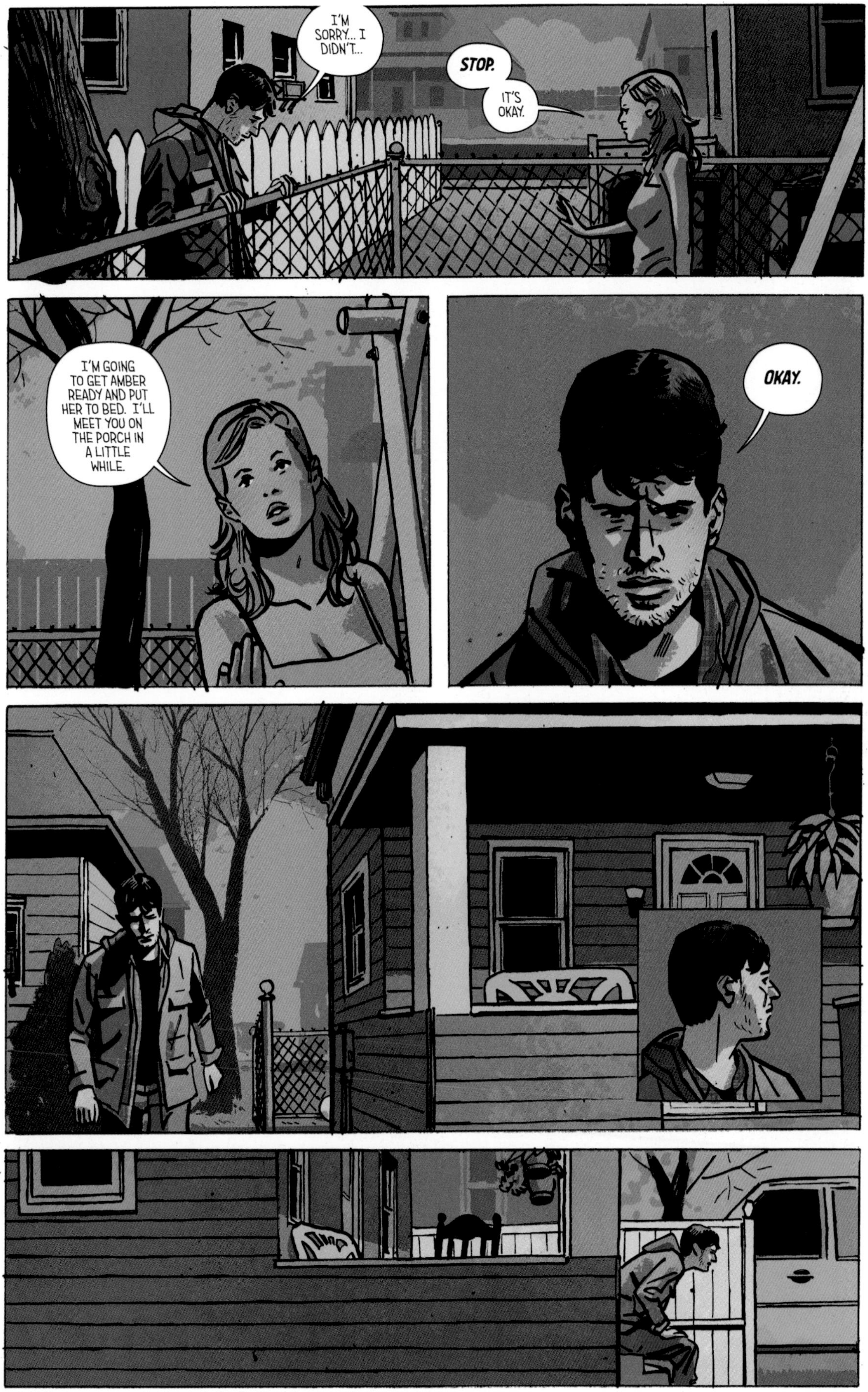
I'M SORRY... I DIDN'T...
STOP.
IT'S OKAY.
I'M GOING TO GET AMBER READY AND PUT HER TO BED. I'LL MEET YOU ON THE PORCH IN A LITTLE WHILE.
OKAY.

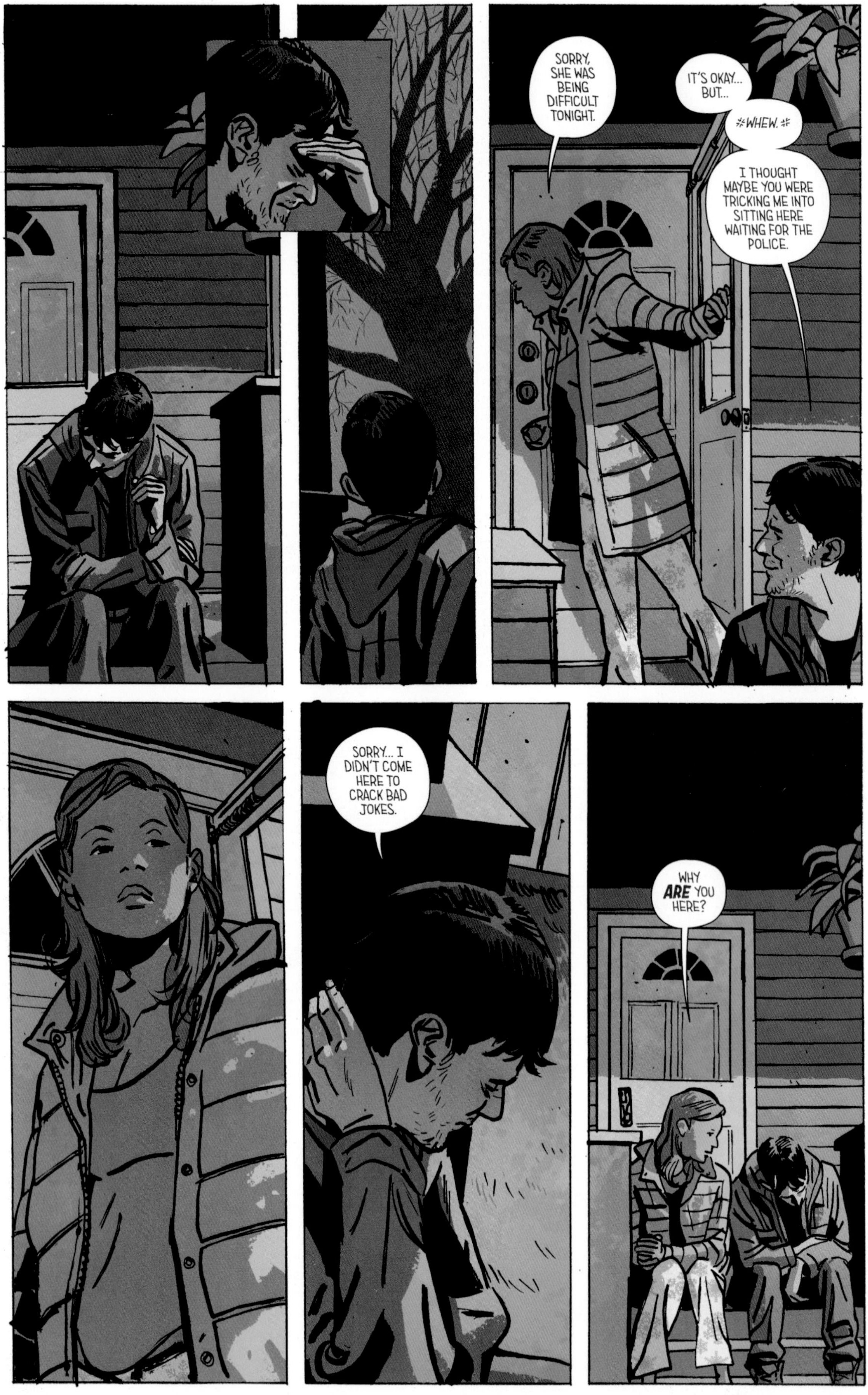

SORRY, SHE WAS BEING DIFFICULT TONIGHT.
IT'S OKAY... BUT...
#WHEW.#
I THOUGHT MAYBE YOU WERE TRICKING ME INTO SITTING HERE WAITING FOR THE POLICE.
SORRY... I DIDN'T COME HERE TO CRACK BAD JOKES.
WHY **ARE** YOU HERE?

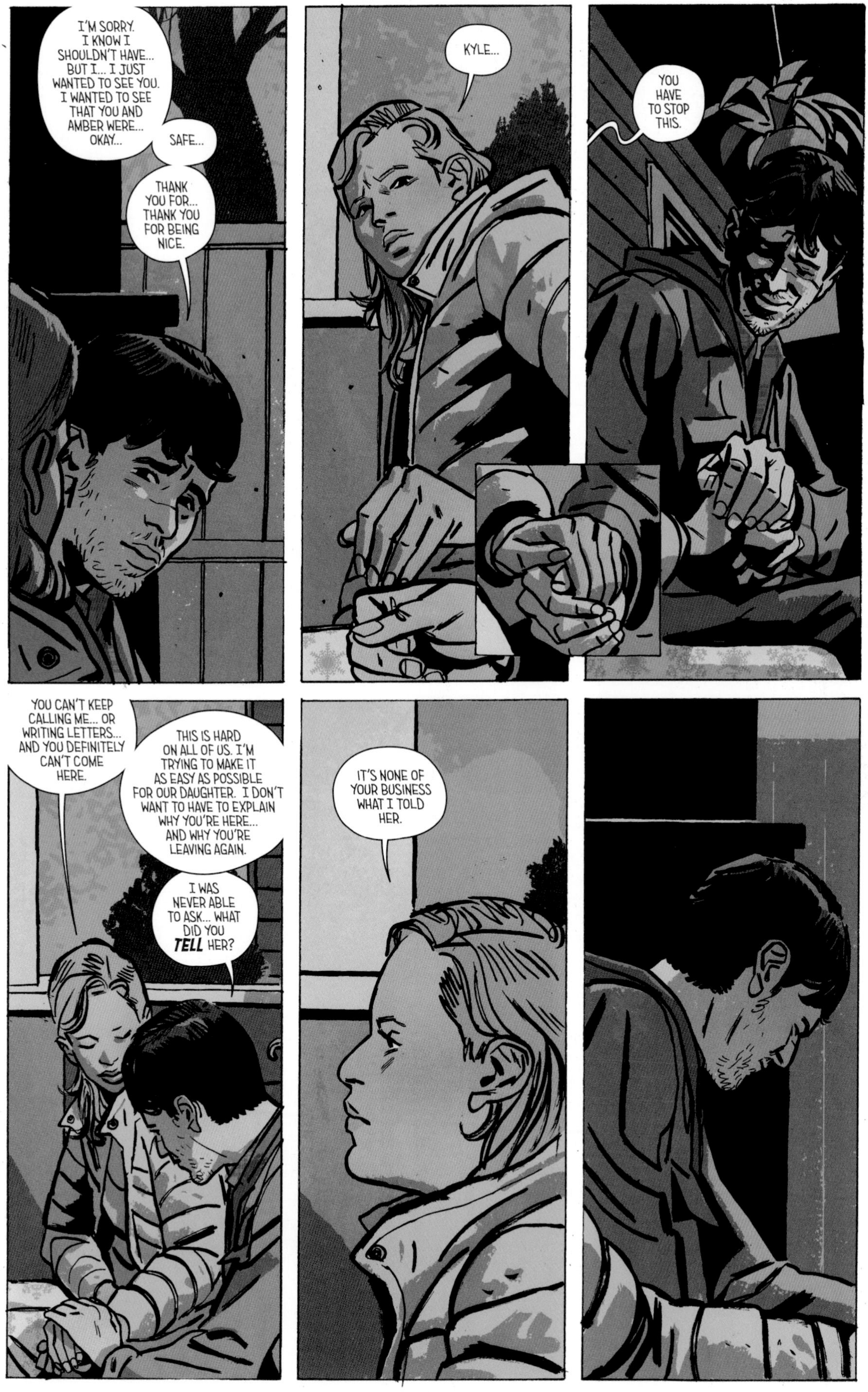
I'M SORRY. I KNOW I SHOULDN'T HAVE... BUT I... I JUST WANTED TO SEE YOU. I WANTED TO SEE THAT YOU AND AMBER WERE... OKAY...
SAFE...
THANK YOU FOR... THANK YOU FOR BEING NICE.
KYLE...
YOU HAVE TO STOP THIS.
YOU CAN'T KEEP CALLING ME... OR WRITING LETTERS... AND YOU DEFINITELY CAN'T COME HERE.
THIS IS HARD ON ALL OF US. I'M TRYING TO MAKE IT AS EASY AS POSSIBLE FOR OUR DAUGHTER. I DON'T WANT TO HAVE TO EXPLAIN WHY YOU'RE HERE... AND WHY YOU'RE LEAVING AGAIN.
I WAS NEVER ABLE TO ASK... WHAT DID YOU **TELL** HER?
IT'S NONE OF YOUR BUSINESS WHAT I TOLD HER.

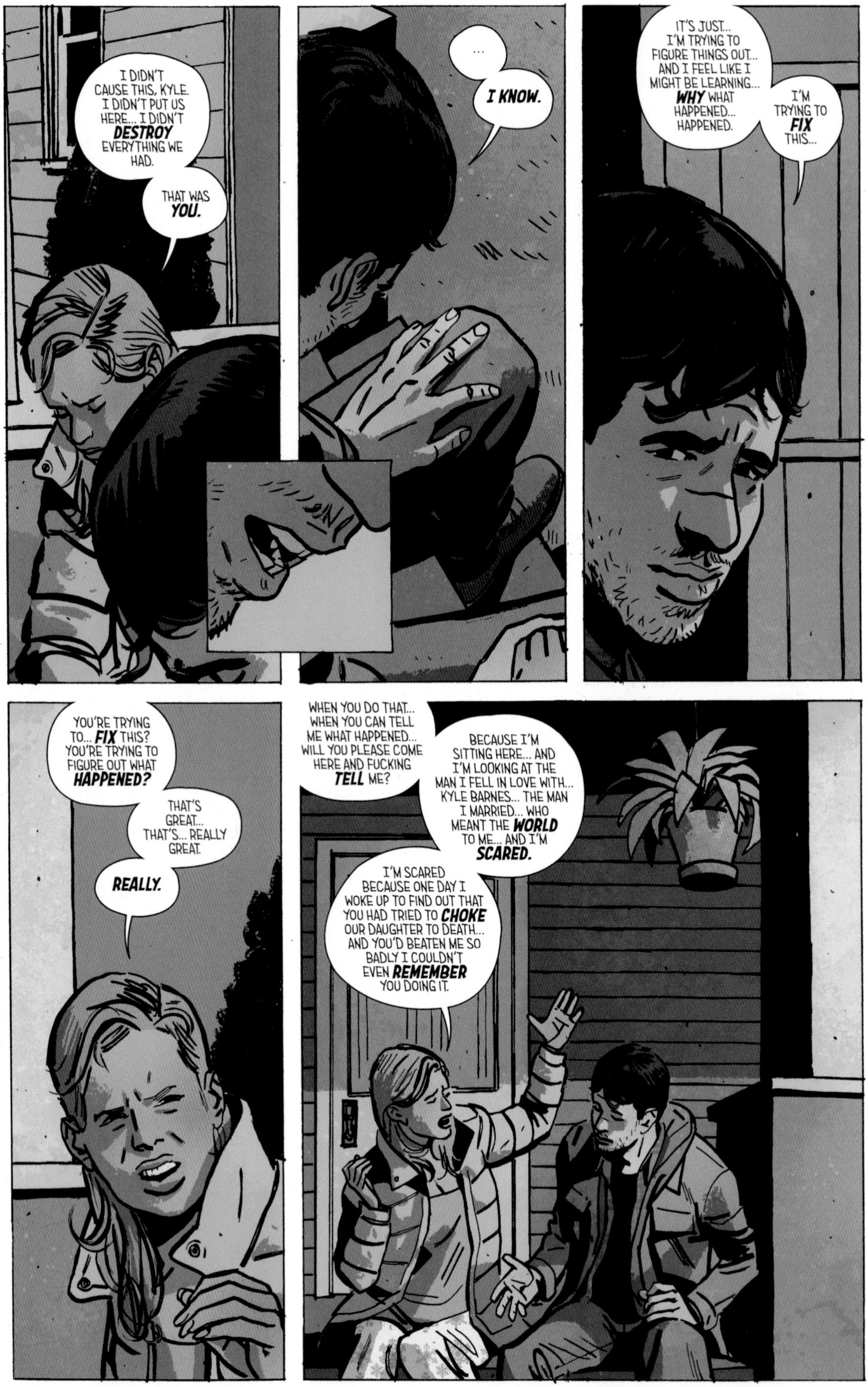
I DIDN'T CAUSE THIS, KYLE. I DIDN'T PUT US HERE... I DIDN'T DESTROY EVERYTHING WE HAD.
THAT WAS YOU.
...
I KNOW.
IT'S JUST... I'M TRYING TO FIGURE THINGS OUT... AND I FEEL LIKE I MIGHT BE LEARNING... WHY WHAT HAPPENED... HAPPENED.
I'M TRYING TO FIX THIS...
YOU'RE TRYING TO... FIX THIS? YOU'RE TRYING TO FIGURE OUT WHAT HAPPENED?
THAT'S GREAT... THAT'S... REALLY GREAT.
REALLY.
WHEN YOU DO THAT... WHEN YOU CAN TELL ME WHAT HAPPENED... WILL YOU PLEASE COME HERE AND FUCKING TELL ME?
BECAUSE I'M SITTING HERE... AND I'M LOOKING AT THE MAN I FELL IN LOVE WITH... KYLE BARNES... THE MAN I MARRIED... WHO MEANT THE WORLD TO ME... AND I'M SCARED.
I'M SCARED BECAUSE ONE DAY I WOKE UP TO FIND OUT THAT YOU HAD TRIED TO CHOKE OUR DAUGHTER TO DEATH... AND YOU'D BEATEN ME SO BADLY I COULDN'T EVEN REMEMBER YOU DOING IT.

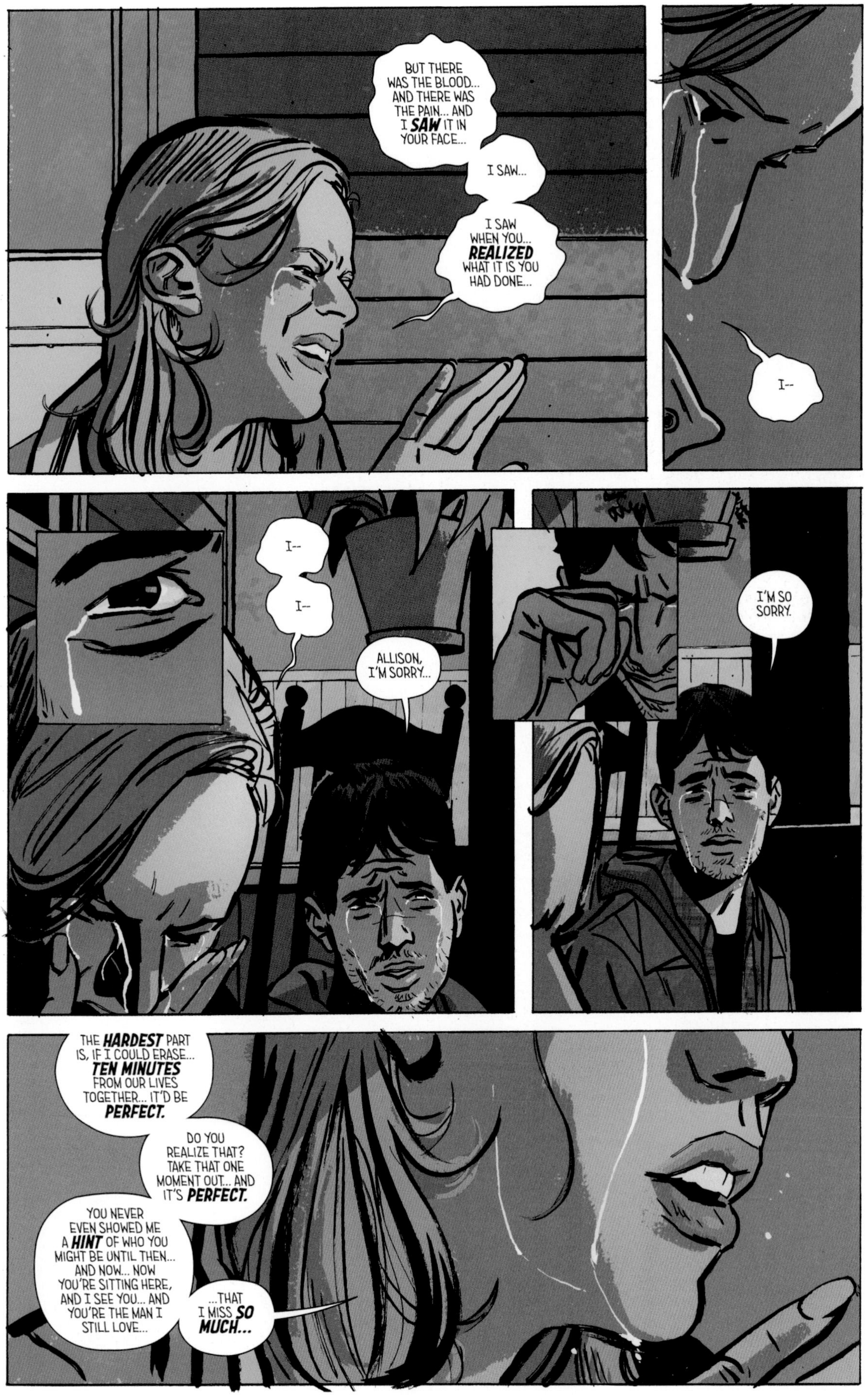

BUT THERE WAS THE BLOOD... AND THERE WAS THE PAIN... AND I SAW IT IN YOUR FACE...
I SAW...
I SAW WHEN YOU... REALIZED WHAT IT IS YOU HAD DONE...
I--
I--
I--
ALLISON, I'M SORRY...
I'M SO SORRY.
THE HARDEST PART IS, IF I COULD ERASE... TEN MINUTES FROM OUR LIVES TOGETHER... IT'D BE PERFECT.
DO YOU REALIZE THAT? TAKE THAT ONE MOMENT OUT... AND IT'S PERFECT.
YOU NEVER EVEN SHOWED ME A HINT OF WHO YOU MIGHT BE UNTIL THEN... AND NOW... NOW YOU'RE SITTING HERE, AND I SEE YOU... AND YOU'RE THE MAN I STILL LOVE...
...THAT I MISS SO MUCH...

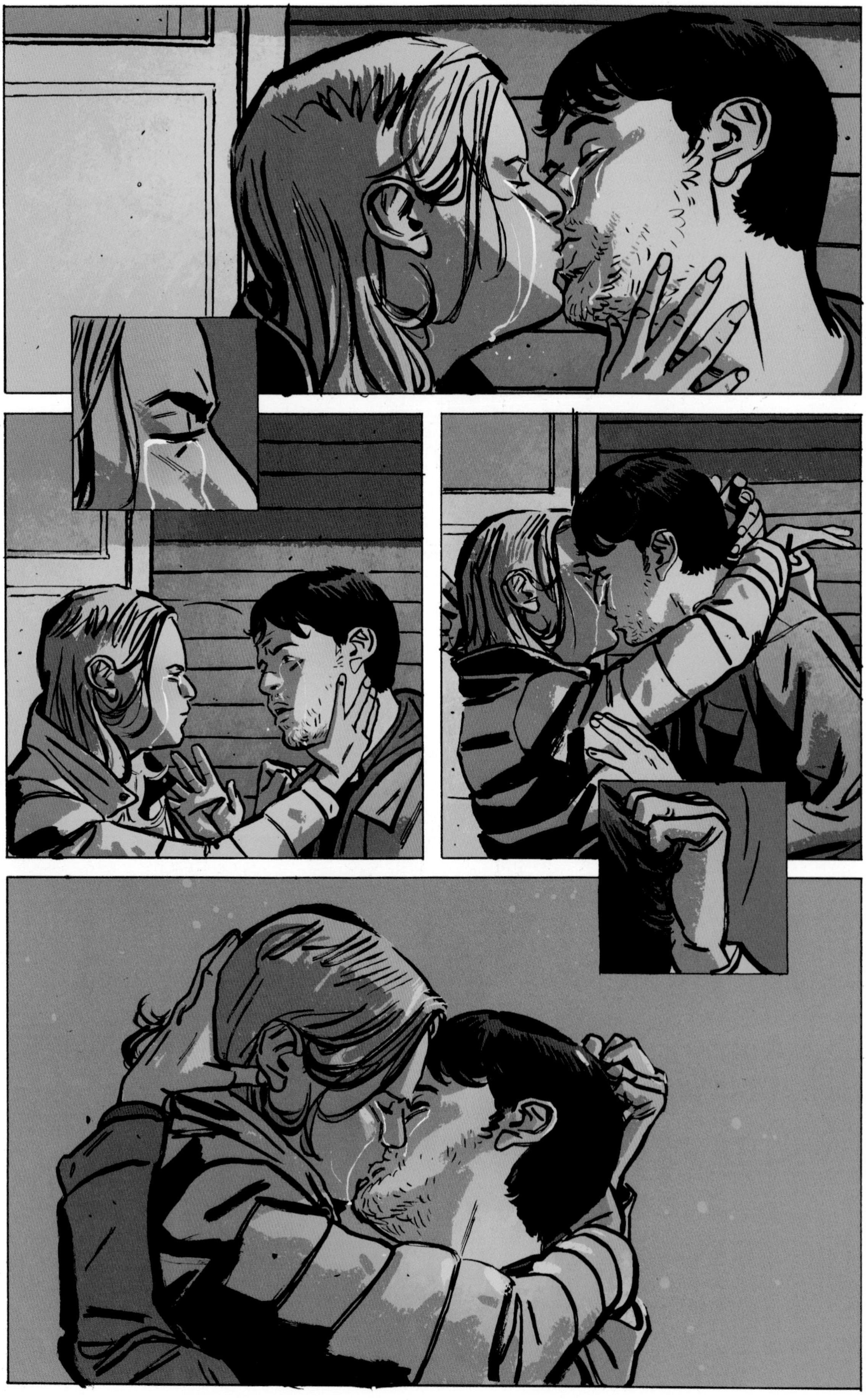

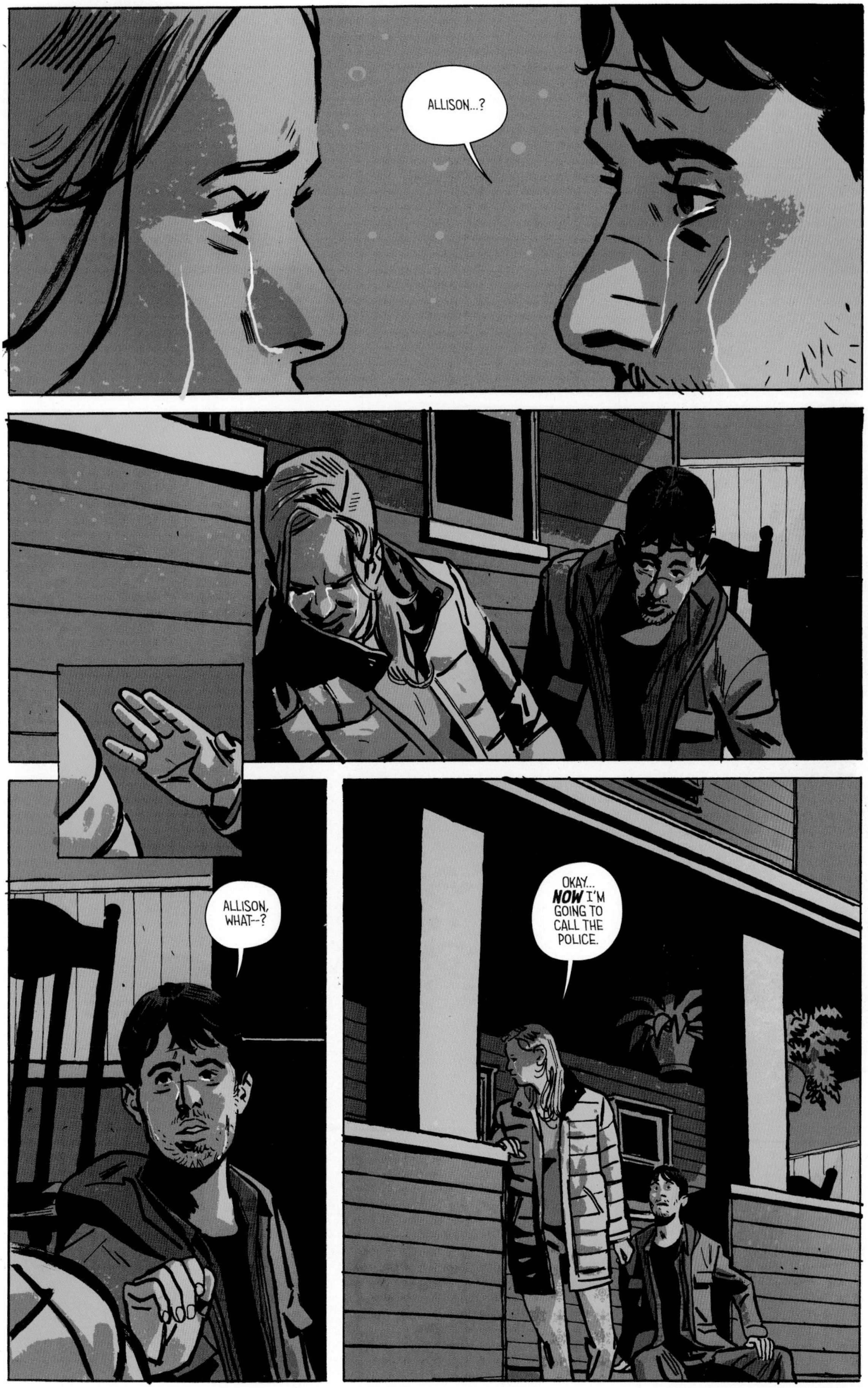
ALLISON...?
ALLISON, WHAT--?
OKAY... **NOW** I'M GOING TO CALL THE POLICE.

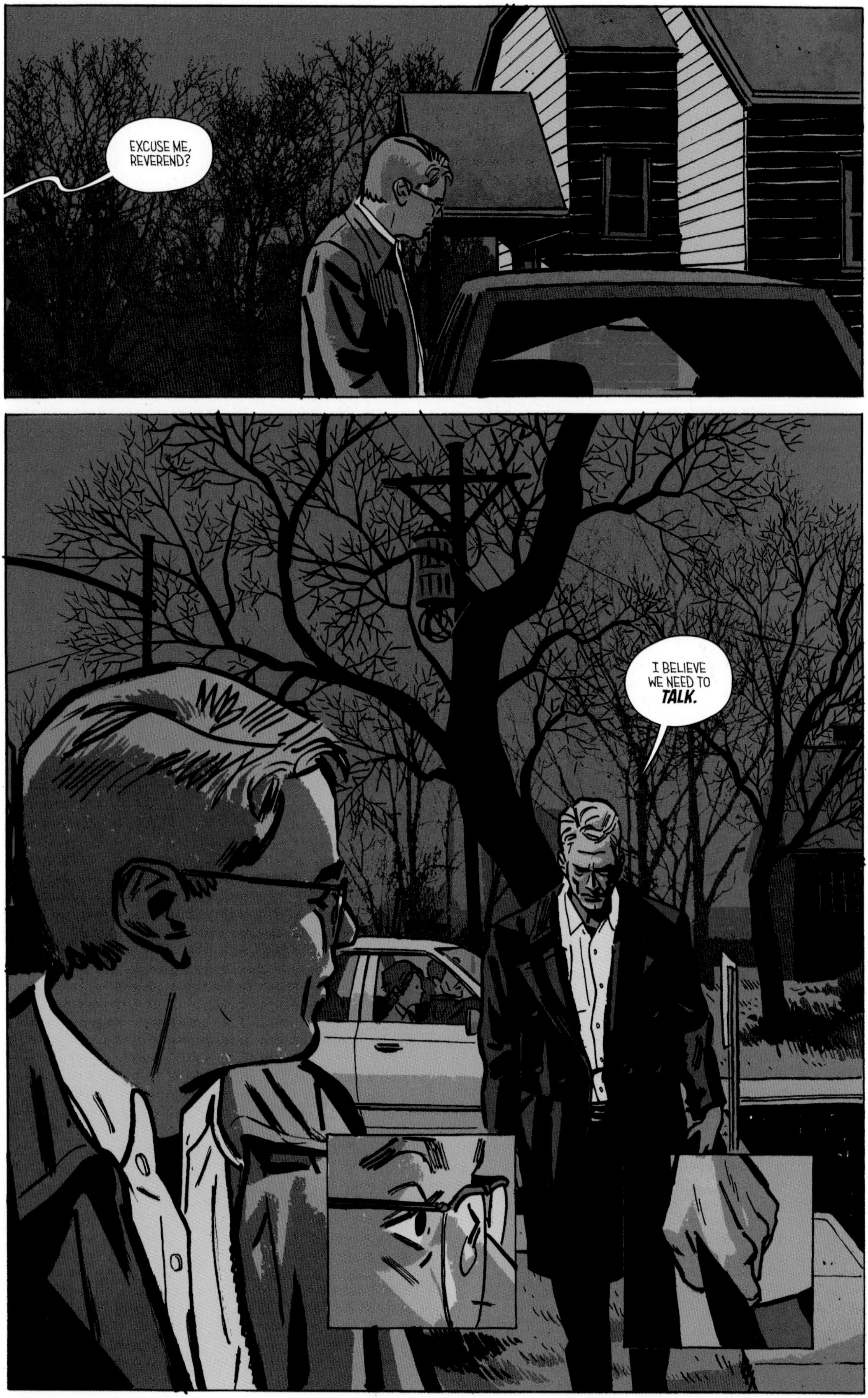
EXCUSE ME, REVEREND?
I BELIEVE WE NEED TO TALK.

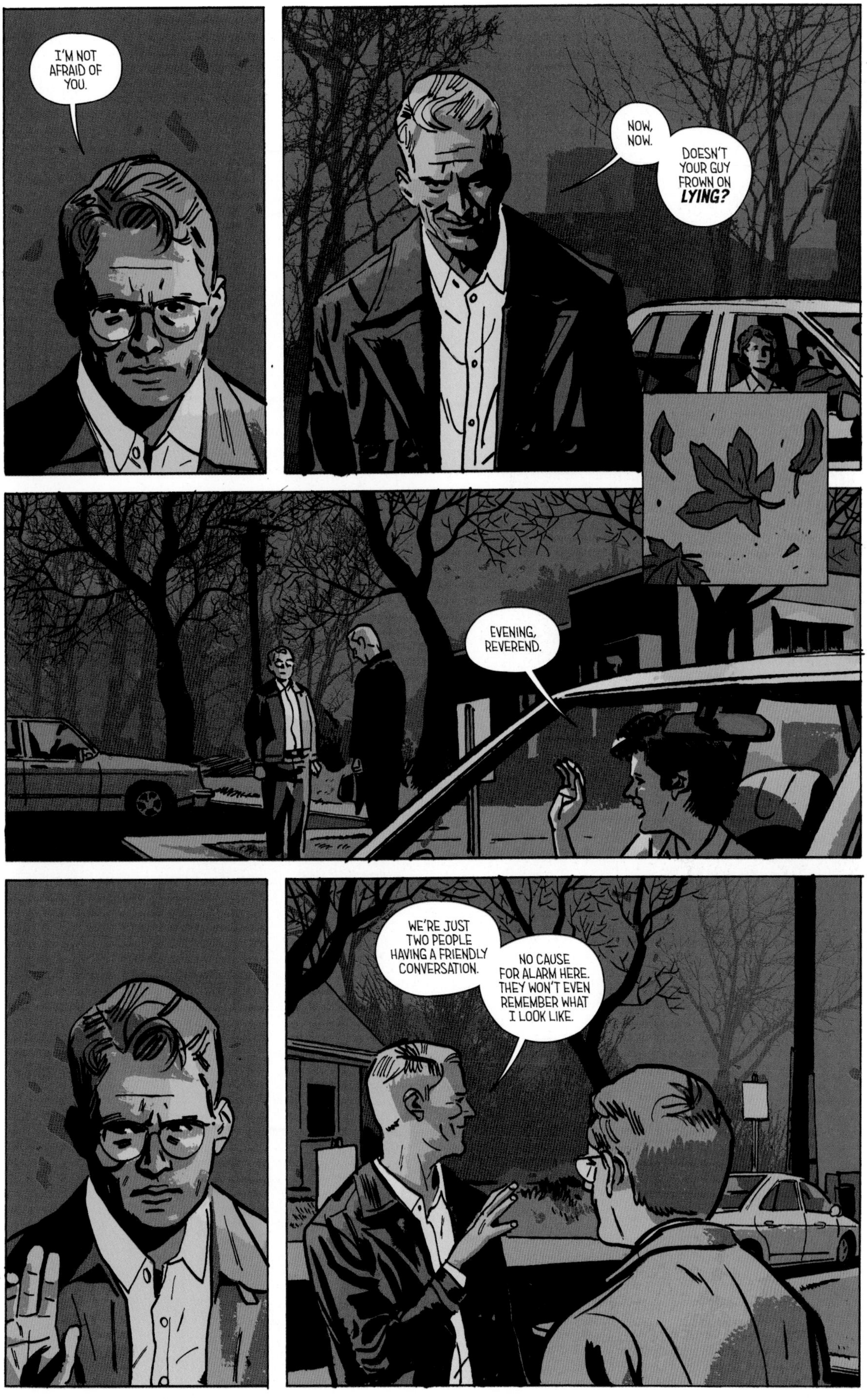
I'M NOT AFRAID OF YOU.
NOW, NOW.
DOESN'T YOUR GUY FROWN ON LYING?
EVENING, REVEREND.
WE'RE JUST TWO PEOPLE HAVING A FRIENDLY CONVERSATION.
NO CAUSE FOR ALARM HERE. THEY WON'T EVEN REMEMBER WHAT I LOOK LIKE.

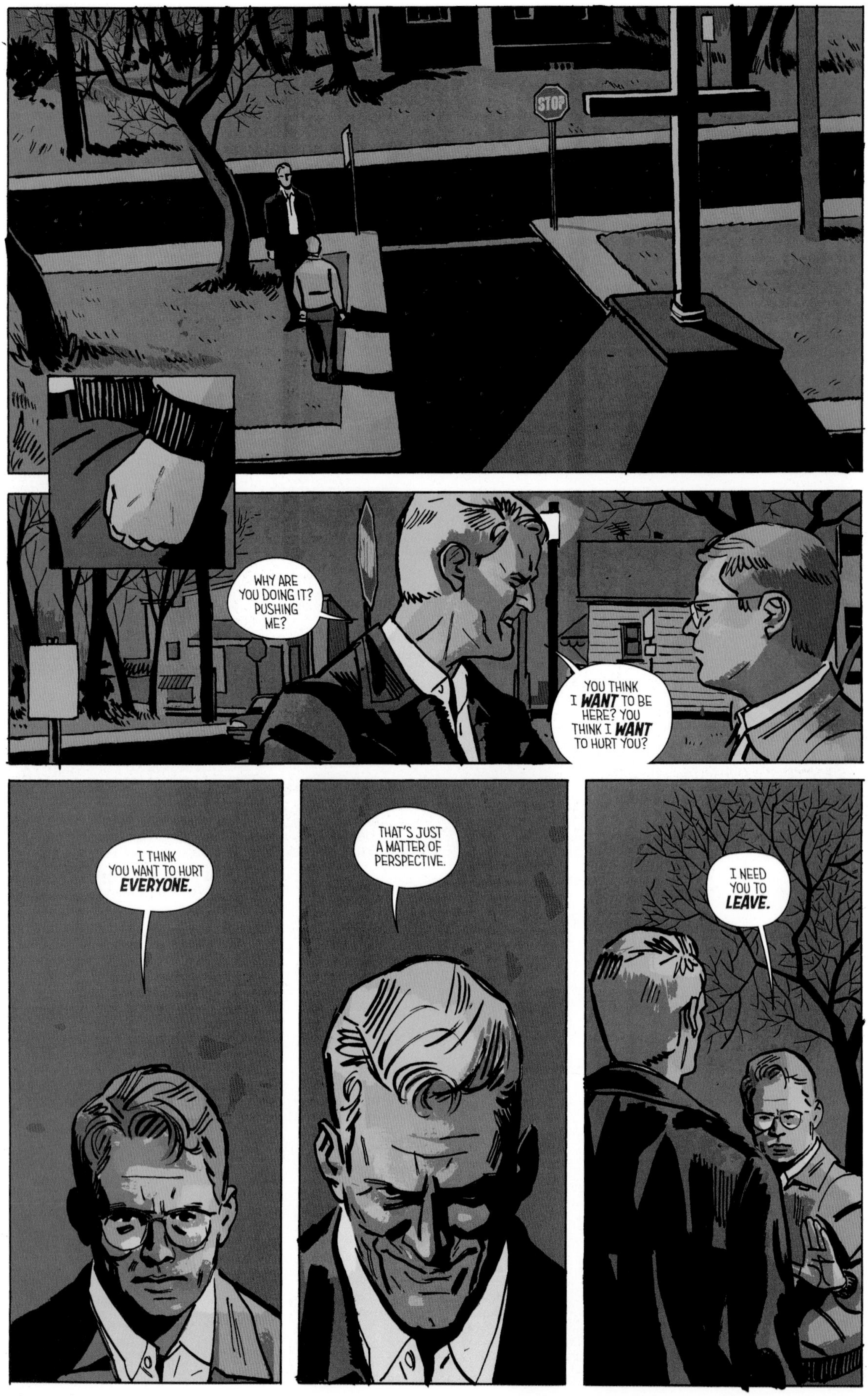
STOP
WHY ARE YOU DOING IT? PUSHING ME?
YOU THINK I **WANT** TO BE HERE? YOU THINK I **WANT** TO HURT YOU?
I THINK YOU WANT TO HURT **EVERYONE.**
THAT'S JUST A MATTER OF PERSPECTIVE.
I NEED YOU TO **LEAVE.**

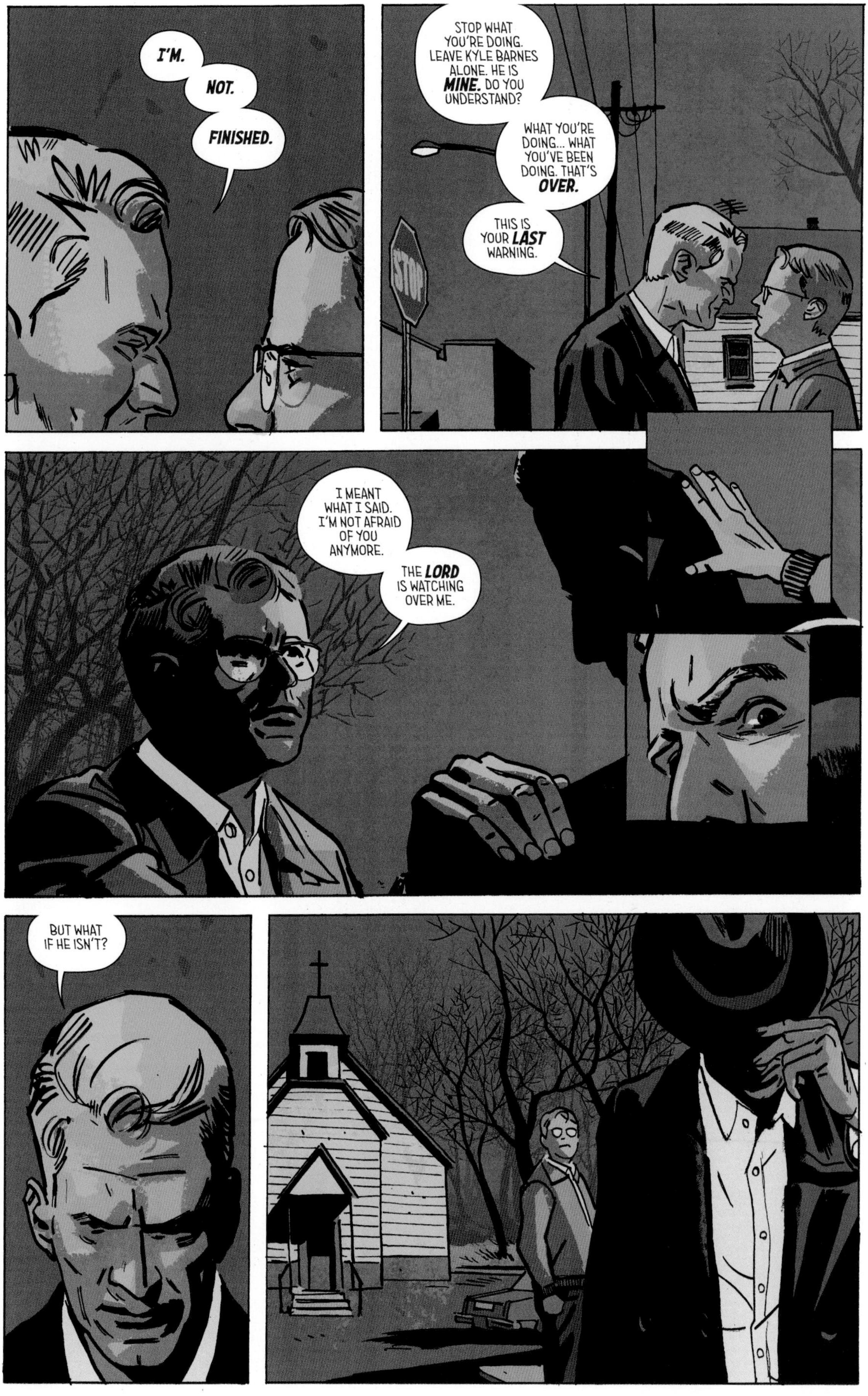
I'M.
NOT.
FINISHED.
STOP WHAT YOU'RE DOING. LEAVE KYLE BARNES ALONE. HE IS MINE. DO YOU UNDERSTAND?
WHAT YOU'RE DOING... WHAT YOU'VE BEEN DOING. THAT'S OVER.
THIS IS YOUR LAST WARNING.
STOP
I MEANT WHAT I SAID. I'M NOT AFRAID OF YOU ANYMORE.
THE LORD IS WATCHING OVER ME.
BUT WHAT IF HE ISN'T?

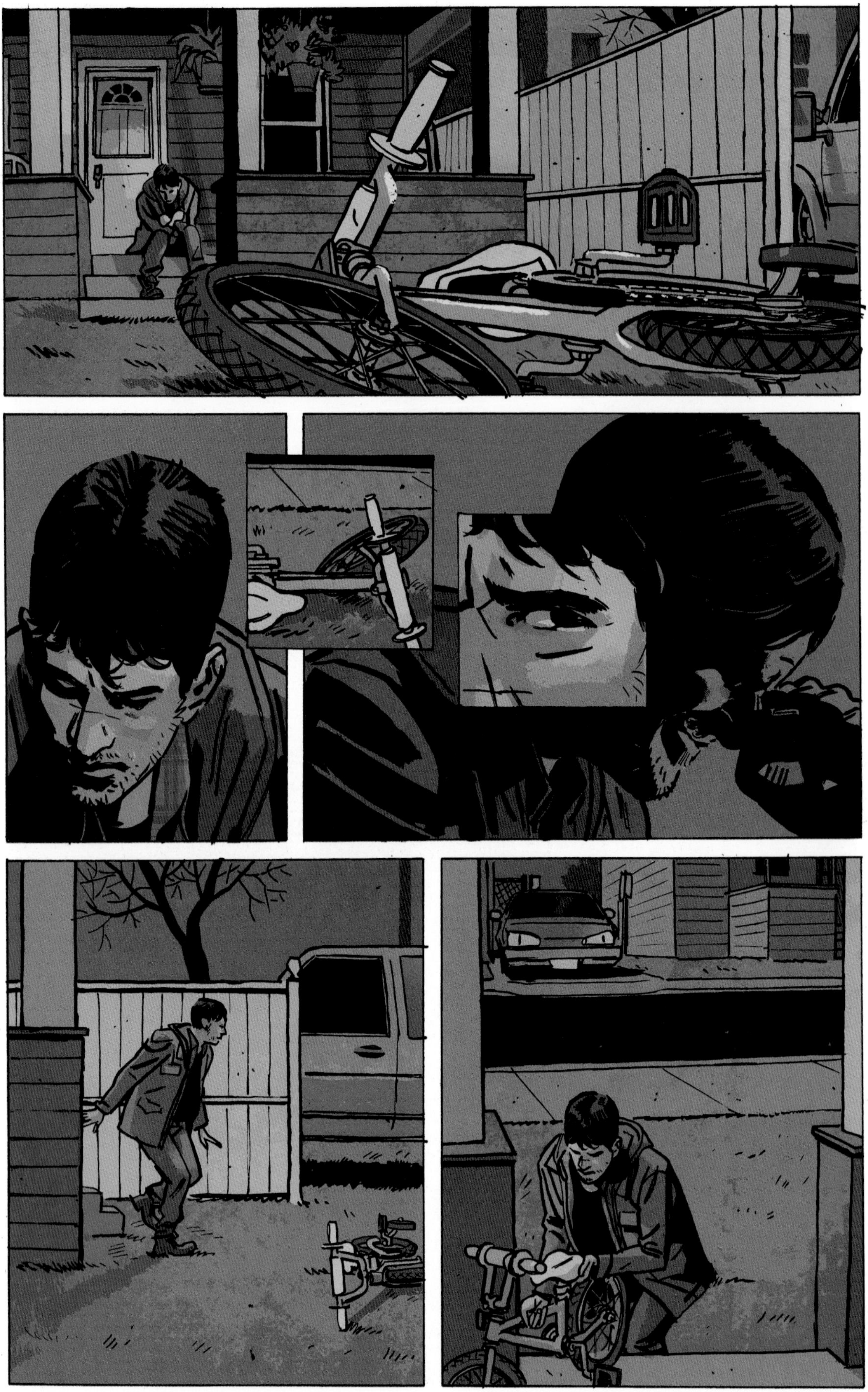

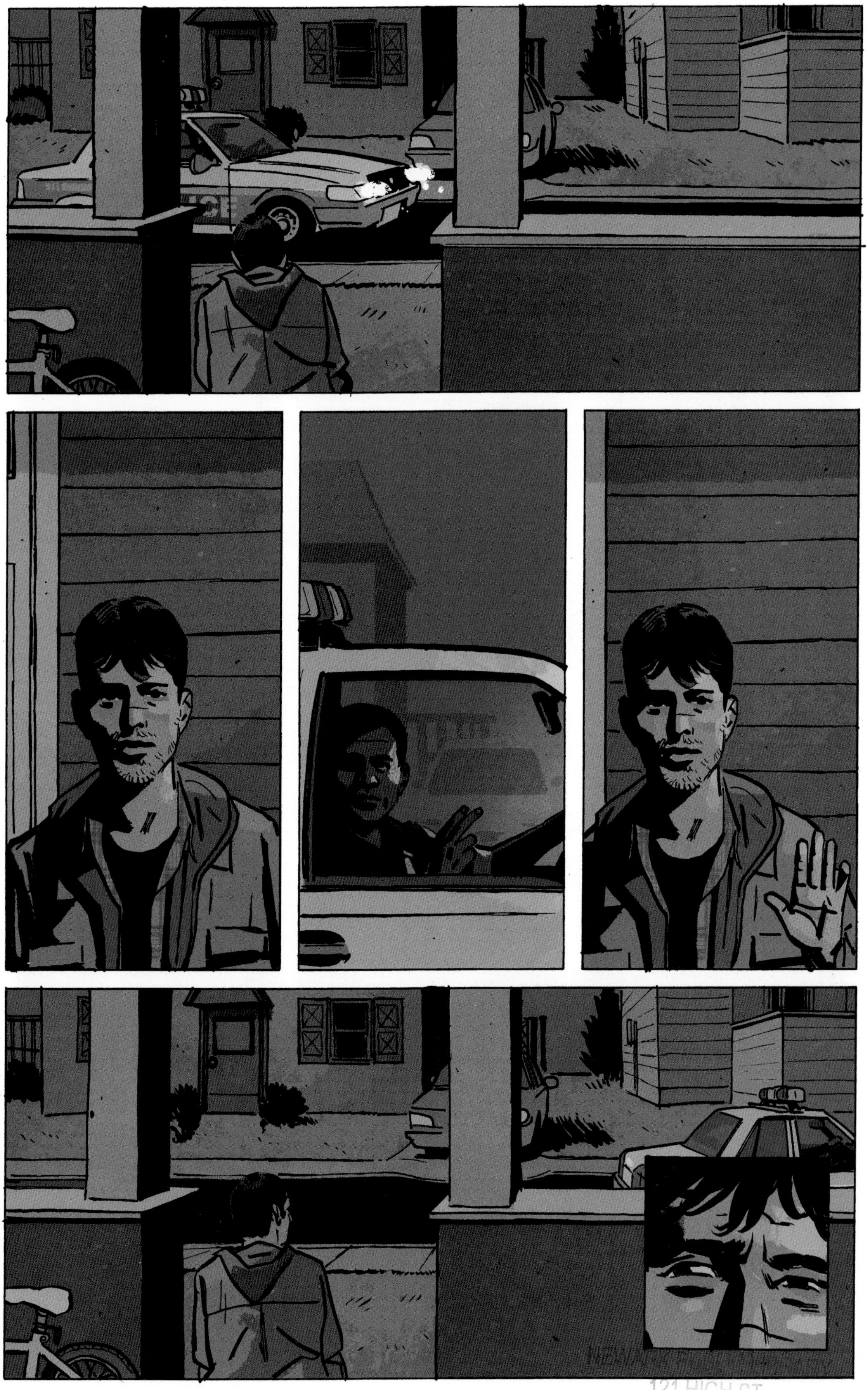

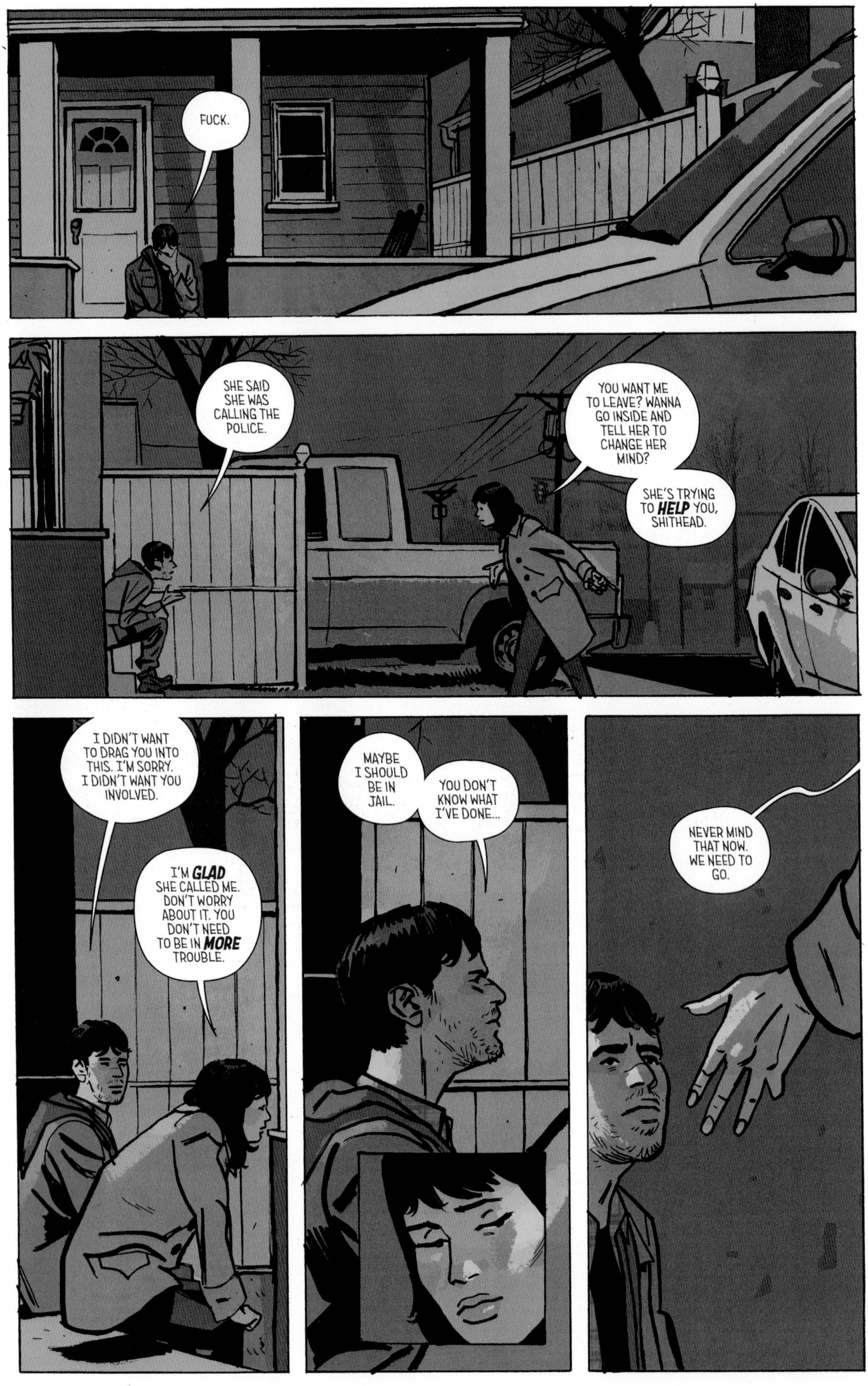
FUCK.
SHE SAID SHE WAS CALLING THE POLICE.
YOU WANT ME TO LEAVE? WANNA GO INSIDE AND TELL HER TO CHANGE HER MIND?
SHE'S TRYING TO **HELP** YOU, SHITHEAD.
I DIDN'T WANT TO DRAG YOU INTO THIS. I'M SORRY. I DIDN'T WANT YOU INVOLVED.
I'M **GLAD** SHE CALLED ME. DON'T WORRY ABOUT IT. YOU DON'T NEED TO BE IN **MORE** TROUBLE.
MAYBE I SHOULD BE IN JAIL.
YOU DON'T KNOW WHAT I'VE DONE...
NEVER MIND THAT NOW. WE NEED TO GO.

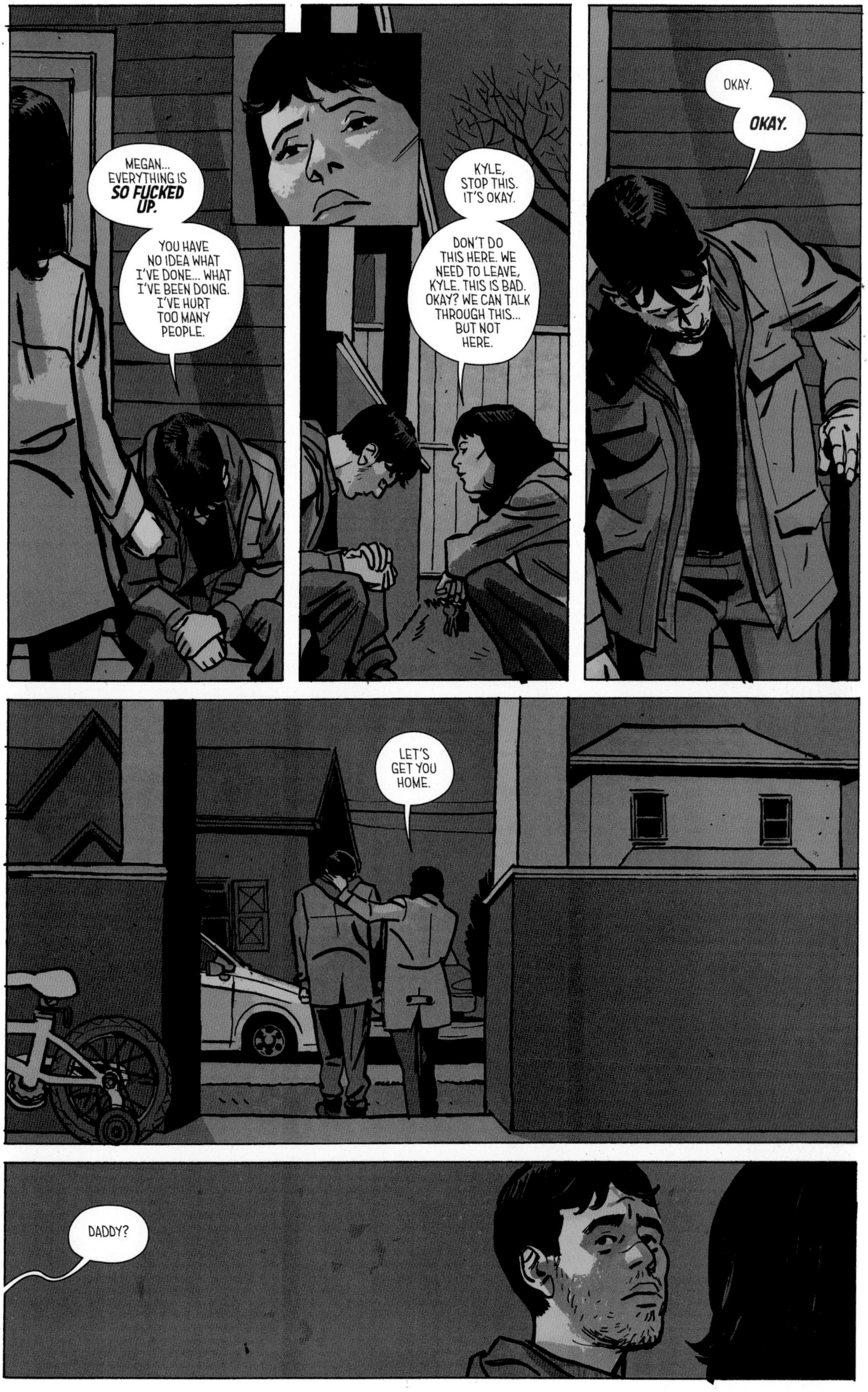
MEGAN... EVERYTHING IS **SO FUCKED UP.**
YOU HAVE NO IDEA WHAT I'VE DONE... WHAT I'VE BEEN DOING. I'VE HURT TOO MANY PEOPLE.
KYLE, STOP THIS. IT'S OKAY.
DON'T DO THIS HERE. WE NEED TO LEAVE, KYLE. THIS IS BAD. OKAY? WE CAN TALK THROUGH THIS... BUT NOT HERE.
OKAY.
OKAY.
LET'S GET YOU HOME.
DADDY?

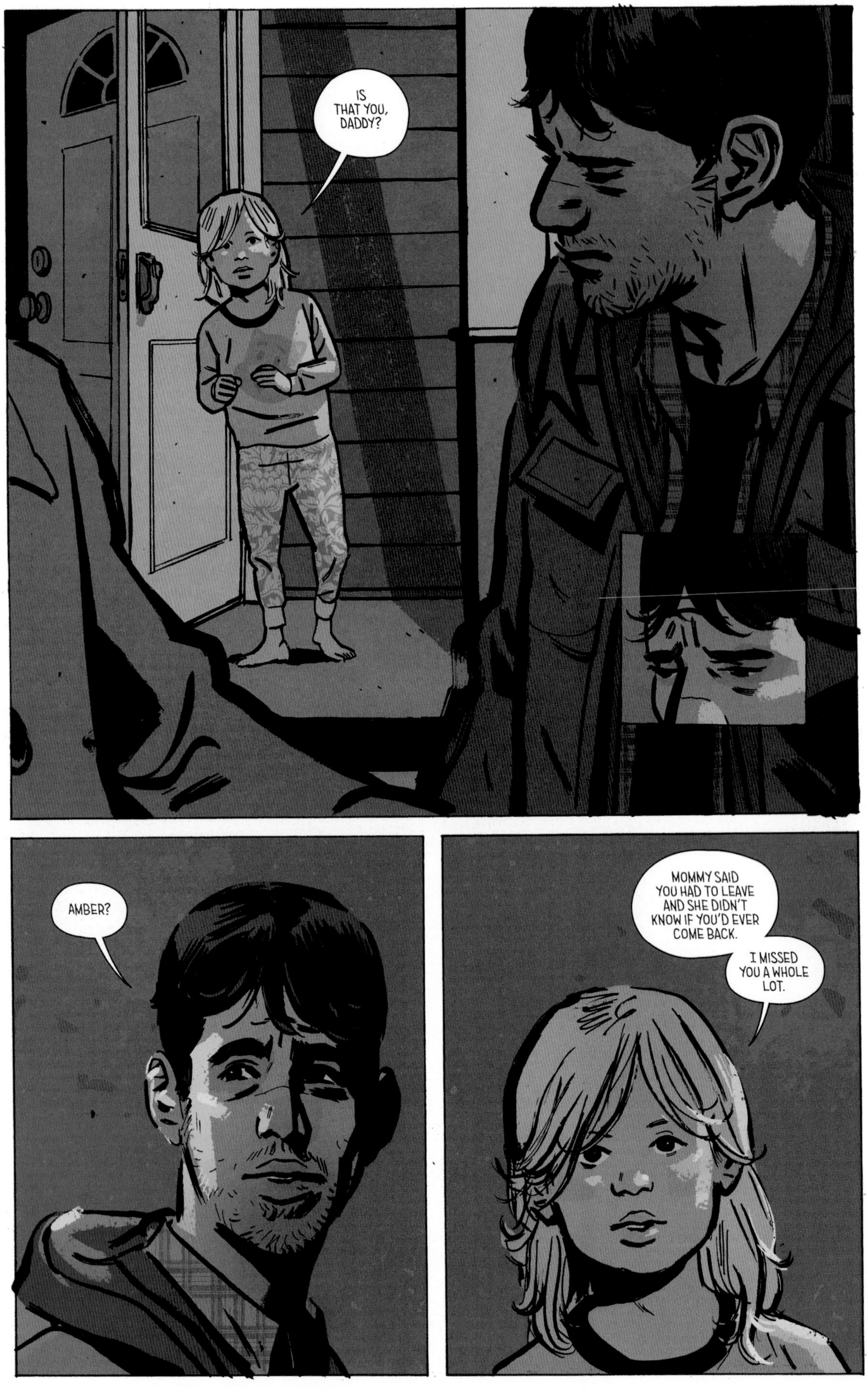
IS THAT YOU, DADDY?
AMBER?
MOMMY SAID YOU HAD TO LEAVE AND SHE DIDN'T KNOW IF YOU'D EVER COME BACK.
I MISSED YOU A WHOLE LOT.

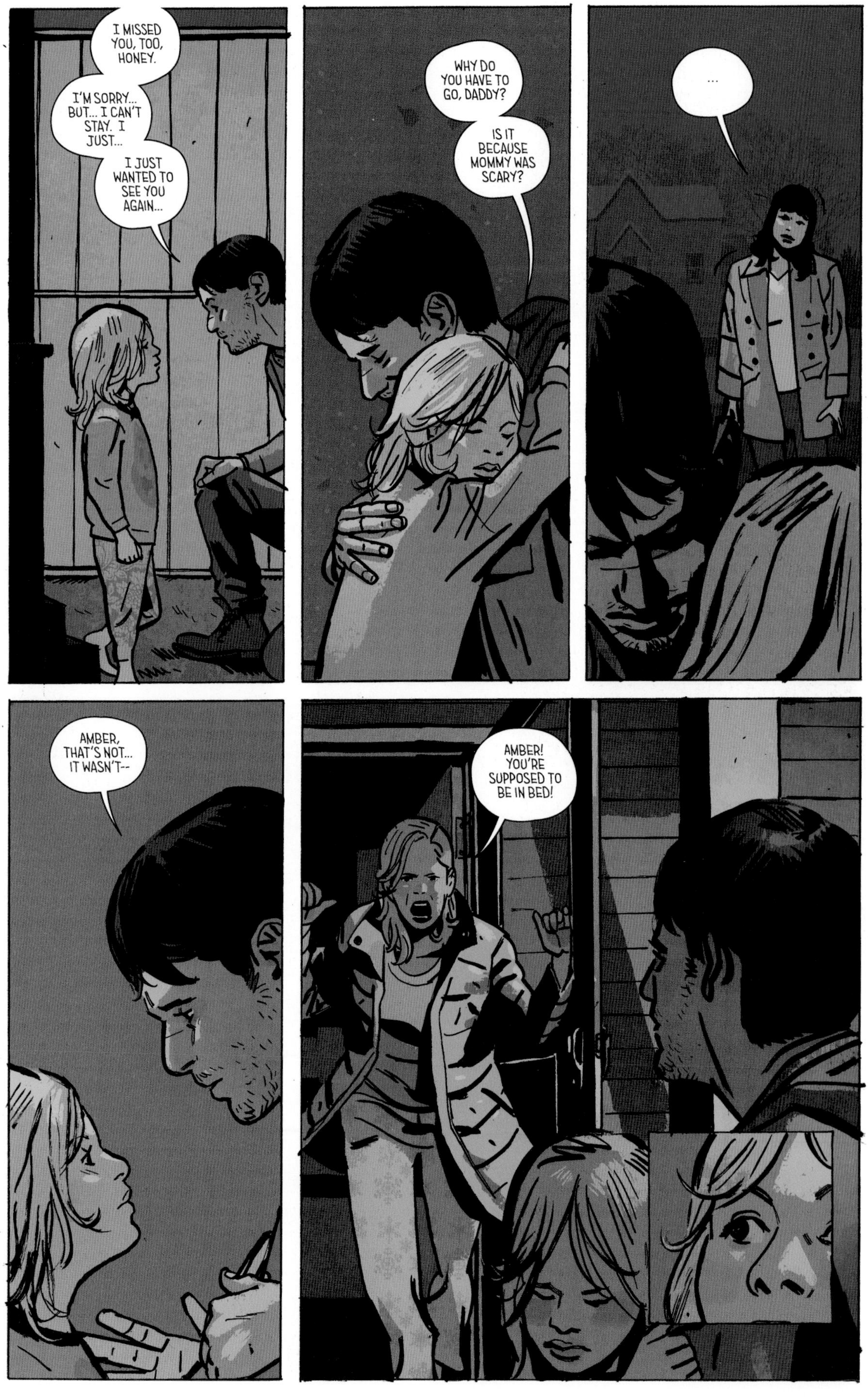
I MISSED YOU, TOO, HONEY.
I'M SORRY... BUT... I CAN'T STAY. I JUST...
I JUST WANTED TO SEE YOU AGAIN...
WHY DO YOU HAVE TO GO, DADDY?
IS IT BECAUSE MOMMY WAS SCARY?
...
AMBER, THAT'S NOT... IT WASN'T--
AMBER! YOU'RE SUPPOSED TO BE IN BED!

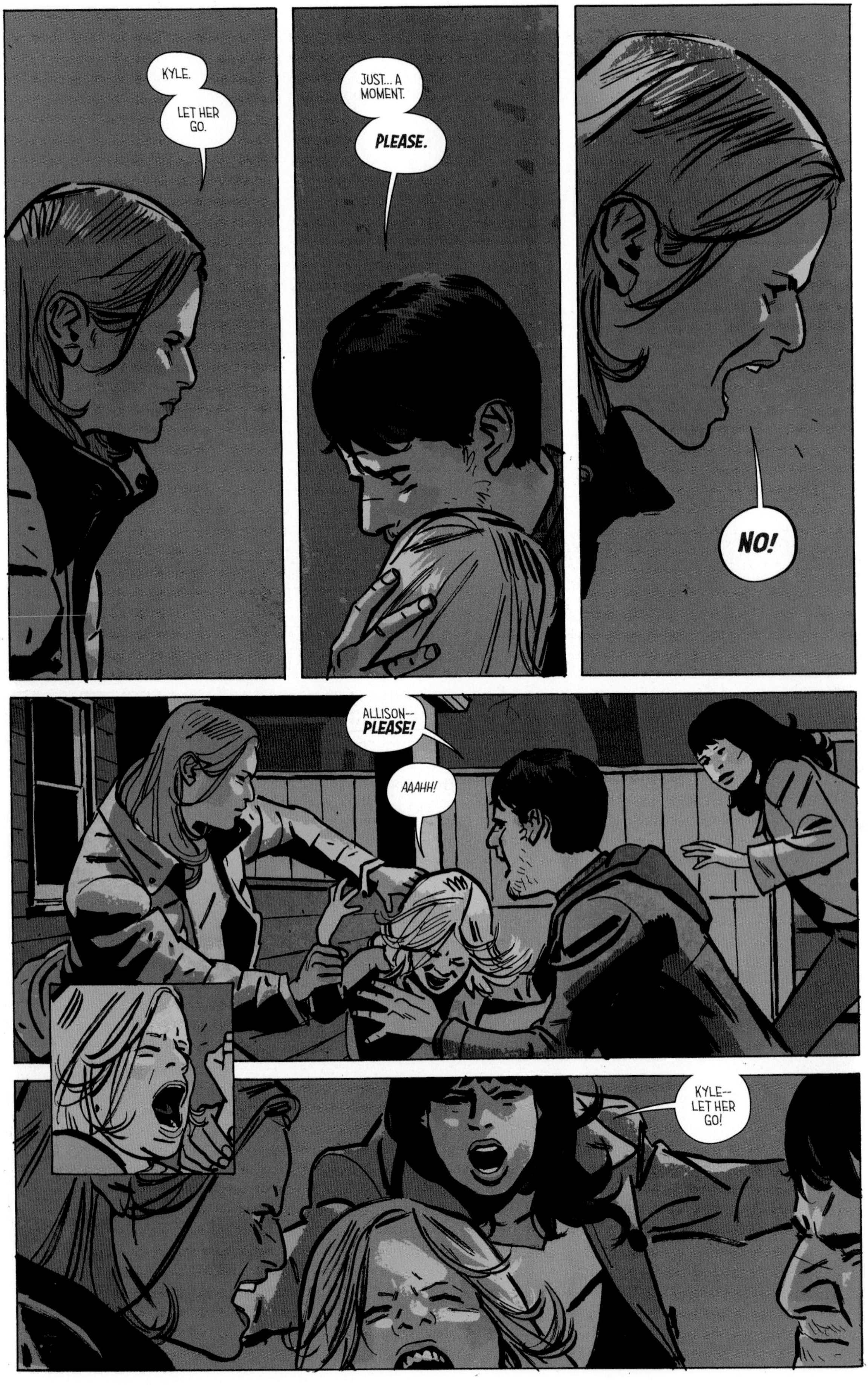
KYLE.
LET HER GO.
JUST... A MOMENT.
PLEASE.
NO!
ALLISON-- PLEASE!
AAAHH!
KYLE-- LET HER GO!

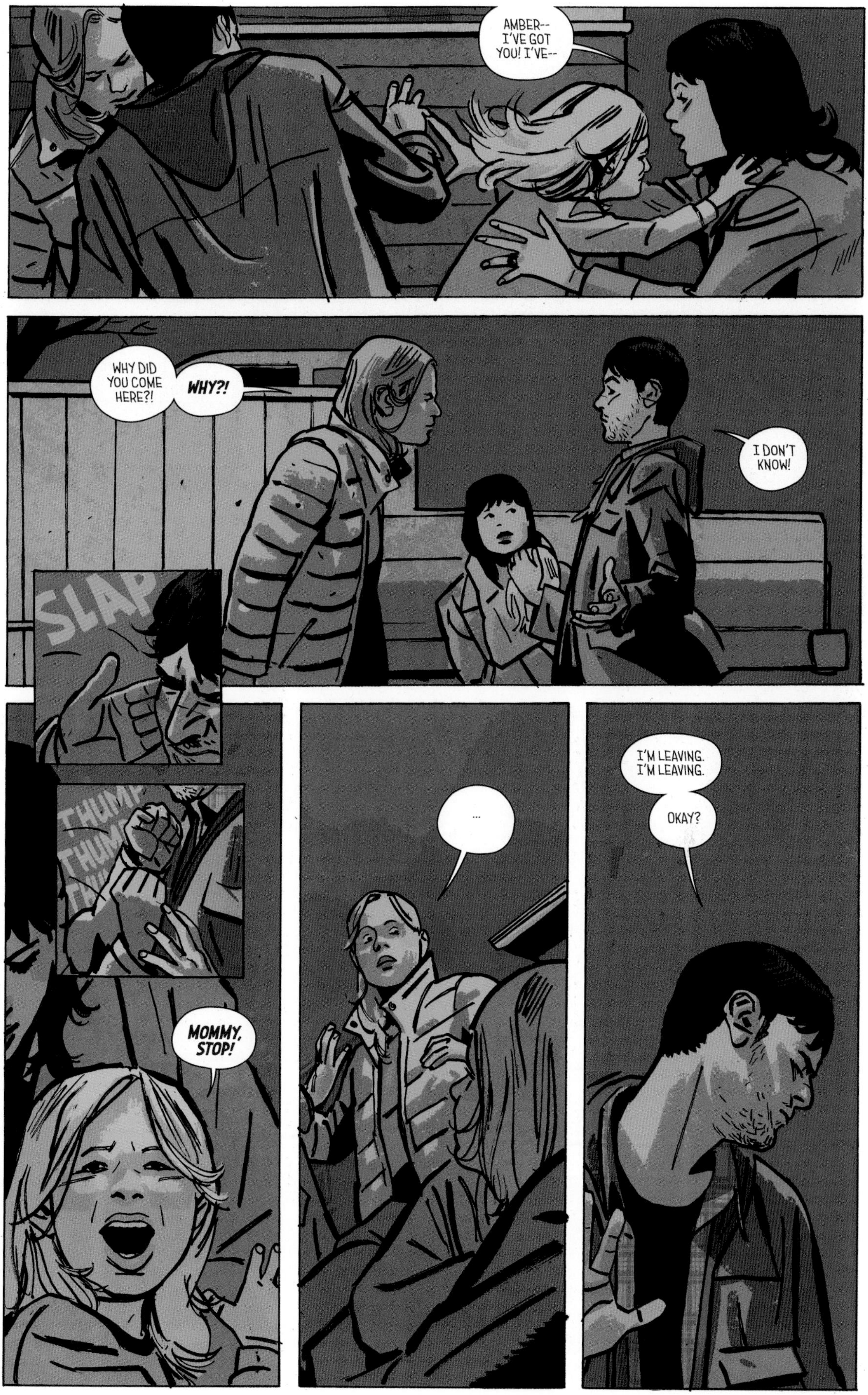
AMBER-- I'VE GOT YOU! I'VE--
WHY DID YOU COME HERE?!
WHY?!
I DON'T KNOW!
SLAP
THUMP
THUMP
MOMMY, STOP!
...
I'M LEAVING. I'M LEAVING.
OKAY?

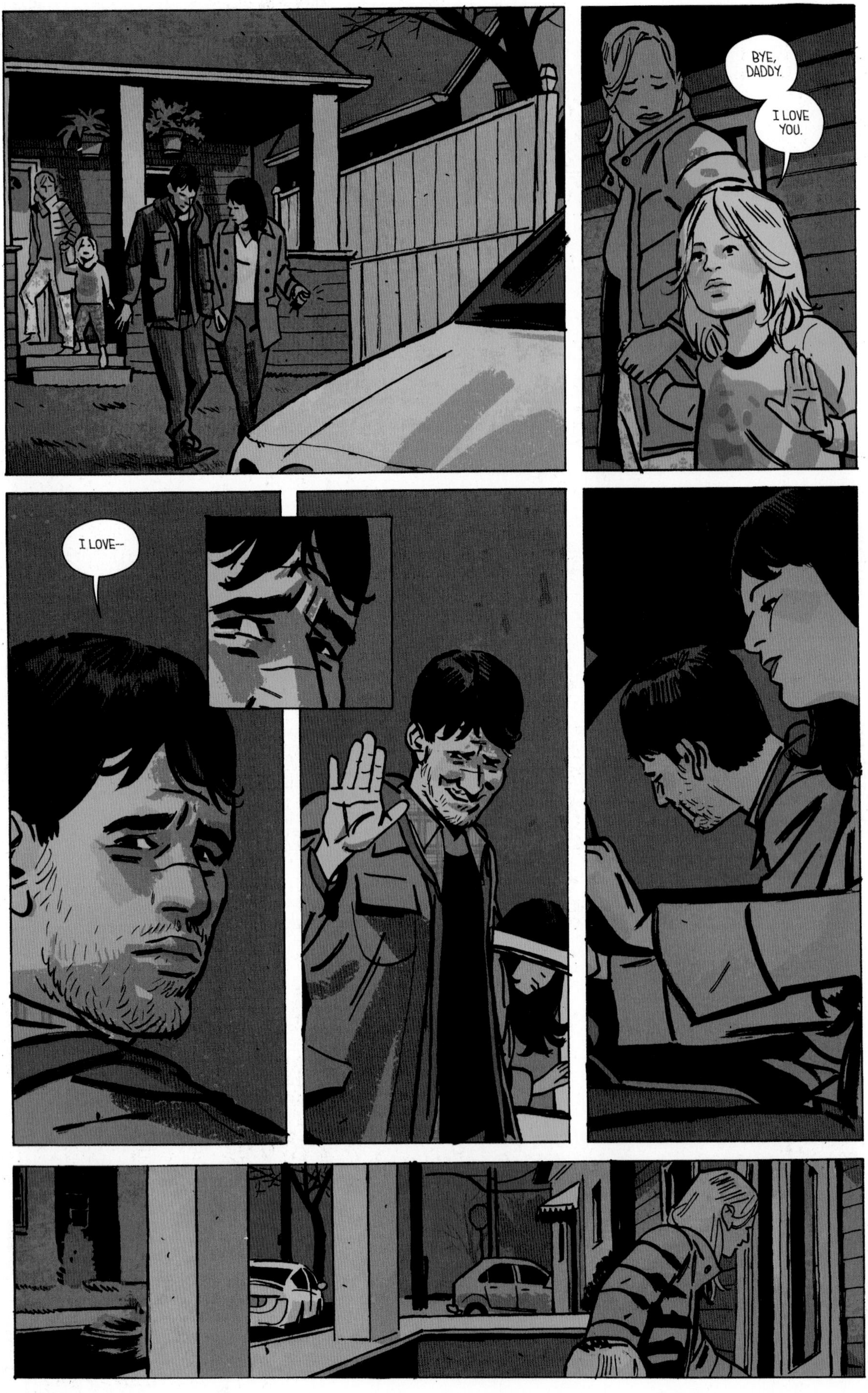
BYE, DADDY.
I LOVE YOU.
I LOVE--

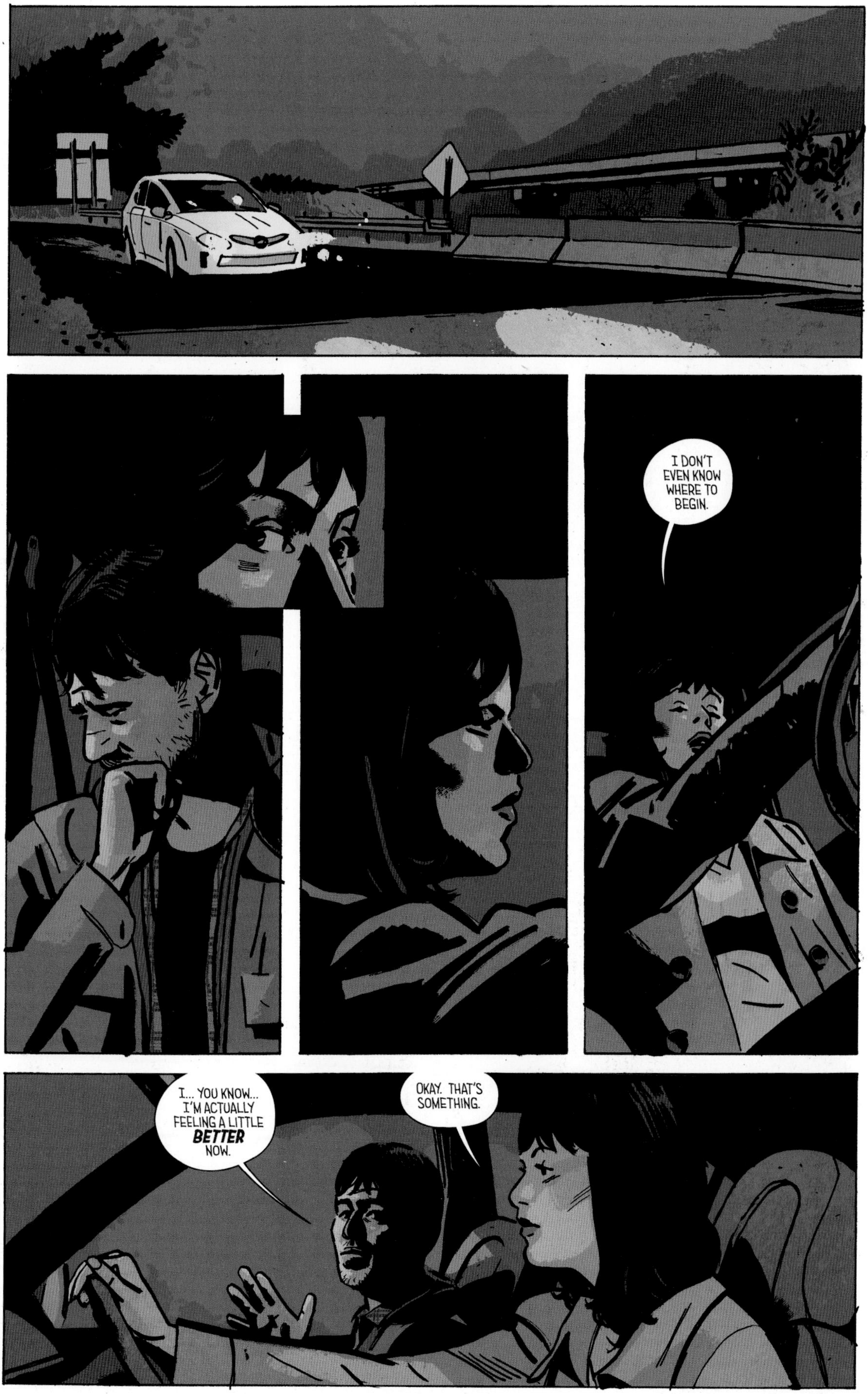
I DON'T EVEN KNOW WHERE TO BEGIN.
I... YOU KNOW... I'M ACTUALLY FEELING A LITTLE **BETTER** NOW.
OKAY. THAT'S SOMETHING.

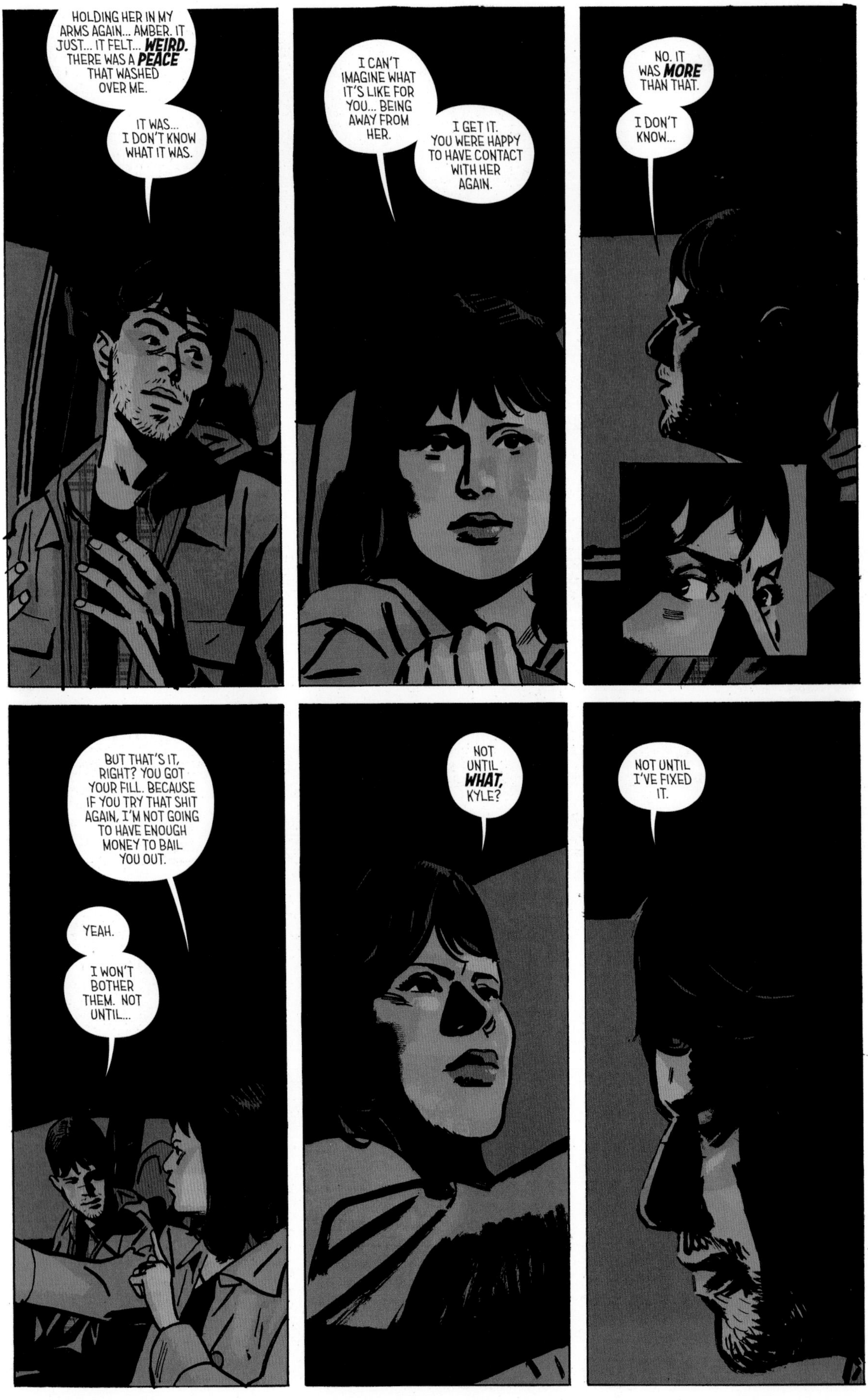
HOLDING HER IN MY ARMS AGAIN... AMBER. IT JUST... IT FELT... WEIRD. THERE WAS A PEACE THAT WASHED OVER ME.
IT WAS... I DON'T KNOW WHAT IT WAS.
I CAN'T IMAGINE WHAT IT'S LIKE FOR YOU... BEING AWAY FROM HER.
I GET IT. YOU WERE HAPPY TO HAVE CONTACT WITH HER AGAIN.
NO. IT WAS MORE THAN THAT.
I DON'T KNOW...
BUT THAT'S IT, RIGHT? YOU GOT YOUR FILL. BECAUSE IF YOU TRY THAT SHIT AGAIN, I'M NOT GOING TO HAVE ENOUGH MONEY TO BAIL YOU OUT.
YEAH.
I WON'T BOTHER THEM. NOT UNTIL...
NOT UNTIL WHAT, KYLE?
NOT UNTIL I'VE FIXED IT.

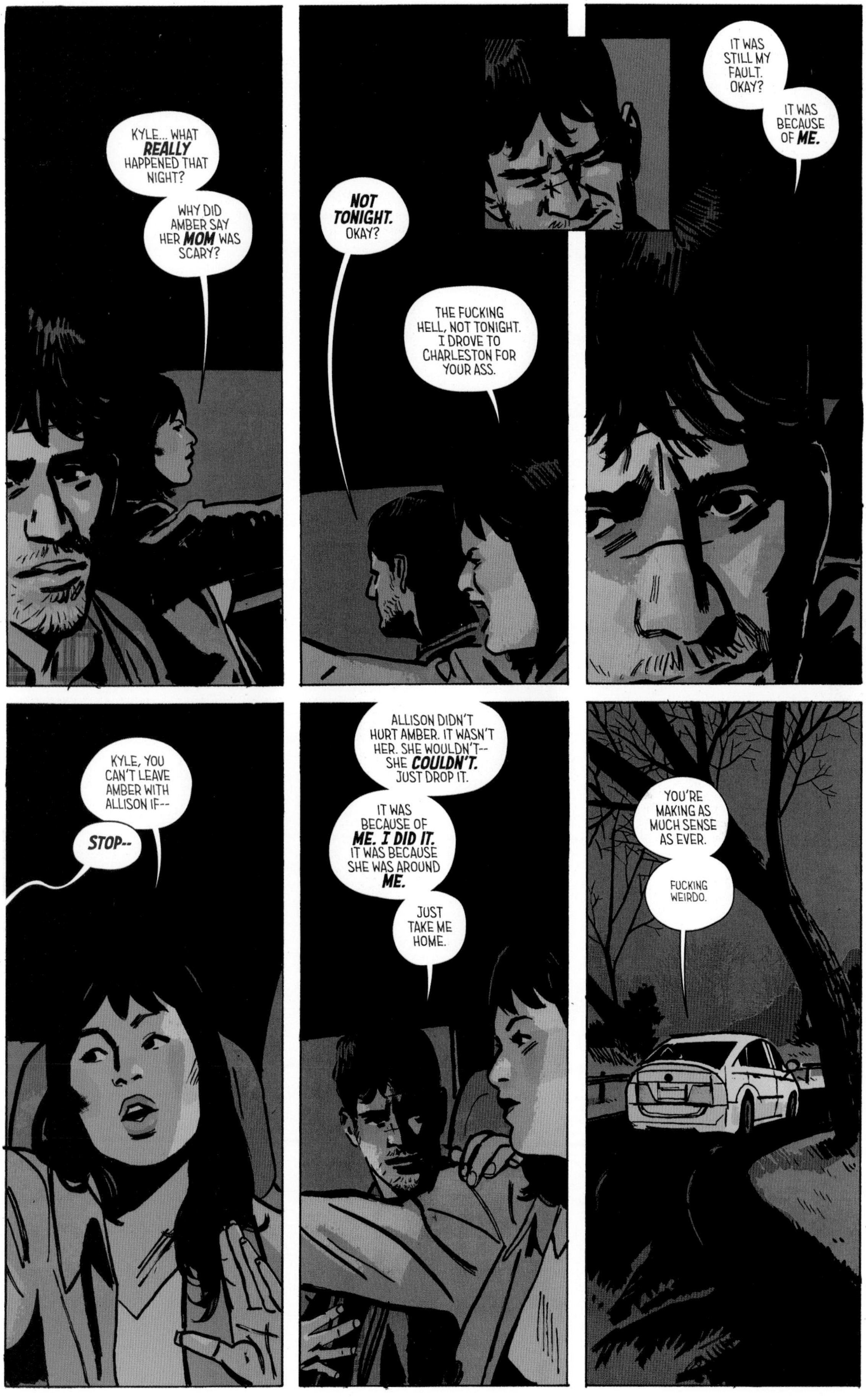
KYLE... WHAT REALLY HAPPENED THAT NIGHT?
WHY DID AMBER SAY HER MOM WAS SCARY?
NOT TONIGHT. OKAY?
THE FUCKING HELL, NOT TONIGHT. I DROVE TO CHARLESTON FOR YOUR ASS.
IT WAS STILL MY FAULT. OKAY?
IT WAS BECAUSE OF ME.
KYLE, YOU CAN'T LEAVE AMBER WITH ALLISON IF--
STOP--
ALLISON DIDN'T HURT AMBER. IT WASN'T HER. SHE WOULDN'T-- SHE COULDN'T. JUST DROP IT.
IT WAS BECAUSE OF ME. I DID IT. IT WAS BECAUSE SHE WAS AROUND ME.
JUST TAKE ME HOME.
YOU'RE MAKING AS MUCH SENSE AS EVER.
FUCKING WEIRDO.

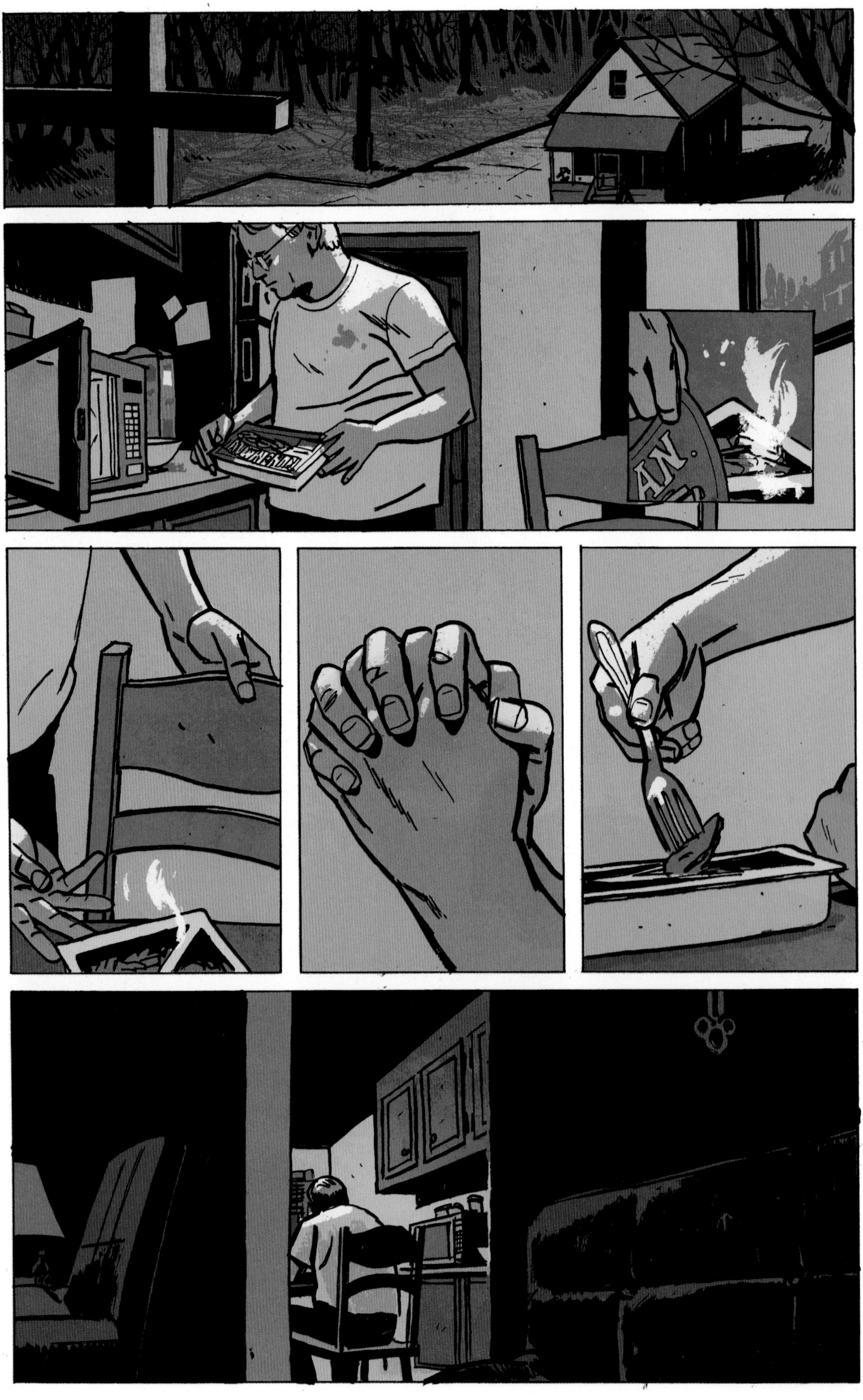

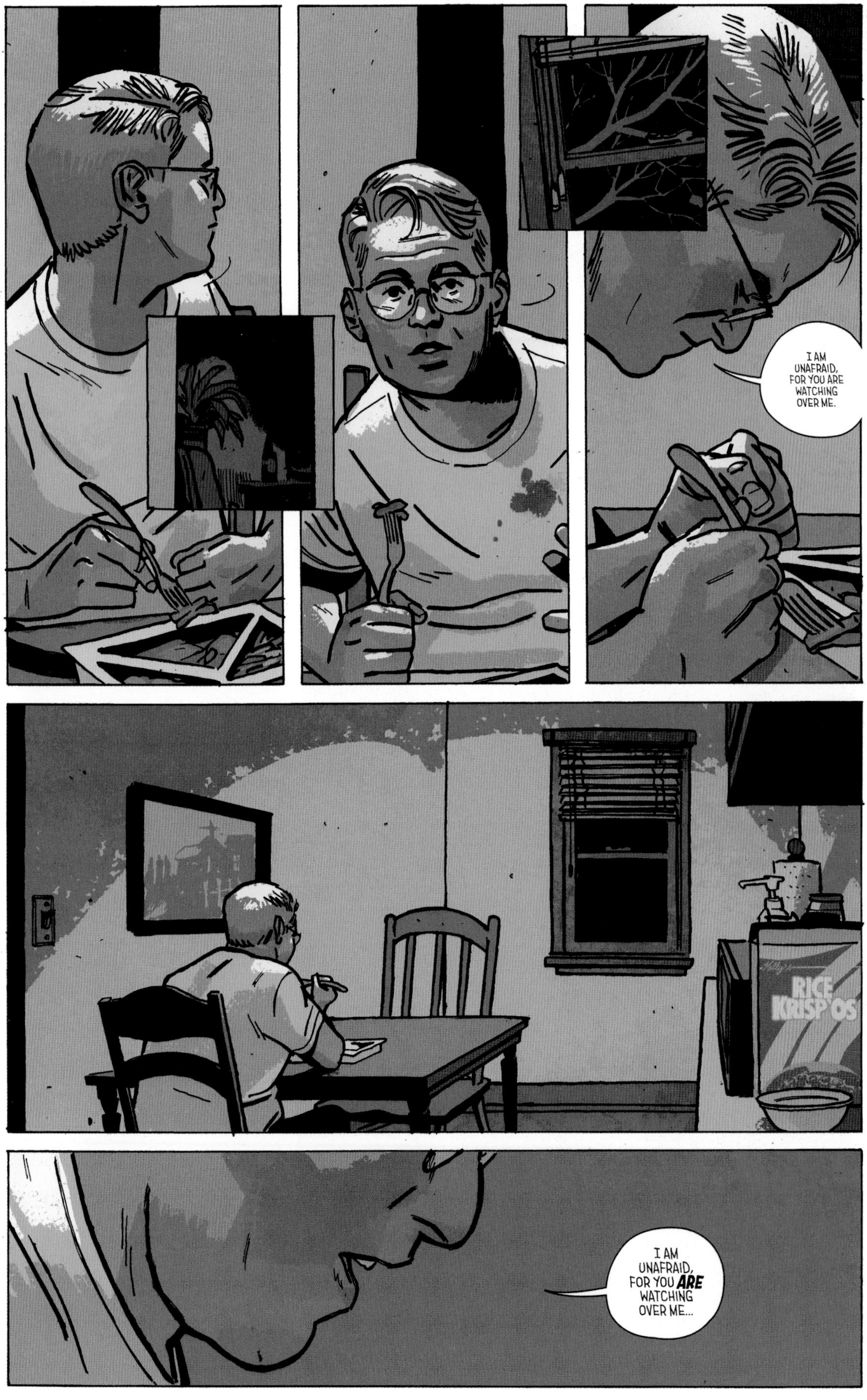
I AM UNAFRAID, FOR YOU ARE WATCHING OVER ME.
RICE KRISP OS
I AM UNAFRAID, FOR YOU **ARE** WATCHING OVER ME...

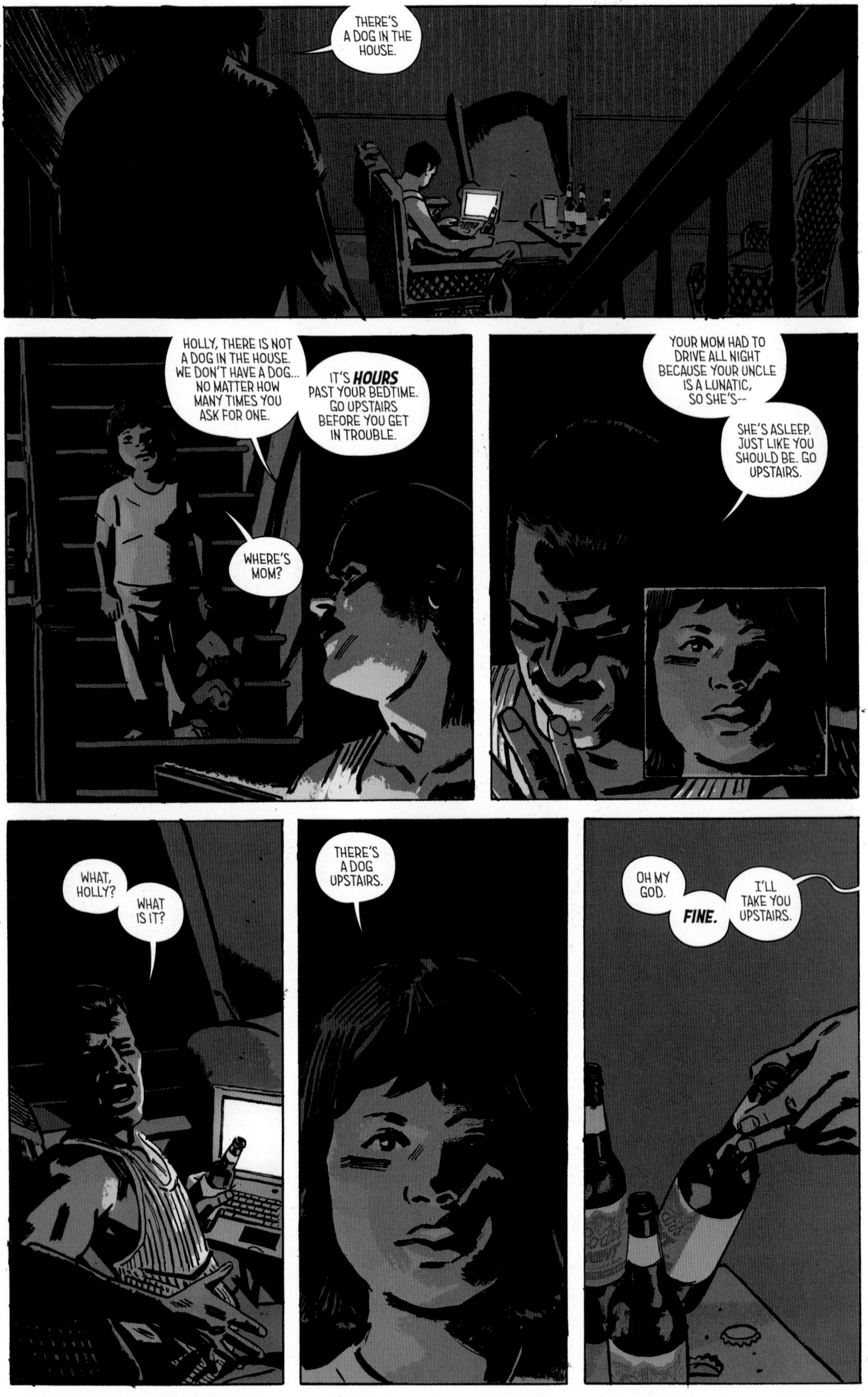
THERE'S A DOG IN THE HOUSE.
HOLLY, THERE IS NOT A DOG IN THE HOUSE. WE DON'T HAVE A DOG... NO MATTER HOW MANY TIMES YOU ASK FOR ONE.
IT'S **HOURS** PAST YOUR BEDTIME. GO UPSTAIRS BEFORE YOU GET IN TROUBLE.
WHERE'S MOM?
YOUR MOM HAD TO DRIVE ALL NIGHT BECAUSE YOUR UNCLE IS A LUNATIC, SO SHE'S--
SHE'S ASLEEP. JUST LIKE YOU SHOULD BE. GO UPSTAIRS.
WHAT, HOLLY?
WHAT IS IT?
THERE'S A DOG UPSTAIRS.
OH MY GOD.
FINE.
I'LL TAKE YOU UPSTAIRS.

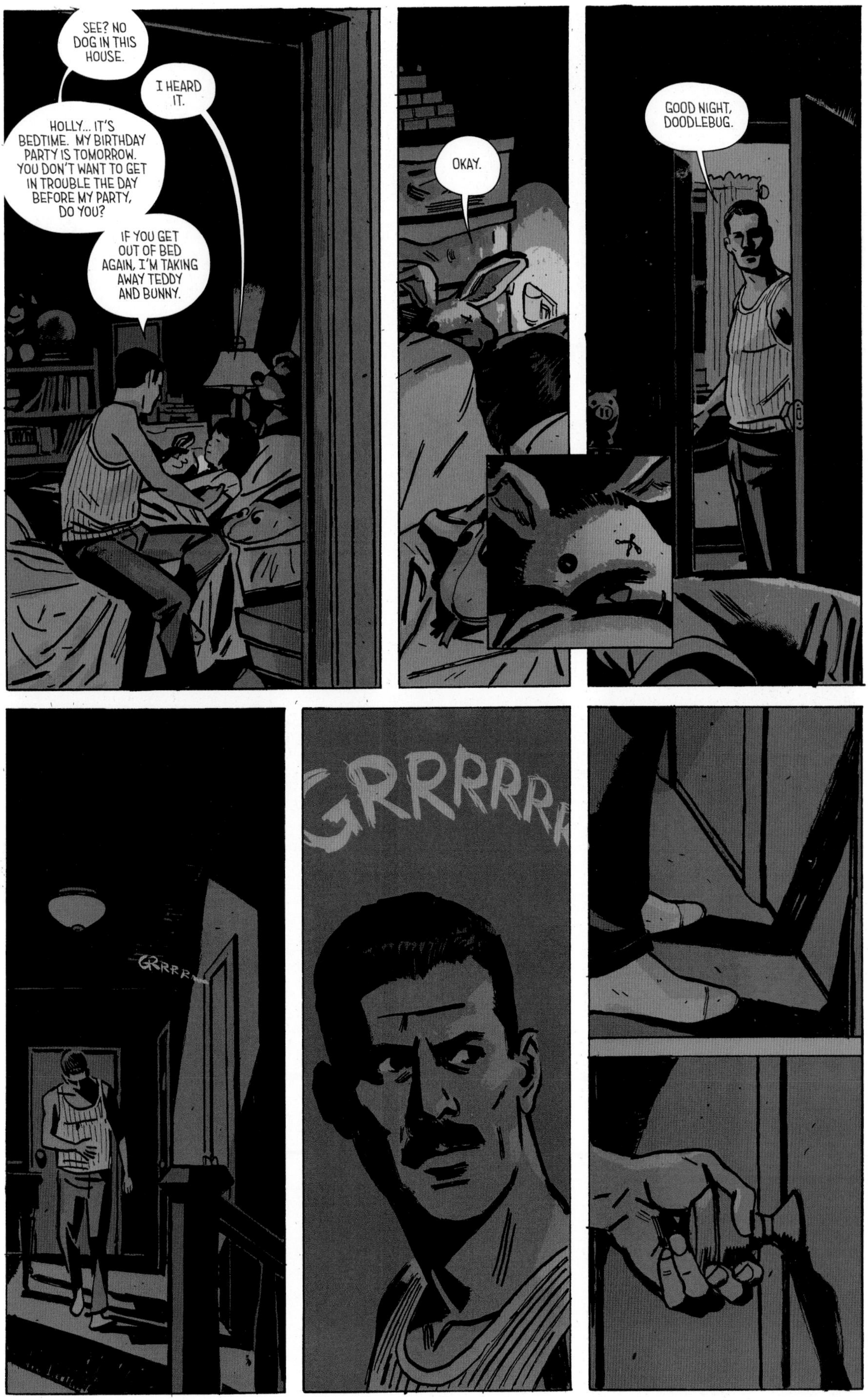
SEE? NO DOG IN THIS HOUSE.
I HEARD IT.
HOLLY... IT'S BEDTIME. MY BIRTHDAY PARTY IS TOMORROW. YOU DON'T WANT TO GET IN TROUBLE THE DAY BEFORE MY PARTY, DO YOU?
IF YOU GET OUT OF BED AGAIN, I'M TAKING AWAY TEDDY AND BUNNY.
OKAY.
GOOD NIGHT, DOODLEBUG.
GRRRRR
GRRRRRR

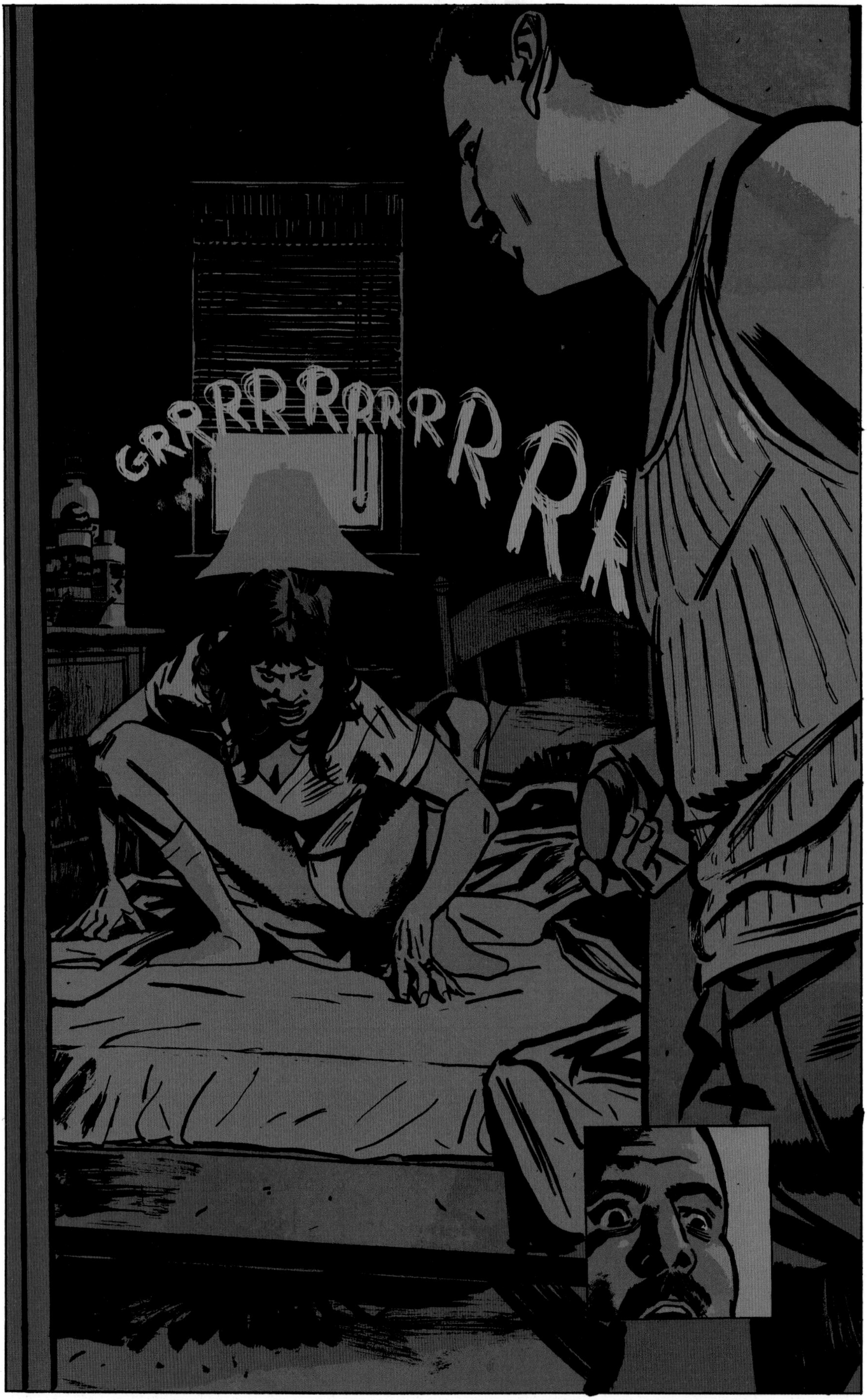
GRRRRRRRRRRRRR

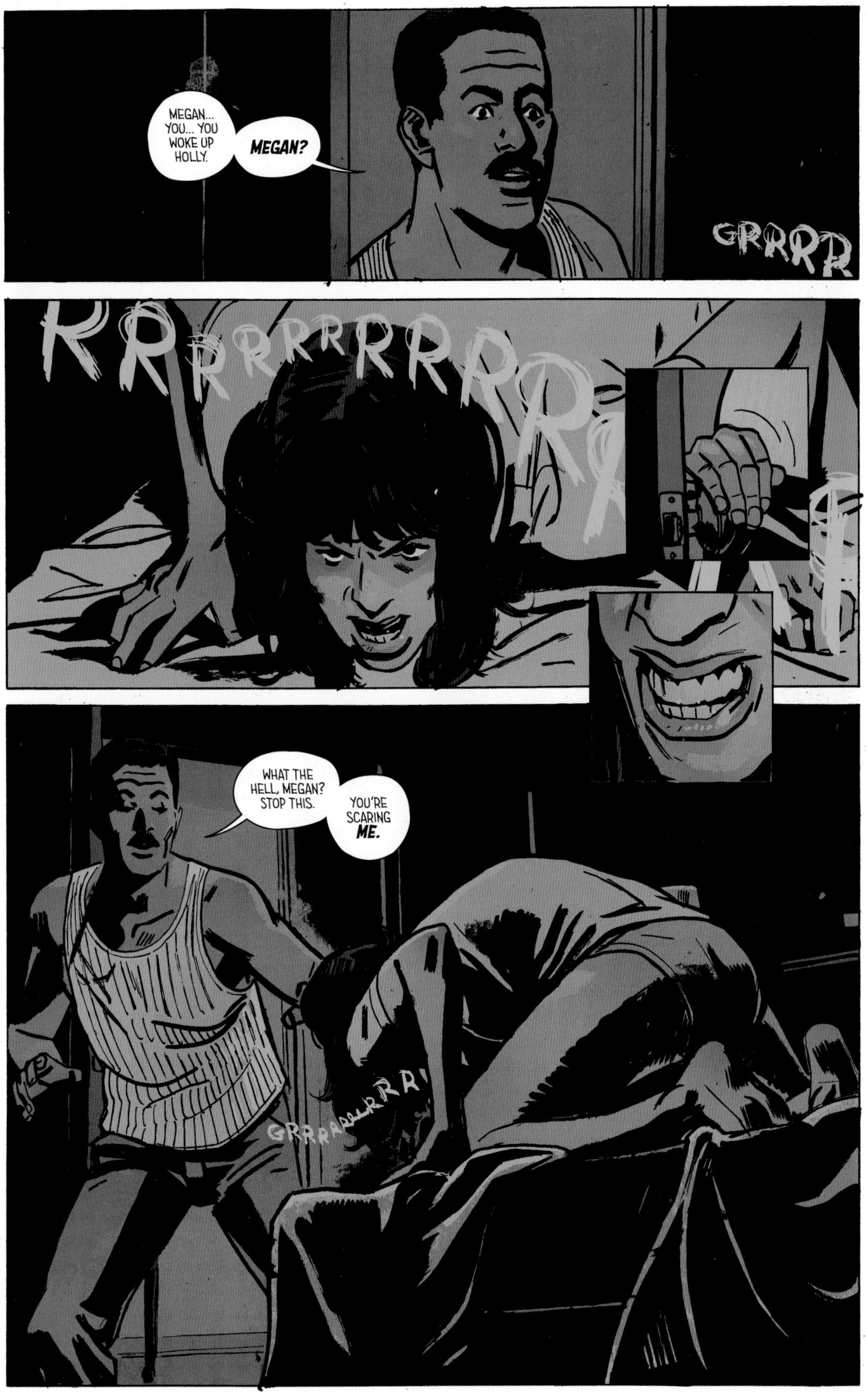
MEGAN... YOU... YOU WOKE UP HOLLY.
MEGAN?
GRRRR
RRRRRRRRRRRR
WHAT THE HELL, MEGAN? STOP THIS.
YOU'RE SCARING ME.
GRRRRRRRR

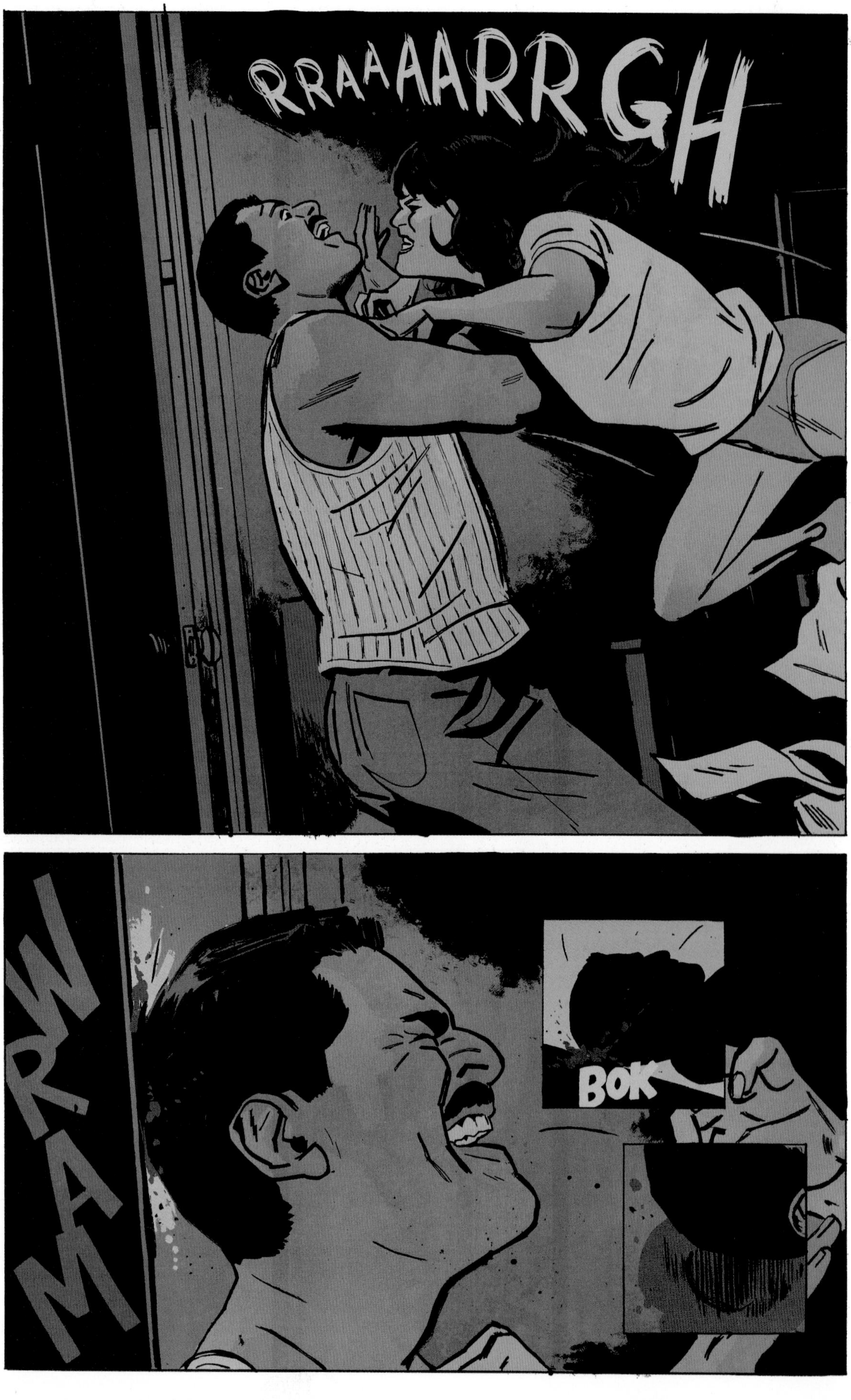
RRAAAARRRGH
WRAM
BOK

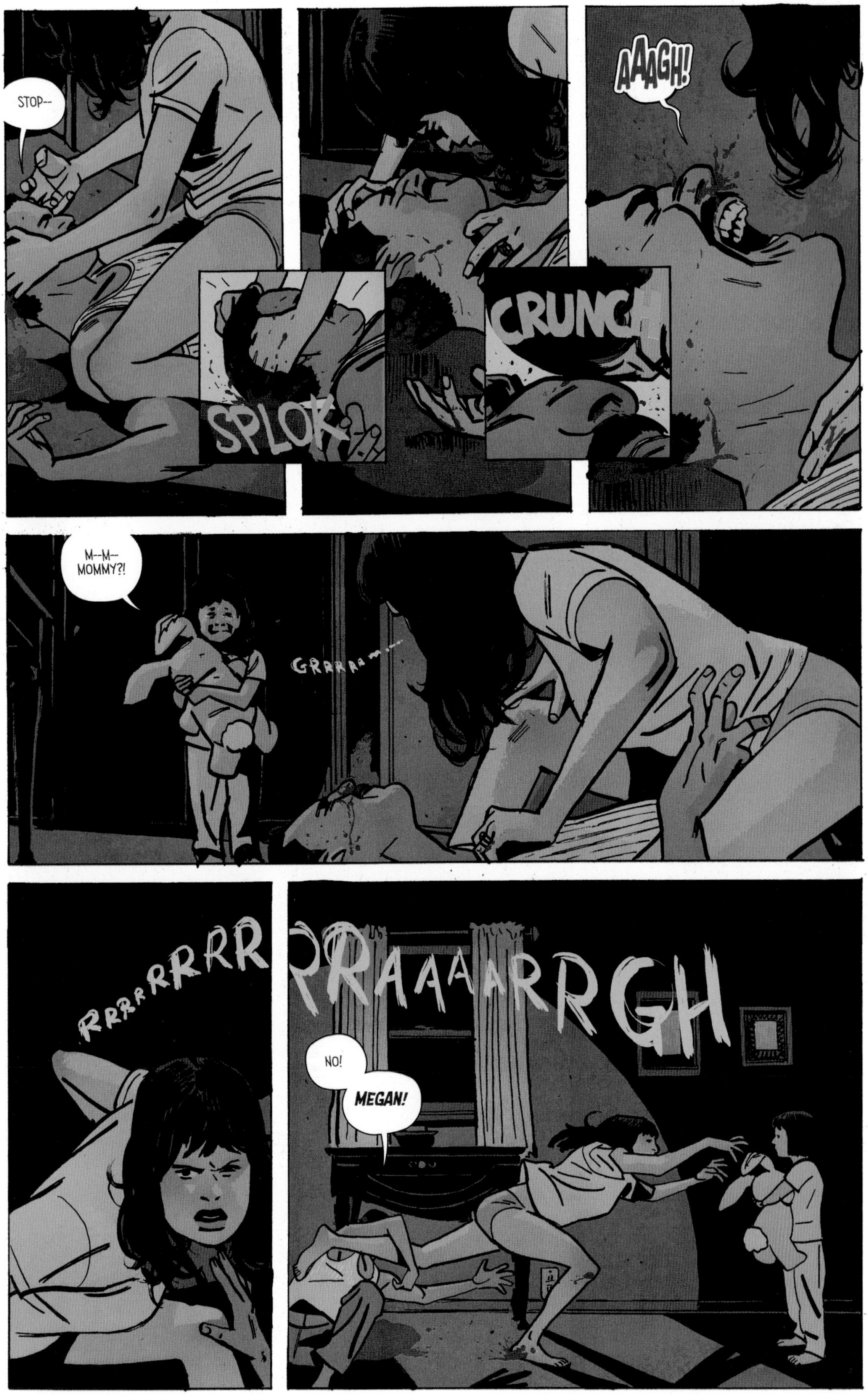
STOP--
SPLOK
CRUNCH
AAAGH!
M--M--
MOMMY?!
GRRRAAM---
RRRRRRRRRAAAARRGH
NO!
MEGAN!

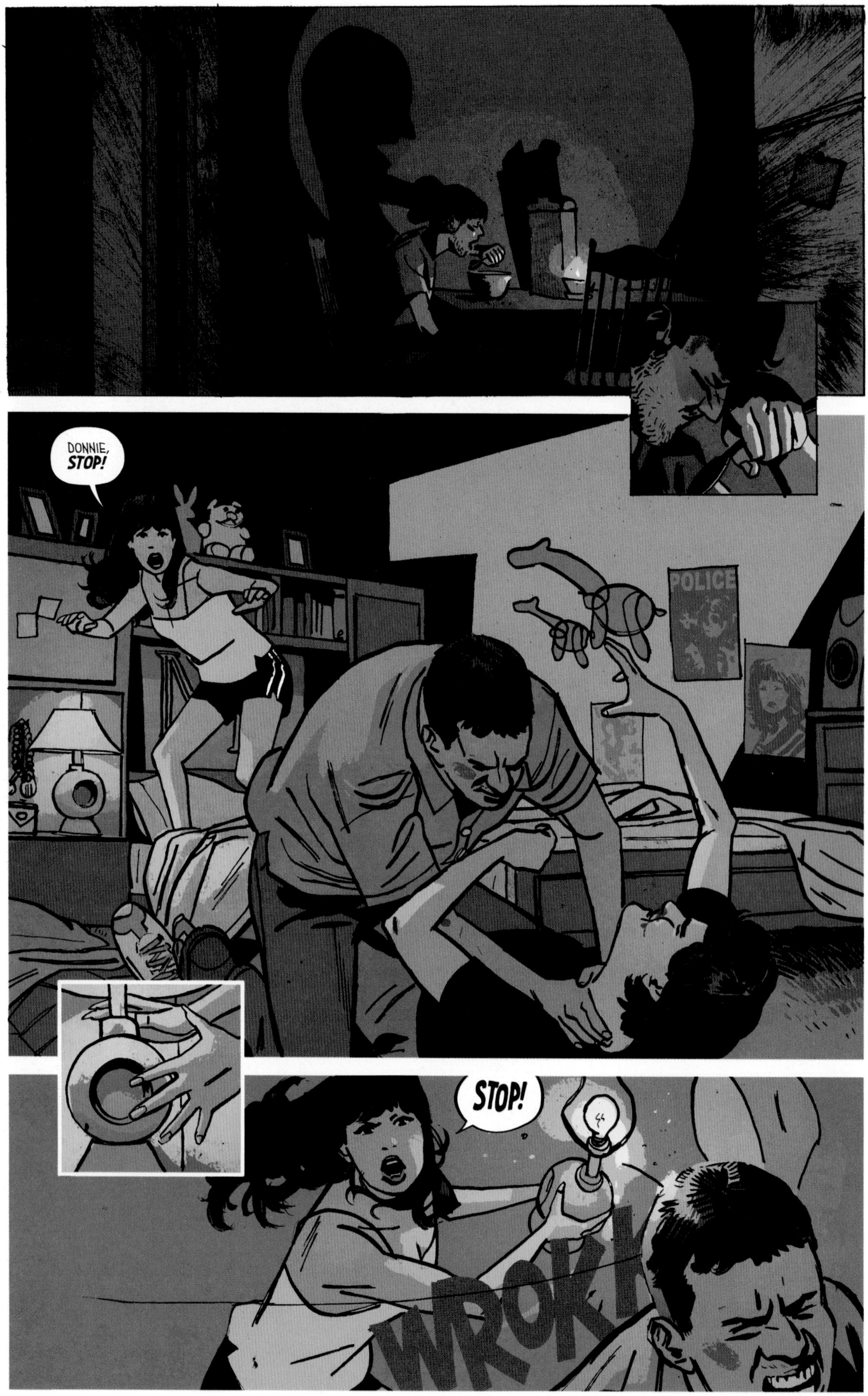
DONNIE, STOP!
POLICE
STOP!
WROK!

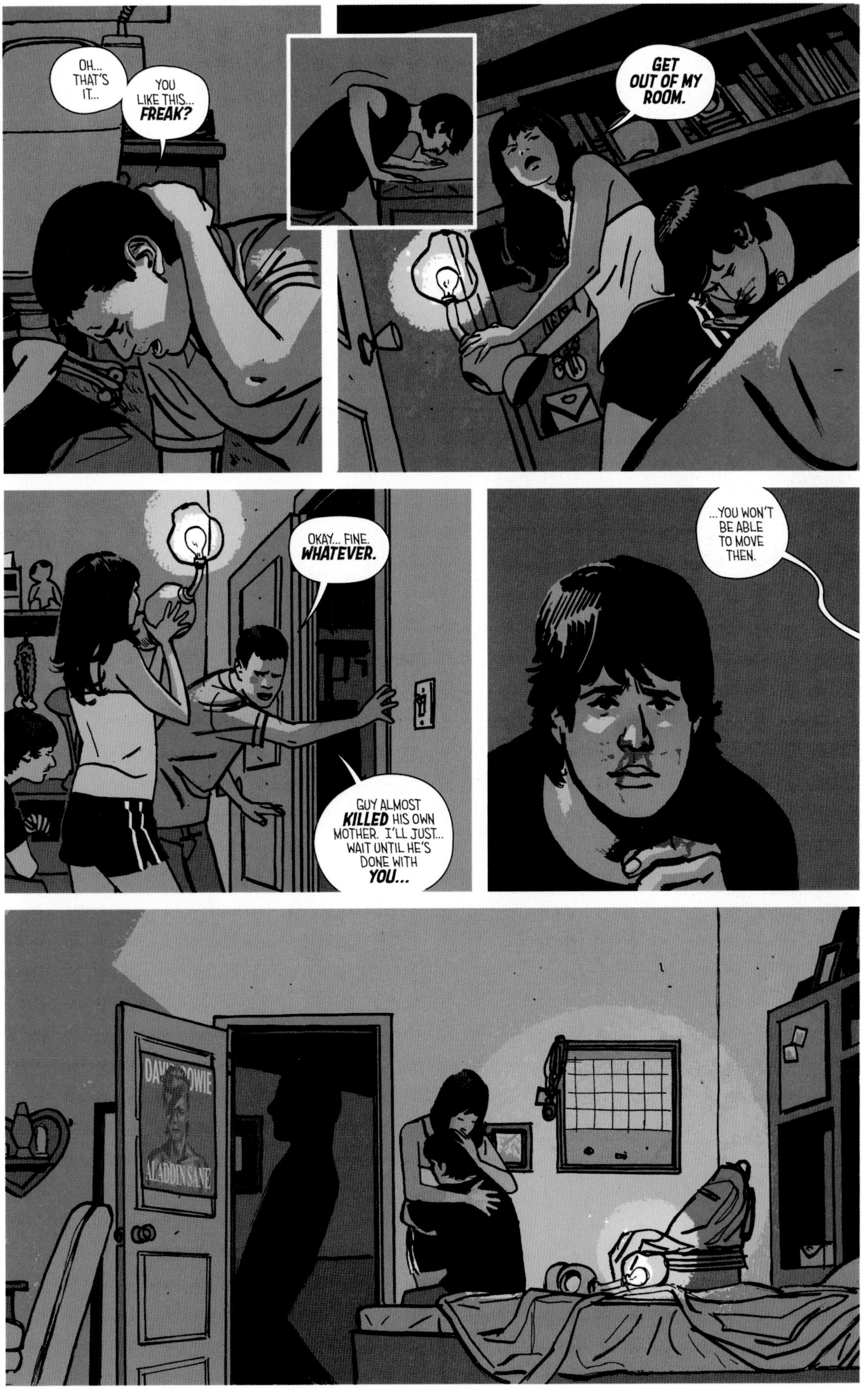
OH... THAT'S IT...
YOU LIKE THIS... FREAK?
GET OUT OF MY ROOM.
OKAY... FINE. WHATEVER.
GUY ALMOST KILLED HIS OWN MOTHER. I'LL JUST... WAIT UNTIL HE'S DONE WITH YOU...
...YOU WON'T BE ABLE TO MOVE THEN.
DAVID BOWIE
ALADDIN SANE

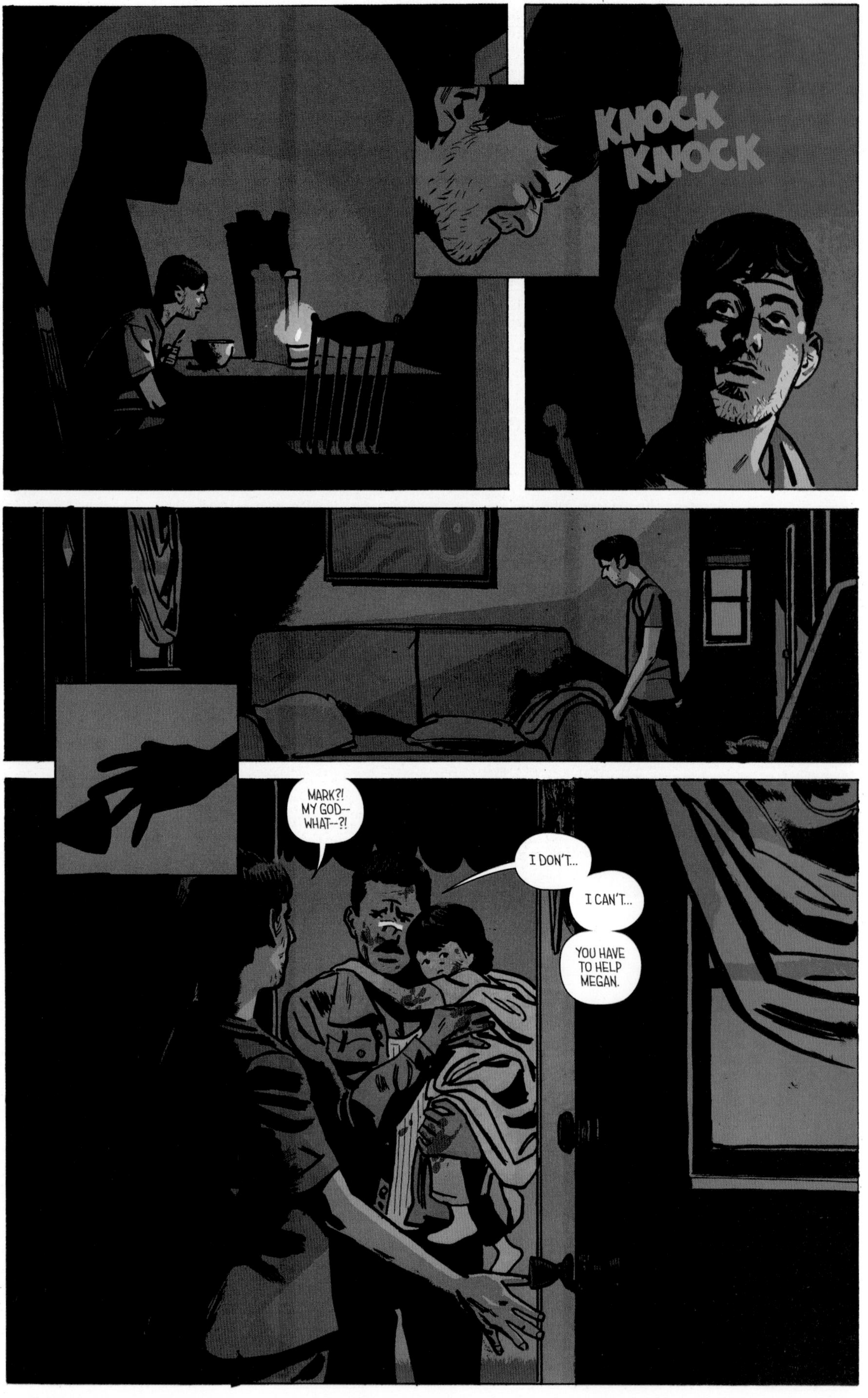
KNOCK
KNOCK
MARK?! MY GOD-- WHAT--?!
I DON'T...
I CAN'T...
YOU HAVE TO HELP MEGAN.

HEAVENLY FATHER... I AM... I AM **LOST.**

I BEG OF YOU... LET KYLE SEE THE **LIGHT** OF WHAT WE'RE DOING. SHOW HIM THAT IT IS IN YOUR PLAN... BRING HIM BACK TO ME.

IF THE WORK I'M DOING TRULY IS YOUR DESIRE... IF I **TRULY** AM... **HELPING** THESE PEOPLE.

I HAVE... DOUBTS, FATHER.

THERE IS SO MUCH HAPPENING RECENTLY.

YOU'VE... **TESTED** ME.

AND I DON'T KNOW IF I'VE PASSED THAT TEST... IF I'M ANSWERING YOUR CALL... IF I AM DOING YOUR BIDDING.

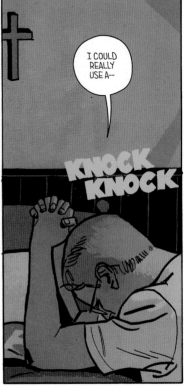

I COULD REALLY USE A--

KNOCK KNOCK

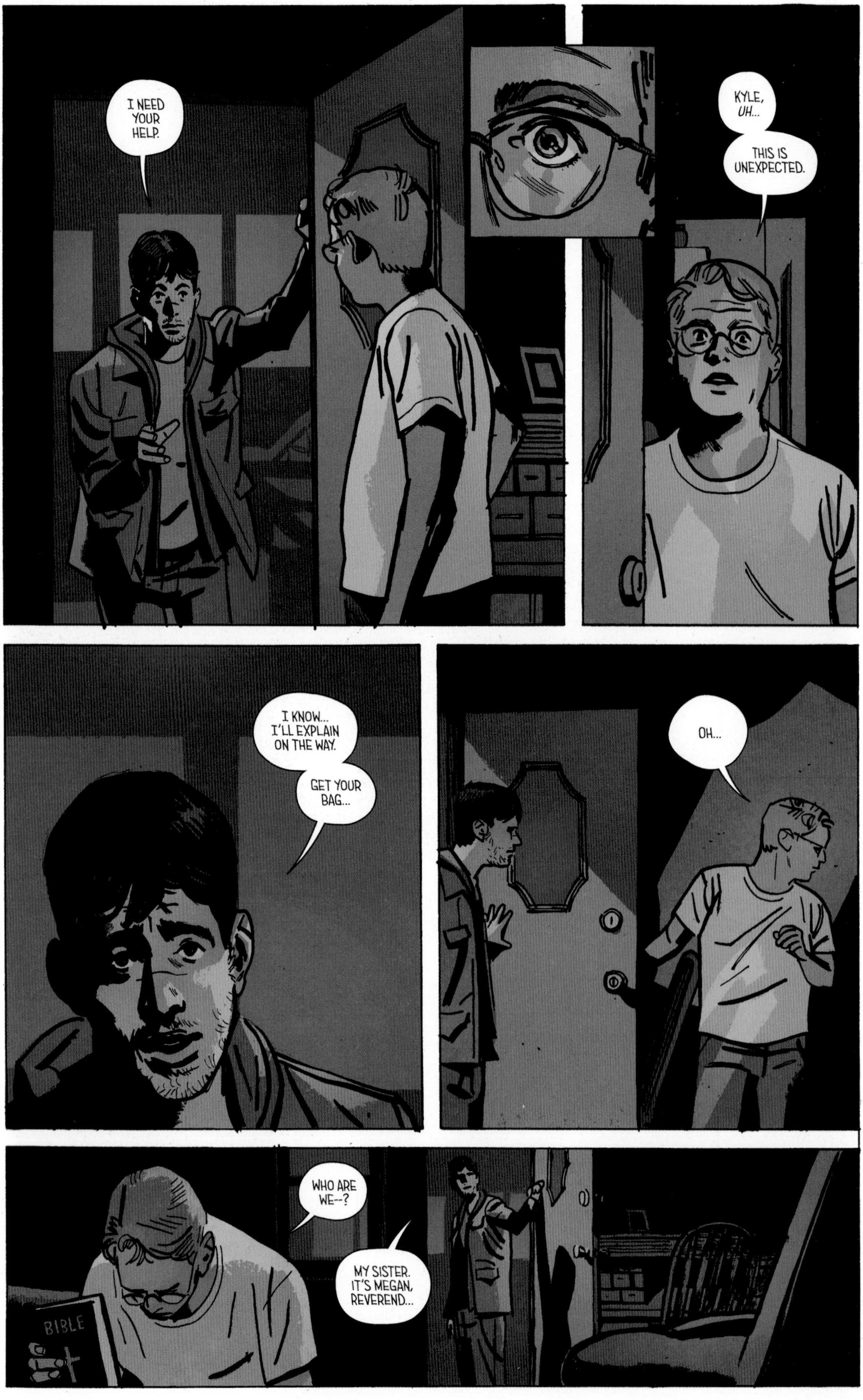
I NEED YOUR HELP.
KYLE, UH...
THIS IS UNEXPECTED.
I KNOW... I'LL EXPLAIN ON THE WAY.
GET YOUR BAG...
OH...
WHO ARE WE--?
MY SISTER. IT'S MEGAN, REVEREND...
BIBLE

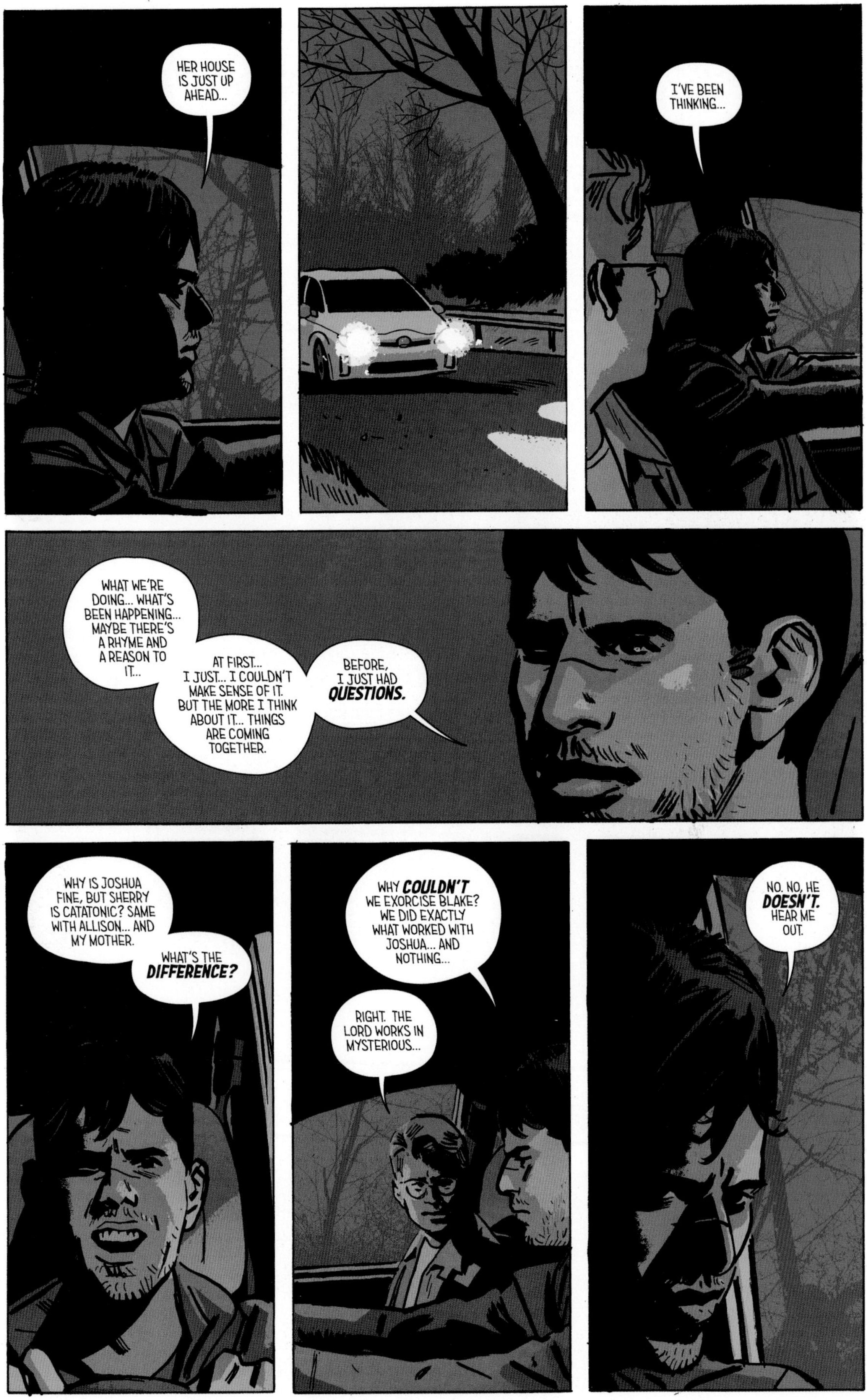
HER HOUSE IS JUST UP AHEAD...
I'VE BEEN THINKING...
WHAT WE'RE DOING... WHAT'S BEEN HAPPENING... MAYBE THERE'S A RHYME AND A REASON TO IT...
AT FIRST... I JUST... I COULDN'T MAKE SENSE OF IT. BUT THE MORE I THINK ABOUT IT... THINGS ARE COMING TOGETHER.
BEFORE, I JUST HAD **QUESTIONS.**
WHY IS JOSHUA FINE, BUT SHERRY IS CATATONIC? SAME WITH ALLISON... AND MY MOTHER.
WHAT'S THE **DIFFERENCE?**
WHY **COULDN'T** WE EXORCISE BLAKE? WE DID EXACTLY WHAT WORKED WITH JOSHUA... AND NOTHING...
RIGHT. THE LORD WORKS IN MYSTERIOUS...
NO. NO, HE **DOESN'T.** HEAR ME OUT.

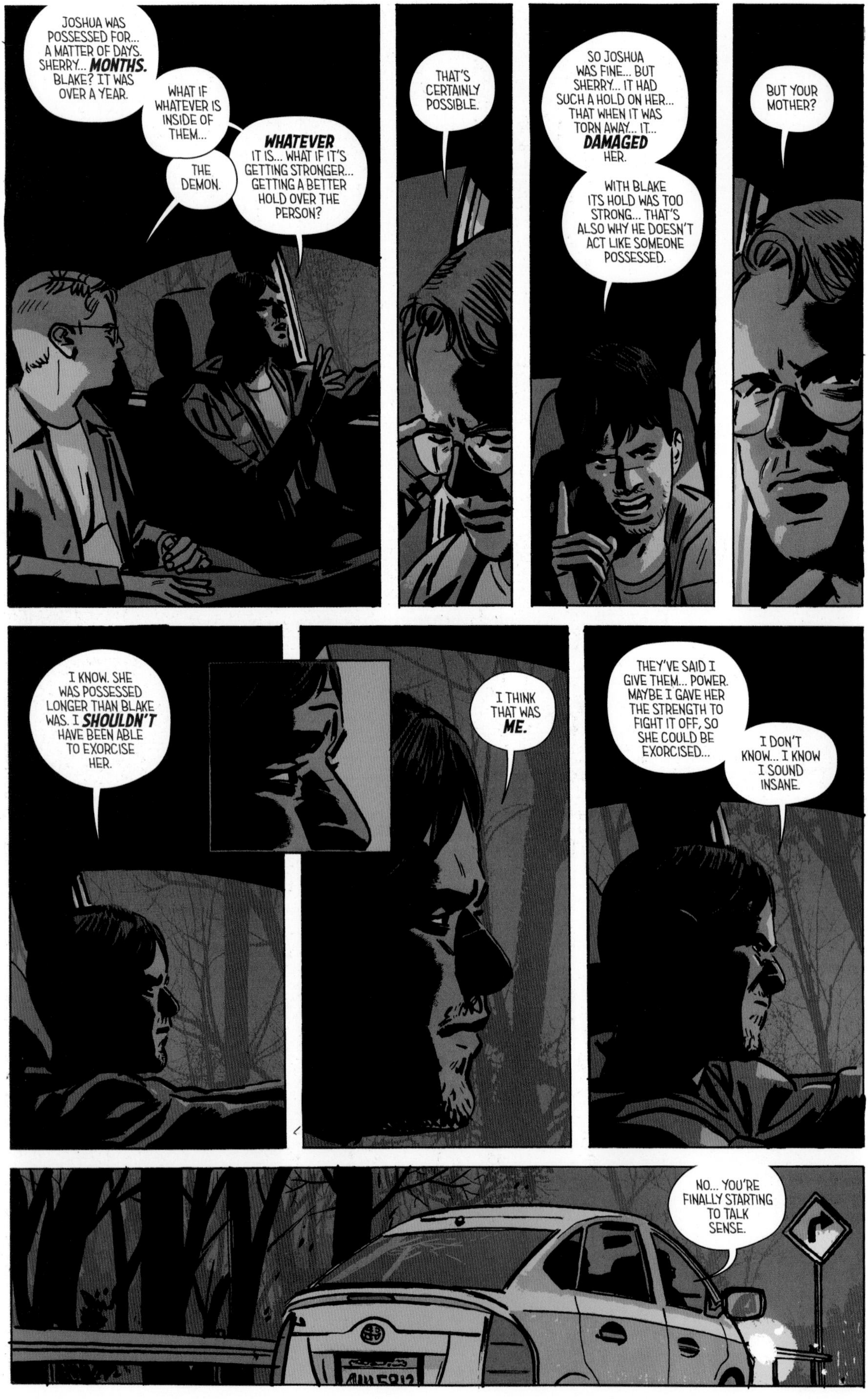
JOSHUA WAS POSSESSED FOR... A MATTER OF DAYS. SHERRY... **MONTHS.** BLAKE? IT WAS OVER A YEAR.
WHAT IF WHATEVER IS INSIDE OF THEM...
THE DEMON.
WHATEVER IT IS... WHAT IF IT'S GETTING STRONGER... GETTING A BETTER HOLD OVER THE PERSON?
THAT'S CERTAINLY POSSIBLE.
SO JOSHUA WAS FINE... BUT SHERRY... IT HAD SUCH A HOLD ON HER... THAT WHEN IT WAS TORN AWAY... IT... **DAMAGED** HER.
WITH BLAKE ITS HOLD WAS TOO STRONG... THAT'S ALSO WHY HE DOESN'T ACT LIKE SOMEONE POSSESSED.
BUT YOUR MOTHER?
I KNOW. SHE WAS POSSESSED LONGER THAN BLAKE WAS. I **SHOULDN'T** HAVE BEEN ABLE TO EXORCISE HER.
I THINK THAT WAS **ME.**
THEY'VE SAID I GIVE THEM... POWER. MAYBE I GAVE HER THE STRENGTH TO FIGHT IT OFF, SO SHE COULD BE EXORCISED...
I DON'T KNOW... I KNOW I SOUND INSANE.
NO... YOU'RE FINALLY STARTING TO TALK SENSE.

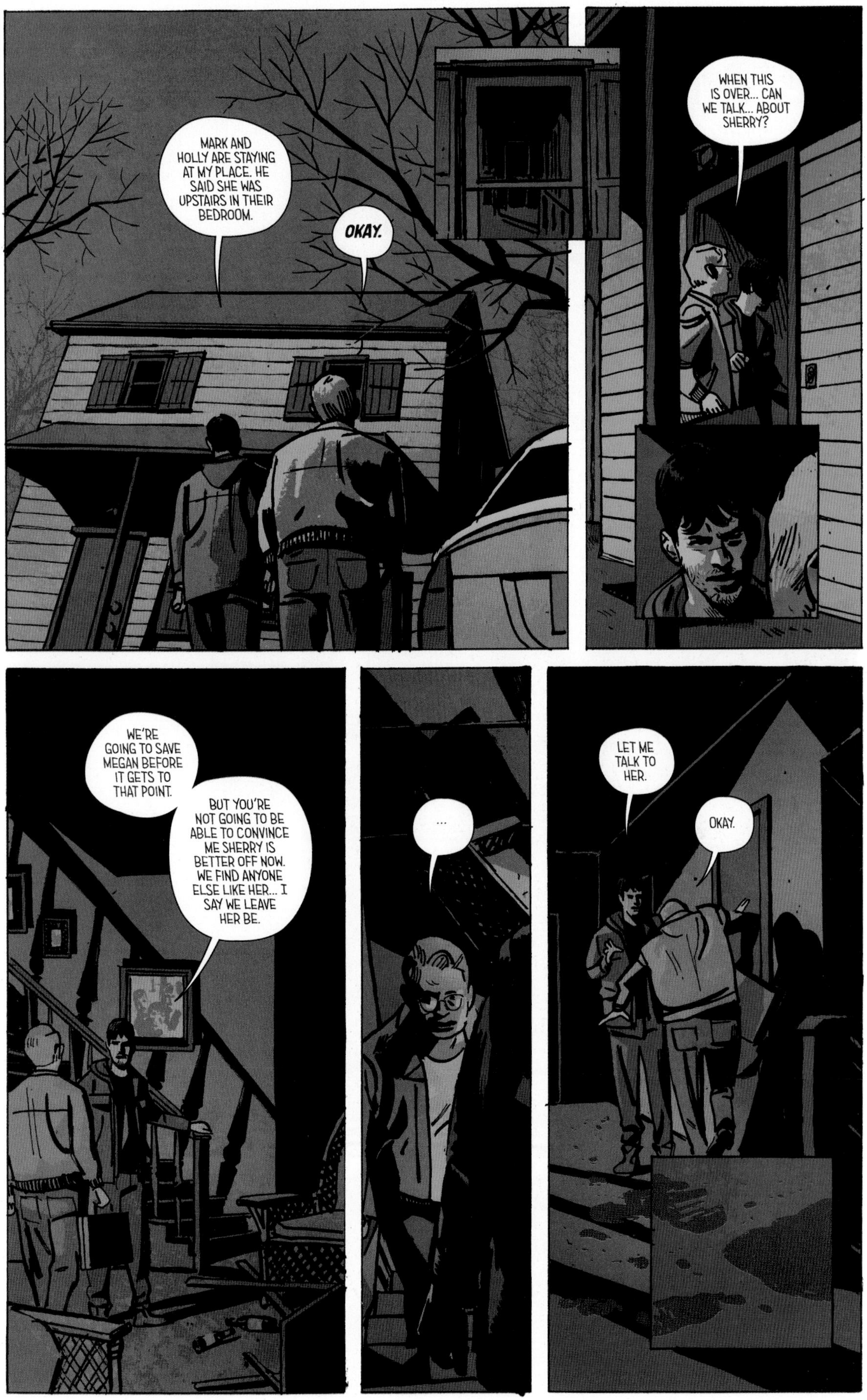
MARK AND HOLLY ARE STAYING AT MY PLACE. HE SAID SHE WAS UPSTAIRS IN THEIR BEDROOM.
OKAY.
WHEN THIS IS OVER... CAN WE TALK... ABOUT SHERRY?
WE'RE GOING TO SAVE MEGAN BEFORE IT GETS TO THAT POINT.
BUT YOU'RE NOT GOING TO BE ABLE TO CONVINCE ME SHERRY IS BETTER OFF NOW. WE FIND ANYONE ELSE LIKE HER... I SAY WE LEAVE HER BE.
...
LET ME TALK TO HER.
OKAY.

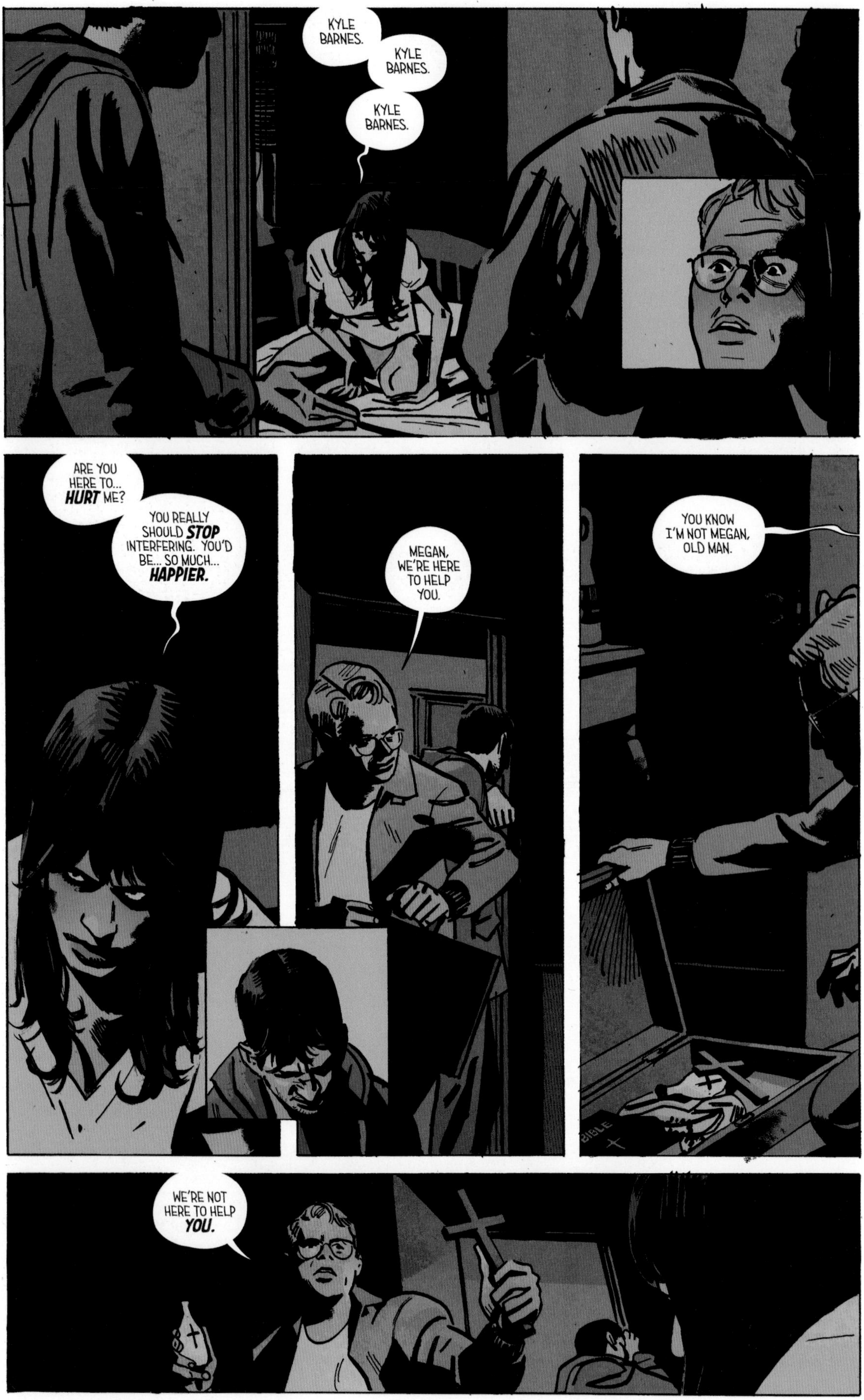
KYLE BARNES.
KYLE BARNES.
KYLE BARNES.
ARE YOU HERE TO... **HURT** ME?
YOU REALLY SHOULD **STOP** INTERFERING. YOU'D BE... SO MUCH... **HAPPIER.**
MEGAN, WE'RE HERE TO HELP YOU.
YOU KNOW I'M NOT MEGAN, OLD MAN.
BIBLE
WE'RE NOT HERE TO HELP **YOU.**

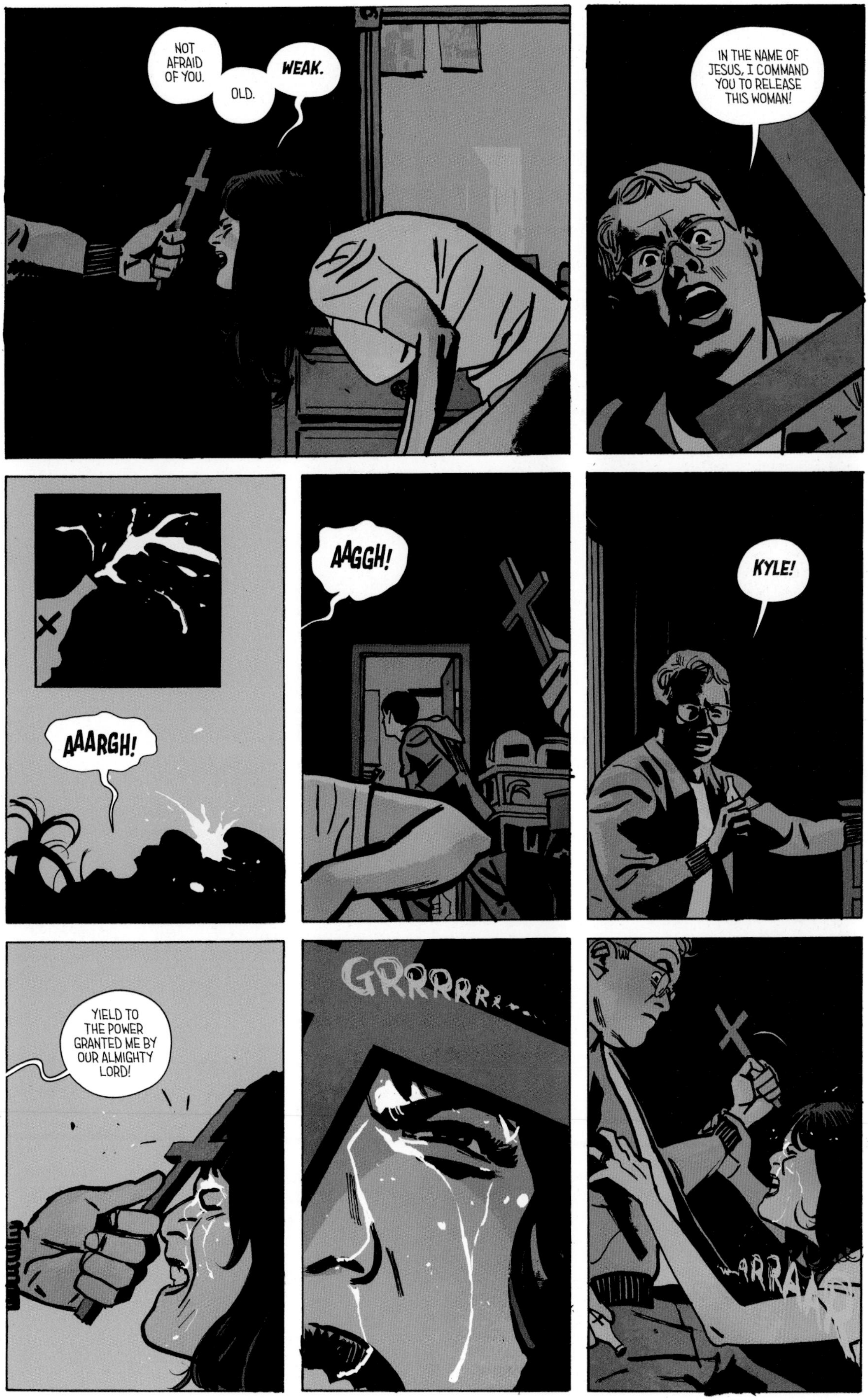
NOT AFRAID OF YOU.
OLD.
WEAK.
IN THE NAME OF JESUS, I COMMAND YOU TO RELEASE THIS WOMAN!
AAARGH!
AAGGH!
KYLE!
YIELD TO THE POWER GRANTED ME BY OUR ALMIGHTY LORD!
GRRRRR

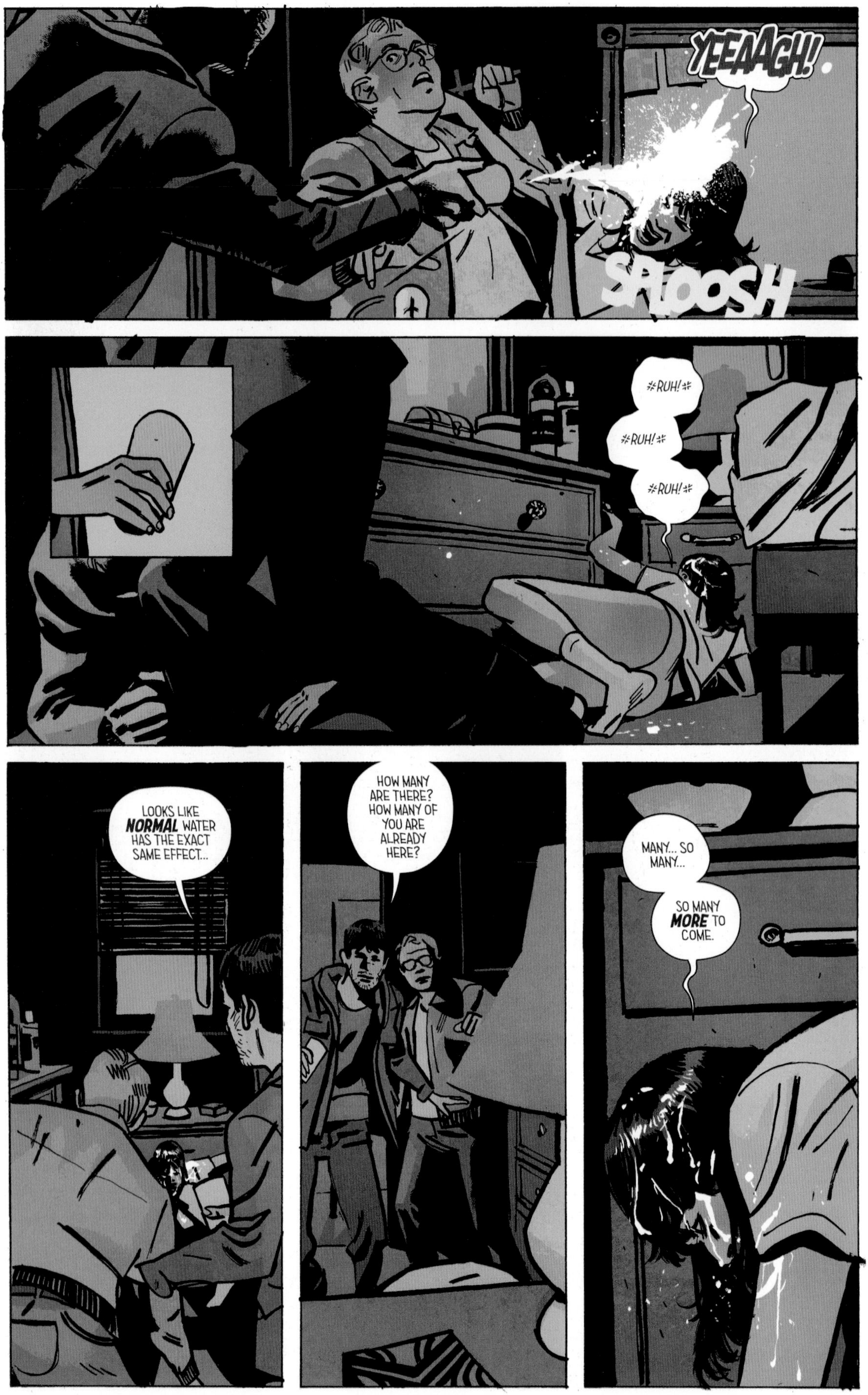

YEEAAAGH!
SPLOOSH
#RUH!#
#RUH!#
#RUH!#
LOOKS LIKE NORMAL WATER HAS THE EXACT SAME EFFECT...
HOW MANY ARE THERE? HOW MANY OF YOU ARE ALREADY HERE?
MANY... SO MANY...
SO MANY MORE TO COME.

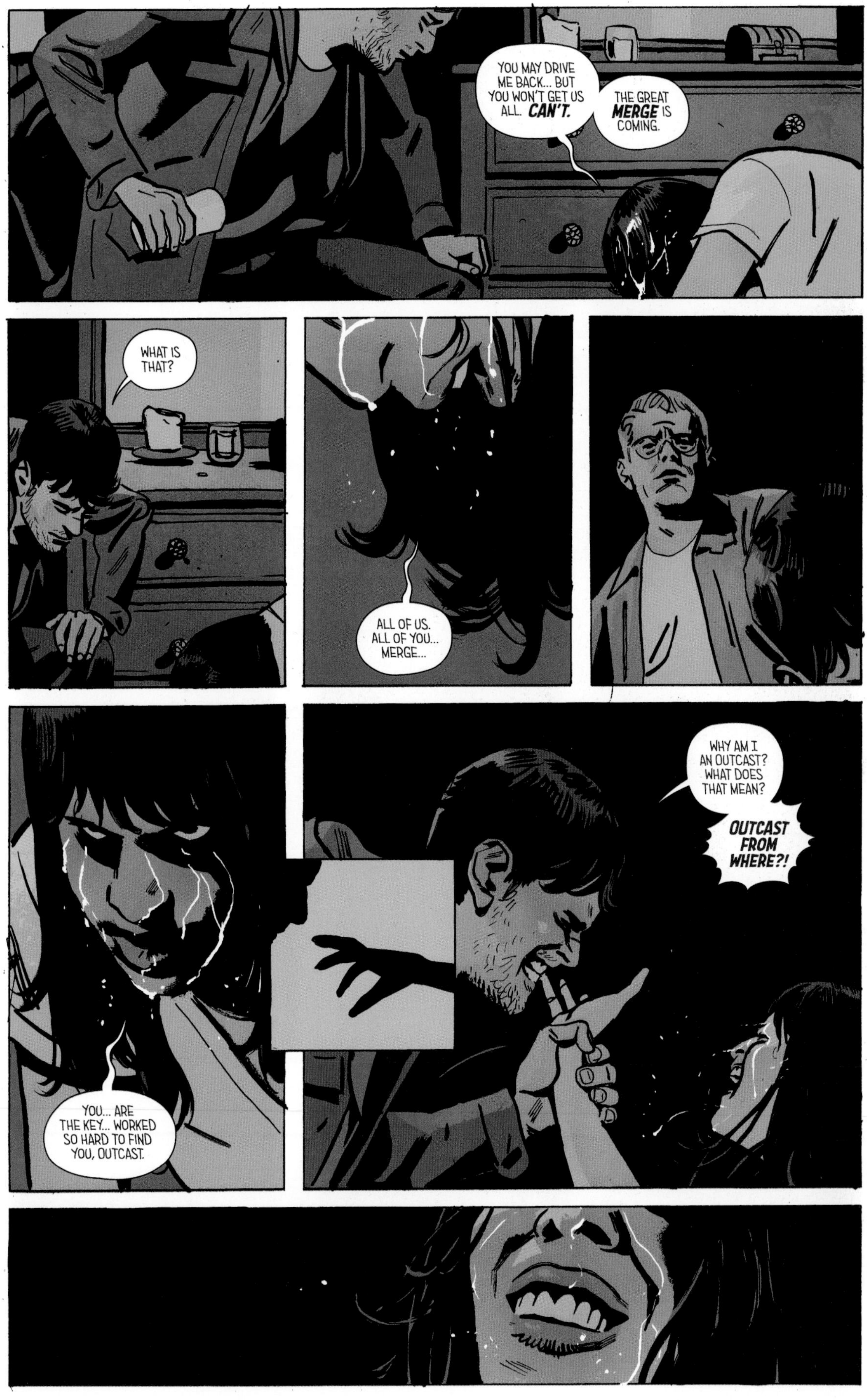
YOU MAY DRIVE ME BACK... BUT YOU WON'T GET US ALL. **CAN'T.**
THE GREAT **MERGE** IS COMING.
WHAT IS THAT?
ALL OF US. ALL OF YOU... MERGE...
YOU... ARE THE KEY... WORKED SO HARD TO FIND YOU, OUTCAST.
WHY AM I AN OUTCAST? WHAT DOES THAT MEAN?
OUTCAST FROM WHERE?!

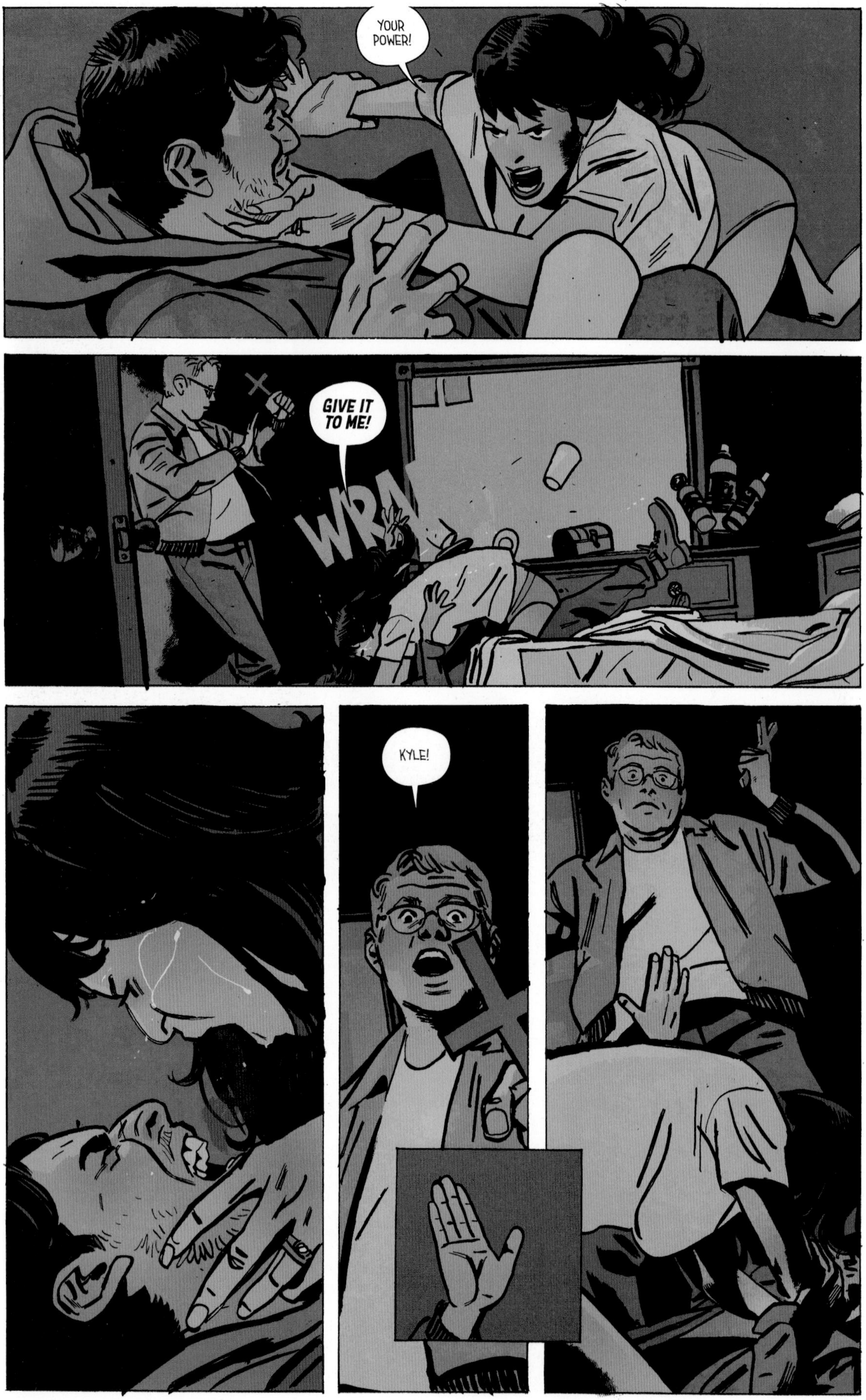
YOUR POWER!
GIVE IT TO ME!
WRA
KYLE!

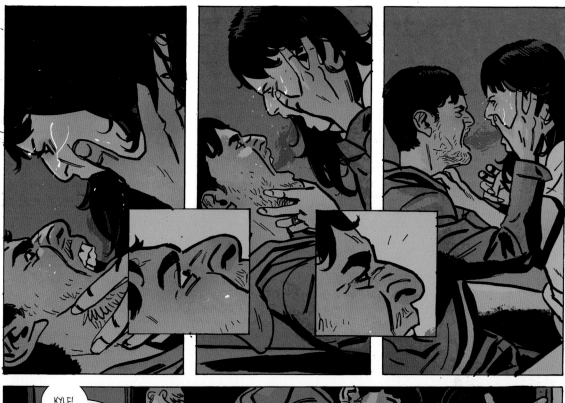

KYLE!

LORD... GIVE ME STRENGTH.

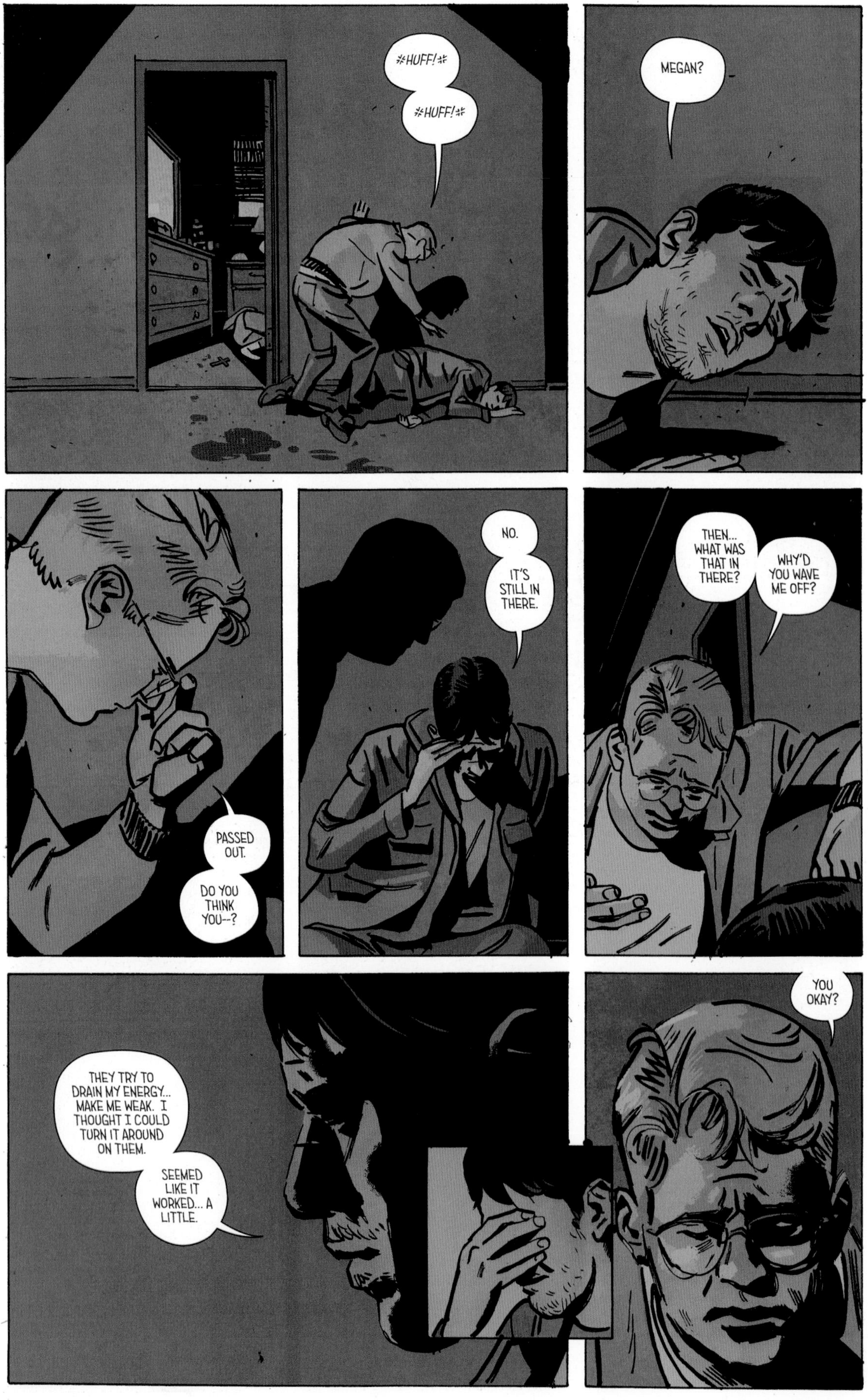
HUFF!
HUFF!
MEGAN?
PASSED OUT.
DO YOU THINK YOU--?
NO.
IT'S STILL IN THERE.
THEN... WHAT WAS THAT IN THERE?
WHY'D YOU WAVE ME OFF?
THEY TRY TO DRAIN MY ENERGY... MAKE ME WEAK. I THOUGHT I COULD TURN IT AROUND ON THEM.
SEEMED LIKE IT WORKED... A LITTLE.
YOU OKAY?

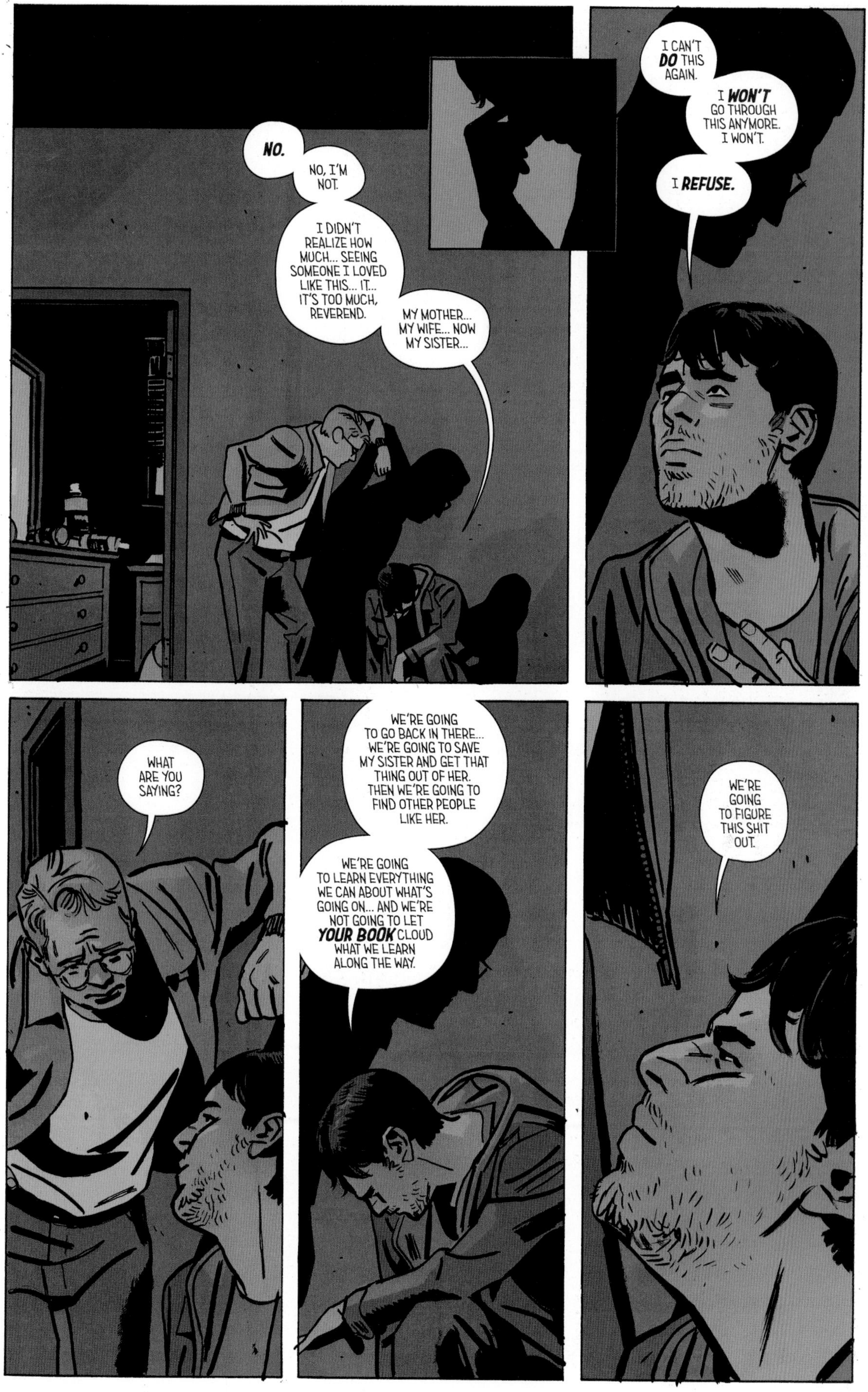
NO.
NO, I'M NOT.
I DIDN'T REALIZE HOW MUCH... SEEING SOMEONE I LOVED LIKE THIS... IT... IT'S TOO MUCH, REVEREND.
MY MOTHER... MY WIFE... NOW MY SISTER...
I CAN'T DO THIS AGAIN.
I WON'T GO THROUGH THIS ANYMORE. I WON'T.
I REFUSE.
WHAT ARE YOU SAYING?
WE'RE GOING TO GO BACK IN THERE... WE'RE GOING TO SAVE MY SISTER AND GET THAT THING OUT OF HER. THEN WE'RE GOING TO FIND OTHER PEOPLE LIKE HER.
WE'RE GOING TO LEARN EVERYTHING WE CAN ABOUT WHAT'S GOING ON... AND WE'RE NOT GOING TO LET YOUR BOOK CLOUD WHAT WE LEARN ALONG THE WAY.
WE'RE GOING TO FIGURE THIS SHIT OUT.

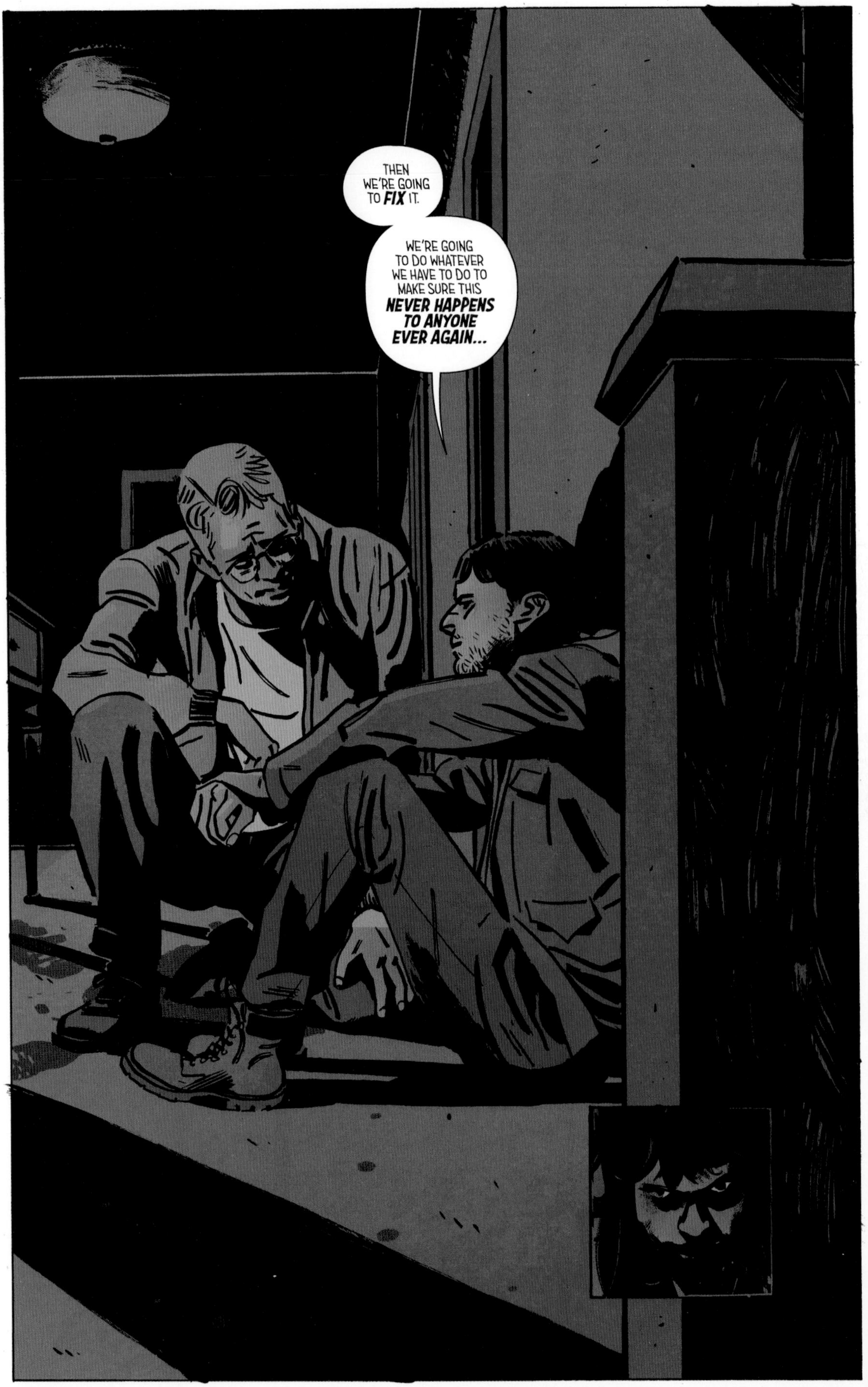
THEN WE'RE GOING TO FIX IT.
WE'RE GOING TO DO WHATEVER WE HAVE TO DO TO MAKE SURE THIS NEVER HAPPENS TO ANYONE EVER AGAIN...

TO BE CONTINUED

"How far could this go?